Mafia Heir

The Mancinelli Brotherhood

Sabine Barclay

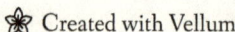 Created with Vellum

Welcome to The Mancinelli Brotherhood, and welcome if you're new to my The Syndicate Wars, an underground world where four organized crime groups vie to control New York City. If you've read any of my other Mafia series, prepare to see the Italians in a new light.

Happy reading,
Sabine

Subscribe to Sabine's Newsletter

Subscribe to Sabine's bimonthly newsletter to receive exclusive insider perks.

Have you read *The Syndicate Wars*? This FREE origin story novella is available to all new subscribers to Sabine's monthly newsletter.

The Mancinelli Brotherhood

Mafia Heir

Mafia Sinner (5.9.23)

Mafia Beauty (6.27.23)

Mafia Angel (8.22.23)

Mafia Redeemer (10.17.23)

Mafia Star (12.12.23)

Do you also enjoy steamy Historical Romance? Discover Sabine's books written as Celeste Barclay.

Chapter One

Luca

This asshole is pissing me off. We've been going around in circles for five minutes, and the longer we stand out here, the greater the likelihood someone will spot us. I have a sixth sense about these things. It's why I'm still alive at the ripe old age of thirty-one.

"Espinoza, enough already. Either sell to us or don't, but we set the price. Your tequila is good, but it isn't nectar from the gods."

I'm watching Carlos Espinoza, some lackey for the Mexican Culiacán Cartel, try to maneuver me into paying more than the agreed upon price. I know it's so he can skim off the top.

"It's as close as you're going to get. You've upped the order, so the price per case goes up."

My uncle, Salvatore Mancinelli, is the New York don. He negotiated this deal, and I warned him it was a bad idea. But what do I know as his underboss and heir? I'm not backing down.

"Haven't you ever heard of a bulk discount? The more I order the better the price should be. No one else around here is buying from you. You know we're your only choice in three out of five boroughs. You aren't going to the Bronx because you won't get more than pennies there. You aren't going to Queens because you don't want to run into the Colombians. You aren't going to Manhattan because then you face the bratva along with us. And what are you going to do in Staten Island? Sell to us anyway? We control Staten Island and Brooklyn when it comes to liquor stores, so take the money and go."

"Luca, there are plenty of liquor stores in Brooklyn that aren't owned by Italians. I'll go there."

We aren't friends. He's patronizing me by using my first name. Fuck him and the horse he rode in on. I have other solutions for this shit.

"And I'll just take what I want from them for free. That's not a half bad idea. The deal's over. Take your shit with the worm in it and go."

"Motherfucking racist. Not all tequila has a worm in it."

"You're selling Mezcal. It's known for the fucking worm. I wouldn't start calling me names, you *penche hijo de puta.*" Fucking son of a bitch.

He has twenty-five crates of stolen tequila that he's trying to offload because he knows he can't sell it at his own liquor store.

"What did you call me?"

Carlos takes what he thinks is a menacing step forward, and his two bodyguards do the same. Not smart. Neither of my two bodyguards nor I react, but the three men in each of my cars open their doors. They won't do more than that. It's just a reminder that the Culiacán can try, but the *Cosa Nostra* still run New York City.

"This is the third and final time I say this. Sell or leave."

Every head turns toward the liquor store's back door as it opens. A gorgeous blonde steps out, and I wish I had the time to appreciate her beauty, but she's about to die. Carlos and his men draw their guns and pivot toward her. My men pull their weapons too, but we keep them pointed at the Mexicans. The woman stands like a deer in the headlights for a second before ducking behind the industrial garbage dumpster like a frightened rabbit. Three shots hit the metal almost at the same moment. That's all it takes for my men and me. The two bodyguards standing with me aim for a guard each, and I set my sights on Carlos. We squeeze our triggers, and the men fall.

Screeching tires tell me Carlos's driver takes off. I hear more gunshots as at least one soldier in my cars tries to shoot the escaping vehicle. Glass shatters, but the sedan keeps going. I hear more tires squeal as one of my SUVs takes off and chases the guy. I holster my gun and wave my men to do the same.

I inch forward toward the trash can, but I see the shadow shift. The woman bolts from the other side. She's still the frightened rabbit, but I'm the fox pursuing her. She's fast, I'll give her that. But she has to be at least a foot shorter than me. My legs are a lot longer and cover a lot more ground with each stride.

She weaves among the cars, most likely believing it's harder to hit a moving object. She isn't wrong, but I have no intention of shooting her. I push myself harder and pounce as she darts out and tries to cross the last stretch of parking lot to reach a better lit area near a bus stop. I lunge.

"Stop running, *piccolina*. I won't hurt you."

I wrap my arms around her and pull her back against my chest, but I'm quick to spin her around and put space between us as I grasp her arms. Of course, she fights me.

"If I wanted you dead, I would have shot at you, too."

"It doesn't mean you won't kill me after."

She's breathless as she continues to struggle. I almost let go to take a step back, insulted at what she implied. But I can't blame her. If I were a woman, I'd be terrified of the same thing.

"I'm not going to rape you. I'm going to talk to you."

"Talk? You are not a man who talks if you just killed a guy."

"To keep him and his men from killing you. I told you, if I wanted you dead, I would have shot at you too. And I wouldn't have missed."

She stops struggling against me, but her eyes continue to dart from one place to another, trying to find somewhere to flee. I know I can keep her in place with only one hand, so I release her left arm. I still have a firm hold on her right one, but I haven't held it nearly as tightly as I could.

"I'm Luca. I know you figured out you interrupted something you shouldn't have. Did that man know who you are?"

"Yes."

"What about his driver? Would he know you?"

"Yes."

"Do you have a name?"

"Yes."

"*Piccolina*, we won't get very far if yes is all you can say. Are you willing to answer me with more than one word?"

"No."

I knew that was coming, and I grin. I can't help it. I wasn't wrong about her being gorgeous, but I doubt she wants to know that's what I think. At least, not if I want her to know I won't assault her.

"Fine. I have more than twenty questions I can ask that you can answer with one word. Do you work at the store?"

"Sometimes."

Ah, an improvement.

"Did Carlos know you were still working?"

"No."

"Do you have a car, or do you take the subway or bus?"

She raises her chin and remains silent. Smart but counterproductive.

"The subway or the bus will get you killed. You're too easy to find and follow. Do you have a car?"

"Yes."

"Can you stay with someone instead of going home?"

She refuses to answer.

"If that man knew you and you sometimes work in the store, then he knew where you live. If he found that out, so will someone in his cartel."

"I know. Let me go. The longer I stand here, the more likely someone is to come back for me."

"No one will touch you while I'm here."

"Arrogant. If he shot at me, he would have shot at you."

"And he would have died, anyway. What's your name?"

"Jane."

"Look, I know you won't get in one of my cars and let me drive you somewhere. In most cases, I would say that's a smart move. But you did nothing wrong tonight except for leave work at the wrong time. I know that, and you know that. But the Culiacán won't see it that way, *piccolina*."

She freezes for no more than five seconds before she trembles so much that I can see it. I don't know what drives me next, but it's the same instinct that's made me call her little girl three times. I pull her to my chest and tuck her head against it. I stroke her hair down to her shoulders, rubbing my hand up and down her back. This is the most inopportune moment to notice she isn't wearing a bra. I will my body not to react.

"What does that mean?"

5

Her voice is barely more than a whisper, but I know what she's asking.

"It means little girl."

"I should be insulted, but the way you say it..."

"It has nothing to do with your height. I know you're not a child."

God, do I know she's not. She feels amazing. Her tits are soft as they press against me, and I can see she has the most delectable ass. I'd love nothing more than to cup it and squeeze until she goes up on her toes and begs for me to wrap her legs around my waist and fuck her. For fuck's sake. Stop, you disgusting asshole. That is not what you need to be thinking about.

"Why didn't you shoot me? Whatever you were talking about, if it was with a Cartel member, then it wasn't completely legal. Carlos didn't want me alive to talk about seeing you together. Why are you letting me live?"

"I told you. You did nothing wrong but try to leave work. He should have checked the building before starting the meeting. That was on him. The only thing I take issue with is you leaving by yourself and walking into a dimly lit parking lot. I suspect you do that often, and that's too dangerous. Jane Doe, I don't hurt women."

She tilts her head to the left as she assesses me. I have a moment of nerves that I won't live up to her expectations, and I have no idea why I care. I should be worried that she's going to call the police the moment she can't see me. I should worry that she'll get me arrested. I should worry about a shit ton besides her safety. But I can't help it.

"I don't like people seeing me leaving the store alone if I go out through the front. The store's been closed for hours, but I was doing some work in the office. You can't see the back-office light is on when you're on the street. I can leave with no one noticing."

"But anyone could lurk here, as you've learned."

"I wouldn't say you were exactly lurking."

She glances around my shoulder to where the bodies were. Her brow furrows, and her gaze swings back to me. In the few minutes that she wasn't looking around, I know my men have already swept the area for bullet casings, wrapped the bodies, tossed them in the trunk of our SUV, and scrubbed away the blood from the concrete. No one will be the wiser that three men died here tonight.

"You said your name is Luca, and you sound like you have an accent with some words. Are you—oh, fuck. You're Luca Mancinelli."

She panics and pushes against my chest, fighting to break loose. She tries even harder than she did before, but my arms around her waist confine her. She tries to stomp on my toes and knee me, but I easily block her.

"Stop."

Most men obey when they hear that tone, but she struggles more. She fears me, yet she doesn't. I'm not the sick bastard who likes to dominate women when they say no, thinking the chase is fun. But I'm not letting go because there's more I need to tell her.

"I do not want to hold on to you like this, but I don't trust you not to bolt. We aren't done talking, Jane Doe. Stop, and I will let go. If you run, I will catch you again. You need to understand how serious this is, and you need to know what to do."

"I know how serious it is. You're the fucking Mafia."

"And I told you Carlos was Culiacán. You looked like you understood what that meant. If I wanted you dead, I would have killed you. If I wanted to rape you, I wouldn't stand around here taking my time chatting. If I was going to kidnap you, you'd already be bound, gagged, blindfolded, and in the trunk."

"Fine."

She stands still, and I let her go. I even take a step back. I'm certain my men are wondering what the fuck I'm doing. I'm wondering the same thing. I know they must be antsy to go, but I feel like I owe this woman something.

"I am Luca Mancinelli. You seem to know who I am, even if I don't know who you are. You said you have a car. You need to drive to someone you know in a different borough. If you know someone in Jersey or Connecticut, that's even better. Do not go to your place. Do not use your credit cards or debit cards. I'm going to give you enough cash for at least three tanks of gas, some food, and some clothes. You can buy non-prescription colored contacts. Your shade of brown is too unique with the amber around the pupils and flecks of green in the irises. You need to get something more muted. Color your blonde hair to a nondescript brown with no hints of blonde. I'll make sure you have enough for that, too. I know you think this is extreme, and it is. But it's what you need to do to escape."

I twist and wave to Gabriele. He's my cousin Carmine's best friend. I can't stand either of them, but Gabriele's excellent at what he does. He was standing to my right when I negotiated with Carlos. When he approaches, I switch to Italian. He was born and raised there until he was ten, and even though I was born in New York, Italian was my first language.

"*Portami duemila dollari e due telefono usa a getta.*" Bring me two grand and two burners.

Gabriele's face barely shows any of his surprise or disapproval, but I see it. I don't give a shit what he thinks. Last I checked, I'm the underboss, not him.

"Two thousand dollars? I can't take that from you."

"You speak Italian?"

"No, but I can understand the number two thousand since it's *dos mil* in Spanish, so close enough, and *dollari* must mean dollars. That's way too much to give me."

"If you know who the Mancinellis are, then you know we won't notice two grand. You're going to need it."

Gabriele hands me an envelope and two burner phones in boxes. I rip the disposable phones open and quickly set them up. I take one of them and pull up the contacts list.

John Doe
212-555-9080

I hand her the phone before I quickly add that phone's number to the one I'm keeping.

Jane Doe
212-555-4103

"Do not store any other numbers in here. Only use it to call me if you have to. Do you have a cosmetic bag in your purse?"

"Yes."

"Let me see it, please."

My sudden rediscovery of manners surprises her. But I hold out my hand for it. I can tell she doesn't want to give it to me, but she does. Her cheeks flame red when I open it and find not only makeup but a handful of tampons and two condoms. That begs an important question that I hadn't thought of.

"Are you single? Is there someone expecting you to go home to them or call them or see them?"

As I ask, I fold the bills long ways. They're all one hundreds, but that still makes twenty bills to fit in the bag. I stack them to make it easy for her to grab one at a time and push them beneath everything else in the bag. I hold it closed and shake it a few times before looking back inside. I pull the sides out, but there's enough stuff in there to disguise the bills if anyone did a quick search.

"I'm single."

Fuck my life. What a time to meet a woman I'd happily spend my life fucking. I hand the bag back to her, and she drops it in her purse.

"Put the phone in your pocket. Never carry it in your purse. That's too easy for someone to snatch. I'd rather you keep the phone than the cash. The cash can be replaced. Being able to call for help can't."

"How long do I have to hide?"

"I will text you one word. Now. When you see that, you'll know I believe it's safe. It may be a few weeks, even a month."

"Do I change my name or something? Obviously, I can't come back to work here. Do I quit?"

"You need to tell me your name and your email address. I can send something to your boss through a VPN. They won't be able to trace it easily."

She stands there staring at me, clearly debating whether to give me that information. She hasn't tried to run, and I can tell she's been locking away all my instructions in her memory. I think she's getting how serious I am. I'm treating her like a CI, a confidential informant, who's done serving my family. That's how I know what to tell her.

"It's Olivia D'Amato."

It's my turn to freeze. I knew something struck me as familiar.

"Are you related to Danny D'Amato?"

"I don't think so."

She's lying. I can tell from her eyes. She's not conveying something through her expression. It's truly her eyes. I've seen the eye color before and only in the D'Amato family. Danny used to come to meetings like this with my uncle, but he got shot nearly two decades ago. A collapsed lung has kept him from being useful since he can barely string a sentence together without wheezing. I suppose she could be related to another person in the family and just doesn't know Danny. He's the only one I can think of who's the right age to be her dad.

"What's your email address?"

I'm repeating it in my head as she tells me. I won't write it down anywhere, and luckily she gives me a work one that has the name of another company in it.

"I'll send it tonight."

"What're you going to say? And won't Carlos's people think it's suspicious that I quit the same night he goes missing? The company I work for certainly will."

"No one's going to know Carlos is dead for a few days. In the meantime, you got offered a better-paying job at another place. What did you do?"

"I'm a marketing rep. I did market research, lined up all the promotions, worked with the ad agency, and oversaw the social media team. You must know this store is part of a chain. It's one of my company's clients and one location I visit."

"All right. You're getting a new job somewhere like Westchester and unrelated to regular retail. Something at a big corporation. You need to hurry and go. Do you have somewhere in mind?"

"Yeah."

Good, because I saw the second car come back. I need to know if they took out the driver or lost him. While I talk to him, my guy is going to follow Olivia wherever she goes until I know she's safe. When I figure out where she's staying, I'll have a team watch her.

"Remember, call me if you think something's wrong. Don't wait to find out if it is. But otherwise, don't use that phone and stick to the cash."

"I will. Thank you, Luca."

"Good luck, *piccolina*."

I watch her get into a Volkswagen Jetta, and I'm glad it's gray. It's unremarkable. I see her chin dip toward me before she pulls out of the lot. What I told her is enough to keep her alive, but she's not used to this. She will trip up somehow. It's inevitable. It's a question of how long she lasts.

Chapter Two

Livy

I have never been so terrified in my life. Not the time I got stuck on a rollercoaster upside down in one of those seats that only has the harness. Not the time I crashed my bike in Midtown and nearly had a city bus run me over. Not the time I watched my dad threaten to beat the shit out of my mom and point a knife at me.

It wasn't the moment I stepped outside and immediately realized what I walked into. It wasn't the moment the bullets hit the dumpster only inches from my head and chest. It wasn't the few moments that I ran. It was the moment I looked into Luca Mancinelli's eyes and realized I was the world's biggest idiot to trust him.

When he held my arms, he didn't hurt me, even though he could have. He held them tightly enough that I couldn't break loose, but I know there won't be bruises. When he hugged me as I was about to freak out, he was so gentle, even though I knew he wouldn't let go. He smelled divine. And fuck me if he isn't the hottest man I've ever seen. Even with the wicked scar that runs along his left cheek, down his neck, and beneath the collar of his button-down shirt. Whoever sewed it did a good job because it's not jagged or puckered, but it is noticeable. It gives him an air of ruthlessness on top of his already dangerous aura. A man who survived that kind of wound is no lightweight.

But somehow I knew from the moment he caught me he wouldn't hurt me. Instinct warred inside. Part of me trusted him the moment I could tell he was being gentle. But the other part said I deserved to die like in a slasher movie for not fighting harder to get away. It was a battle between what I should do and what I wanted to do. In any other situation, I might have tried my inept version of flirting. That wasn't possible since I witnessed a triple murder, and one killer was giving me instructions on how to get away from the victim's bosses. What the ever-loving fuck?

I just took the BQE—Brooklyn Queens Expressway—from Williamsburg in Brooklyn and jumped off at Sunnyside in Queens. I need to get gas. I'm watching all the cars I pass or those around me. I'm looking in my mirrors as often as I'm looking through my windshield. I keep my back to the pump the entire time. I've watched enough of those crime drama shows to know I should do that.

The moment my tank's full, I jump back on the road. I get back on the BQE until it turns into the Grand Central Parkway, which takes me to the South Bronx. From there, I wind through the borough on local roads to Hutchinson Parkway and head north to Connecticut.

I don't know where I'm going. I just feel like Connecticut is a less likely place to flee to than New Jersey. Do Brooklyn murder witnesses hide out among yuppies in the burbs? I've lived in New York City my entire life. I know which stereotypes about Jersey are true and which aren't, but right now, I'm buying into all of them. I'm less likely to be swimming with the fish wearing concrete shoes if I head north. Then again, that's supposedly the Mafia's hallmark, and Luca said I was safe from them. The Culiacán will behead me and leave me in the street. It's how they handle things in Tijuana and Chihuahua. I know what that cartel is like, and I know TJ is the most dangerous city in the world. I want nothing to do with it.

Where the hell am I going? Luca said to color my hair and to get colored contacts. I definitely have the cash to do that, but I hate he gave me such big bills. That sounds so fucking unappreciative, but breaking one hundred-dollar bills draws attention. I'm on Interstate 95 now, so I get off in New Rochelle and find a chain pharmacy. I'm still looking around everywhere I go. It's night, so it's not like I can use sunglasses to disguise myself. It's late winter, so I pull up my hood, but it doesn't hide my face. I'm just going to keep my head down as best I can. Even with my chin tucked, my eyes are sweeping my surroundings.

I force myself to stroll through the drugstore rather than rush straight to the hair color. I grab a can of men's shaving cream and a stick of men's deodorant. I don't need them or anything, but maybe it'll make it less obvious who I am if someone searches for me. Paranoid much? How can I not be?

I'd like to think I'm a nobody that the Mexican Cartel will take no interest in, but Luca didn't make it sound that way. It feels a bit egotistical to think I need to go to so many measures to disguise myself, but someone doesn't give you two thousand dollars and a burner phone if it isn't important. So, I keep reminding myself of that as I wander over to the hair color aisle and grab a washout box of medium brown color. If I grab some cold medicine along with the hair color, is someone going to think I'm cooking meth or making a bomb or something? All right. I really have binged too many of those cop dramas. Regular people have allergies or get sick and want to have colored hair.

I swipe a box of cold medicine and head to the self-checkout. Of course, there are four machines, and three say debit or credit only. The only one that takes cash has someone at it. Patience is a virtue, my mom used to say. I'm apparently an unvirtuous person because I'm fighting the urge to fidget and get irritated as the guy takes forever to ring up his forty million things. For fuck's sake, dude. Come on.

Finally, it's my turn. I'm quick to scan and bag everything before I reach into my purse and dig into the cosmetic bag. I grab my change and drop the coins into my purse and shove the bills in the little bag. I'll sort them out once I'm on the road again. I repeat the same process, buying a few other odds and ends, when I stop in Mamaroneck. I switched highways to be a little unpredictable because I think I saw the same car at the first pharmacy as I did at the gas station. I look around, but it isn't here at the one I just came out of with the colored contacts.

I'm crossing into Greenwich and praying I can find a twenty-four-hour Walmart since it's now three a.m. I'm nervous about using my GPS on my car or phone to find it, but I need clothes. Shit. My closest choices are White Plains, which is back in New York or going to Norwalk, which is just past Greenwich. Lucky for me, I had promo materials in the back of my car today, so I still have the backseat folded down. I have a couple bottles of rum in the back. I pull into the Walmart parking lot and reach into the back to snag a bottle of Malibu. I pour just enough in my lap to look like someone spilled a drink without looking like I'm a sloppy drunk who might be driving. I'm careful not to get any on my car seat.

I dash into the store and grab one of the hand baskets and

make my way to the women's clothes. I grab a shirt, a pair of leggings, a bra, and a pack of panties. I pretend to see something that snags my attention and take a step back. I look at a sweater top, then a shirt next to it. I grab both and toss them in my basket. I walk past some jeans and stop to look but skip them. I go to a different jeans rack and tilt my head as though I'm considering them. I grab two pairs.

The store pretty much only has self-checkout lanes open. Thank God.

"Ma'am, I can take you over here."

"That's all right. I've got it. Thanks."

The one cashier I pass offers to check me out. Son of a bitch. She's smiling and waving me over. I can't ignore her.

"I can do it faster than those machines that always need someone putting their employee number in when they freeze." The woman's brow scrunches as she looks at the stain on my clothes. "That sucks."

"Yeah. I know, right? A guy turned around and didn't see me right behind him. My drink landed on me without a drop hitting him. He didn't even say excuse me. I couldn't handle the smell, so I stopped to grab a couple things."

"A couple?"

The woman is bagging up my stuff as we chat.

"I'm a horrible impulse shopper. I can't turn down a deal."

That is the furthest thing from the truth. I'm thrifty to the point of rarely buying new clothes. I have stuff from high school that is still in great condition. I find clothes shopping demoralizing too. I'm short. At five-foot-two, I can practically shop in the kids' section. It's why Luca calling me little girl rankled at first. I'm also pear-shaped, so pants rarely fit well with a narrow waist and wider hips. I'm taking a leap of faith with the ones I'm buying. At twenty-eight, I've given up waiting for my boobs to grow in. I'm a B cup, which fits my frame, and I'm not exactly part of the itty-bitty titty committee. But neither am I what anyone would consider busty.

I hand her the cash and wait for my change. Thank God I thought to break another hundred-dollar bill at the last pharmacy. I don't need Chatty Cathy here, who's telling me about the deals she got at Target, to notice a big bill. I grab the bags, say thanks, and hurry out to the car. I toss everything in and leave. I pull off onto a residential street where there are no streetlights. I strip down, quickly changing all my clothes. What the fuck am I going to do with what I was wearing?

Do I just keep driving around until it's really morning? I can't stop at a motel because they'll ask for ID. Now I really am being paranoid. I need some sleep. I need something to eat too. Okay. I'm going to find a drive thru, then I'm finding a hotel. I'm not going to some skeazy roach motel either. I want somewhere with a few floors and a proper front desk staff that'll notice if a bunch of mobsters walk through. There has to be a Marriott or something.

I grab some fast food, grateful the burger place is open 24 hours, and I'm back on the road, scanning the highway exits for hotels.

Bingo.

Shit.

I don't have luggage or anything. Not true. My gym bag. I forgot about that, which is fine because I didn't want to put sweaty clothes that have been damp all day back on. I pull in, park, pop the trunk, and reach in. After I pulled out what I needed to get changed, I flung the Walmart bags onto the backseat far enough that I can reach them through the trunk. I quickly switch over the stuff and shut the trunk.

"Hello, welcome."

The receptionist is way too perky for this time of night.

"Hi."

"Do you have a reservation?"

"No. I got too tired driving and decided it would be better to pull off for the night."

That's not entirely a lie. I'm fucking exhausted all of a sudden. I want nothing more than to eat my food and crash. Oh, shit. I didn't think about the fact that they'll want a credit card to hold a deposit on the room. Fuck. Luca said not to use any. Even if I pay in cash, they'll want it for incidentals. I have a company credit card that doesn't have my name on it, but accounting will see a hold put on it for whatever amount even if they charge nothing.

"Do you have a credit card and ID?"

"I don't. The reason I'm driving so late is that I got mugged in the city. They got my wallet while I was in the Guggenheim of all places. I didn't notice until I left and tried to buy subway fare. I only have the money I had in my hotel room, so I can pay in cash."

"That's horrible."

"It's a mess."

I can tell she's debating whether to believe me or whether to turn me away. I run my hand through my hair and over my face, showing how tired I am. My shoulders sag, and I can tell the moment she takes pity on me.

"Do you have a car in the lot? I'll need the license plate number."

I give it to her, and I can tell she's wondering why I'm in Connecticut if I have New York plates. She looks up at me.

"Luckily, I had a rental because I can't fly home without my ID."

I make up some random address in Vermont of all places. Whatever. I'm banking on the fact she won't check. I pull out the amount she tells me, and I grab my key. I have never been so glad to lock a door behind me after I put the Do Not Disturb sign on the door handle. I flop onto the bed after dropping my bag on the floor. I lie back for a moment, but my stomach grumbles. I devour my food. Thank heavens for hotel toiletries. There's a toothbrush and toothpaste. There's shampoo and soap too. I'm tempted, but hair color takes better on dirty hair. I'm going to take care of that in the morning.

I put the burner on the bedside table beside my regular phone, which I turned off once I got away from the liquor store parking lot. I didn't want my location services to ping anything, but I want it close just in case. I strip naked and climb between the clean sheets. I'm out within five minutes.

I'm a brunette now with plain brown eyes. I barely recognize myself since I also bought some self-tanner while I was getting the contact lenses. It's just enough of a tan to make me look like a completely different person. I'm banking on the desk clerk from last night not being there now that it's mid-morning. I get ready to head out to buy some food to keep in my room.

I guess I'm going to be watching a lot of TV for the next week. I have enough to cover seven days at the hotel and still have money for food and more gas. I'm going to have to go out somewhere every couple days, so housekeeping can get in and tidy the room. I don't want to draw attention by not having them come in, nor do I need them doing a random wellness check to be sure I'm not a corpse stinking up the room.

What if that woman from last night looks me up? I'm supposed to be on my way home to Vermont. Damn. I need to move somewhere else. This is so much more complicated than I thought. I gather the few things I have, including the used-up hair dye stuff and the contacts packaging. I check out and get back on the road. Where to now?

"What the—"

I lay on the horn as the car in front of me slams on its brakes for no reason on the interstate. I swerve to miss it, but a car rams into me from the back while I swear another car speeds up to nail my front driver's side. I can't help it. I rear-end the car that randomly stopped. It's after the morning commute, so the highway is relatively quiet. There aren't cars whizzing by. I lean over to get my registration out of my glove box, and a damn good thing I do. The driver's window shatters before the front passenger one does too. Someone just shot them.

My door flies open, and a man grabs me. My seatbelt keeps him from pulling me out.

"Come on, *chica*. Don't be stupid. Get out on your own. You won't like it if I do it for you."

I know that Spanish accent. I look over and nearly shit myself. It's Carlos's brother, Arturo. And that is a gun pointing at my head. I close my eyes for a moment. After everything I did to follow Luca's instructions, I didn't even make it a day.

"I'm going to reach down and undo it."

I put my left hand up in the air as I ease my right hand to the buckle. The moment it releases and the belt moves past my right hip, Arturo yanks me out. I can't get my feet under me, so he drags me away from the car. I'm looking around, but all I see are the cars that boxed me in and a swarm of men. They're speaking Spanish, and I can understand all of it. I may look like a gringa with my blonde hair—at least when it was blonde—but my mother's Mexican. Like actually born and raised in Mexico. I grew up speaking Spanish at home.

"*Mátala ahora y déjala.*" Kill her now and leave her.

A guy standing across my car snaps as he looks around. He glances down at me and sneers. I struggle to my feet as Arturo pulls up on my arm. He continues barking orders.

"*Estamos aquí por dejar cabos sueltos. No la vamos a dejar*

21

al costado de una carretera." Leaving loose ends is why we're here. We're not leaving her on the side of a highway.

This guy—the one on the other side of my car with a gun pointed at my chest—sounds like he's in charge.

"*¡Date prisa! Si ese hijo de puta idiota no hubiera perdido tanto tiempo escondiéndose, podríamos haber llegado a ella anoche antes de que Luca la ayudara.*" Hurry up. If that dumbass motherfucker hadn't wasted so much time hiding, we could have gotten to her last night before Luca helped her.

He must mean Carlos's driver hid. How did they know about Luca helping me? I know he wouldn't tell him that.

"Maybe if you spent less time using your own product, you might have figured things out faster. Put the guns down."

My head snaps around, and my eyes nearly fall out of my head. Luca's walking toward me as though there aren't half a dozen guns pointed at him. He's looking at me, and his expression makes me wonder if *El Diablo*—the devil—is his father.

Chapter Three

Luca

I had Gabriele follow Olivia last night. I don't like him, and I don't trust him about most things. But he's our best enforcer, which means he's damn good at tracking someone down. He's a hunter, and I made Olivia his prey. But he knows that he's not to touch her, not to scare her; just keep an eye on her. I had to meet with Uncle Salvatore and give him a heads up on what happened. If it had been a man who screwed up the negotiations by disrupting them, he wouldn't have given a shit when Carlos shot at him. But a woman—Uncle Salvatore would have castrated me for not protecting a woman.

I've done some shitty things lately, especially to Niko Kutsenko's woman, but I learned my lesson. I learned I will never trust Carmine ever again, and I will never let that *stronzo* —asshole—control me again. He can tell my secret for all I care. I'm not going down with him again. I'm still redeeming myself with my uncle, so I knew he would understand, and he did. *Grazie Dio.* Thank God.

Once Gabriele told me she stopped at a hotel in Norwalk, I went out there. I needed to see for myself that Olivia was safe. I could have let it go and just had Gabriele watch her for a few days, but I couldn't. Something compels me to watch over her myself. I'm glad I did. I knew Carlos's brother, Arturo, and his boss, Manuel, would figure shit out way too soon.

"Maybe if you spent less time using your own product, you might have figured things out faster. Put the guns down."

I watch her head swing around to me and wince since Arturo now has his hand fisted in her hair and is steering her to stand in front of him. The only man who should have his hand in her short hair is me. And it should be while I make her scream with ecstasy, not whimper in pain. I'll kill him just for that.

"Let her go, Arturo. Manuel, you don't want to do this. The woman is under my protection after your cousin fucked up. If he hadn't tried to screw me out of what *you* agreed to, we would have finished before she came out of the store. We had a witness because of him. She's my responsibility."

"She's just some bitch that you'll fuck and forget. But she won't forget. We don't need her going to the police. You should have had the *huevos* to put a bullet in her head. I have no problem doing that."

"You say I don't have the balls to do it, yet you think I'm going to fuck her. It's been my experience that you need one—both—to do the other. It also means I'll put a bullet between your eyes like I did Carlos. Put your gun down."

I'm still walking toward Olivia and Arturo. I'm watching Manuel, who's standing on the other side of Olivia's car with a gun pointed at her. My gun is pointed at him. If I see his trigger finger even twitch, I'll shoot. I can see Olivia in my peripheral vision, and her terror is obvious. But the closer I step, the more I realize she's actually afraid for me. She thinks they'll kill me. It would be a grave mistake for them to kill the *Cosa Nostra's* next don. I may not take that position for a few more decades, but I will.

Manuel smirks at me before delivering his lame comeback.

"I'd like to see you try."

I know my men are in position. They were already calling out who they'd each target before our cars stopped. They each have a man to focus on. I swing to point my gun toward Arturo and squeeze the trigger. Before the bullet even reaches his skull, I pivot and do the same thing to Manuel. Arturo falls and brings Oliva down with him. She screams and tries to scramble away while my men take care of the other Mexicans. A shootout on a Connecticut highway is hardly ideal, and I can already hear sirens from passersby calling the cops. I sprint to Olivia and pull her into my arms.

"Shh, *piccolina.*"

I scoop her up and carry her to the SUV I rode in. There are three others with enough room for the two guys who rode in the back with me to find seats in a different one. I help her into the backseat before I climb in. I holstered my gun as I ran to her, but I pull it out again as the car door slams behind me. I put it on the seat next to me and lift her onto my lap.

"It's all right, Livy. I'm here now. I never should have sent you off on your own. I'm sorry."

"All right? It's never going to be all right. I've witnessed two shootouts and seen at least a dozen men die in the past two days. I may as well give up now. There is no way I'm going to survive this."

I grasp her shoulders and push her away from my chest, giving her a little shake.

"Do not say that. *Not ever.* You will *not* give up. I won't let you."

The vehemence in my voice shocks me, but I hate the idea

that this life of violence has come anywhere near her, and I loathe the idea that it will defeat her. She doesn't deserve any of this. She had so much fight in her last night, and now she seems a shadow of the woman I met less than twenty-four hours ago. For some inexplicable reason, I need to bring that strength and courage back to her. There's something I can't name that draws me to her. She's a stranger, so it's utterly ridiculous.

Five months ago, I was trying to arrange a marriage with the Chicago don's daughter. I loved her no more than anyone would love a bad case of the flu, but it would've been an advantageous deal to strengthen the *Cosa Nostra* from the East Coast to the Midwest. I wasn't heartbroken when it fell through. I was more pissed by the consequences of going behind Uncle Salvatore's back and getting the bratva from Russia involved with the New York bratva. The Chicago woman was pretty and intelligent, but she did nothing for me. The woman on my lap—she's doing everything *to* me.

"Only because you're worried I'll go to the police, too, Luca. You wouldn't care otherwise."

I tuck hair behind her ear, so I can lean in and whisper. Our town cars and limos have privacy glass, but our SUVs don't. I don't need my driver listening in.

"I can't name what's driving me to protect you. But I can tell you that worrying about you going to the police isn't it. You were so brave last night. I know it scared you shitless, but there was so much defiance in you when I caught you. Then there was so much resilience as I explained what you needed to do. The idea of that going away—that this shitshow extinguished any of that—I can't stand it."

"But why? Why does that matter? You say you can't name it, but there has to be a reason."

"Fate."

She stares at me, but I pull her back against my chest and kiss the top of her head.

"Rest, *piccolina*. We'll talk when we're somewhere safe."

"Where are we going?"

"To my house."

I feel her freeze, then she inhales a shaky breath. It surprises me when I feel her body go lax against mine. I glance down to find she shut her eyes as she burrows closer. She draws her legs up and tucks her arms between us as though she's curling into a protective ball.

"Livy, I'm going to protect you. Relax and sleep, little girl."

"First it's *piccolina*. Now it's Livy. Why the pet names as though I'm someone special to you?"

I tip her chin up and gaze into the plain brown eyes. They're a disappointing shade after seeing her natural color. It doesn't stop me from pressing a soft kiss to her lips. The words slip from my mouth, and I have no explanation for where they come from.

"No one is more special to me."

Her eyes well with tears before she presses an equally soft kiss to my lips. Then she burrows against me again. The vehicle is silent except for the radio, which my driver keeps low, all the way back into the city.

My house in Queens is modest compared to my uncle's, but it suits me as a bachelor who never entertains. The only people who come over regularly are my brothers, Lorenzo and Marco, and Marco's best friend, Matteo. My little sister, Maria, comes by the least, but I enjoy her company the most. My brothers and Matteo usually come to discuss work. My home is my sanctuary, and I insist that my office is the only place where our

Mafia life permeates my otherwise peaceful place. I say it's modest because it only has four bedrooms compared to the mansion Uncle Salvatore and Aunt Sylvia own. But I still have a gate with bodyguards to patrol the grounds.

"Wake up, Livy. We're home."

Not we're at my home. Just home. Why on Earth does that sound right to me? Did all that Sicilian sun bake my brain? For my royal fuck up with the Chicago deal, Uncle Salvatore sentenced me, Carmine, and Gabriele to working at a Sicilian winery. Life at that vineyard was a hard labor camp, not a vacation, despite how the Kutsenkos taunt me about it. Eighteen—sometimes twenty—hour days, working outside among the vines. The owner was a sick bastard. He enjoyed beating Carmine, Gabriele, and me. He knew we wouldn't fight back. He knew we wouldn't complain to Uncle Salvatore.

That's exactly why Uncle Salvatore sent us there as our punishment. I doubly deserved it, and I can accept that now. I allowed Carmine to influence me, and I contributed to the shit that put Anastasia Kutsenko in the hospital then got her kidnapped. I don't want to think about that anymore, but it's constantly on my mind. That must be why I feel so driven to protect Livy. I need to redeem myself more than I realized.

"Where are we?"

Livy rubs her eyes as she looks out the window. It took nearly a half an hour, but she fell into a deep sleep.

"Queens."

"Queens? I thought being in the city wasn't safe for me."

"Look around. The place is practically Fort Knox. No one is coming in without getting past my security."

"Am I prisoner?"

"No. We have to sort some things out, and you may need to stay here for a while. But you are not a prisoner. I won't hold you against your will, Livy. But I hope you'll stay here until we have somewhere safe for you. I have three guest bedrooms, and they all have an ensuite bathroom. I have a living room and a den, plus a fully finished basement. I will keep you company, or I will give you space. Whichever you want. There's plenty of room for us to never see each other if that's what you want."

"That sounds like solitary confinement."

"I just don't want you to think I expect—"

I know what I hope, but I don't want her believing I'm going to take advantage of her. She watches me before she nods.

"Can I call my mom? We don't talk every day, but we do a couple times a week."

"Of course."

"What do I tell her? We both live in Brooklyn, and she knows I'm single. How do I explain this?"

"We'll figure that out together, but I don't have an answer right now."

I ease her off my lap and open the door. Once I'm out, I offer her my hand as she climbs out. I let go, but I don't want to. She's a fraction of a second slower to release my hand than I expected. Does she like holding it? I lead her into the house and start pointing out the rooms on the first floor before showing her the basement. I have a theater down there and a gym. I let her know she's welcome to use either whenever she wants. When we get to the second floor, I stop at the top of the stairs.

"My room is to the right, and the guest bedrooms are down here to the left."

She glances toward my door before following me in the opposite direction. I show her each of the three rooms, and she chooses the one that looks out over the backyard. One of my guys grabbed her gym bag before we left the accident scene, so someone brought her bag upstairs while I was giving her a tour downstairs. It was waiting beside the railing that looks over my living room.

"Thanks for having someone grab my stuff. What about my car? The police are going to know it's mine. Then they'll want to know how I'm involved in the shooting and the crash."

"They won't find your car. Gabriele—the guy who stood to my right last night—will have made sure we took the plates off and fakes replaced them before a tow truck brought it to one of our salvage yards. I can already tell you it's totaled."

"I figured, but how do I file an insurance claim? I can't just get a new one. I don't have the—"

"Livy, we will sort all of this out. I don't have answers to everything yet. You're going to be here for a few days, and I think it's best that you don't leave the property. But if you do, I have more than one car you can use."

"I can't—"

I hate not touching her when we have these kinds of intense conversations. Yet another thing I have no way to explain. I slide my arm around her waist, but I keep my hold loose as I interrupt her. I don't want her to get the wrong idea about my intentions since we're standing in a bedroom.

"You can. I get that this is a bizarre situation. I'm asking you to trust me when you don't know me. I know that's no small thing. I told Manuel that you're my responsibility, and you are. But only because I want that. I'm not looking for some Stockholm Syndrome shit where I kidnap a woman to make her fall for me. But I want to take care of you, Liv. I feel protective of you, and I not only need to know you're safe, I want to do what I can to make you happy while you're here."

"I still don't understand why. I don't get why you're doing this. And I sure as hell don't understand why I'm agreeing to any of this. It's insane."

I sigh. I'm going to muddle my way through the truth as best I can when I'm not sure what to say.

"When you stepped out of that building, I thought you were the most gorgeous woman I've ever seen."

"You must not have had a very good view."

Anger pulses through me at her flippant comment. It's unreasonable, but it vibrates within me. My arm is still around her waist while my other hand fists her short hair. I'm not trying to hurt her like Arturo did. But I want her to understand the man she's about to share a home with.

"I know exactly what I saw, *piccolina*. I have eyes like a hawk and ears like a dog. Do not contradict me about how I feel. I said I saw the most gorgeous woman I've ever seen, and that's what the fuck I meant."

"You think I'm gorgeous? I'm short, and I'm too—"

What the fuck possesses me? My lips slam down against hers as I lift her off her feet. My tongue presses against her lips, demanding entrance. She's hesitant—smart girl. But she lets me in with a sigh. I'm ready to devour her—heart, body, and soul. I want her like an addict wants his next hit. I crave it now that I've started. However, a sliver of reason tells me to slow down. I pull away and put her back on her feet.

"Whatever you think are your flaws may be very real to you, but I don't see them."

I'm panting as my heart races from our kiss. I'm no monk, but I don't date. I don't do random hook-ups at my age. There's a woman I fuck when the mood strikes us. We don't go on dates. We don't snuggle on the sofa and watch movies. We don't chat about our days. I tie her up and fuck her until we're both too tired to keep going. The sex is amazing. But nothing with that woman or any before Livy can compare to that kiss. Holy fuck.

"Luca."

She trails her finger softly along my scar as she stares into my eyes. I want her to take those fucking contacts out right this fucking minute.

"You're the hottest man I've ever seen. Men who look like you don't hook up with women who look like me."

I lean forward and whisper in her ear much like I did in the SUV.

"Argue with me one more time, *piccolina*, and I will spank you." *And fuck you until my eyes cross.*

"Spank me?"

It's a breathless whisper that shoots straight to my cock, which is fucking hard and uncomfortable. I know she felt it while we kissed. She pressed her hips forward.

"With great pleasure—at least for me." I squeeze her ass. "I wouldn't tolerate anyone else insulting you, so I won't listen to you do it. I'd beat the shit out of a guy, and I would have nothing polite to say to a woman. Don't test me, *piccolina*. Your ass wouldn't like the outcome."

I watch her, and the heat that flares in her eyes tells me she might like it very much. I know lust when I see it.

"Or is that exactly what you'd enjoy?"

"I—"

She shakes her head. We're moving way too fast. She's not ready to confess her sexual desires to me, and I can't blame her. I'm not ready to tell her I like my sex kinky and hard.

"You asked me why, but I didn't get to finish explaining. There's a fire in you I saw last night. It draws me like a moth to a flame. You intrigue me, but I also admire your strength. It took a lot to witness what you did and not fall apart. Most people couldn't handle it with that calm and rationality. My guy followed you last night. He watched you in both pharmacies and at Walmart. He said you were methodical in making it look like you weren't there for just the things you needed. You kept your back to the camera at the gas station. Somehow, you got a hotel room without using your ID or credit cards. I hacked the hotel and know you gave a false name and address. You're resourceful. I admire you, and I refuse to let anyone extinguish that flame or diminish you in any way. That's why I'm so protective. You went to a hotel because you have no one else to protect you or because you refuse to endanger anyone else. Right now, you're alone in this if I don't help. That's why I want to take care of you."

"Are you always like this?"

"Never."

The word comes out harsher than I intend. Her eyes widen a fraction. I'm no longer fisting her hair but cupping her skull and supporting its weight as she tilts it back to look up at me.

"What do you mean take care of me? That you're offering me a place to stay and food to eat?"

"Yeah. But I want you to know you can rely on me when you're scared, that you can come to me when you're worried."

"If I do that, then you'll have a second shadow."

"I wouldn't mind."

She smiles, and the angels sing.

"I'd be underfoot like a chihuahua."

"Hardly. I don't take you for the yappy type, and I don't think you'd bite." I wink. "Unless I asked you to."

I can't help the innuendo. I don't flirt, but I find I want to with Livy. I want to lighten her mood, but I also want her.

"Luca, I'm scared. This all—it's too much. I'm scared that the Culiacán won't give up. I'm scared that I don't have a job or a car. I'm scared because I can't go to my place. I'm scared they'll find my mom. I'm scared to trust you. I'm scared of how attracted I am to you at the worst possible time. I'm scared of dying. I'm just fucking scared of everything."

I think about sitting next to her on the bed, but she's just told me being attracted to me frightens her. The bed isn't the right place to take her. I slide my hand into hers and lead her to the love seat positioned to see the TV. I sit, then pull her onto my lap. She curls up like she did in the car on the way here.

"If this were a normal situation where we met at a bar or store or coffeeshop or wherever, then I would have chatted with you and asked for your number. I would have called you—not texted, but actually talked to you—and asked you out. I would have prayed you'd say yes. If you had, I would have taken you to dinner and maybe a movie, or to a museum, or for a walk, or whatever you wanted. I would have prayed for a goodnight kiss and that you would agree to another date and another and another. But that's not what fate dealt us. But I can make dinner for you, or we could order in. We can watch a movie in like five different places in this house. We can walk around the backyard. It's not ideal, but it's what we have. Livy, would you go out with me?"

"Are you trying to distract me?"

"No. I'm trying to find a normal way for you to trust me and get used to me. I'm trying to take care of you. I know you're scared, and I hate it. I caused this as much as Carlos and his family. I'm trying to make it better."

She's silent a long time as she digests what I said.

"Luca, I don't have trust issues, despite watching my father intimidate my mother and having him threaten me more than once with a knife. But neither am I too trusting and naïve. Something in me is telling me I can and should trust you. If you disappoint me, I'll never forgive you. If you're saying all this just to fuck, then you don't need to."

"Are you saying you'd fuck me even if you didn't trust me?"

I'll deal with that first.

"I mean, if this is just about sex, then let it just be about sex.

You don't have to win me over. You're hot, and you know I desire you, even if this is such a fucked-up time for this."

"Is that all you want? Someone to fuck until you can move on with your life? Is that how you want me to distract you?"

"I'm just saying don't play me for a fool, Luca. If you want to fuck me, then forget about me, then just say so. You don't have to woo me."

"That is not what I want. I don't lie, Liv. I have plenty of faults, and you know I sin without remorse. But I have been honest with you since the start. I told you what you needed to do to get away. Yeah, I followed you to be sure you were okay, but I didn't plan to contact you so soon. I was prepared to watch you walk away because I thought that was the right thing to do. I thought that was the best way to protect you. It's never been about fucking and forgetting you. You're utterly unforgettable."

"You'd really like to date me?"

"Yes."

"I've heard of staycations, but is this stay-dating?"

"I suppose so. If you don't enjoy my company after our stay-at-home date, then I'll back off. You can friend zone me or tell me to give you space. I'll respect either."

She kisses my cheek before cupping my cheek with the scar. Usually, I hate anyone touching it. It doesn't hurt, and I'm not embarrassed by it. I just don't like the reminder.

"What time are you picking me up for dinner, Luca?"

Chapter Four

Livy

I'm fucking certifiable, and so is he. He said he doesn't want some Stockholm Syndrome woman falling for him. He hasn't kidnapped me exactly, but this is like a forced proximity romance book. Except, there's not just one room at the inn. There's no winter blizzard forcing us to share a cabin in the woods. The hotel didn't accidentally mix up our reservations. I'm staying at a mobster's house because another group of mobsters tried to kill me.

Are we into each other because of convenience? We're clearly attracted to each other. I think he's exaggerating—by miles—how good looking I am, but he's fucking *fine*. I'm certain he's probably better than a porn star in bed. He radiates it. I think I'm a pretty good lay, if I do say so myself. Is that all this is about? We're stuck here together, so we may as well fuck? It could be worse.

But I don't want it to just be about sex. And that makes me fucking certifiable. Nothing can come of this. This is not grounds for a solid relationship. What happens when I don't need him anymore? Does his protectiveness wear off, and he's done? Do I realize I was using him just to survive?

I don't have answers to these questions, and the shower I'm taking isn't relaxing. I hoped it would be, but I'm not someone who can just stand under running water for ages. I'm a wash and go kinda girl, so I'm already done washing my hair and giving myself a good scrub. Maybe I thought I could wash away the memories of the dead bodies and of Arturo touching me. I can't.

I hurry to towel dry my hair. I appreciate that someone grabbed my purse and my gym bag. I have clean clothes to put on. I wear little makeup most days, so what I have in that cosmetic bag is enough for me to feel presentable. Once I'm dressed, I make my way downstairs. I smell something divine, and my stomach rumbles. It's midafternoon, and we missed lunch. It's too early to call this a dinner date, but I'm excited.

As I walk into the kitchen, it shocks me to see Luca in jeans and a polo shirt. He was in a suit last night and one this morning. He looks just as hot in something casual, but it doesn't look like comfy clothes you'd wear around the house. I'm in a pair of the jeans and the flowery shirt I grabbed. I feel under dressed, especially with the sneakers that were in my gym bag. He's in what looks like designer Italian leather loafers.

But it surprises me even more to find him standing at the stove with two pots and a pan in front of him. I walk over to him, and I have this overwhelming urge to wrap my arms around him and rest my cheek against his back as I hug him. It would be the picture of domestic tranquility. He must be thinking something similar because he puts down the wooden spoon and turns to me, drawing me into his embrace.

"I'm neither barefoot nor pregnant, but I am in the kitchen, *piccolina.*"

"Ha. I hardly see you with the title househusband."

He chuckles, and it makes my pussy ache. I've been a mess since he kissed me. The hot water did nothing to relax me in the shower, and neither did getting myself off twice. The feel of him holding me just soaked another pair of panties. This just feels so damn natural, and I bet the feel of him inside me would be divine.

"Maybe not a househusband, but I like the idea of cooking for you. It's definitely better than making all this just for me and knowing it'll be leftovers for the next three days."

"Don't you know how to make single servings?"

"That's rhetorical, right? I'm Italian. Like fully Italian. Both my *nonnas* were from Sicily, and my *nonno* on my mom's side was too. My dad's dad was second generation Italian American. So, three-quarters of my grandparents were from Italy, born and raised. A single serving means enough for at least a family of six to eat all at one meal."

"What're you making?"

"I didn't think to ask whether you have any allergies or whether you like seafood, so I stuck with something I figured was safe. In other words, nothing with sardines. They're popular in Sicilian food, but I know not everyone likes them. I'll eat them since I've been doing it since before I could talk, but I don't like them. This is *pasta alla Norma*. It's named after some opera. I have no idea why. But it's salted ricotta, eggplant, garlic, basil, and tomatoes over pasta."

"It smells delicious."

"It's one of the first dishes I learned to cook. My mom made sure my brothers, my sister, and I could all make it. She said if we could prepare at least this, we would never starve. She warned my sister to never make it for a man unless she was already married. She said it would be enough for any guy to drag Maria to the altar. You know, the whole the way to a man's heart is through his stomach. She was joking, but Mama's recipe is that good."

"How many brothers do you have?"

"Officially? Only two. Lorenzo and Marco. But Marco's best friend, Matteo, may as well be my third brother. They were born on the same day, and our mothers are best friends. Marco and Matteo have been inseparable since they were three."

"You're the oldest?"

"Yes. Maria is the youngest."

I can tell he hesitates before he lets go to stir the eggplant in the pan. I can see the pasta is boiling in one pot while the other ingredients for the sauce are in the other pot. I look up when he speaks.

"You recognized my last name. What do you know about my family?"

"Only what I've heard gossiped. I grew up in Brooklyn, so I've heard speculation my entire life. After what I saw last night and this morning, I realize some of it wasn't far off."

"Have you seen someone die before?"

"No. Why?"

"You saw me kill last night and today. You saw men who work for me do the same thing. Yet you aren't running for the hills. You might think I'm attractive, but I doubt my looks would be enough to keep you if you believed me a psychopath."

"I was thinking about that while we were on the highway. Part of me rationalizes it would be the ultimate sign of being unappreciative if I took umbrage with what you did after you kept me alive twice. Part of me figures you live a life I don't know and don't understand, but it's obviously kill or be killed. I can't blame you for wanting to live. A huge part of me is glad it was those fuckers who died rather than me. You've been kind and gentle with me from the start. I guess, somehow, I'm able to separate the man I've seen handling a gun with the man you are with me. Am I naïve to do that?"

"No. I never want to be that man around you. I hate that you've seen what you have because I never, ever want you to fear I would be violent with you. I didn't miss you saying you saw your father mistreat your mother and that he threatened you. I am not that kind of man, even though violence surrounds me outside my home. Where is your father, Livy? You mentioned it was only your mom and you."

I wondered why he didn't react earlier. I suppose he figured it wasn't the right time, but I knew it would come up. He doesn't seem like the forgetful or oblivious type. I take a deep breath before I sigh.

"My parents divorced when I was nine. My dad still came around because the court granted him joint custody despite knowing he kept intimidating my mom even after their marriage ended. I have no idea how that happened because that can't be typical in family court. He never struck me, and he wasn't even verbally abusive, except for the threats. It was enough for the courts to believe I was better off with a father in my life than a deadbeat."

"Threatened you? That's the definition of abusive."

"I meant he didn't swear at me, call me names, or tell me I was worthless. None of that. But he would threaten me to get me to do what he wanted. He'd point knives at me if I didn't want to go for my weekends with him. He'd do it to make sure I knew my curfew or to make sure I didn't hang out with the wrong people. He would just point them at me and wave them. He never said he would slice me or kill me. He never touched me with one."

"You didn't answer my first question. Where is he?"

"When I turned eighteen, I cut ties with him. I don't see or talk to him anymore. It's been years since—"

"Olivia, answer me."

"Don't call me that."

It shocks me to not only hear the words come out of my mouth but also how sad I sound.

"What?"

Luca's brow furrows, and he's not sure what I mean. Maybe he didn't notice.

"You never call me Olivia. I—I don't like it. It sounds—"

All I can do is shrug. My cheeks are ablaze, and I feel like a fool. I'm completely embarrassed. He wraps me in one of his hugs, and it's like the world is back to rights. His hugs make me feel safe, like I really am protected.

"*Piccolina,* I'm sorry. I guess I wanted to make sure you knew I was serious when I told you to answer me. I didn't mean to sound distant, or that I was telling you off or something. I call you little girl, but I don't think you are one. I wasn't scolding you."

"I know you weren't. But it just sounds so—cold."

"Considering you make me overheat, I didn't mean to sound cold."

"Overheat? Are you sure it isn't just you sweating over an open fire making me my meal?"

He squeezes my ass, and I love it.

"You know what you do to me, Livy."

"Do I?"

I'm trying my abysmal flirting skills, but they seem to work since he chuckles again. He turns off the burner for the eggplants and lifts me, pulling my legs around his waist before turning toward the kitchen island. He places me on it, and I'm ready to drop my legs, but he holds them in place. His hard cock presses against my pussy, and my nipples are hard.

"If you tease me, I'll tease you right back."

He kisses along my neck and up behind my ear as he palms

my breast. He squeezes it just like he did my ass cheek a moment ago before his thumb and forefinger catch my nipple between them. He adjusts to pinch it as he sucks my earlobe. I moan as my legs tighten around him, trying to draw him closer. But he resists. He pulls back, actually. The moment I give up, he pulls me off the island and swings me toward a wall. My back slams against it as he grinds his cock against my pussy.

"Don't tease, little girl, unless you're ready to get what you ask for."

"What do you think I'm asking for?"

"Do you want me to answer that with words? Or do you want me to show you?"

"Show me."

I blurt my answer before I can think better of it. He carries me to the kitchen table and sits in a chair after he puts me on my feet. Before I know what's happening, my jeans are at my ankles. My lacey thong is practically in shreds, and I'm over his lap. His hand lands across my ass, and I yelp. It's from surprise. When the second lands, I'm prepared—ish. I know he's not spanking me nearly as hard as he could, but it leaves a sting.

"Kick your jeans off and widen your legs, turn your feet inward."

I'm quick to follow his directions, and I know he has a clear view of how wet I am. He spanks each cheek twice more once I'm free of my sneakers and pants. Then his fingers dive into me. He thrusts two in, and they slide with ease. I'm fucking dripping.

"You like the feel of my cock against your pussy. You love the feel of my hand on your bare ass as I spank you. And you sure as fuck love me finger fucking you."

"Yes."

I can barely croak my response before I moan. He's rubbing my g-spot and my clit. All I can think about is how badly I want to come. I can't even think about what this makes me to be hooking up with this guy in his kitchen barely more than twelve hours after we met.

"Tell me where your dad is, and I'll let you come."

That's a bucket of cold water.

"Let go of me, Luca. Stop."

He does immediately. He draws his hands away until I struggle to get upright. He helps me, then lets go again. I'm standing there with my socks on, but no underwear or jeans. I feel ridiculous.

"Don't do that. Don't use sex to manipulate me into doing what you want. That's not all right."

"I shouldn't have done that. I apologize. I regretted it as soon as I said it. I'm sorry."

His apologies always sound genuine, but it's almost like they're foreign words to him. Ones he hasn't said that often. He holds out his hands to me, and I place mine in his. He guides me to straddle his legs before I sit.

"I still want to know the answer. And I enjoy playing with you, including orgasm denial. But I shouldn't have put the two together. Livy, I like my sex rough and kinky. If you prefer vanilla, then I'll try. But it's not what I'm used to anymore."

"Used to? Do you have a girlfriend?"

"No. I have a fuck buddy, but I've never been married. I don't have kids. And I haven't had a girlfriend since college."

"A fuck buddy."

I don't like that. Actually, I viscerally hate it. Jealousy pumps through me as I sit half naked on his lap.

"Am I going to become your second one?"

"No. Had. I should say had. I texted her it's over while you were in the shower."

He pulls out his phone and unlocks it. He pulls up some contact called Diana and shows me.

LUCA

I've met someone. Our arrangement is over.

DIANA

Over? Met someone? You don't date. That's why we fuck. A lot. We'll just put it on pause like we do when I'm dating someone.

No. No pausing. There won't be any coming back. It's serious.

The fuck it is. We were together yesterday afternoon.

It's done. You know it's not a good idea to argue with me.

Yes, sir. I'm sorry, sir.

Holy fuck. Holy fucking shit. There's no more to the conversation. But I don't like most of it. I hate knowing he was fucking someone else yesterday afternoon, only hours before meeting me. So what if I hooked up with my ex-boyfriend the night before last? I'm not telling Luca that, so I don't want to know about this Diana chick. And sir?

"Are you a Dom?"

"Yes."

"Is that what—"

"No, Livy. That is not what I want with you. Diana was a fuck buddy who likes it kinky, too. Our relationship was entirely based on kinky sex whether it was a prelude to it or the actual thing. There was no romance or tender feelings involved. If you prefer vanilla, then I'll work hard to never be too rough with you. I will never ask for anything you don't offer."

"Do you realize we have some intense conversations? Like shit most couples don't discuss for weeks, if not months, into their relationships. Or at least not before the first date. I'm sitting half naked, reading texts from a woman you fucked yesterday, and now we're discussing how you and I are going to have sex."

"We are. I'm in over my head with you. Even if we don't work out—though I wholeheartedly believe we will—I can't go back to her now that I've tasted you. I want you in a way that makes my heart ache. I've never felt that before."

He sighs as he looks out the kitchen window before his gaze meets mine again.

"I've never admitted to anyone who—or rather what—I am in my family. I told you about my brothers and sister, which I never do. I don't name names. Ever. You know I'm *Cosa Nostra*, and you know that means I'm in the Mafia. I'm the underboss. One day, I will become the don when my uncle Salvatore dies. That won't be for at least twenty or thirty more years. But I will run our branch one day. You've seen what I can do. I think you know last night wasn't the first time I've done that. You also saw that I make life-changing decisions quickly. I consider my options—all of them—but I'm decisive. I have to be. I don't have the luxury of hemming and hawing over things. I've spent the last twelve hours thinking about you, about us. I know that doesn't sound long to a regular person, but in my world, that's practically a lifetime when you make split-second decisions that could kill you or end a dynasty. I'm not impulsive, Liv. I'm purposeful. I wouldn't tell you any of this, let you anywhere near my life, if I didn't think there's something real and special between us."

"Aren't all Italians romantic? Don't you all love *love*?"

"Hardly. But neither are all Italian men philanderers who can't keep it in their pants. Diana is the only woman I've been with in four years. I know what you read. When we were together, we were together for a reason. But we went weeks, even months, without seeing each other. I didn't see her every day. I definitely never would have given her an open-ended invitation to stay here. I've never done that before, but I did for you because I want to know if we can have something as special as I think."

I listen to everything he's saying. I thought about him the entire way to the hotel. I dreamed about him when I slept in the hotel bed and while I was in his arms on the drive here. I thought about him fucking me as I rubbed my clit and got off in the shower. But before and after that, I thought about what we could be. If we could be. I might not be his level of decisive. I doubt many people are. But I'm not wishy-washy either.

I kept telling myself over and over all the reasons this is wrong. All the reasons I should find him morally repugnant. All the reasons I should sneak away. All the reasons I should call the police. No matter how many times I did, my mind reverted to one simple fact. Being with him feels right. I know I'm safe in this house. The guards everywhere prove that. I don't need to keep hugging him or letting him hug me. I want it. I need it because it feels like this is how life should be, not because I'm struggling to keep from falling apart. I'm shockingly calm as I consider all of this.

"Livy?"

"Sorry. I was just thinking about how I've spent almost every minute since I met you thinking about you. I've thought about why I trust you and haven't tried to escape or turn you in. I've thought about why you make me feel safe and why you've offered to protect me. I've thought about you saying you want to take care of me and what that might mean. I've thought about how much I want to sleep with you. I've thought about why I'm thinking about it all. And the only answer I can come up with is that there is something special between us. You said you haven't had a girlfriend since college. My guess is you're about thirty. That's a long time. I get why you haven't with what I assume your life is like. If you're letting me in, then you must want me to stay."

"I do, Livy. Very much. I'll never force you, though. If this isn't right for you, if you want out, then I'll let you go. But not before I beg you and try to be what you need."

"I don't think I want you to change, Luca. I think I need you to be who you are now. It's the man I'm drawn to."

"Do you believe I won't trap you?"

"Yes." I look down. "I need to send a text similar to what you sent Diana."

"You said you don't have a boyfriend."

"I don't. But I hooked up with an ex-boyfriend the night before last, and we agreed to be friends with benefits. I'm supposed to see him tomorrow night."

I feel him tense beneath me. I run my hands up his abs and over his chest, hoping to soothe him. It's my turn to kiss up his neck to behind his ear. I flick his ear with my tongue.

"If you don't want me inside you, fucking you until you scream, you need to stop."

I tug his earlobe between my teeth. I whisper to him.

"Warn your men because I'm going to be loud."

I cling to Luca as he jolts out of his seat. He strides over to the stove and turns everything off. I'd forgotten about the food. He walks back to the chair, holding me like a chimp clinging to a tree, and swipes at my jeans and panties. He looks down at the clothes in his hand.

"Wear panties again, *piccolina*, and I will shred them just like I did these. Your pussy is mine."

Chapter Five

Luca

I need to slow down before I embarrass myself. Just the feel of her pressed against me as I walk up the stairs, the way she's rubbing against me, is driving me mad. When I get to the second-floor landing, I look toward her room. Fuck that. She can keep her stuff there and even sleep there if she needs space, but she's going to scream my name in my bed. Our bed if I get what I want—need. What is wrong with me?

When my family finds out—which they will—that I brought a woman here and plan to have her stay indefinitely, I won't hear the end of it. It's not like every woman in my family was a virgin when she got married, and the men definitely weren't, but no one lived together before the wedding. Most of the couples were arranged, anyway.

Uncle Salvatore and Aunt Sylvia were. She arrived from Sicily only a couple weeks before they got married. She barely spoke any English. But she and Uncle Salvatore were a match made in heaven. They fell for each other right away. At least

Uncle Salvatore was infatuated by their wedding. Love came a little later.

Maybe that's what I'm doing. I know I'm not in love. Obviously. I don't know Livy well enough for something that serious. It must be infatuation. But infatuation doesn't last. I want this to. I want it to become more. In my family, the couples who have fallen in love—and that sure hasn't been all of them—look at Carmine's parents—didn't take years to get there. Maybe I'm more like Uncle Salvatore than either he or I think.

"*Piccolina*, what do you want?"

"You."

I chuckle.

"I know that. You already told me, and your wet little cunt proves it. I mean, do you want vanilla? Do you know what that means?"

"Yes, I do. And no, I don't."

"Are you into kinky?"

As much as I want to rip her shirt and bra off like I did her panties, this is yet another time for a serious conversation. If this were a one-night stand, then I'd figure it out as we go. But I'm praying this is the first of many times. And I have never wanted to pleasure a woman more. Not just physically.

Before Diana, I had a couple other subs, so we knew from the start what we wanted. It was just a matter of setting limits. I tried romance with the few girls I dated in high school and college, but I could never commit emotionally. They were pretty vanilla with me—just holding their hands above their heads or at their lower back, maybe a mild spank here or there. Maybe that's what Livy means.

"Yes, but there's never been the opportunity to try the things I really want."

"You've only had vanilla, but you want BDSM. Do you know what types of things you're into?"

I sit on the bed with her still wrapped around me. She pulls off her socks while I unbutton the cute shirt she's wearing and slide it off her shoulders as I kiss the top of her tits. She's left only wearing her bra. She reaches back to unfasten it, but I snag her hands and hold them against her lower back. When she relaxes into my hold, I unfasten it and release her hands to pull it off.

"I know the things I want to try. But I need to know something before I tell you that, because I think it might influence my answer."

"You can ask me anything, anytime, Livy. With my work and my family, there are things I can never tell you, questions I can never answer. I think you can understand why. But I don't want to keep things from you when I don't have to. I want you to know I'm not being closed off because that's what I want. It's only when I have to be."

"I get that. That makes a lot more questions pop into my mind, but I know it would be pointless to ask, and I don't want to put you in that position. What I want to know right now has to do with us and sex. You said you're a Dom, so I suppose Diana was your sub. If I'm staying here with you, do you want a 24/7 Dom/sub arrangement?"

"I don't want a Dom/sub arrangement at all."

I don't. I hadn't pictured that with Livy. Not even once.

"Liv, I'm a dominant man by nature. I need to be in control to feel normal. I have my lifestyle to thank for that, and I get it. Being a Dom is about more than just being in control during sex. It's about providing for a sub's emotional needs, too. But in a limited context. It's not about romance. Some couples mix the two, but that's not what I want. Outside of the bedroom, I want you to know we're always equals. You can disagree with me, argue with me, speak freely with me. If it's about anything but your safety, then I'm willing to compromise or give in. But I'm inflexible about protecting you. That's the only time when I will punish you outside of sex."

"Punish me? That sounds a hell of a lot like domestic discipline."

"No. I won't set rules for you about how you behave. I won't insist that you do exactly what I say about everything. Only when it comes to your safety. You've entered a world you don't understand yet. It happened because of what you saw, but it's going to get harder before it gets easier because you're with me now. If you willfully disobey me or do something foolish because you didn't think about the consequences or danger, then I will punish you. But I won't spank you for not eating your vegetables or staying up too late or talking back. Can you live with that?"

She watches me as I speak, and I know I'm throwing a lot at her. She's vulnerable being naked while I'm fully dressed. We both know that, even though I can tell we both find it arousing as hell. She's going to make herself even more vulnerable by agreeing to what I'm saying, but I hope she trusts me at the same time.

"What if I break your rules or don't meet your expectations, but it's an accident? What if I don't know that I'm doing it?"

"Most likely, I will still punish you. But I will always explain why. The spanking I gave you downstairs was mild, and we both know it. We both know it aroused us together. You enjoyed submitting, and I enjoyed dominating. I'm going to make you come when we're done talking, *piccolina*. But if it's a real punishment, then I probably will not. But I also won't leave you alone after. You already know I like to hold you. I need to. I can't seem to let you go. After a punishment, I won't abandon you. All will be forgiven, and I'll always prove it by staying with you."

I watch her bite her lip.

51

"You know a lot about this. Is this how a regular Dom/sub relationship works too?"

"To an extent."

"Can I ask you how you know so much?"

"Of course. I realized what I'm into while I was in college. I started reading about it and discovered it was what I'd felt was missing in my sex life. I joined a BDSM club that had voyeurism rooms. I watched other couples. I even tried out being a sub to a couple Dommes. I hated it because I hated relinquishing control, but I needed to know how a sub feels, at least in part. Then I practiced. That's where I met Diana."

"Do you still go to that club?"

"Yes."

I watch her stomach suck in, and it's a visceral reaction. I cup her face with both hands and bring her head toward me. I'm slow with my kiss. It only takes a moment before she melts against me.

"*Piccolina*, I told you I've had other Dom/sub arrangements. They were always monogamous. Diana was a fuck buddy. We were free to do what we wanted with other people, and we did. I told you, I want a romantic relationship with you. I want it to be monogamous. I sure as fuck am not leaving you in this house to go out and fuck someone else. If I go back to that club, it's because you want to come with me. If that doesn't appeal to you, or you're not comfortable knowing I'm still a member, then I'll cancel it."

"You don't have to give up your regular life for me. We haven't even had our first stay-date. This is moving too fast, Luca. It's too much to take in."

"I know, Livy. You don't have to agree to anything right now. I'm just putting all my cards on the table, so you know where I stand. I don't want you to worry about or have to guess what I want or expect."

"It sounds like you want me to be your girlfriend."

"Yes. Eventually. If that's what we want as we get to know each other, then that's what you'd become. I know I want to be your boyfriend."

She nods as she continues to absorb it all. I wonder what's going through her mind. She appears contemplative not scared. She runs her fingers over my chest and down my abs to my belt. As she eases her hands to my waist, I know she's considering pulling my shirt free. She's watching herself, but she freezes and brings her gaze to mine.

"Do I call you sir?"

"No. I'm not your Dom."

"But I don't think you want me to call you Luca."

"You can always call me that."

She nods as she fists my shirt, but once more she stops.

"Would you please take your shirt off, Luca?"

She's ceding control to me, and I love it. The question sounds so natural that I can tell she's not forcing it.

"Take it off me, *piccolina*."

She pulls it free from my belt and jeans and inches it up my ribs, but she stops halfway. Is she trying to torture me?

"Is there something I can call you besides Luca? I—I—It doesn't feel right."

"What do you mean?"

"You call me *piccolina* and little girl. I want something too."

One day, I hope she's calling me *amore mio*, my love, or *cuore mio*, my heart.

"*Caro*. It means dear."

It's easy for her to say, and it's a pretty common form of address. It doesn't feel right to tell her that last bit, since I don't want her to think it doesn't mean much to me. But it's not too heavy or significant. She's not ready for that.

"*Caro*. I like that. May I take your shirt off, *caro*?"

"*Si.*"

I raise my arms, and she pulls the shirt over my head. Her eyes widen as they sweep over my abs and up to my chest. She swipes her tongue across her lips as though she's hungry enough to devour me. I'll happily be her lunch instead of the pasta we left. But her brow furrows as she takes in my scars. She trails her fingers over one on my left ribs. I can thank Jorge Diaz for that. He's the nephew of the Colombian Cartel's *jefe*. He can thank me for a matching one on his right ribs. We were sixteen when we got into that knife fight. From the twenty-five stitches we each got, I'd say it ended in a tie. Really, they just mean we both lost. She sees the puckered gunshot scar near my belly button, and her eyes shoot up to mine.

"These are from a long time ago, Liv. They don't hurt, and I don't think about them anymore."

I don't. I'm just used to them. But I can tell how much they trouble her. If she doesn't like those two, she won't like to see my back or my right thigh. I have other fine white scars from knicks and cuts that weren't deep enough for stitches but were left as reminders.

"How long ago did you get your last scar?"

"You don't want to know, *piccolina*. It's better if I don't tell you how I got any of them."

"This is a gunshot wound."

She covers the scar by my belly button with her fingertips. Her touch is so light I barely feel it.

"Yes. I have a couple other ones, Livy. But they were from a long time ago."

"What does that mean? A year? A decade?"

I sigh. I'd been off and on with Diana for four years, and she learned not to ask personal questions. I didn't have most of them when I had subs before her.

"This one and one on my back are from five years ago. The one on my thigh is from fourteen years ago."

"Your thigh?"

That one was thanks to Aleks Kutsenko, the fucking bastard. The one time his aim was off. We were in a fucking melee when we were in high school. He's a year younger than me. I was a senior, and he was a junior. We were in a fight against each other but fucking Dillan O'Rourke and his band of fucking merry men started it. Aleks was aiming for Finn O'Rourke and got me instead. It was close range, too. I'm lucky I didn't fucking bleed to death or lose the leg. At least he had the decency to put pressure on it and slice Finn before the fucking Irish dipshit could kill me. We all had hell to pay with our respective leaders for that shitshow.

"Yes. It was over ten years ago, *piccolina*. I'm telling you the truth. They don't hurt, and I don't think about them."

Her eyes shift to the scar on my cheek, but she only nods.

"May I kiss you, *caro*?"

"Today, you can do whatever you want without asking."

She dives in and pushes me backward until I lie on the bed. Her kiss is desperate and needy. I made her wait too long. We talked too much, even if it was all necessary. She rises with her knees on the bed as she reaches between us to unfasten my belt and pants. I kick off my loafers before raising my hips to push down my jeans and boxer briefs. The gun I had holstered at my back is in my office, where I put it while she showered. I have another in my bedside table. I have weapons scattered throughout the house. I know she saw I was wearing it earlier, so at least I don't have to hide it from her.

She climbs off me and kneels beside me. Her hand wraps around my dick. Fuck. I place one hand beneath my head as I watch her. She once more sweeps her gaze over my muscles, liking what she sees. I pull her right knee wider before I slide my fingers into her. She's so wet I can see it on her thighs.

"I know you said I can do whatever I want without asking today. But I like to."

"And if I want you to surprise me?"

She laughs.

"I don't think you're the type who likes surprises."

"I like you. You've been one surprise after another."

Her cheeks pinken, and it's sexy as hell. She leans forward and with no preamble, takes me deep in her throat. Christ. Where the hell did she learn to do that? Doesn't she have a fucking gag reflex? She draws back until she swirls her tongue over the tip before sinking down on it again. She practically swallows me, and I can't help my groan. It spurs her on as she sucks and strokes me with her hand. I can't take it. I'm going to come, and I don't want this over until she's come first.

I sit up and flip her onto her back as I reach toward the bedside table. I pull it open as she turns to see what I'm doing. I know she spots the gun at the same time as she sees the strip of condoms. I grab one and tear it with my teeth. She's watching me now, but her eyes dart back to the drawer I just slammed shut. We'll talk about that later. We're done discussing shit. As I roll the condom on, I realize I need to ask her one more thing.

"What's your safe word, Livy?"

"Um...Uh...Museum."

I didn't expect that. She shrugs and smiles sheepishly.

"I can't imagine museums coming up during sex, so I figured it would work."

"True. All right. You can say your safe word at any time. It won't upset me or disappoint me. The moment you say it, we stop. No questions asked."

"Do you need a safe word?"

I stare at her. I haven't had one since I trained to be a Dom, and I just used red back then. I don't want to use that with her. It's too generic, and I used it with other people.

"Do you think you'll be too rough with me, little girl? Are you too much for me?"

"I hope so."

Her eyes twinkle with mischief, and I can't help but give her a wolfish grin before I ease down the bed. I have a new set of plans now. I slide my shoulders between her thighs and latch my mouth onto her clit. She screams, unprepared for the suction and my teeth grazing her sensitive flesh. My tongue flicks over and over mercilessly.

"*Caro.*"

It's a breathless plea. Is she begging for more? Begging to come? Begging for both? I'm not letting go until I make her come. She clenches the comforter as her hips try to buck off the mattress, but I pin them down. She fights me, and I only redouble my efforts. Our eyes meet, and I see how much she needs to get off. She moans, and I flick my tongue inside her pussy. She does it again, a little louder. I reward her with two fingers thrust inside her. Her third moan fills the room, and my cock feels like it's going to explode. A third finger slides in, and she writhes, her cries getting louder until she screams.

"Luca!"

I push up until my left forearm is beside her shoulder. My right hand grabs her leg as I thrust my cock into her. She clings to me and sighs. I'm not gentle as I pound into her. The bed bangs against the wall, and that only drives me more. I'm losing that vaunted control, and I've never been like this before. I watch her as I work her pussy, and I feel her fingertips press against my back, then her nails digging into my skin. That's always been a no-no with other women. I never allowed them to mark me. They're mine to do with as I want, not the other way around. But I want Livy to mark me as hers.

With her leg over my hip, I let go and move my hand to her tits, squeezing them, going back and forth. Sweat drips down my temples and glistens between her breasts. I watch as they bounce, and I'm turned on even more.

"More, *caro*."

I want to, but I know if I do, I'll harm her. That's the last thing I want.

"No, *piccolina*. If I get any rougher, I'll hurt you."

"No, you won't."

"I warned you I would tell you my expectations for keeping you safe. This isn't one of those times where I'll back down or compromise. I won't risk hurting you."

"I know what I can take. You want me to trust you, but it has to go both ways. Please. I need you to be as rough as you can."

I slow my pace and lower myself onto both forearms, resting my chest against hers. She whimpers and shakes her head.

"Livy, look at me. You don't have to prove anything to me. You don't have to take more to make me want you more than any woman I've ever been with. I already do. I'm already being rougher than usual. You push me to the last thread of control before I forget you're a person and I just fuck for the sake of getting myself off. I will never do that. I would hurt you in more than one way, and it would disappoint me that I made it all about me. I'm too much bigger and stronger than you. I wouldn't forgive myself for that."

She cups my face and draws up to press a soft but quick kiss to my lips before lying back. She wraps her hands around my hips and grabs my ass, pressing my hips toward her.

"Then at least go back to what we were doing before. I was so close."

I bury my head beside her neck, licking and nipping as I start up that relentless pace again.

"Fuck, Luca. Yes...I'm so close."

"Me too. I want to feel you come on my cock. I'm the one making you come, little girl. Your pussy is mine."

"Just like your cock is mine."

"Completely yours and only yours."

I thrust and circle my hips before pulling back and doing it again. I feel her tense as her pussy clamps around my cock. Fuck me if I don't blow my load as I feel her come. Goddamn, can this condom hold how much cum I feel shoot out of me? I have a moment's worry that I might have ripped it with how rough I was. Shit. I tense for an entirely different reason. She must read something on my face.

"*Caro*, I'm on the pill if you're worried the condom broke. I took it yesterday, so we should be good. But I missed it this morning, so we have to be careful from now on."

I'm not sure how I feel about her reading my mind. But I'm sure I've never felt better after sex. I roll us until she's draped over me. There's a lot more to our kiss than the usual afterglow. What have I gotten myself into?

Chapter Six

Livy

Yup. Completely nuts...And happier than a puppy with two peters.

That was the best sex I've ever had. Hands down. Bar none. T.H.E. *best*. And I've had enough to know. I wouldn't consider myself a slut, and what does that even mean these days? But I've had plenty of partners. I'm old enough now to understand why I've done what I've done. It's the same insecurity that drove me to beg Luca to be rougher with me. I wanted to be the best. Yes. I'm competitive. Like unhealthy levels sometimes. But I wanted to be the best, so he'd keep wanting me.

At five-feet-two and curvy, I just wanted to look like the other girls. The hot ones. Self-reflection wasn't my forte back then. I hated it when people called me thick. I think of thick slices of bacon, thick slices of ham—not the comparison I wanted. Ah, the stupidity of youth.

I had a boyfriend in college who was into porn. Like lots of porn. I wasn't comfortable in my skin yet, so I hated he wanted to watch it. It made me feel like I wasn't hot enough, good enough, if he wanted to watch other women have sex to get himself off. It felt like cheating in a way. I told him I would end things if he didn't stop watching. He convinced me to watch with him.

I learned a lot from all those hours. Needless to say, I took those skills with me when I dumped him. I believed he was out of my league, so I was desperate to keep him when we started dating. Now I should have known he must have thought I was attractive because he was shallow as fuck, but we were together for six months. It was all my insecurity that kept me with him for even that long.

That's the same reason I slept with several of the guys on the list I don't keep. I wanted to prove to myself that I was attractive enough to get them. I look back now and think about how handsome many of them were. That should have been enough to give me the validation I needed long before I got so many metaphorical notches on my headboard. I guess I just didn't put two and two together.

But I didn't have enough self-esteem to figure that maybe they liked me for my personality *and* that was what should have mattered. I've slowed down over the last few years. I keep it to relationships now, not hook ups or short-term liaisons. I only agreed to a fuck buddy because I've been too busy with work to consider a commitment. I don't judge my worth by the attractiveness of the men I date.

But Luca...Fucking hell, he's hot. Like Armani model hot. And his scar on his cheek—that's like James Dean bad boy hot. I want to know how it happened, but I'm worried that is the one scar that's too personal to ask about. The other scars made my heart hurt. I hate thinking about him in that kind of danger. It's been the only time so far when I've had difficulty reconciling that he's a mobster with how he's been with me.

Now I'm lying on top of him as his hand strokes my ass cheek. It's about the most soothing thing I've ever felt. My eyelids feel so heavy. I would happily fall asleep in his arms and stay here until morning. My cheek is resting on one pec while my hand is over his heart. I can hear the steady rhythm, and it's like a lullaby pushing me toward the Land of Nod. I sigh, completely content.

And it's shattered a moment later.

"Luca! Luca, where you at?"

Luca eases me off him and sits up.

"That's my brother Lorenzo."

He rolls off the bed and reaches for his jeans. He kisses me as he puts them on. I look around for my clothes and scramble to get them as the voice gets louder downstairs.

"Let me go down there before he comes up here."

He hurries out of the room as he buttons his pants. He closes the door behind him, and I wonder if that's merely for my privacy or because he expects me to stay here. He didn't tell me to, and I suddenly don't want to feel like a dirty secret. I yank on my clothes, then ease open the door. For someone who wants to be acknowledged, I sure am acting like I'm spying as I creep toward the stairs.

"*È di sopra? Ho sentito che hai portato quella ragazza a casa con te. Che diavolo ti viene in mente? Mamma e papà si incazzeranno quando sapranno che hai una ragazza che vive con te.*" Is she upstairs? I heard you brought that girl home with you. What the hell are you thinking? Mama and Papa are going to be pissed to hear you have some chick shacking up with you.

Often Spanish and Italian are close enough to understand one if you speak the other. But not this time. I catch the word *casa*, which must be house in both languages. *Diavolo* must be *diablos* or devil. *Che diavolo* sounds like *que diablos*. What the devil? What the hell? I obviously understand Mama and Papa.

Con te probably means the same thing as *contigo*, which is with you. Wonderful. Something about his parents, the devil, and me being here. That sounds promising.

"*Ho trentanni. Posso avere un ospite se voglio. E non chia-marla ragazza. Si chiama Olivia.*" I'm thirty-one-years-old. I can have a houseguest if I want. And don't call her some chick. Her name is Olivia..

The only parts I can get are that he's saying he's thirty-one and my name. But their tone tells me way more than the words. Lorenzo sounds accusatory, and Luca is defensive. He sounds like he's about to get angry. That's not what I want. Do I let them know I'm here? Or do I sneak back into the bedroom and let them deal with it themselves?

They're brothers. Clearly, this isn't their first argument, but I don't enjoy being the cause. I go back to the bedroom door and close it just loud enough that they must hear it without me slamming it. I know they're in the living room, and that if either of them looks up, they'll see me cross the landing. If Luca says anything, I'll go down. If he doesn't, then I'll go into the room I picked earlier.

"Liv, will you come down here, please? I'd like you to meet my brother."

I realize as I'm halfway down the stairs that I'm barefoot. That makes me look pretty at home here since Luca said nothing about being a shoes-off house. I saw him wearing his loafers earlier, even if he's barefoot now, too. I'm also coming from the direction in which only his bedroom lies. I plaster a smile on my face as I round the corner and walk toward the guys. When I get close, Luca wraps his arm around my waist. I glance up at him, and defiance radiates from his expression. Is he daring Lorenzo to say something against me? Is he doing this to prove a point?

I feel his fingers press into my waist for a second before

they rest lightly just above my hip. I keep my smile in place as I look at Lorenzo. He's even hotter than Luca in looks. Like almost too good looking—too perfect—to be real. But there isn't the same air about him that Luca has. He's a big guy too—tall and built—but he seems way more laid back than Luca. Not as intense. I guess that comes from not being the heir to the New York Mafia.

"Hello, Ms. D'Amato."

How does he know my last name? And such formality.

"It's nice to meet you, Mr. Mancinelli."

"Enough, Lorenzo. Don't be a dick."

Luca sounds more annoyed than defensive now. I shift my hip to bump his.

Relax, dude. An argument isn't how I want to meet your family.

"It's Lorenzo." He flashes a smile. "Is it Liv instead of Olivia?"

"No."

Luca answers before I do. He's right. No one else calls me Liv or Livy but him, and I don't like the idea of someone else doing it.

"My mom calls me Ivy because I loved to climb as a kid. Some of my friends still do."

I hate it. I don't know why, but it sounds like a stripper's name to me. But I can live with it. I don't know why I just shared that since I don't want new people to call me that. I guess I want to break the ice because it's the fucking Arctic in here right now.

"Olivia works for me, though. That's what I'm most used to."

There. Maybe that fixed it. Luca's brother nods before shifting his attention back to Luca. I shouldn't have come downstairs. This was a mistake. Neither one of them is moving the conversation along, and it's obvious that's because I'm here. We stand in silence for what feels like a few minutes, but it couldn't be more than twenty seconds.

"I'm going to check on the food we left. Nice to meet you."

I step away from Luca before either of them can say anything. I hurry into the kitchen and look at the stove. The eggplant has withered and looks rubbery. The tomatoes look mushy in the sauce, and the pasta is clumped together. That might be salvageable, but I don't know that the sauce is. I turn the burner on beneath the pasta pot. I scrape the rest of the food into a compost bin. I didn't take Luca for being so green. Maybe it's a neighborhood thing. Then again, what the fuck do I know about him? He fucks like a porn star, which I know since I've watched so much. But beyond that, I know little about who he really is.

And I've agreed to live in his house and practically be his girlfriend. And back comes the same question: what the fuck am I doing? Obviously, Lorenzo disapproves. A normal person would.

As I wait for the water to boil, I consider why I keep questioning what's going on. I need to because my life spun out of control yesterday. I need to think about why I'm in hiding, and I still haven't called my mom. That stops me in my tracks. I just had sex instead of thinking about whether my mom is safe. Guilt washes over me, and it ruins the last rays of my afterglow.

I'm not just certifiable. I'm selfish and self-centered. I look toward the living room, but I know the guys went somewhere else because I can't hear them anymore. Fuck. I really want to call my mom, but I don't know if I can use my regular phone or the burner. I look down at the water that is finally boiling and hurry to stir the clump. It breaks apart fairly easily, so I snag one of the tubular noodles and taste. Yeah, no coming back from that. Gross.

I look around and find oven mitts and spot the strainer already in the sink. I dump out the water, then toss out the noodles. I'm still debating the phone issue as I check the dishwasher. It looks like the stuff is dirty, so I do a quick rinse and stick the two pots and pan into the machine.

I need to end things with Luca. I'm causing him to argue with his brother. I've forgotten about my mom. I've lost my job and my car. This is not how normal people live. I can't go to the police because then I'd have to report Luca, too. But I need some other way to protect myself and go back to the way things were. He said I can end things with him if I want, that he wouldn't force me to stay.

I tilt my head back and sigh. I also don't want to die. I'm physically safest here. Distance would make ending my infatuation easier. If I can't put actual space between us, then I need to use some fucking willpower. One and done. I scratched an itch, and now I'm over having sex with him.

Bull-fucking-shit. It's like fucking hives. I still have that itch and scratching it once doesn't feel nearly enough. But I need to ignore it. The sex, the being taken care of, the wanting to date. All of it. Done.

I leave the kitchen, and it's suddenly easy to know where Luca and Lorenzo are. They're arguing, and I can hear it. They're back to speaking Italian, so I can't follow what's going on. As I get closer, I keep hearing the name Kutsenko. I don't know who that is, but at least I don't hear my name. They've moved on. I stop in front of Luca's office door, but then I knock lightly.

"Olivia?"

That's Luca's voice. My gut reaction is that I hate hearing him use my full name. But I decided there's nothing between us. Maybe he's come to the same conclusion.

"Yes, Luca. May I come in?"

The door opens, and concern etches deep into Luca's face. Is it for me? Or is it because he worries I might have understood something I overheard?

"What do you need, Livy?"

That's better. His voice is low and discreet, even though I'm certain Lorenzo can hear. Hearing the pet name shouldn't make me feel this way. Calmer. Safer. Like the world is back on its axis.

"I'm sorry to interrupt. I really need to call my mom, but I don't know if I can use my phone or the burner."

"The burner. Tell her you're staying with a friend on Long Island for the weekend."

"Is she safe, Luca? What if they go after her?"

"I already have men watching her place and following her. No one's gone near her, and no one else appears to be paying attention."

I nod, not sure what to say, needing to gather my thoughts.

"Thank you. I'm sorry someone has to babysit my mom."

"It's not babysitting, Livy."

I glance around Luca's shoulder, and Lorenzo's expression tells me that's exactly what he thinks it is. He looks irritated. Is he on the rotation or something?

"Enzo."

Luca's back to sounding pissed. There's a warning in his voice as he says his brother's name. How does he know?

"I can see it in your face, Livy. However he looks, he's upsetting you."

"I'm not upset."

Luca leans forward and whispers in my ear.

"Don't lie to me, *piccolina*. Your ass won't enjoy the conse-quences."

Fuck if that doesn't make my pussy ache. I clench my ass,

both anticipation and dread causing my reaction. No. It's over before it goes any further.

"That's not an option anymore, Luca."

My chest tightens as I force myself to draw the line. Something sparks in his eyes, and I'm frozen in place as he stares at me. Dominance radiates from him, and I want to give in. I want to look away, throw myself into his arms, tell him to forget what I just said. The world tilts again.

"Lorenzo, deal with what we talked about. I don't like it, but you are right. We do it your way."

"*Davvero? O vuoi solo che me ne vada, così puoi tornare a letto con lei?*" Really? Or do you just want me to leave so you can hop back into bed with her?

The only thing I get out of that is Lorenzo asking if Luca wants him to leave, but I don't know what he said after that. Luca swings around and storms over to Lorenzo. For a moment, I fear he's going to punch his brother. Lorenzo grins, but it's mocking.

"*Ho ragione, vero?*" I'm right, aren't I?

That I can guess. I'm right, aren't I? What's he right about? I look between them, and I can tell Luca's ready to throttle his younger brother. I suck in a deep breath and walk over to them. It's like going to stand between two lions battling for who will lead the pride. Which one will chew me up and spit me out first?

I rest my hand on Luca's upper arm, but he doesn't acknowledge me. That's fine. I keep my eyes on Lorenzo.

"I know you disapprove of me being here and of someone watching my mom. I can guess a few of the reasons you're not thrilled that I've entered your life, but I didn't have much say about part of that. I don't know how long I'm going to stay here, but it won't be too long. I'm going to be a houseguest, and that's all."

Luca shoots me that look again, and I feel like he nailed my feet to the floor. But I don't back down this time either. His left eye narrows, and I'm sure that's made plenty of men cave. But he told me we would be equals outside of the bedroom. I could disagree or argue with him if we were in a relationship. If we aren't, then I should be able to do that, anyway.

Luca's practically snarling now.

"*Se mandi tutto in rovina per me, ci vorrà molto tempo prima che ti perdoni. Vai.*" If you fucked this up for me, it'll be a long time before I forgive you. Go.

I'm still only getting bits and pieces. Something about a long time before Luca forgives him. He told him to go. What was the first part? What won't he forgive? So much for Spanish and Italian being as much alike as I thought.

"*Bene. Ma la mamma sa già che è qui.*" Fine. But Mama already knows she's here.

"*Può farmi la predica quanto vuole, ma siamo con la mafia. Non siamo così buoni cattolici come diciamo.*" She can preach at me all she wants, but we're in the Mafia. We're not as good Catholics as we claim.

Mafia and not being as good Catholics as they say they are. Shit. That isn't hard to figure out if they're talking about their mother. She won't be pleased I'm here. This needs to end.

"Luca, I don't want you to argue with your brother over me being here. There has to be another option."

Lorenzo responds before Luca can.

"She can stay with Uncle Salvatore and Aunt Sylvia."

"No."

Luca's response begs no argument, but I push on.

"I don't want to impose on them, either. I meant a hotel somewhere."

Luca turns and wraps his arm around my waist, pulling me

against him. He cups my cheek, and it's as though his brother is no longer there.

"How well did that work, *piccolina?* They found you in less than twelve hours. They won't back down next time."

"Back down? You shot them."

"And more will come. They will try harder. Even if I send men to guard you, you'll still be in more danger than being here. I know you're scared now but think how much worse you'll feel when you're alone. Even if your bodyguards are outside your hotel door or in a car in the parking lot, you'll be doing this without help. Is that really what you want?"

"I don't want any of this."

A moment of hurt flashes in his gaze. His arm loosens but doesn't let go right away. He nods, then steps back. Lorenzo finally stops looking pissed.

"I'll talk to Uncle Salvatore, Ms. D'Amato. We'll set up a new rotation and pick a safe house."

"The fuck you are. Stay out of this, Enzo. If I want your help, I'll ask."

Lorenzo slips out of the office and shuts the door behind him. Luca's on me before I know what's happening. His arms go around my waist as he yanks me against him. He urges me backward until I bump into his desk. He nudges my feet apart and steps between my legs. He presses me until I'm bracing myself on his desk. Then his right hand trails up my body, over my breast, until his hand rests on my throat. It's heavy but there's no pressure. It's just a reminder that he's in control in moments like this.

"Didn't take much for you to give up on us, *piccolina.* I misjudged you."

"Because I'm thinking of someone other than myself? Because I don't want to cause problems for you with your family? Because they're more important than I am? This isn't about giving up. It's about doing what's right. And it's ridiculous to make more of this than it is. We're infatuated and we're attracted to each other, but this isn't a relationship."

"You haven't given it a chance. Maybe we should have waited to have sex for the first time, but you enjoyed that as much as I did. It's been brewing since the moment I stopped you in the parking lot last night. If you don't want to do that again, then we won't. But don't put up walls that don't need to be there."

"Don't want to? It's the only thing I want to do."

I snap my mouth shut. That shouldn't have come out. Fuck me. Literally and figuratively. That wolfish grin that makes me horny as fuck is back.

"At least you're honest about that, *piccolina*. If you really don't want to see if there's anything romantic between us, then I can accept that. But don't cut off your nose to spite your face. You need the safety I can provide. Don't pretend you don't, even if you're going to pretend you don't want more with me than a place to sleep and a good fucking."

He's right. I slide my hands up my face and over my hair, resting them on the top of my head. I close my eyes as I clench my jaw.

"All right. I'll stay for a few days until *you* find somewhere you're comfortable with me going. I know you don't want Lorenzo involved in this, but if there's a safe house, then that would be best. Maybe my mom could stay with me."

"How're you going to explain that? I told you that you're not a prisoner here. If you want to go somewhere, I have cars you can drive. I have men who can drive you. But if you leave the house, then you take three bodyguards if I'm not with you. I still recommend you stay out of sight for a few days."

"Fine. You're right about it all. But no more talk about us

being in a relationship. It's too much, Luca. It's too fast, and it's not real."

I hadn't noticed that his hand dropped away from my throat until he puts it back. He brings our bodies together as he lays me flat on his desk. I can feel how hard he is against my pussy, and it's taking all my restraint not to rub against him.

"Then a goodbye kiss, *piccolina*."

Never have I faced such temptation. I want to wrap my legs around him, dig my heels into his lower back, and push his dick closer. He still doesn't have a shirt on, so I run my hands over him until I catch myself. I rest them on his chest, but I don't have it in me to push him away. The kiss carries on, getting deeper and more urgent as the minutes tick by. It's not until he feels a tear slip onto his hand that he stops. He jerks back, and I look up at him with watery eyes.

"Livy."

He sounds distraught. He's quick to lift me off the desk and carry me to the leather sofa. He tucks me against him and strokes my back. All of my resolve crumbles as I listen to his racing heart. His entire body is pulsing. Some of it may be lust, but he's anxious. I can just tell. I use my index finger to turn his face toward mine. I press a soft kiss to his mouth as more tears fall.

"I'm trying to do what's right, Luca. It's not what I want."

"What do you want?"

"You. I know this is a fucked-up situation, but I also know I'm not in any immediate danger. I'm not looking over my shoulder, expecting someone to burst in here. I feel calm when you're not holding me. I'm not terrified, even if I'm scared. I guess I feel fairly normal when I'm not touching you. But everything feels infinitely better and righter when I am."

I try to sit up, but he holds me against him. I settle, closing my eyes, and sighing. He's not trying to control me right now.

He needs me. He's slowly relaxing the longer I sit on his lap, and he runs his hand up and down my back. A wave of protectiveness washes over me. I want to make everything better for him, reassure him. But the only way to do that is to end this. To get out of his life.

"Luca, I speak Spanish. I couldn't understand everything you and Lorenzo said. But I gleaned enough to know that not only is he pissed I'm here, but so are your parents. I think it's as much about me being a woman as it is an outsider. Lorenzo didn't tell you to abandon me. He said I shouldn't be here. I don't want to cause trouble for you."

"Livy, I'm thirty-one-years-old. No one is telling me who I date and who I can have stay in my home. I'm an adult despite what my parents might still wish. All of their children are. Whether you're strictly a houseguest or my girlfriend staying with me, I don't need permission to have friends over. You haven't officially moved in, and we haven't said we're living together. Maybe one day. But until there's something permanent, they can all calm the fuck down. My brothers have had women stay overnight, and so have I. No one's said a damn thing about that. Whether you stay one night or thirty, it's the same thing. It's no one's decision but mine, and no one else's business. My family has plenty of traditions I respect and appreciate, but this is not one. It's fucking hypocritical. No one thinks I'm a virgin."

"You might think it's not a big deal, but obviously it is. I don't want to cause trouble, Luca. You work with them, and my guess is your life depends on you getting along with your family. If you're at odds with them, will the men you lead think less of you? Respect you less? I don't want to endanger you. That scares me as much as the Culiacán coming after me."

"As much as I want to tell myself there are some things about my life that are totally normal, there's not. I hate putting you in this position, but I think you're going to have to meet my parents soon. At the very least, you'll have to meet Uncle Salvatore. Aunt Sylvia will probably be there because she'll worry that a bunch of Italian men observing you will scare you shitless. Uncle Salvatore is intimidating even when it's just him."

"Do you think meeting me will make them approve of me?"

"If nothing else, at least it'll take away the mystery. But I think my parents are going to like you a lot. Uncle Salvatore probably won't let you know what he's thinking. I'm positive Aunt Sylvia will love you, if for no other reason than she's always trying to get my family to let go of some of their old-fashioned ways of thinking. And she's the one who's actually from the old country."

"Can I ask one favor, please?"

"Of course. Ask anything."

"Before I meet your family, could I get something to wear that makes me feel more presentable? Jeans and a top don't feel right. I'll be embarrassed."

"Of course."

"How soon will I meet them?"

"I can set something up for tomorrow."

"Okay. I'll look on Amazon and see if I can get—"

Shit. I'm not supposed to use my credit card or debit card. Or doesn't that rule apply now that I'm staying with Luca?

"What's the matter?"

"Can I shop online now that I'm staying here? Can I use my credit card or debit card again?"

"We'll keep everything on my account."

"No. I've already taken—"

"Stop, Livy. My home is pretty modest compared to what I can afford. I'm a very wealthy man. No matter who I date, there are few people who have what I do. I'm not saying this to imply that I want some arm candy, or kept woman, or whatever. I'm saying that it won't break the bank for me to continue to help you."

"Thank you."

I'll be gracious, but it still doesn't feel right. No doubt, I appreciate everything he's doing for me.

"Come on, *piccolina*. We have our first stay-date tonight. We missed lunch. Let's start with ordering dinner."

Chapter Seven

Luca

I knew better than to ask Livy to share my bed last night. We ordered Chinese and watched a movie together in my basement theater. After our hands brushed against each other for the fourth time, we entwined our fingers. But neither of us of acknowledged it. There was no kiss goodnight before she went up to her room. My bed has never felt so lonely. I hated missing her after only spending such a short time in my room with her yesterday.

But she's wearing a calf-length dress that she ordered and arrived this morning. We're heading to Uncle Salvatore and Aunt Sylvia's. I can tell she's nervous, even in the modest dress. I can't blame her. Meeting someone's parents can be nerve-wracking enough, but she's about to meet my entire family. And we're not exactly your typical family at that. She's meeting the man who runs the most powerful crime syndicate on the Eastern Seaboard.

I'm driving us, but we have men in the car in front and behind us. I hoped being in my car would make it feel more normal, but I don't think it makes a difference. She took one look at my gun metal G-Wagon, and I know she remembered what I said in my study yesterday. I'm a very wealthy man. I am in my own right. Sure, it helped having my parents pay for college, and Uncle Salvatore got me launched with *Cosa Nostra* funds, but I have businesses outside of the ones we run for the Mafia. Most of my income is from the legit stuff I do. I own six different rental car franchises and four gas stations. The rental car businesses are completely on the up and up. The gas stations launder our money sometimes.

"*Piccolina*, it's going to be fine. No one's going to say anything hurtful or be rude to you."

"They'll just think it. Your parents already don't approve of me, and they haven't met me. There's no way they're going to believe I'm not shacking up with you. I have no job and no home to go to. How is anyone going to think I'm not using you?"

"They'll know you aren't within two minutes of talking to you. You are not a gold digger, and nothing about you gives off that air."

"They're still going to think that and believe I'm an expert manipulator to be using you and not look like it."

"I get that you're nervous, Livy. But you're believing the worst about yourself and people you haven't met yet. Do you really think I would put you in a situation where I set you up to fail?"

"No. I just think that this is something beyond your control. If they don't like me, then fine. I won't be around for forever, but you still have to deal with your family and the fallout."

I'm fighting to keep my cool. I want to drive my fist into

Lorenzo's face, and I want to shake Livy. If my brother hadn't shown up and run his mouth, then she wouldn't be putting this distance between us. Sure, she might have doubts. I have some too. But nothing before Lorenzo showed up made me think she disagreed with what we talked about. I thought we made huge strides and were on the same page.

It fucking pisses me off because I've never felt this way about someone. I've never felt any potential for something more than sex. I've never felt as comfortable around someone as I do with Livy. But Lorenzo shattered that, and now I feel completely stressed out. I am going to have to deal with my family when all I want is to hide away with Livy and fix things.

Won't be around for forever. What if that's exactly what I want? What if I want to at least see if that's possible?

I'm going to get shit from my parents for having a woman live with me who isn't my wife, not even my fiancée. I'm going to get shit from Uncle Salvatore and my brothers because she's not Italian, despite the last name. I'm going to get shit from everyone for being into her so soon after meeting. I feel like a gorilla ready to fling all that shit back at them.

"And I will deal with my family just like I always have. I have obligations to them I can never walk away from. I can't and don't want to. But I'm still my own person. Not everything I do or choose revolves around the *Cosa Nostra*. When I become don, then everything will have to revolve around that, but for right now, I have leeway. I intend to make the most of it."

"For what? A week, maybe two, just so we can fuck?"

I grit my teeth. I guess we're not going to dance around this after all. I inhale slowly, so I don't regret what I say.

"Livy, I made my position pretty clear yesterday. We talked about a lot of serious shit, and I thought we'd come to an agreement. My brother showed up and guilt tripped you. Now you think—what—that I lied about what I want? That I'm foolish and naïve? I promise you, I am neither of those. I don't have the luxury to be. I told you, I've given this a lot of thought. A day might not seem like much to you, but it's a lifetime in my world."

"A day is only a day in mine. And a shit ton happened in less than twenty-four hours. I gave it a lot of thought, and my thoughts were all over the place. Luca, I've never said I don't like you, and it would be an obvious lie to say I'm not attracted to you. It's because I like you I feel like this is wrong. I had a shitty father and divorced parents. That doesn't mean I don't get how important family is. Just the opposite. Family is everything to me. I don't want to cause trouble with yours. That's my issue here. It's not you."

"So, you'll reconsider when you see it's not a big deal?"

"But it is a big deal. Lorenzo wouldn't have come to see you if it weren't."

"Is that what you think? Liv, he didn't come to see me because you're staying with me. He led off with that. Asshole. He came to see me about a business matter. We went in my office because we had some documents to review, and I needed to read some files he'd just sent me."

"But you spent more time arguing about me than you did talking about work."

"No, we didn't. You were in the kitchen longer than you realize. We were in my office for like twenty minutes. We talked about you in the living room and then when you came in. In between, it was strictly work."

I'm telling the truth. Lorenzo wanted to talk about Livy more, but I refused. I know my little brother is looking out for me. If the situation were reversed, I know I'd be doing the same thing. I get that, and I can admit that. But it rankles. I have a sex life, but I have no love life. It's fucking unfair, but that's the life I was born into.

Every woman I went out with only lasted a few dates. They complained I'm emotionally closed off. I am. I trusted none of them well enough to tell them more than just superficial stuff about my life. I wanted to do fun things and enjoy their company at dinner, or the movies, or working out, or whatever. The moment they wanted to delve deeper, I shut off.

I haven't felt like that once with Livy. I'm not ready to spill state secrets or anything. But I don't feel the oppressive need to be guarded around her. I have no rational way to explain it. It's intuition.

"Luca, I'm guessing you wouldn't let me Uber back to your place if things go poorly. Would you agree to letting one of your guys take me back if I ask to leave?"

"You're not leaving without me, Livy. If you want to go, then we leave. No questions or arguments from me. But I'm not sending you away or letting you walk away."

"I thought you only wanted to be controlling in the bedroom. Since that's not happening..."

"This isn't about that kind of control. I trust my guys, but I'll worry the moment you're gone until the moment I see you. Unless it's one of my brothers or someone in my family circle, I won't relax. I told you, I take your safety seriously. And I'm not letting you come home to an empty house while you wait for me to leave the people who made you uncomfortable."

"You cannot choose me over them, Luca. I keep saying that, but you refuse to listen. You're being obstinate, and it's not cute."

"I'm being obstinate? Hello, pot. Meet kettle. You're being just as stubborn. I know my family. I know there's going to be some hesitation at first, but I also know that they'll like you and respect you."

"That's not—"

"Lorenzo can fuck off. Liv, he's my younger brother. Half of what he said was to bust my balls. He was goading me. It pissed me off because he used you to do it. That's what I objected to."

She sits back and looks out the window. I glance over in time to see her jerky nod. Fuck this keeping our distance. I rest my hand on her thigh. She looks over at me, and I wait for the rejection. But it doesn't come. She leans her head back and closes her eyes. Temptation to inch up her skirt and slip my hand under it is so real I can practically see it. I want nothing more than to slip my fingers into her and make her moan, get her off before we get to Uncle Salvatore's.

How big a setback will it be if she refuses? I'll only know if I try. I inch her skirt up her leg. She looks forward but doesn't stop me. I pull it high enough for my palm to rest on her bare thigh. When she does nothing to stop me, I slide my hand under the material until the back of my fingers rubs against her pussy. She still doesn't tell me no.

"Open your legs for me, *piccolina*."

She obeys as my fingertips caress the inside of her leg. I feel her shiver. We have five minutes until we get to my uncle and aunt's place, but I'm in no hurry. I'll circle the fucking block if I have to. My middle two fingers glide along her pussy before dipping inside. She's soaked. She's also not wearing panties. What the fuck?

"Nothing underneath your dress, little girl. Did you expect someone to play with you?"

"Hoped, *caro*."

It's a whispered confession. I'll take it.

"You need this, don't you? You need me to reassure you. You need me to want you. You need me to take care of you."

Only the first sentence was a question. The others are fact.

"Yes."

She's still speaking so softly I have to strain to hear. I press farther into her cunt, and her hips tilt to let me in. I thrust in and out a few times before I withdraw. She clamps her legs together, and I chuckle. It's not amusement. It's something darker, and I feel that shiver again.

"Open your legs, little one. I'm going to make you come."

She does as I say, and my slick fingers rub her clit. Her left hand grips the side of her seat while her right hand clings to the door. Her eyes are closed again. Uh-uh.

"Pull your dress up and watch me finger fuck you, Livy. What did I tell you yesterday about that pussy?"

"It's yours."

Her voice is stronger when she answers this question. It's decisive.

"Are you going to remember that after I get you off? Or will you conveniently forget when you're no longer aching to come?"

"Luca, don't do this to me. Please. I can only do what I can do. I want you, but you're toying with me. You're asking the impossible."

"Only you are making it impossible. You're the one who craves us but is so quick to give up."

"Us? I crave you fucking me. There's a difference."

"You can't have one without the other, Livy."

I'm still rubbing her clit, and her body is humming even while her mind rebels. I work her into a frenzy as she thrusts her hips to meet my fingers.

"*Caro.*"

She fills the single word with need, sadness, and ecstasy. How can it be all three? But I know she's coming. She grabs my wrist and presses it against her cunt. I dip my fingers into her again as her orgasm wanes. I pull my hand away and lick my ring finger.

"My favorite flavor."

I reach over and run my middle finger against her lips and press into her mouth. She recoils, and I know she doesn't like her own taste as much as I do. But it's only a second later that she's sucking on my finger. Fuck. I'm so hard it hurts. I'm two blocks from my uncle and aunt's, and there's a parking lot I pull into. The car ahead of me circles back, and the one behind me follows. But they keep their distance. I'll signal if I need something during this unexpected stop. My tinted windows are so dark they're almost not street legal.

I unfasten my seatbelt before I unfasten Livy's. I'm reaching across her and dropping the seatback before she knows what's happening. It's not the easiest maneuver, but I climb across the center console. I pull out my wallet and grab a condom. Cliché, but smart. I hold it up to her and cock an eyebrow. She can always say no.

She yanks it from my fingers and tears it open. I fumble, but get my pants undone as she pulls the condom out. She rolls it down my dick as I grab the seatback above her shoulders. I thrust into her and freeze. Our gazes lock. We both know how good it feels to finally have me balls deep inside her. I'm in control of our kiss, just like I'm in control of how fast we fuck. I'm rough, and I'm certain my car shakes. I care what my guys think only so much as I don't want them thinking Liv's some whore. But I don't care enough about what anyone thinks to make me stop needing her.

She cups my jaw as our kiss draws on. Then her right hand trails down my body until she grabs my ass. She moans each time she feels the muscles flex. She draws her feet up to the end of the seat to give her leverage to meet my thrusts.

"*Caro*, fuck me. Do whatever you want with me. Just don't stop. I'm so close."

"I'm not stopping until you come with me buried inside you. I'm the one making you come. I'm the one you want, Livy. We both know it because you want it just as much as I do. You need it like I do. You want me to get you off, but you also want me to be the one who gives you what you need beyond fucking."

"I know. And that's so fucking scary."

"I know, little one."

My tone's softer as I kiss her cheek and along her neck. I brush my lips over the sensitive skin behind her ear before I whisper to her.

"Don't push me away anymore, *piccolina*. Don't let what you fear other people might think keep us from what we know is right."

"I did it because I thought I should, not because I want to. I still worry, and I still feel guilty. I feel selfish. But maybe it's *la mano di Dio* that's brought us together. You said your family aren't great Catholics, and neither am I. But I think we both believe He's real. Maybe it's Him or fate. I don't know. I can't explain why I feel calm when I think about an us, and I feel—off—every time I push us apart. I feel wrong."

"Then stop pushing."

As I kiss her, I thrust twice more, and I feel her pussy spasm around me. Both of her hands squeeze my ass as I grind my pelvis against her clit and keep her coming as I shoot my load. We watch each other until we can't hold back our grins. I give her three quick pecks before I pull out. Fuck. I hate that feeling with as much passion as I love the feeling of slipping into her. I get myself back in my seat without banging my head or knees before I pull the condom off and grab a couple napkins from the center console. We do what we have to, so we're presentable again. I wrap the spent condom in another napkin. I'll deal with it later.

My hand goes back onto her thigh as I put the car in drive. She slips her hand beneath mine, and I wrap my fingers around hers before bringing the back of it to my lips. She pulls my hand to her lips before it rests back on her leg again.

"Luca, I can't promise my doubts won't come back or that my fears won't get the better of me at times. My guilt about coming between you and your family isn't gone, either. But I won't keep pushing you away. You're not the only one it hurts."

"Let's get through the next few hours, and then we'll reassess. Fair?"

"Very. Thanks for being patient."

"Livy, I know I'm asking more of you than you're asking of me. Thanks for keeping an open mind."

We pass through the gate to my aunt and uncle's property. It's a full-on mansion. I recognize all the cars in the driveway. Everyone is here. I mean, family and beyond. Fuck. I suspected as much, but I hate seeing that I was right. This is going to be even more intense than I wanted for Livy.

"Livy, one thing I want you to get used to is that you don't open your own car door. Not to get in or out. It's not just chivalry. It's safety. Unless one of my guys or I am standing outside your door or have checked the car, you don't get in or out. All right?"

"Yes, *caro*."

"Do you want me to call you Olivia around my family?"

"No."

She's quick to answer. She really doesn't like it when I use her full name.

"Liv or Livy is fine. Whichever you feel is right. If it's possible, I don't want anyone else to call me that, though. I'd prefer Olivia."

"You mentioned Ivy before."

"And I hate it when anyone but my mom calls me that. I think it sounds like a stripper or porn star. I only mentioned it because I got nervous and was trying to break the ice."

"All right, *piccolina*. I'll make sure people only call you Olivia. Are you ready?"

"I suppose."

Chapter Eight

Livy

I don't know what I expected when I walked into the don's house, but it wasn't what I find. Perhaps I expected ostentation or grandeur, excessive wealth dripping from the rafters. I discover a comfortable home with spots that make you want to curl up and take a nap or sun yourself like a content kitten. I find furniture that surely cost a fortune for each piece but is comfy and cozy. I find the clearly lived-in home of a family with two young kids. There are toys in the backyard and backpacks near the door. It's so normal.

Salvatore Mancinelli is broad-shouldered but lean. Not skinny, just not the same bulky musculature I discover all his nephews and their friends share. I would still put my money on him in a fight, if not because of his sheer aura of victory, then because he still looks in great shape considering he must be getting close to his mid-fifties. Sylvia Mancinelli is breathtaking. Just stunning. She has some fine lines around her mouth and eyes, but they increase her air of elegance instead of detracting from it. Her clothes are definitely designer, but she doesn't look frigid. She looks like an Italian Martha Stewart, I guess. I only catch glances of the couple's daughters in the backyard.

I recognize Lorenzo, and the man standing next to him must be Luca's other brother, Marco. They're three peas in a pod. Luca and Marco could be twins, even though I find out there's eighteen months between them. After that, the siblings are a year apart almost to the day. Their younger sister is standing behind Luca and Lorenzo with a smirk that makes me want to grin. She steps forward after I'm introduced to Salvatore and Sylvia, but before anyone else can talk.

"They're the pretty ones. I'm the smart one."

Maria thrusts out her hand, and I take it.

"I don't know. I think it might be age before beauty."

She laughs at my attempt at a joke, and I feel like I might have won over at least one person in the family. Luca and I haven't touched since before we got out of the car, but he's standing near me. We're keeping a respectful distance, but I watch his parents watch us. I force myself to remain composed when I keep worrying that somehow they know we just had sex on the way here.

"I'm lucky. I have good genes."

Maria steps aside, and Luca guides me to stand before his parents. I offer them a warm smile and shake their hands, too. Massimo looks as much like his older brother, Salvatore, as Luca and his brothers look alike. Good genes? Freaking dominant, just like all the men's presence. Nicoletta is still an attractive woman, but there's suspicion in her eyes that gives them a hard edge.

"It's nice to meet you, Mr. and Mrs. Mancinelli."

"The same to you, Ms. D'Amato."

It's Luca's dad who greets me. His tone is warmer than his

expression. Progress? I turn toward Sylvia when she comes to stand next to me.

"Would you like something to drink? Wine? Beer? Soda?"

"Water, please."

I can feel a headache coming on. The last thing I need is booze to add to it. As I watch everyone, I wonder if I insulted them by not accepting wine. Is it an Italian thing? Do they think I'm just trying to suck up?

"Perhaps wine with dinner."

Did that make it better or worse? Hell, if I know.

"Ms. D'Amato, you look familiar."

I turn toward Salvatore, and he's peering intently at my eyes. I don't have those fake contacts in. I know my eyes are unusual. I often think they're my best feature. But Salvatore's looking at them with suspicion.

"I don't think we've met before, Mr. Mancinelli."

"Salvatore, please. And it's Sylvia, Massimo, and Nicoletta. Otherwise, you'll have a dozen men answering and at least three women. It gets confusing in a family our size."

"Thank you."

"Are you related to Danny D'Amato?"

"Luca asked me that. I don't think so. The name isn't familiar."

I live in New York where there's about a bazillion people with Italian last names. I can't possibly know all the ones who have the same one as mine. I don't know any Daniel D'Amato.

"Maybe it's a distant relation."

Salvatore continues to look at me after he speaks, but I turn toward a man I recognize from the other night. I think Luca said his name was Gabriele. Luca's ignoring him, but I feel like I should say something. There's another guy standing with him who looks a lot like Luca and his brothers, but I can tell he's not directly related. Maybe a cousin. When Luca stops to talk to a man I'm introduced to as Matteo, Marco's best friend, I step away. I'm trying to be brave and not cling to Luca.

"You're Gabriele, right?"

"Yes."

His Italian accent is the heaviest of them all. Maybe he was born there and lived there for a few years. He's built like an ox. There is no way he doesn't spend half his day at the gym. His clipped answer isn't rude, so much as hesitant.

"I wanted to say thank you. I remember you from the other night, and I know you kept an eye on me when I tried to hide. I don't think Luca gave you a choice, but I still appreciate it. I'd be dead if it weren't for both of you."

"Just doing my job, Ms. D'Amato."

Oh. Well, that doesn't sting. I nod and back up. I feel like a complete idiot. I glance down at the floor not sure what to do next.

"Don't be an ass. I'm Carmine. Forgive Gabriele. He's a man of few words."

"And you're a man of far too many."

I twist to see Luca glowering at Carmine. He slips his arm around my waist, and I can't think of it as being anything but territorial. Luca appears even more pissed at Carmine than he did at Lorenzo yesterday. That I got. They argued. But he's said nothing to Carmine yet.

"This is my cousin Carmine. Gabriele is his best friend."

Luca says nothing I didn't just already learn. He presses against my waist and draws me away. Apparently, he and Carmine aren't friends. The look he shot Gabriele makes me think he barely tolerates him, too. Maria goes to stand with them, and she's the only one who seems to have any warmth toward Carmine or Gabriele. Luca, his brothers, and Matteo basically ignore the other two guys.

It's not until we're walking to the dining room that Maria slips beside me and whispers.

"Carmine's the black sheep in the family. No one will hold it against you for being polite, but Luca won't appreciate you making friends. Same goes for Gabriele. He's guilty by association."

"You don't sound like you see Carmine that way."

"I don't. But it helps that I'm a girl. My relationship with my cousin differs from the one he has with my brothers. He's a good guy, but he's done some super stupid shit over the years. Gabriele tagged along."

I glance at Luca, who's holding my hand, but talking to Salvatore in Italian. I didn't think he heard Maria until he shoots her a dirty look. She rolls her eyes and keeps whispering to me.

"I can tell you're trying to be discreet, and Luca's a bull in a China shop. Mama and Papa will warm up. They're being way nicer to you than they are to any of the guys I've tried to date. If it's not Papa scaring the poor guys away, then it's the six Hulks I have around me all the time. I suspect they already really like you but feel like they're supposed to be the disapproving and stern Italian parents. Aunt Sylvia definitely likes you, which means Uncle Salvatore does, too."

Hmm. I watch the couple as they lead the way into the dining room. Salvatore's arm is around Sylvia's waist, and his hand is precariously close to his wife's backside. He may be the head of the family, but I suspect she's the hand that turns it. It's not like I think he's pussy whipped. That's not a phrase anyone could associate with Salvatore Mancinelli. I think he respects his wife's opinions and trusts her more than most.

"Are you Luca's girlfriend?"

I peer down at a little girl who must be about eight. She's

the older of the two sisters who came inside when Matteo went to tell them it was dinner time.

"I'm a friend of his."

"He doesn't hold Matteo's hand or Gabriele's. They're his friends."

I don't know about the latter. I smile at her and try to come up with an answer.

"We can have different kinds of friends, and we can show them they're important to us in different ways. Luca holds my hand. I bet he works out with Matteo and Gabriele to show he's friends with them."

"What—"

"Pia, how about you introduce yourself before playing twenty questions with my—friend?"

Luca sounds like he's ready to choke on that word. He's looking down at the little girl with the long brown braid running down her back. She shoots him the same smirk Maria gave her brother when we arrived. Fucking genes. I swear.

"I'm Pia, and that's my sister, Natalia. That's our Mama and Papa."

She points to Sylvia and Salvatore. I look at Natalia, then back to Pia. They're the best of both of their parents.

"I'm Olivia. Thank you for having me over for dinner. You have a very nice backyard. I wish I had swings."

Natalia chimes in as she shoots me a disdainful look. So much attitude for someone who can't be older than six.

"Aren't you too old for swings?"

"You are never too old for swings or slides. They're always fun."

Luca leans over to whisper in my ear.

"If you're a good little girl, I might play hide and seek with you when we get home."

"Why would I hide?"

I keep my voice just as low.

"I'm talking about your tight little pussy and amazing tits. They're hiding under those clothes, and I intend to seek them out."

"*Shh. Luca.*"

Please don't let anyone have heard that. I dart my gaze around, but no one's paying attention. Maria is back to talking to Carmine, and the little girls have gone straight to their seats at the dinner table. Luca pulls out a chair for me, and I slide in. He sits to my left, which puts him to Salvatore's right. Massimo is sitting on the don's other side. As I look around, I realize there's a hierarchy to the seating arrangements.

Sylvia sits at the foot of the table across from Salvatore. To my other side is Marco, then Lorenzo, then Carmine. Nicoletta sits between her husband and Maria, who is next to Matteo, then Gabriele. Pia and Natalia sit on either side of their mother. Despite there being an odd number of people at the table, someone spaced the seats evenly as though my chair was always there. That begs the question: who usually sits in my seat?

Luca leans toward me and answers that very question.

"You're in the seat of honor for guests. We usually spread out a little more because Aunt Sylvia only puts the chair there when someone comes to dinner."

No wonder I'm so warm. I'm in the hot seat.

I already have my hands clasped in my lap when I realize Salvatore is about to pray. I dip my head and close my eyes.

"*Benedici, o Signore, noi e questi doni che la tua bontà ci elargisce. Per Cristo nostro Signore.*" Bless us, O Lord, and these gifts that Your goodness bestows upon us. Through Christ our Lord.

I catch the first couple of words and the last sentence, but I don't understand the rest. But I guess it's something about being thankful for gifts given to us.

"Amen."

I make the sign of the cross without thinking, but when I open my eyes, half the table is staring at me. My face flushes. I assumed if anyone would make the sign of the cross after praying, it would be Italian Catholics as much as Latin American Catholics.

Nicoletta finally smiles at me. Score!

"Did you understand the blessing?"

"Some of it was close enough to Spanish for me to follow."

Salvatore interjects before Nicoletta can say anything else.

"You speak Spanish?"

"Fluently."

Nicoletta draws my attention back to her.

"That's certainly useful in New York."

"It is. I switch back and forth at work all the time. I write some content for advertisements, and I do most of them in both English and Spanish. It also gets me the best kept secret foods at my local bodega. The lady who owns it loves that *la gringa rubia* can speak as fluently as she does since she was born in Puerto Rico. She says I make up for being a gringa by being a good Catholic. We go to the same church."

Natalia leans forward with a gap tooth smile.

"What does *la gringa rubia* mean?"

"The blonde gringa. Basically, the blonde foreigner."

"But you're not blonde."

"I usually am. I'm trying something new."

I smile and shrug one shoulder. I retreat a little because I don't want to get into why my hair is different. I'm pretty sure all the adults know. Nicoletta rescues me, but it's with another question.

"Which church do you go to?"

"Our Lady of Guadalupe in Brooklyn. Actually, it has an Italian Mass on Sundays. There have been a couple times when I've missed the English one before it and the Spanish one on Saturday nights. I've gone to the Italian because it's close enough to the Latin Mass for me to follow, and the routine is the same regardless of the language."

Massimo's eyebrows shoot up.

"Latin Mass?"

"It isn't Christmas without it. My mom insists."

We've been passing around dishes as we talk, but now everyone has served themselves. We grow quiet for a few minutes as we eat. It gives me a couple moments reprieve. Luca offers to pour me some wine.

"Just half a glass, please. Robust reds give me headaches."

"Would you rather have something else?"

"It's all right. Just a little wine and some more water."

"I can get you—"

"It's okay. I promise."

We've kept our voices low, but with no one else talking, everyone hears us. I don't notice Sylvia get up from the table, so I nearly jump out of my skin when she offers me a larger water glass than the small tumbler in front of me. Luca's already handed off the wine bottle and is filling my water glass nearly to the brim. I'll be lucky if I don't spill it down the front of me.

"Thank you."

I meet his gaze as he leans back after putting the water carafe down. He's more anxious than I realized. I'm not sure how I can tell since he looks relaxed. I just sense it. Maybe it's because he's trying so hard to make sure I have what I need and want. I felt his forearm tense next to mine when Massimo asked me about the Latin Mass.

The meal progresses onto other topics, and Luca and I both breathe easier. The brothers and Maria banter throughout the meal, and it makes me wish I wasn't an only child. Carmine keeps Pia and Natalia entertained throughout the meal. I notice Salvatore watching his nephew as though Carmine is as much a stranger as I am. He's trying to get a read on both of us. Maria mentioned Carmine wasn't the favorite family member, but he seems great to me. Maybe he's turned over a new leaf, and Salvatore doesn't know what to make of it. For the black sheep of the family, Carmine looks like he might actually make a good dad one day.

"Don't be fooled." Luca leans toward me. "He says and does all the right things to get what he wants."

"What could he want from Pia and Natalia? Their lunch money?"

"Uncle Salvatore's forgiveness."

There must be way more to that story, but this is definitely not the time. And I think Maria is likely a better source than Luca. I think she'd be unbiased. The meal continues, and by the time dessert is served, I'm stuffed. It amuses me that all the men stand and clear the table as though they're pre-programmed machines.

Nicoletta laughs as she speaks to me.

"One daughter and three sons, plus Matteo. There was no way I was going to clean up after all of them once they weren't toddlers. If they can make the mess, they can clean the mess. Once Sylvia realized my boys can do chores as well as anyone else, she made sure Carmine and Gabriele joined in when they came over. She guilted Salvatore into it, and Massimo went hungry for nearly a month when we first married. He made a flippant comment about my wifely duties. My father was a union leader. Massimo learned what it means to strike."

Maria giggles and shakes her head.

"Mama got Papa and my brothers—including Matteo— monogrammed aprons for Christmas a few years ago. You should see them in their suits with their Betty Crocker-looking gingham aprons. They're all so tall that it looks like they're wearing ones made for kids. It's hilarious."

"Did Matteo grow up with you?"

Everyone keeps acting like he's an extra brother. Did I miss something? Nicoletta shakes her head.

"No. Matteo's father is Massimo and Salvatore's second cousin. Domenico was adopted at birth, so there's no actual blood relation. Matteo's mother is my childhood best friend. Marco is two and a half hours older than Matteo. They've been best friends since they were three. They used to nap together in the same crib as babies. If Matteo wasn't at our house, then Marco was at his. Matteo has his own room at our house, and Marco has one at Matteo's parents' house."

"Wow. Two and a half hours?"

"Yes. Massimo and Domenico have been best friends for as long as I've been friends with Carlotta. The men have always been competitive, so of course, they bet each other who could get their wife pregnant sooner. Matteo has an older brother, Emilio, who's six months younger than Luca. Apparently, God smiled on those two fools on the same night. Matteo and Marco were born on their due date, which had been the same since Carlotta and I found out we were pregnant within a week of each other."

"Kismet. It destined them to be best friends. Are Luca and Emilio close?"

Nicoletta glances at the kitchen and shakes her head. She draws her index finger down her cheek where Luca's scar is on his. I turn to look at the men in the kitchen, and I can see Luca flicking dish soap bubbles at Lorenzo, who snaps a towel at his older brother.

"They were."

That's not nearly enough information, but I don't dare ask

for more details. And before I could if I wanted to, the men come back. Luca slides into his seat, and I reach for him without thinking.

"No dish pan hands? Are you sure you did a good job?"

As soon as I realize what I've done, I let go and mentally kick myself. Things were going so well. It doesn't help when Marco chimes in.

"Be glad he doesn't. My brother would be demanding you kiss his boo-boos if he did."

"*Zitto.*"

"Luca, don't be rude to your brother. Marco, don't antagonize your brother."

"Yes, Mama."

I cover my mouth to keep from laughing at the two disgraced little boys in overgrown man bodies. I lean toward Luca, not sure if I dare repeat what he said.

"What does *zitto* mean?"

"Shut up."

"You don't take teasing well."

He leans closer to me, and his breath on my neck sends goosebumps down my arms.

"The only teasing I like is when you're naked and sitting on my lap while I'm still dressed. Maybe you'll tease me mercilessly later."

"You at my mercy? I doubt that."

"You have no idea, *piccolina.*"

I clench my pussy. The promise in those words and that purely masculine voice is enough to make me worry I'll stand up with a wet spot on my dress. I guess the wall I put up crumbled. Not a stone left standing.

We move into the living room, and I watch the entire family drink espresso. I'll be up all night if I do that. I decline and explain why. I accept a *digestif.* It's a small glass of

Amaro Averna, a Sicilian liqueur. The name should have prepared me for the bitter taste. *Amaro* in Italian and *armago* in Spanish. I try not to curl my nose as I swallow. Just like the espresso, no one thinks twice about the shot of liquor. I know it's a palate cleanser after coffee, but I can't imagine one bitter drink getting rid of the taste of another bitter drink. I think it just compounds it. Either way, I take mine to be polite, but I won't ask for it again. Limoncello next time if I get a choice.

Luca takes my glass from me and puts it on the coffee table.

"Not a favorite? It's an acquired taste."

"If you say so."

"Have you had sambuca before?"

"Yes, at work to taste it for a product promo. I've seen it served with coffee beans, so it doesn't appeal to me by choice."

"We'll find an after-dinner drink you like."

"I prefer sweeter drinks in general. If I drink coffee, it's with plenty of cream and sugar."

"Don't tell me you like Frappuccino."

"No. That's way too much sugar."

"Good. They're coffee sacrilege. They give Italian coffee a bad rap. They don't even exist in Italy."

"You sound deeply offended by their mere existence."

I chuckle, and he exaggerates his aggrieved expression.

"They're a personal slight against all Italians. Just like pizza from anywhere outside Italy or New York."

"Chicagoans would disagree."

I cock an eyebrow, but it drops when Luca's smile falters. My brow furrows, but he shakes his head.

"It's nothing, *piccolina*. I just had a bad business trip to Chicago a few months ago. Not a place I want to think about."

I sweep my gaze over everyone in the room before stepping closer to Luca.

"Did something happen there? Is that where you got the fresh scar on your back?"

His eyes widen.

"I saw it when you were walking out of the bedroom yesterday, Luca. It looks pretty new."

"No. That's not where that happened. I made some bad choices thanks to Carmine, and I had a deal go really, really bad in Chicago. But in the end, it falling through was a blessing in disguise."

"Oh?"

"Among other things, I wouldn't be here with you if it had gone through."

"You wouldn't?"

"No. I'd be married."

I can only stare at him. Married? What the fuck?

Chapter Nine

Luca

Chicago and everything to do with it were not my shining moments. My dad had been pushing me to prove myself more and to show the world I deserve to be the underboss. As Uncle Salvatore's younger brother and an attorney, my dad is our *consigliere*. He's Uncle Salvatore's chief advisor and sometimes his conscience. My dad suggested I stick it to the bratva, or Russian organized crime. He said it would show Uncle Salvatore that I'm ready for more responsibility. I thought I was doing just fine.

Of course, Carmine wormed his way into it like he does everything else. I had a couple deals about to go down in New Jersey that would have cost the Kutsenkos, the heads of the bratva, millions. But Carmine put a bug in my ear about striking bigger and harder. The Chicago bratva has made some moves to usurp the Kutsenkos' shipping routes from Mexico to Canada. They got in bed with the Guadalajara Cartel and thought that would guarantee them leverage.

At the same time, I knew the don in Chicago was considering marrying his daughter to a guy in London. I've known Cecelia since we were kids. She doesn't want to leave the U.S., and an alliance through marriage would strengthen my family. Don Edoardo considered me because he assumed an alliance would elevate him. What he didn't realize was an alliance would have allowed us to take over most of the Midwest. We are far more influential and powerful than he is.

But he had a stipulation—a test—for me to prove myself worthy of Cecelia. It coincided with my dad's suggestion that I make a move on the Kutsenkos. Before I knew what was happening, Carmine was leading me by the balls because he knows a secret I never want shared. It's the only thing I truly regret in life, and I don't want anyone to know. I don't even like admitting it to myself. He threatened to tell everyone, especially Uncle Salvatore, if I didn't go along with his plan to involve the Podolskaya, a Moscow bratva, and the Kutsenkos' personal enemy.

It blew up in all of our faces. I never wanted to hurt Anastasia Kutsenko, the woman who married Nikolai. He's the third brother out of four in the Kutsenko family and part of their Elite Group. That's the bratva's top leadership. His oldest brother, Maksim, is equivalent to Uncle Salvatore as their *pakhan*. Carmine, Gabriele—of course, because Carmine can't shit without his bestie up his ass—and I spent four months in Sicily as our punishment. Despite what the Kutsenkos call it, it was not a vacay under the Tuscan sun. That scar Livy noticed came from the vineyard owner who took a shovel blade to my back for not picking as many grapes as the other men. I already had an arm in a sling.

"Luca?"

I turn a blank stare to Livy until I snap out of my thoughts. I tuck hair behind her ear as I gaze into her unique eyes. Thank

God for unanswered prayers. Actually, no. I prayed things would work out and I would impress my uncle and dad. I prayed I would impress Edoardo, so I could marry Cecelia. I'm glad those went unanswered. But I'm way gladder that he answered me when I prayed to find some way out of marrying Cecelia once shit started. I prayed to survive Lucenzo and make it home. God answered that. I prayed Uncle Salvatore would forgive me, and I'm almost back in his good graces.

And my most secret prayer has been to find someone like Maksim, Aleksei, Nikolai, Bogdan, and Pasha Kutsenko have. Five out of the eight most senior members of the Russian syndicate have found women to love them and marry them. Maybe I can have that with Livy.

"Sorry, *piccolina*. I was lost in thought. It would have been an arranged marriage, and I'm happy it never happened. I've known the woman since we were children, and she's what many men would want. But I knew I would never love her. It would have been business. I'm grateful things fell through."

I want nothing more than to link our hands and bring hers to my lips. But we're standing too close, and I already touched her hair. Whispering is only drawing attention. I think my mom and dad have warmed to her, but I don't need to flaunt anything in their faces. I take a step back, but I watch Livy. I can tell what I just said threw her. She doesn't like it.

"Livy, there was nothing between that woman and me but a business arrangement I tried to make with her father. She's been in love with the same guy since high school. She didn't want to marry me, and she made sure her father—everyone —knew it."

"Then why'd you pursue her?"

"It would have been good for my family."

I can't say more than that, but I should have known that wouldn't suffice as an explanation.

"Is that why your parents don't like me? Because they think you should have married this woman?"

"No. It's a long story, Liv, and not one to tell you right now. It was my idea, but I'm eternally grateful it didn't work out. My parents don't dislike you at all."

She raises an eyebrow at that. I don't know which part she's skeptical about. Probably all of it.

"If you say so, Luca."

"Are you ready to go home?"

I see the moment she's about to argue that it isn't her home, but she bites her tongue. Good. I'm not in the mood for that argument or any variation of it. My place is her home for right now.

"Yeah. I'm exhausted, and I can't wait to take these heels off. I don't know how I ran in them the other night in the parking lot."

Fear gives you superhuman powers. She ran in them because she thought it was the only way she would survive.

"Let's say goodnight to everyone, then go."

I steer her to my parents and my aunt and uncle. She offers them all a warm smile, but I can tell she's more at ease with Aunt Sylvia than anyone else.

"Thank you so much for including me in your family dinner. I had a wonderful time."

"Olivia, you are welcome here whenever we gather. I hope you'll join us again soon."

Aunt Sylvia offers her a loose hug. Livy returns it, and I can tell she's genuinely happy. But she grows wary again as soon as she steps back. Uncle Salvatore wraps his arm around my aunt's waist, but his smile is sincere when he directs it at Livy. I breathe easier.

"It was nice to meet you, Ms. D'Amato. I second what Sylvia said. I hope you will join us again in the future."

Not as warm as it could be, but I'll take it. I know my uncle, and I know his tone of voice. His words might not have been effusive, but he was sincere. It's my parents' turn now, and I hold my breath as my mom speaks.

"Olivia, the boys and Maria come over every Wednesday for dinner. I look forward to seeing you there. I know this arrangement was unexpected, so if there is anything you need that you don't have with you, please let me know."

My mom leans in and kisses Livy on each cheek. Livy's uncertain what to do at first, but she quickly catches on and returns the air kisses. My dad watched me while my mom spoke, but now his attention is on Livy. He wasn't an affectionate father to his sons, only his daughter. But he did his best to nurture in his own way, and I've never doubted that he loves my brothers and me as much as he does Maria. I know he regrets pushing me to stand out, and I know he feels guilty for some of what I did. That only makes me feel more ashamed because it wasn't his ideas I followed.

"Ms. D'Amato, I enjoyed your company this evening. You remind me of Maria, which means you are far more interesting and funnier than any of the boys. I suppose you can bring Luca along on Wednesday, but I look forward to seeing you again soon."

"Thanks, Papa."

I pretend to scowl as he offers Livy air kisses too, but he pulls me into a loose embrace, clapping me on the back several times. I'm unprepared for him to whisper to me.

"You've found the one."

I step back, and my gaze meets my dad's. He wraps his arm around my mom's shoulders because they've always been more modest than Uncle Salvatore and Aunt Sylvia. Just like my aunt and uncle, my parents were an arranged marriage. But they were already in love when they got engaged. Calling it arranged is more a technicality than an explanation.

My mom looks up at my dad, then she looks at me. She opens her arms to me, and I accept her hug. I don't care how old I get. I always find immediate comfort in her arms. I close my eyes for a moment as I lean down to rest my head on her shoulder.

"I like her, *cucciolotto*." Little puppy. "Take care of her and make her happy."

"I will, Mama."

I let go with a sigh. I really don't want to. If only I could be six again and crawl onto her lap to listen to her tell me stories about when she was growing up. I noticed Maria and Livy chatting, so I turn toward my little sister. Her giggle is still the same as it was when we were all kids. It's infectious. I grin as I listen to her talk with Livy.

"If your warden ever paroles you, we should go out. Lorenzo owns a nightclub that's one of the hottest places in Manhattan."

"That sounds like so much fun. Have you been to Ivy or Envy? I love both of them."

Everyone goes silent, and Livy looks up at me. I know she can't figure out what she said wrong. I shoot Carmine a glare.

"Those are rivals. We keep our distance."

I don't want to explain more than that, and fortunately, Livy just nods before she looks back at Maria. When we returned from Italy, we drove past a Kutsenko-owned nightclub to flaunt we were back. Uncle Salvatore booted all of our cars. I admit that was my showboating because I resented what I'd just experienced. I knew better, but I did it anyway.

"Let me know when you want to go out. I'll see whether I can be let out on good behavior."

I'm trying not to twitch. The last thing I want is to imagine

Livy in a crowd with loud music and too many drunk assholes. My hand slips into hers as I shake my head. I shoot my sister a look that tells her not to argue. Maybe there's ever so slight a chance that she doesn't know Livy's backstory about how we met.

We say quick goodbyes to everyone else. We don't linger after that, and we go straight home. We keep the conversation light and laugh about some things Pia and Natalia said during dinner. When we get in the house, we move to the kitchen where I put a few containers of leftovers in the fridge. Aunt Sylvia always makes sure there's enough for all of us to take something home. I jest I don't know how to cook for less than six people. She can't cook for less than twenty-five.

"Who owns Ivy and Envy?"

"The Russians."

I don't want to get into this. I don't want to explain all the rival syndicates, but as I think about it, I realize this might be the best time to start educating her. If we're going to be together, she needs to know who to steer clear of.

"Russians?"

"You know who my family is. You know the Culiacán are a cartel. The Kutsenkos run the Russian bratva. There are four brothers: Maksim, Aleksei, Nikolai, and Bogdan. They own Kutsenko Partners and several nightclubs and strip clubs. They have four cousins who are always with them. Sergei and Misha Andreyev and Anton and Pasha Kutsenko. If you hear those names, you stay away. If you see four men who are almost identical with dark hair and icy-blue eyes, you stay away. Their cousins are from opposite sides of the family, but they look just like their shared cousins. If you spot men who look like the Kutsenkos but either have blond hair and blue eyes or brown hair and brown eyes, you'll know you've met the Andreyev brothers or the other set of Kutsenko brothers. Their family tree is a little complicated, but you won't miss how similar they all look."

"Luca, your tone is scaring me. Would they hurt me if they found out I know you?"

"No. They will never hurt you. That's one thing you can guarantee with that family. They never touch women and children."

"But aren't Russians known for…"

She's too uncomfortable to say what I know she's thinking.

"Yes. As a whole, the bratva is known for human trafficking. However, the Ivankovs, that's the Kutsenkos' branch, remains steadfastly against threatening or harming women. However, I—"

Fuck me in the ass with a pogo stick. This isn't what I want to admit right now. We had such a great evening.

"You what?"

"I did some shit not that long ago that endangered Anastasia Kutsenko, Nikolai's wife. It was bad enough that she wound up in the hospital. It was my connection with the Chicago *Cosa Nostra* that led to the Moscow bratva kidnapping her."

"Kidnapping her? She lived?"

"Yeah. Just barely."

I watch Livy as she digests everything I just said.

"Luca, what did you do? Tell me right now."

I scrub my hands over my face and blow out a breath. It's only fair she learns now. It'll be far worse if I wait, our relationship deepens, and then she finds out. Considering everything I can't tell her, I should share this.

"Let's sit in the living room. Of all the intense conversations we've had in three days, this is probably the hardest."

We walk to the sofa, and she sits as far into the corner as

she can. She pulls her legs up, creating a barrier between us. I take a fortifying breath before I launch into it.

"At the beginning of last summer, the Kutsenkos did some things we couldn't ignore. We—"

"What are 'some things,' Luca? Don't be evasive."

"I need to back up. Livy, there is information I can never share with you. Not only would knowing endanger you with our enemies, but with the cops and feds. What you don't know, you can't tell. Not knowing will keep you from incriminating yourself, but it'll also keep many members of my family and me off death row. You saw what I did. You know that wasn't the first time I've done that. Do you know what RICO stands for?"

She shakes her head. Of course not. Most normal people don't.

"It stands for Racketeer Influence and Corrupt Organizations Act. It's the law that brought down a bunch of Mafia members from the 1970s through the 1990s. It's still enforced and would be the way to end most of my family's businesses. To avoid leaving anything for the feds to use against us, we go through a lot of measures to protect ourselves. All the syndicates do. While we leave clean trails law enforcement can't follow, sometimes it gets messy among us. It got really messy last summer."

I pause to see if she's following along despite how vague I'm being. I will not tell her any of the illegal dealings we're into. I draw the line there. She can't know about the money laundering, loan sharking and extortion, the fencing, illegal gambling, and a shit ton more.

"Last summer, the bratva found out about a deal we made with partners in several Eastern European countries. They like to think they have a monopoly in that region. They don't. The oligarchs and organized crime organizations are free to deal with whomever they want. Some of them wanted us. The

Kutsenkos put a hit on several top members of our organization. These men were family members a couple times removed. They were men I grew up with. Men Uncle Salvatore and my dad grew up with. They did it to prove a point. That's all. It was unnecessary, but they did it because they could."

Livy's frozen in her spot. She's barely moved enough to breathe. Now I'm doubting the wisdom of saying any of this. But it's her right to make an educated decision. If I'd married Cecelia, yes, it would have been arranged. But the entire point would have been to marry within the Mafia. Cecelia knows this life because it's all she's lived. Livy knows none of it.

"Livy?"

"Keep going."

"How scared are you right now?"

"Plenty. Tell me the rest of it. How did you risk this woman's life?"

I can't help but sigh each time I talk.

"We needed to strike back hard. It wasn't something we could ignore, and not making an equal strike in return endangers us all because we look weak. I know what that sounds like, all machismo and toxic masculinity, and it is. But that's our life. I hold a very senior position, but I'm still young. People still expect me to prove myself. We took Anastasia to make a point: don't take family members from us, and we won't take them from you. But the Kutsenkos responded with guns blazing—literally. To end the shootout, one of my guys pushed her out the front door. She fell down the steps and injured her spine, but she fully recovered. I punished the guy, and he can never make the same mistake twice."

"Did you hurt her before you let her go?"

"Do you mean did I beat her, or do you mean did I rape her?"

"For fuck's sake, Luca. I definitely didn't think about the latter. Is that what I have to fear if someone takes me?"

"Depends on who it is. Any American syndicate, I don't think so. But you dying isn't my only fear and the only reason to protect you right now."

I watch as she absorbs everything. She's so pale it's scaring me.

"Livy, do you need me to stop telling you this? Is it too much for right now?"

"Finish."

"I told you I ended up making a deal with the Chicago don. He wanted me to prove myself worthy of marrying Cecelia. I did some asking around with the Chicago bratva to see if they'd want Anastasia. They could hold it over the Kutsenkos and demand a ransom. I never planned to follow through. I wanted to make it look like I would strike the New York bratva that hard, but I would have stopped it before she could leave the city. But word spread to Russia, and it fed an old feud with a Moscow bratva. They got involved personally to hurt the Kutsenkos. They kidnapped Anastasia while she and Niko were on vacation in Greece. I don't know the details, and I don't think Uncle Salvatore does either, but whatever Anastasia did to protect herself scared the shit out of my uncle. He's terrified to be in the same room as her."

That's the truth. We suspect she resorted to a level of violence even the men in all the syndicates rarely do. She's thin as they come and looks like a good gust of wind would knock her over. She killed at least one man who was double her size. I'm certain about that. But no one outside the Kutsenko family knows the specifics. That adds to the air of danger.

"Did you get away with all this?"

"No. I barely survived. If I weren't Uncle Salvatore's nephew and heir, I would be dead. I ended up at a vineyard in

Sicily. He sentenced me to hard labor with a man who owed my uncle a favor. It pissed the owner off that he had to pay the debt by employing my co-conspirators and me. I got that recent scar from him."

"How?"

"I won't tell you that, Livy."

"Yes, you will. How, Luca? If I'm in for a penny, then I'm in for a pound. I want to know what kind of danger you face. I want to know what to expect. What kind of injuries will you come home with?"

"Livy, I don't want you to know those details. It's not something I want you to think about, picture. I don't want you to hold your breath, expecting me to always come home injured. The scars you've seen are old, and that was a rare circumstance."

"Fucking tell me. You want me to stay in a relationship with you. I deserve to know what the fuck I'm accepting. This isn't protecting me. It's treating me like a child. I'm feeling like one demanding an answer. I resent that."

"The vineyard owner took a shovel blade to my back when I didn't pick grapes fast enough. One of my arms was already in a sling from Uncle Salvatore's punishment."

"Your uncle beat you?"

"In my world, I deserved what I got."

"Your world. So, one I'll always be outside of."

"No. You're still learning and deciding if this is what you want. With what I'm telling you now, I'm not assuming you'll forgive me."

I want nothing more than to pull her into my arms and reassure her I'm not the man I've been. Plead momentary insanity to have done those things to Anastasia.

"Livy, I will always regret what I did. There is no amount of redeeming myself that will make the Kutsenkos, my uncle, or me forgive myself. I have to live with this for the rest of my life. But before that and since then, I have lived by the unwritten code among the syndicates. Women and children are off limits. When we violate that, we endanger our own women and children. That's why Uncle Salvatore was livid and why he sent us away."

"Us?"

"Carmine and Gabriele."

"That's why you hate Carmine."

"That's way more complicated. He's my cousin. I love him, but I don't like him. I never have. I didn't trust him much before, but I don't trust him at all now."

"Why? You're the heir. Aren't you the leader, and he's the follower?"

"Only by appearances. Carmine is a master manipulator. He's pretended to be useless while quietly inserting himself into everything. I knew what he was doing, but I was stuck. I truly can't tell you why. He's far smarter than anyone outside my family knew. He doesn't want my position, but he thought he could connive his way into controlling me."

"Sounds like he did."

"I know. And it sucked extra hard because I knew it the entire time."

"Luca, is what I've seen you do just a typical day for you? Is that what you do every day?"

"No. I obviously did nothing like that today."

"If I weren't here?"

"No. My typical day is boring. I run several businesses, so I do things like payroll, inspecting inventories, generating reports. I meet with my uncle and other leaders to discuss other business matters."

She only nods to that last part. Is she shutting down and retreating? Or is she realizing she's better off not knowing?

"Luca, I don't know if you can really understand how overwhelming this is for someone so new to this. I think you can guess, but I don't think you can know. I don't know what to make of all of this. I feel super conflicted. I need to think about this. A lot. I'm going to bed."

"Livy—"

"No. I need to be alone."

Do I sleep outside her door? Post a guard under her window? She's going to bolt. I can tell.

Chapter Ten

Livy

What the fuck kind of living nightmare have I entered? How the fuck do I wake up from it?

Luca's just admitted shit that he rightly says is unforgivable. What kind of person does that make me to be romantically involved with him? How can I possibly overlook that he kidnapped a woman and created a situation where other people kidnapped the same person?

Morally gray doesn't even begin to describe this shit.

I sit on the end of the bed and close my eyes. I'm so fucking exhausted I can barely think straight, yet my mind is abuzz. The contradiction is giving me a headache. The hardest part to all of this is reconciling the man he's been with me to the man he just described. It's like two separate people.

If I stay with him, will his kindness wear off, and I'll see a different man beneath? If he could do this once, could he do it again? He said Carmine and Gabriele were involved. He said Salvatore beat him and sent him off to be beaten by someone else. Violence engulfs his life completely. Mine will be too if I stay with him.

He said I can't tell what I don't know. I can't incriminate myself or him. But what if people don't believe I know nothing?

There are more questions than answers. I won't resolve anything tonight, so I may as well try to get some sleep. I slept naked last night because I really had nothing to wear. When I ordered the dress, I picked out some pajamas. I'm quick to brush my teeth and hop into bed. I don't fall asleep as quickly as I hoped, but it doesn't take long. I almost wish I hadn't shut my eyes. Dreams—or rather nightmares—of finding Luca dead, seeing someone murder him, having a family with him and watching someone kill our children fill my sleep. That makes me wake in a cold sweat. My heart's racing.

There's a lot to unpack with this last nightmare. Is my mind trying to scare me? Or am I batshit crazy after all? Why am I dreaming about having a family with Luca? What the ever-loving fuck? I don't know him nearly well enough to picture that scenario. I'm not some middle school girl doodling Mrs. Mancinelli in my notebook. I need to get these thoughts out of my head, but they refuse to budge as I lie here looking at the ceiling and the inside of my eyelids.

We've had unseasonably warm weather for late winter, so I climb out of bed and pull on a pair of socks and my sneakers. I have flannel jammies on, and I grab my coat. I need more air than I'm going to get with just my window open. I need out of these four walls. I need to see the stars and just take a break from being even remotely in the same space as Luca. I mean, I'm only going to his backyard, but at least I won't be in the same building.

I half expect him to be camped outside my door, but I see and hear nothing when I open it. I refuse to creep down the stairs like I'm doing something wrong. I move quietly, but I'm not hiding. I know there are a couple of throw blankets in the living room, so I grab those. I get to the French doors that open to the garden and freeze. He probably has an alarm. Now what? Do I try anyway and risk setting it off? Or do I abandon this and just sit down here for a while?

I really don't know what to do. I look for any sensors around the door frame and see nothing. But maybe they're hidden somehow. Fuck it. The more I think about an alarm, the more trapped I feel. I want out. I just hope I don't wake the entire neighborhood or trigger some alarm company. I twist the lock and push down on the handle. Nothing happens. I open the door an inch and still nothing. I immediately realize why Luca doesn't have an alarm. He doesn't need one. I knew he had guards at the gate to his driveway, but I didn't realize how many patrol the grounds. Two men approach me with heavy New York accents.

"Is something wrong, Ms. D'Amato?"

The first man has a beak nose that's clearly been broken several times.

"No, not at all. I just needed some air. I'm going to sit on one of the lounge chairs and look at the stars."

"If you need anything..."

"Thank you."

I see the second guy hang back and tilt his head slightly down. Is he about to speak into one of those earpiece radios I've seen on cop shows?

"I don't want to disturb anyone. I can go back inside."

The second guy shoots me a quick smile before he explains.

"I'm just letting the other men know not to bother you."

"Thanks. I'm just going over there."

I point to the chairs near the covered pool. I don't know why I feel like I need to explain myself. They're only checking on me. Do I feel guilty because I'm out here or because I'm worried

I'm disturbing them? I don't know. It's one more thing to puzzle out. I adjust the back of one, so I can recline and look up at the stars. I wrap myself in the blankets and pull up my hood. I'm cozy in my little cocoon. I pick out the constellations I remember from my middle school astronomy class. A few deep inhales calm me, and I feel myself grow tired again. But I'm so comfy.

"Livy! ... Liv! ... Olivia! ... Liveee!"

I come awake to Luca's voice bellowing at me. I sit up and look around. It's already morning, but not that late. I'd guess seven something.

"Luca?"

I spot him as he comes around the side of the house and wave. He sprints to me, then comes to a dead stop beside my chair and stares.

"Luca, what's wrong?"

"What's wrong? I go knock on your door, and you don't answer. I think that you're still sleeping, but I don't want to leave for the gym without letting you know in case you wake up, I'm not here, and panic. Just like I fucking did. How long have you been out here? Do you have any idea how fucking terrified I was that somehow someone got you?"

He scrubs his hands over his face. I pull my legs in and tap the chair. He sinks down and cups his face in his hands with his elbows resting on his thighs. It takes a moment before he looks at me.

"I thought you ran. I thought you might after we finished talking last night. Then I reasoned you knew it was too cold out. How long have you been out here?"

"I think it was like two when I came out."

"Five and a half hours? You could have frozen to death. I can't believe my men let you stay out here."

"Let me? Do I need permission from you or them?"

"Of course not. But it's way too cold. Common sense should have had them wake you."

"Don't get mad at them. I would have stayed even if they woke me."

"You wanted to be as far from me as you could without leaving."

"No. I needed more air than I could get with an open window. I needed space."

He isn't completely wrong. I couldn't be in the same house as him last night, but I didn't want to get as far away as I could. I wanted to stay close while still having that space. As he nods, I know he's tacking on "from me" in his mind, but he says nothing.

"Luca, I had nightmares about you dying in front of me. That someone would tell me you were dead. That we had a family, and I watched someone murder our children."

I can't believe I admitted any of that, especially the last bit. This is all too serious for knowing a guy for a few days. He scoops me into his arms and nestles me against him. I feel him sigh, and I realize he's not just comforting me. He needs this. He needs to hold me and feel me close. I can't deny how comforting it is. Maybe if I hadn't curled up on the sofa and let him hold me instead, I wouldn't have felt so adrift.

"*Piccolina*, I'm sorry I scared you so badly you had nightmares. I don't know what to tell you and what to avoid. I'm figuring this out as we go along. I've admitted things to you I've told no one outside my family. But something compels me to be as honest with you as I can. I think it's because I know there's so much I can't tell you. I want you so badly that I can't think straight. But I never want you to think I trapped you by keeping things from you."

"Are you scared I'll hate you, *caro?* Are you afraid I'll turn you in?"

"The first part, yes. The second part, maybe. This is the most abnormal way to—I don't even know. Most abnormal everything. To meet. To want to date. To find out the truth about the guy you're living with. To be living with a guy the day after you meet. I'm so sorry, Livy. God knows, I'm glad to have you in my life, but I wouldn't wish these circumstances on you, because along with all of it, your life is in danger. Now that you've met Uncle Salvatore and Aunt Sylvia, would you rather stay with them?"

"No."

I blurt my answer and wrap my arms around him. I'm clinging to him for dear life. It's pure instinct. My rational mind would tell me to consider the offer.

"Are you more afraid of them than me?"

"I'm not afraid of any of you. That's what's scary. I should be. But you seemed like such a normal and happy family last night."

"In a lot of ways, we are."

"Do you want me to leave?"

"No."

He blurts his answer just like I did mine. I lift my head from his chest and twist to look at him. My right hand cups his left cheek, covering the scar. My fingers press lightly against it as I bring my lips to his. I initiate the kiss, but he soon takes control. The moment I open my mouth, his tongue dives in. The kiss is not only passionate but possessive. I love it. It's like he can't get enough of me, and he refuses to let me go. He's proving I'm his, and I can't *not* accept it.

When we pull apart, I gaze into his eyes. There's lust, but

there's still a lot of worry. I'm driven to make it go away. I don't enjoy seeing him so uncertain after the way he's been. It's unsettling, and I hate being the cause.

"Let's go inside, Luca."

"Are you cold?"

"Far from it. I think I need to take all these layers off. I'm suddenly overheated."

"All?"

"Yes, all."

"Livy?"

"Your room or mine?"

Luca stands with me in his arms as though he's not lifting anything. It feels like he's going to lower my legs, but then he thinks better of it. He carries me back to the house, a guard barely opening the French door in time. Lucky for us, he was patrolling the patio. I'm not even embarrassed. I've never met a man in as good shape as Luca. He carries me up the stairs with ease, not even one heavy breath.

We head to his room, and he kicks the door shut behind him. I look around, and I wish I'd spent the night here. I suspect I would have slept through the night without the dreams if I'd been in Luca's arms. He sets me down and pulls off the blankets, which he tosses on the foot of the bed. He unfastens my coat as I push back my hood. It lands on top of the blankets. He smiles when he sees my pajamas. He saw them arrive since security opened the box. But I think he likes the way they look. They have little dolphins surfing waves. I never wear cutesy stuff like this. Like ever. I prefer plaid or stripes, but it was an impulse. I guess I wanted something fun after the couple days I'd had.

"*Piccolina*, I told you already that I want to take care of you and that I desire you. Nothing has changed. What do you need? Vanilla? Rough? Kinky?"

"I don't know. Just you. Can we figure it out as we go?"

"Of course. But I need to know how you want to start? Rough or gentle?"

"I want another kiss like we just had. Whatever happens from there is what I want."

He moves fast, his hand sliding into my hair and fisting it. His hand lands hard against my ass before his mouth devours me. He spanks me again and again, pushing my pussy against his rock-hard dick. Fuck me. Like *please* fuck me. He holds my head in place, kissing me how he wants. His arm is wrapped tightly around me now that he's squeezing my ass. I know without a doubt that if I pushed away, he would stop immediately. That's part of what feeds my hunger and why I accept his control. Ultimately, I decide, even when he seems so dominant.

"Do you know why I spanked you, little girl?"

He whispers beside my ear, and it sends shivers throughout me. I shake my head as best I can with his hand cupping my skull now.

"I have told you over and over that I want to keep you safe. You made yourself a target being out there in the open like that. I trust my men implicitly to keep anyone from coming into my yard or into my house. But they can't protect you from a shooter they can't see in the dark."

"I didn't know."

"I get that. But I also told you I would punish you for breaking my expectations, and I'd do it even if you didn't know ahead of time. I'm explaining it to you now, Livy. I need you to know how serious this is. You can go outside during the day and move around the yard however you want. But at night, you stay inside. Even with guys stationed around the yard with night vision goggles, it's too easy for someone to get into a tree and them not notice. If you want to look at the stars again, there are a couple of places close to the house where you'd be nearly out of sight from anyone close enough to hurt you."

I lick my lips and nod. I feel guilty, and a part of me feels unresolved. I don't feel like the spanking he gave me was enough to make amends. I shift my weight from one foot to the other.

"Livy?"

"Yes, *caro*."

"You don't seem satisfied with that explanation."

"I am. What you just explained is more serious than I realized. That spanking—it didn't feel like enough."

"Do you want to be punished more?"

I nod.

"How severe do you feel the punishment should be?"

"Is a spanking the only type of punishment?"

"That or orgasm denial."

That sounds way more agonizing than a spanking.

"You decide, *caro*."

"Take off your pajamas. Lie on the bed, *piccolina*."

I hurry to obey. I watch him take five ties out of his closet. He prowls over to me.

"Raise your arms."

I'm quick to follow his directions. He binds my wrists with one tie, then connects them to the headboard by looping a second tie around a wood crossbar. A third tie becomes a blindfold. I wait to find out what he'll do with the other two, but nothing happens. He's so still, it's almost as though I'm alone in the room. My heart rate speeds up. I strain to hear any clue to what he'll do next, but the room is silent except for my labored breathing.

I shriek when his teeth capture my nipple, and he bites. It's not hard enough to harm me, but it shoots pain down to my belly. He licks and swirls his tongue, taking away the sting. He pinches and twists the other.

"Remember to use your safe word if you need it, Livy."

"I will, *caro*."

His hand trails over my belly to the inside of my thighs, grazing the skin in just the right place to make me shiver. He feathers his fingers over my entire torso and thighs over and over. I feel needy and unsettled, waiting—for what? I don't know. Whatever will come next. I shriek again when he pinches my clit.

He's neither rough nor gentle when he flips me onto my belly. His hand lands across my ass five more times before he nudges my legs apart and pulls me up onto my knees. The palm of his hand slaps my pussy over and over, managing to rub my clit each time before he pulls it away. I'm moaning as I pant.

Then I'm on my back again, my legs suddenly stretched wide, my ankles tied to the footboard. I wait, but nothing else happens. I turn my head toward where I think he might be, but I can see nothing. I jump when I hear the door close.

He left me?

I need to come, and I ache everywhere, and he just left.

I don't know how long I wait, but I hear the door open. Then his mouth is on my pussy, his morning stubble scraping my inner thigh and bare pussy lips. His tongue delves into me, lapping me up. Then his teeth graze my clit, and I try to raise my hips to him, gain more friction. He pulls away, then slaps my pussy.

Once again, there's nothing. I wait a few seconds, then I hear the door close once more. We go around and around like this three more times. He brings me to the edge, then leaves. He's never gone more than a few minutes, but the uncertainty —the inability to know or control what's happening—is scary and exciting. It heightens my lust because I enjoy knowing

Luca is in charge. He decides how this will go, and all I have to think about is what he might do next to pleasure or taunt me.

I'm almost sad it's over when he unties my legs, then my arms, and finally removes the blindfold. He helps me off the bed, then he sits down. He guides me over his lap like he did in the kitchen two days ago.

"Livy, I'm going to spank you, and it will hurt. Then this is over. I'm giving you the two things you said you wanted—needed. I know you believed I left the room, but I didn't. This is still way too new to you for me to leave you alone. If you'd panicked or something had happened, I wouldn't have been here to help you if I left. I won't put you in that position. I was here with you, *piccolina*, in case you needed me. Just like I'll always be here if you need me."

I think in the back of my mind, I knew he never left, which is probably why I didn't get scared. But I liked the idea that he had. It added to the experience, and he understands that.

"Turn your feet inward, little girl."

I follow his instructions. The moment I'm positioned how he wants, he lands ten hard slaps that land all over my ass. He doesn't miss a single spot. Then he's so gentle. His hand caresses my heated flesh, rubbing out the burn. I kicked my feet more than once, and I had to hold his ankle to keep from reaching back. Tears stream down my cheeks, but I sigh. Stress from the last few days drains away, and I'm left feeling boneless. He eases me off his lap, then guides me to sit down. He widens his legs, so my ass is in between and not rubbing against the material of his warm-up pants.

"I'm sorry, *caro*. I really didn't mean to scare you. I thought I'd go back to bed. I didn't think I would fall asleep out there."

"I know. It's all forgiven. Please just ask, and I'll do what I can to accommodate your request."

He's so soothing when he strokes the hair back from my

face. His next kiss is the polar opposite of the two we've just shared. It's so incredibly tender. It makes my heart ache. His hold on me isn't looser, but it's gentler. I cup his face, savoring this moment. It's *this*—how we are right now—that makes me crave a relationship with Luca. It makes me think there can be one. How is it possible to feel this deeply without it being fate?

"I don't want to be an inconvenience. I—"

"You are not an inconvenience. Just the opposite. I want you around, Livy."

"I can't commit yet, Luca. There're still too many confusing things, and they're scary. But I know I want to be with you. And not just because I need your protection. I like the man you are with me and with your family. I just have a lot of reconciling and accepting I need to do, and I don't know if I can."

"That's fair. If you ask my sister, I've always been over-the-top protective of her, but I've never worried about anyone as much as I do her. Until now. If you feel suffocated at any point, tell me. We'll talk about whether I can back off."

"That's fair too."

As we continue to gaze at each other, the need surges back. We're tugging at his clothes until we're both naked. Luca picks me up, and I wrap my legs around his waist. Every muscle I feel is as hard as his cock. He's chiseled marble. A woman's dream toy. But there's nothing playful about the ways he's looking at me now.

"*Piccolina*, there isn't an inch of you I won't know by the time I'm done with you. I'm going to make you come on my fingers, on my tongue, and on my cock. I'm going to suck your tits and finger fuck you until you can't take it anymore, until you're begging for my cock. And once I'm inside that tight little cunt, I'm going to fuck you until you scream."

"What if I'm ready to beg for your cock now? What if I can't stand the idea of waiting?"

There's a tremble in my voice, and he catches it. He gives me a jerky nod before he climbs onto the bed. I'm clinging to him like a koala. The moment I'm settled onto the mattress, he's reaching into the bedside table and pulling out a condom. Goddamn, I wish I had my pill. He rips the wrapper and tosses it aside. I reach for him, but he's much quicker than I could be. He rolls it down his dick, and then he's lined up with my pussy. He thrusts hard, and my back arches. Fucking hell. Goddamn for an entirely different reason. He feels amazing.

I'm way too short for him to suck my tits while pounding into me, but he squeezes my breast harder and harder, testing me. He lets go long enough to draw my hands over my head, then supports himself on the other arm, giving my other tit as much attention. He pins my hands to the pillow, and he increases the force of his thrusts. The bed's shaking, and he's fucking me so hard that I can barely keep up. I try to lift my hips to meet each time he surges into me, but he weighs too much more than me. My knees grip his hips as he fucks me. Hard.

"Is this what you want, little girl? Your moans tell me you do. The way you can barely keep your eyes open tells me you do."

"Yes. Don't stop. Just like this. Harder even."

"Any harder, and I will hurt you. You know I won't do that."

"You won't hurt me. Please, *caro*. Please."

He growls. *Growls*. Then he's moving so fast and so hard I fear we'll break the bed.

"You want me to prove I can't get enough of you. Prove that I have never wanted a woman as much as I crave you. You are mine, Livy. We will figure out all our shit, but no couple fucks like this without there being something real between them. Admit it."

"Luca, I—"

"Don't you dare fucking lie to me right now, or I will pull out, come all over you, and leave you crying. I will brand you with my cum, and I will make you beg for me."

"Please, no. I do want this, you. I need all those things you said. It scares the shit out of me. But I need you to not only fuck me but to—"

I catch myself. Holy shit. That was way too close. I almost admitted that I need him to love me.

"I know what you were going to say, *piccolina*. I need that from you, too. Give us a chance, and we will get there. I know it."

"All right, *caro*."

Our mouths fuse, and he pushes me into my orgasm. I squeeze my pussy around him as tight as I can. Thank you, Kegels. He can't pull back, so he rocks inside me. I feel him shudder and flex as he comes, too. We rest our foreheads against each other as we pant. I pull him closer, but he hesitates.

"You call me little girl, but I'm not one. You won't crush me."

"You're my little girl. I've been rough with you. Now I want to be more considerate. You won't be able to breathe."

"I'll breathe easier if we're touching more."

He lowers only a portion of his weight onto me. I know he's supporting most of it on his forearms. But being chest-to-chest lets me hug him. I need this post-coital affection. As he relaxes, his dick still inside me, I can tell he needs it too. He presses feather-soft kisses along my cheek and jaw as I run my hand over his back before he asks me a question that takes me a moment to remember what he means.

"What did you say all right to?"

Luca rolls us, so I'm draped across him, my head resting

over his heart. The steady beat is a lullaby every time I hear it. I rouse myself enough to answer.

"I'm saying all right to us. You spoke the truth when you described us. I can fight this, or I can make peace with this. But what's between us isn't going away, and I don't want it to. I want to figure out how to live with it. I'm not promising that I can. I can't commit that seriously yet because there's way too much about each of us and this life that we need to learn. I'm saying I won't fight it or put space between us again."

"Thank you. Whatever happens, we figure it out together. You're not alone in all this, Livy."

"I know."

His hand rests on my ass as my eyes drift closed. I sigh with a contentment unlike anything I've ever felt. I'm at peace with my decision, and I'm soon sound asleep.

"Weren't you going to go to the gym?"

We finally made it down to the kitchen for breakfast after I slept on top of Luca for an hour, and we had another round of mind-blowing shower sex. That man...The things he can do.

"Do you think I still need to work out?"

"I didn't mean to interrupt your plans. I know you have to work and get other things done."

"I do. I was thinking about asking Maria to come over today. She could keep you company while I'm gone. I need to visit a couple of the businesses I own to check on payroll."

"Doesn't Maria have things to do?"

"She does, but she can work from home. She might need to be on her computer from time to time, but when she isn't, you can chat. Maybe watching a movie would make it easier."

"What does she do?"

"She's a radiology resident. She gets the images sent to her, then she reads them and sends her findings back."

"A radiologist?"

I never would have guessed she was a doctor. I figured something in, maybe, advertising or marketing like me. I don't know why medicine never occurred to me.

"Yeah. It's her day off from the hospital, so she's moonlighting."

Moonlighting? Um, isn't she rich like Luca and the rest of his family? Why the hell does she need to moonlight?

"I know what you're thinking, Livy. There are four of us. Our parents put all of us through college, but advanced degrees are on us. Yes, they can afford to pay for it, but my brothers, sister, and I are adults. We can't have Mama and Papa pay for everything our entire lives."

"Is she the only one with an advanced degree?"

"No. Lorenzo has a Master's in Accounting. Matteo is finishing up his MBA, and I have an MBA too."

Not a dumb one in the bunch, apparently. All gorgeous and all intelligent. If they weren't all born into the Mafia, I would say one family shouldn't have so much good luck. But I doubt they'd consider themselves fortunate to live with so much danger surrounding them.

"Can I ask you something about your brothers?"

"Of course."

He says that, but he doesn't sound encouraging at all.

"I saw Gabriele with you, so I know he's done what I've seen you do. Is it the same for your brothers?"

He just stares at me for a long time. The longer I wait, the more obvious the answer becomes.

"Livy, that's one of those questions I won't answer. But you already know the truth. It's easy to figure out."

"Can I ask about you?"

"Yes."

Even less encouraging, but I want to know.

"How old were you when all of this started? I mean, the stuff I've seen you do."

"Young. This is the only life I've known. It has surrounded me since birth. It wasn't until I was in my early twenties that it became more obvious that I would likely be Uncle Salvatore's heir. He loves Pia and Natalia, and I know he's glad he didn't have sons. But it means I have no choice but to fill his shoes one day. I've been training for that since even before we all realized it. Just having my family name made me a target. I didn't have a chance to choose what to get involved with."

"Are you talking eight or like fifteen?"

He takes such a deep inhale that I see his chest rise.

"I was in my first knife fight when I was fourteen. A kid pulled one on me while I was walking home from school. He was seventeen and thought he could humiliate me simply because I'm Uncle Salvatore's nephew. My brothers and sister were with me. Lorenzo and Marco kept Maria between them and shielded her from seeing what happened. That guy survived that fight. He didn't survive the next one six months later."

"Were you still fourteen?"

"No. He thought he'd beat the shit out of me as a birthday gift."

"You know this only creates more questions, right?"

"I know. Ask what you want. If I can't answer, I won't."

"Does that mean you officially became a mafioso at fourteen?"

"Something like that. I didn't have a title or job when I was that young. That didn't come until after grad school. But I started doing things for my uncle when I was thirteen."

Sabine Barclay

Things for his uncle. I know better already than to ask what those things are.

"Were you much older when you shot someone for the first time?"

Something flickers in his gaze that I can't read. Then it's gone. I want to press, but I can tell that would be a horrible idea.

"Around the same age."

"Thank you for telling me. I got Maria's number last night. Can I invite her over? Or should you?"

"I know she'd love it if you did."

Luca carries our plates to the sink and rinses them before putting them in the dishwasher. I offer to make him another cup of coffee, but he declines. He comes around the kitchen table and stands in front of me when I rise.

"Maria knows the rules. I'd really prefer you to stay here while I'm gone. But if you and Maria decide to go out, you'll have three guards with you. Maria will have two. If anything happens at all, listen to my sister. She knows what to do. Don't ask questions, just do as she or our men say. Can you promise me?"

"Of course. I think I'd rather stay here."

He slides his arms around my waist and draws me against him.

"I'd rather you didn't go out, but you're not my prisoner here. I don't want this place to feel like a jail."

"It's a little too luxurious to feel like a jail."

"Why? Because we have hot water?"

"Yup. And the comfiest pillow."

I tickle his ribs before straining to kiss his neck. He lets go and gives me a playful smack on my ass before he heads upstairs to get dressed for work. I head into the living room and text Maria.

> Luca's headed to work but he suggested I
> see what you're up to. If you're free maybe
> you could come over. He said you might need
> to work a bit but we could hang out or watch
> a movie.

Was that too long? Did I ramble? Too late now. I already hit send. I wander over to the window and look out at the yard. I picture sitting on the same lounge chair but in the middle of summer with the pool water glistening in front of me. Luca has the perfect patio for entertaining, too. He has a massive grill and food prep area. I saw the speakers for the surround sound as we came inside. All of his lawn furniture looks super inviting, and it's arranged in a way that a large group could still chat easily. I wonder if his family comes over a lot. Maybe not because it also looks completely unused.

I spin around as the front door opens. No one knocked. My eyes dart around, uncertain what to do. But I breathe easier as Maria waves. Marco and Matteo follow her inside. She holds up her phone.

"Great minds. I was just going to text you and say we were coming over. I'd love to hang out with you. I'm on call, but I don't think I'll be that busy today."

I cross the living room and into the foyer to greet Marco and Matteo, but Maria snags me into a loose hug before I can say hi to either guy. I return the embrace before smiling at the best friends.

"Good morning. Luca's upstairs. He'll be down in a minute."

"Cool. Can you let him know we're working out?"

Marco glances up the stairs as he speaks. Huh? Why'd they come here to work out? Matteo grins.

"We're Maria's detail today. Marco and I will work out and occupy ourselves while you ladies—do whatever."

He shrugs at the end. Neither Marco nor Matteo seemed bothered by the fact they're going to have to entertain themselves while Maria and I watch a movie or something. I remember what Luca said. He told me Maria would come with two guards. I didn't think it would be guys who seem to have such senior roles. I could tell at dinner last night that Matteo is just as important as Lorenzo and Marco.

Maria watches me before she speaks.

"Did Luca not explain the rules?"

"About having guards? Yeah, he did. He said you would come with two, and I have to have three if we leave. I didn't realize your guards would be family."

How do I ask don't you have better things to do than babysit Maria?

"Livy?"

I turn toward Luca as he walks down the stairs. He shoots his siblings and friend a look they understand. The guys head to the basement stairs, and Maria goes into the living room. She grabs the remote and already has a streaming service up by the time Luca stops in front of me.

"Marco and Matteo are guarding Maria today because no one in my family trusts anyone outside the family as much as we do each other. If it weren't them, then it would be Lorenzo, Carmine, Gabriele, or me."

"Carmine and Gabriele?"

"Yeah. Carmine and Maria are really close. She's the only one who can tolerate him most of the time. And Gabriele is like Carmine's sheep. Carmine has a little lamb, and everywhere he goes, Gabriele is sure to follow."

"You trust them enough to guard your sister?"

"For all Carmine's faults—of which there's a fucking

laundry list—there's nothing he wouldn't do to protect Maria. I can give credit where credit is due. I don't want him anywhere near you, but if you're ever with Maria, and Carmine or Gabriele are her guards, you're safe. I trust them with you, but only if you're with Maria."

"You said I have to have three guards. Should I meet them or anything?"

"Giuseppe, Francesco, and Dario are the guys I'm going to assign. Francesco will help Marco guard Maria, and Matteo, Giuseppe, and Dario will guard you. You don't go anywhere without my brother or Matteo. I won't bend on that, Livy. One of them must be with you at all times."

"But you have the three guys. Why can't they just do it? Why rearrange what's already set for Maria?"

Luca pulls me tightly against him and leans down to whisper in my ear. His breath is warm and minty.

"Because I don't trust anyone in this world as much as I do my family. No one else is good enough to protect you. No one else understands how important that trust is when it comes to protecting the people we care about most."

I gaze up at him as he straightens, and he offers me the softest smile.

"I count you in that small group of people, Livy. I hate knowing I won't be with you if you leave the house, but you and I can't be glued together all the time. I get that. If I can't be with you, then it's one of the men from my immediate family. Matteo and Gabriele are extended family, but they're both as good as brothers to me."

He gives me a quick, hard kiss as he taps my ass.

"Have fun with Maria. Don't get too wild."

He winks as he lets go.

"Should I make dinner? What time will you be back?"

"I should be home by six. I'll let you know if that plan

changes. We still have plenty of leftovers from Aunt Sylvia. Though you may want to hide them in the back of the fridge from Matteo and Marco. *Porcellini.*"

At my confusion, he laughs.

"It means little pigs."

"Be nice. Have a good day at work, honey."

I laugh, but fire sparks in his eyes. He lifts me off my feet and kisses me, and I wonder for a moment if he plans to abandon going to work.

"Bye, little girl."

"Bye, *caro.*"

I watch the front door close, then I head into the living room. Maria just shoots me a knowing look before we decide on a movie.

Chapter Eleven

Luca

This has been the longest day ever. And it's not just because I'm away from Livy. That definitely doesn't help. The fucking payroll system for all my car rental places crashed. It's been down for three hours, and tomorrow is payday. I can issue paper checks, but who does that anymore? People want direct deposit, and I like making sure the IRS thinks everything is on the up and up for these businesses.

"Luca, I don't know what's going on. I've done everything I know how to do and even made some shit up. The best I can offer is to create a new program, but I won't finish until tomorrow afternoon. It's going to take me some time."

I look at Lorenzo and can only nod. He has a Master's in Accounting, but his bachelor's is in computer science. Fucking Sergei Andreyev and Anton Kutsenko aren't the only ones with Ivy League level educations in computer science. Lorenzo went to fucking MIT. They're not the only hackers who can get into anything. My brother has hacked into banks all around the world, and he's better than just about anyone with managing the money we—found. He's our on and off the books accountant. He handles the financials to all our mergers, acquisitions, and investments. The man could memorize pi to infinity.

"What do you need from me to make a new program?"

"A little time. Then I'll need all the employee information. That's what's going to be a pain in the fucking ass. All that fucking data entry. If only I could have an intern."

He's been saying that for years. If Pia continues her interest in math, in twenty years, she might be our accountant for all our legal businesses. But until then, Lorenzo's SOL.

"Why do you think this happened? Were we hacked?"

"No. This was some sort of manual data entry error. An object variable or block variable wasn't set. The system is basically spinning its wheels, trying to figure out what's missing. I told Uncle Sal this piece of shit program was antiquated and obsolete. If our payroll people can't handle learning a new program, then it's time for them to fucking retire. I could waste more time trying to restore this shit, or I can start on the new program. If you can get your people to do the data upload once I'm done, then it won't take as long. But if I'm left to do it for all six rental sites, then issuing paper checks is your only option for on-time payday."

"Motherfucker."

Lorenzo has been telling our uncle for months that we need to update this program we use across almost all our legal enterprises. It's not that our uncle refuses a more modern system. It's that he hates creating more paper trails, which are inevitable when migrating systems that connect to the IRS. The fewer types of contact we have with them, the better.

"I'll get Jessica on top of it. She can deal with the individual sites. Just create the program and be ready to train her on it.

And try not to get sidetracked fucking her. I don't have time for this shit."

"One time at a Christmas party three years ago, Luca. I haven't and am not going back for seconds."

"Doesn't stop her from offering or you from flirting."

"Leave me alone and let me get to work."

"You're in my office, jackass."

"If I'm going to be at this for a few hours, you owe me the comfortable chair."

"Get your own damn chair. You can have it just for today."

"*Anch'io ti voglio bene.*" I love you too, brother.

I flick him off.

"*Ti amo anch'io.*" Love you, too.

There's a shit ton we can't and don't talk about in my family, but one thing our parents insisted upon since we were little is that we never leave each other or hang up a call with each other without saying we love them. It could be the last time we get to say it, so they insist we never waste the opportunity. Lorenzo and I might give each other shit, but we both know we mean what we said. Maybe the fact that my family talks about feelings with shocking ease for being in the Mafia is why I feel comfortable discussing how I feel with Livy.

But that's only part of it. I'm certain if it were another woman, it wouldn't be the same. It hasn't been the same. I can talk to her with ease because I actually feel something. I don't remember the last time I liked a woman enough to even consider for a second letting her into my world.

I wonder what she's doing right now. I'm tempted to text or call her, but I don't want to be a stage five clinger. I'll see her in a few hours. I have more than enough to keep myself occupied. There's a restaurant in Queens that's giving us trouble. The owner seems to forget who's his landlord. He's late on three months' rent. I let it slide when he gave me some sob story about his mother dying and her pension ending because he knows he's accruing interest on this debt. He was late this third time, and now I'm collecting.

I'm about to leave the office and shut the door so Lorenzo can work in peace, but my phone rings. I notice a text message icon I missed.

"Matteo, what's—"

"You need to get here now. We brought Maria and Olivia to the Queens Center so Olivia could get some more clothes. Everything was fine until we stopped at a restaurant a few blocks away. I'd just shut Olivia's door when someone shot at us."

"What the fuck? Lead with that next time. Where the hell are you?"

Lorenzo is standing next to me now, so I put the call on speakerphone.

"Headed to Uncle Sal's."

"How far away are you?"

"Like ten minutes. Whoever this is, is following us."

"Is Livy hurt?"

"Scared but not hurt."

"Put her on the phone."

I hear the phone exchanging hands. I point to the door, but Lorenzo shakes his head. He hurries to gather up his computer and whatever other devices he has. We head out together, leaving our office in Manhattan. It's going to take us at least forty-five minutes to get to our uncle's place. No one ever points it out, but we pass four Kutsenko homes on the way to Uncle Salvatore's. They all live in the same neighborhood. We could spit and hit like five more. They've practically taken over the area now that half of them are married, plus their various parents live near them, too.

"Luca?"

"*Piccolina*, are you all right? Did you get hurt?"

"No, *caro*. Matteo was right next to me. I don't know how he didn't get hit. I saw a bullet strike the front passenger door right in front of me. Matteo got me back in the car before anything happened to me."

"Where's Maria?"

"Next to me. Marco's sitting on the other side of her. Dario is in the front passenger seat. Giuseppe is driving. Matteo and Francesco are in the third row."

Our SUVs are like tanks. They're reinforced everything. Bullet proof, crumple proof, whatever proof. The tires will still roll, even if they're shot. Steel plating protects the undercarriage too. Short of a landmine, nothing is stopping them once they're moving. I'm glad they went out in one. I didn't think to mention it, but now that I do, I'd be in a real panic if they were in town cars or a limo. All of ours have shatterproof windows and are bullet resistant, but they aren't geared up the same way as the SUVs. We take the SUVs on ops with us, so that's why they're souped up. It also means I know they have high-powered rifles with them in the back.

"*Piccolina*, put Marco or Matteo on, please. I'm leaving my office in Manhattan right now. It's going to take me about forty-five minutes, but I'm coming straight to you. I promise."

"I know. Just be careful. Maybe these people are after you, too. I—"

She stops herself from whatever she was going to say. I wonder what it was.

"I'm coming, little one. My family will protect you no matter what."

"I know. Here's Marco."

I switch to Italian. Anyone else in the car will understand if they hear me, but I don't want to freak Livy out even more.

"Pensi che si tratti di noi o di lei?" Do you think it's about us or her?

"Lei. Li ho sentiti parlare in spagnolo, ma sicuramente non erano i ragazzi di Enrique. Era lei l'obiettivo. Hanno aspettato che fossimo fuori dall'auto. Nessuno ha sparato dalla parte di nostra sorella." Her. I heard them speaking Spanish, but it definitely wasn't Enrique's guys. She was the target. They waited until we were out of the car. None fired on our sister's side.

He's careful not to say Maria's name. He knows I don't want Livy to understand what we're talking about. If she heard Maria's name, she'd be even more suspicious.

"La sua voce non è forte come al solito. Sta piangendo?" Her voice isn't as strong as usual. Is she crying?

"No, è solo molto scossa." No, just really shaken up.

Lorenzo and I are getting into my car since I picked him up on the way into the office. The phone switches to Bluetooth when I turn on the car. I toss the phone into the center console, then put the car into reverse. The tires squeal as I pull out.

Lorenzo grunts.

"Non fateci ammazzare per strada." Don't get us killed on the way.

We're in my Mercedes AMG GT Coupe. I can weave through traffic much better in this than my G-Wagon. Lorenzo sits back and relaxes. He's used to my driving. I'm usually behind the wheel for most of our ops. I'd be driving an SUV like the one Livy and Maria are in.

My heart's pounding, worrying about both of them. My brother might look at ease, but I know beneath the surface he's as desperate to get to Maria as I am. Add Livy to it, and I'm ready to go out of my mind. Lorenzo and I are anxious about Marco and Matteo too, but they're better equipped to protect themselves.

Maria knows what to do, and she's a better shot than any of

us. But she's eighty to a hundred pounds less than most of the guys we face. She may have the technique, but she simply doesn't have the strength to go up against guys that are ten inches taller than her and work out twice a day. Marco and Matteo aren't immortal, but if it comes to hand-to-hand, I know they can hold their own. I've seen them too many times.

"Livy, you still there?"

It's gone quiet, and I don't like it. I don't hear anyone talking in the background.

"I'm here, Luca. Whoever this is, is still following us. Maria and I are hiding on the floor. Some car pulled alongside us."

I don't think I wanted to know that. Lorenzo and I glance at each other. Excessive lane changes doesn't begin to describe what I'm doing. I'm breaking every law but running red lights. I'm not hellbent on getting us killed. I hear Marco, but something muffles his voice until Livy must hold the phone up.

"*Luca, stiamo per attraversare quella zona morta. Ti chiamiamo quando arriviamo dallo zio Sal. Lui sa che stiamo arrivando.*" Luca, we're about to go through that dead zone. We'll call you when we get to Uncle Sal's. He knows we're on the way.

"*Va bene. Ti amo.*" All right. Love you.

"*Ti amo.*"

What else can I say until we get there?

Five minutes later, my phone buzzes. I hit the button on the steering wheel to read my text.

MATTEO

We're safe. My mom was already here. Maria and Olivia are in the kitchen with Mama and Aunt Sylvia.

My car asks if I want to respond. Of course, I do.

ME

About twenty minutes out. Any trouble going through the gate?

I want to know if anyone sped up and shot at them when they slowed down to turn into the gate. The house has a semi-circle driveway, but I'm certain they pulled straight into a garage. No one would get the women out of the car in the open.

No. They stopped a block before we got there. They didn't drive past.

Okay. Be there as soon as we can.

"You think it's the Culiacán, don't you?"

Lorenzo has his phone out while he speaks, and I'm sure he's texting Maria to hear from her they're all right. I would do the same thing.

"Yeah. If they only shot at Livy, then who else would it be? The only other possibility is Dillan and his shitbag crew. We know Maks would never sanction going after Maria or any woman. Enrique wouldn't do it either. Juan acted on his own, but Enrique's still trying to get back into Laura's good graces. She's more apt than Maks to go to war with the Colombians. That only leaves the Irish. But why would they target only Livy? They would have gone after at least Maria, if not both."

Enrique's brother lives next door to Maks's wife's parents. She grew up with Enrique's nephews. Things soured with Juan when Laura and Maks got together.

"No. Finn wouldn't allow it. They all know Maria tried to save that girl Finn was with at that party. The poor dipshit went to get a beer, and the girl OD'ed on Fentanyl his family probably sold the guys hosting the party. Maria did what she could, and Finn knows that. He wouldn't let anyone come after

Maria. She dealt with the paramedics and the cops, so Finn didn't have to get involved. They never should have been at the same place at the same time, but Finn's still grateful."

"Then it leaves the Culiacán. They're watching her. They knew she's staying with me. But why'd they wait until today? Why not yesterday when only she and I were in the car?"

"They wanted you apart. Someone must have spotted you or has been watching your place. They saw you go out together, and that confirmed she was there. Then they saw you leave alone. They waited and got what they wanted. It's obvious they won't make a move with you near her. They should have known the same goes for the rest of our family. She didn't say anything, but you know Marco or one of the other guys got a few rounds off before getting back in the car."

"That's what I keep telling myself. But there won't be shit left at the scene for anyone to find. Not the police and not us. We won't learn a damn thing."

"You know who we can ask."

"No."

"Really? You wouldn't ask Mrs. Kutsenko if her men saw anyone strange parked on their block. You know they will have seen anyone, and they'd have security footage. Let Uncle Sal ask then."

"All right." I blow out a breath. "It's more important to protect Livy than to deal with my ego."

I don't want to ask any Kutsenko for anything. Ever. But Maks's mom lives on the same street as Uncle Salvatore. Maks and his three brothers have their mother's place locked down like they're guarding the fucking Vatican's gold. They take no chances since she's a widow. If anyone would notice strangers on their street, it's the bratva security. None of them wants a Kutsenko brother to get their hands on them for failing to watch out for their mom. The guy would be better off killing himself than letting Maks, Aleks, Niko, or Bogdan punish him.

I glance out my driver's side window as we pass Galina Kutsenko's house. I recognize Niko's car in the driveway. Wonderful. Just the one I need to have at her house when I grovel for help.

"Let Uncle Sal or even Aunt Sylvia call. I'll call if need be."

The Kutsenkos aren't ready to castrate Lorenzo, Marco, or Matteo. And if they find out Maria was there too, they'd probably help even if they knew I'm involved. I nod as I turn my attention back to the road. We pull into my uncle's driveway, and I appreciate push starts. I hit the button, and my car is off. No turning the key in the ignition and pulling it out. The three seconds it saves me feel precious. I'm out of the car before the engine's quiet. I bolt to the door and throw it open.

"Livy!"

She comes out of the living room and launches herself into my arms. I engulf her, and neither of us wants to let go. We cling to each other as my family filters in around us. Lorenzo is hugging Maria while talking to Marco and Matteo.

"Luca?"

I don't release Livy, but I turn to look at my uncle. He glances at Livy before tilting his head toward his office.

"*O mi lasci qualche minuto con lei, o lei viene con me e parliamo in italiano.*" Either you give me a few minutes with her, or she comes with me, and we speak Italian.

"*Se non crede sia scortese parlare senza che comprenda, allora portala con te.*" If she doesn't think it's rude for us to talk without her understanding, then bring her in with you.

"*Glielo chiederò, ma possiamo stare un paio di minuti da soli nel suo ufficio? Ho bisogno di sapere come la pensa davvero.*" I'll ask her, but can we have a couple minutes alone in your office? I need to know how she really feels about this.

Uncle Salvatore nods, and I slide my hand into Livy's. I lead her down the hallway until we reach what would normally be a den but is my uncle's office. It's big enough to fit ten large men easily. It's where we hold our meetings that we don't want anyone to bug.

I shut the door and pick her up. She wraps herself around me just like she did this morning. I carry her to the sofa and sit down.

"What do you need from me, Liv?"

"Hold me."

She says that, but she's restless. I'm hard as a plank and have been since the moment I touched her. Her pussy is rubbing against me and driving me crazy. I grasp her hips and hold her in place, but she tsks in annoyance.

"Little girl, tell me what you really need. The only way we can get any closer is if I'm inside you."

She leans back and our eyes meet.

"Is that what you want? Do you need a quickie?"

"No. Yes. I don't know. It's not like all I can think about is getting off. I just—I was so scared, Luca. Scared I was going to die. That your family was going to die because of me. I know those men were only shooting at me. It scared me, thinking I would never see you again, see my mom again. I haven't talked to her since before I went to bed after watching that movie with you the night before last. I know I'm safe here, and I feel even safer in your arms. But I just can't get close enough to you. I need the comfort I get from being with you."

I reach back to my wallet and grab the condom out of it before putting it away. Good thing I replaced the one I used last night. She's unfastening my pants as I rip open the wrapper. Then we're adjusting our clothes until she's able to slide down me.

"No more panties, little girl. I want to get to your pussy without those damn things in the way."

"And if I want to get to your dick without your boxers in the way?"

"I won't wear them if you don't want me to."

She moans as I settle into her completely. She rests her head against my shoulder, and I hold her.

"How is it comforting to feel your cock in my pussy? I'm aroused, but more than anything, I just want to snuggle closer."

"Is it reassuring? You know I won't let anyone get near you. You know I like to hold you like this."

"I finally feel like I can breathe again. The only place I want to be is here with you. I hate that this happened, but I love knowing that you can make everything better. When everything feels utterly out of control, I know that you'll look out for me."

"Always, Livy. You're my *piccolina,* my little girl."

"That's what I want, D—"

She gasps, and I look down at her. She presses her lips tightly together between her teeth. She's fisted my shirt and gone completely still.

"Go ahead and say it, *piccolina.* You know I've never called a woman that. No woman has ever called me what you were going to say."

"I'm too embarrassed. I can't believe I almost called you—"

She tries to shake her head, but she's resting it against my chest, so she can't move it much.

"Have you thought it before?"

"Yes."

"What if I like the idea of hearing you call me that? What if that's what I want to be?"

She sits back.

"Luca, I know I bought those cute pajamas, but that's not who I am all the time. I'm not into that."

"I didn't think you were. Nothing about you makes me think you want age play between us. But I think you really enjoy having a man who's bigger than you, stronger than you, and more knowledgeable about this shit looking out for you. I think you want to let go of trying to grab control of a situation that's way over your head. You trust me to be that protective and knowledgeable guy. I think you also know I won't take advantage of the vulnerability that goes along with using that word."

"But is age play what you want? Do you want a little?"

"No. That's why no woman's ever called me that word you still refuse to say. I've never looked for or wanted that dynamic. That's not what I want now. But I've called you little girl from the beginning. I told you it has nothing to do with your height, and it doesn't. You stir every protective and possessive urge I have. I want to make you happy, Livy. I want to give you the security you need, but I also want to share the weight of this colossal fucktastrophe. You know that about me, and that's why you nearly said it."

"Daddy, I'm so glad I can call you that. I did in every dream last night."

My chest aches when I hear her call me that. Never did I imagine that word would do anything for me. It's fucking arousing as hell, but it also reminds me of what I'm pledging to Livy. The man I'm promising to be for her, and I never want to fail her, disappoint her.

"Can I call you that whenever we're in private?"

"Of course."

"We have to let your family in. I think your uncle wants to talk to you."

"He does. You can go back out with Aunt Sylvia, Maria,

149

and Auntie Carlotta, or you can stay in here. But we'll be speaking Italian if you stay. We have to discuss stuff you can't know about."

"I'd rather stay with you."

"I'd rather you do that, too. Little one, I'm ready to blow my load being inside you. Do you want me to get you off?"

"Good God, yes."

It's hurried as we move together, and she rides me. It's an embarrassing two minutes before I'm coming inside the condom while her pussy squeezes me. She kisses me like there's no tomorrow, but I know it's keeping her from screaming as her orgasm takes over. The moment the euphoria subsides, we're hurrying to put our clothes back in place. I grab a couple tissues from the coffee table and wrap up the condom. There's no way I'm throwing it out in my uncle's office.

Livy stays on the sofa while I go open the door, shoving the tissues in my pocket as I turn the handle.

"Uncle Salvatore?"

"*Arriva.*" Coming.

I return to the sofa, but instead of leaving Livy to sit beside me, I lift her onto my lap. I tuck her head against my chest. She tries to scramble off as my family joins us, but I hold tight. She gives in, but she sits upright. But as the meeting begins, and she can understand nothing, she rests against me. I know the minute my little girl falls asleep on her Daddy's lap.

Chapter Twelve

Livy

I wake to loud voices arguing in Italian. I must not have been asleep long because, even with my eyes closed, I can tell all the men in Luca's family are still in the room. I was too shaken earlier to piece together any of the Italian I might have understood. Now I listen quietly as they go back and forth. I recognize Massimo's voice.

"*Abbiamo già abbastanza problemi. Non vogliamo trascinarla a lungo.*" We have enough problems already. We don't want to drag this out.

I got nothing. The only thing I understand is Luca's dad sounds pissed. Marco sounds like the voice of reason when he responds.

"*Non potete abbandonarla ai lupi. Luca ha ragione. Non è stata colpa sua. Se avesse saputo che c'era ancora qualcuno nell'edificio, non avrebbe mai iniziato la riunione.*" You can't leave her to the wolves. Luca's right. It wasn't her fault. If he'd known anyone was still in the building, he never would have started the meeting.

Something about Luca being right, in the building, and never start the meeting. My guess is, if he'd known I was there, Luca wouldn't have met with Carlos. Luca's chest rumbles beneath my cheek as he speaks.

"*Beh, lei era lì. Abbiamo bisogno di un modo migliore per proteggerla. Sai che non l'avrei messa nel mio mondo, in questo mondo, se non significasse qualcosa per me.*" Well, she was there. We need a better way to protect her. You know I wouldn't have brought her into this world, into *this house*, if she didn't mean something to me.

"*Non è passata neanche una settimana.*" It hasn't even been a week.

Salvatore is scoffing at Luca for only knowing me a week. It doesn't take much to get that. But why's Luca laughing at him?

"*Lei dice che ci sono voluti cinque minuti per innamorarsi di zia Sylvia. Mi dici sempre che dovrei essere più simile a te. Credo di aver finalmente ascoltato.*" You say it took five minutes to fall in love with Aunt Sylvia. You're always telling me I should be more like you. I guess I finally listened.

"*Tua zia viene da questa vita ed è arrivata qui per sposarmi proprio per questo motivo.*" Your aunt came from this life and arrived here to marry me because of that.

"*Ti comporti come se non avessi riflettuto su ciò che significa.*" You're acting as though I haven't thought about what this means.

"*E tu?*" Have you?

Luca tenses beneath me, and I feel his heart rate accelerate. He's getting pissed. Lorenzo steps in before Luca can answer.

"*Zio, stai lasciando che una cosa ti faccia dimenticare il modo in cui è sempre stato. Non è un tipo avventato. Può prendere decisioni in fretta, ma ci pensa sempre bene prima di fare qualcosa. Anche se ha fatto una scelta sbagliata, ha comunque pianificato una strategia."* Uncle, you're letting one thing make you forget the way he's always been. He's not impetuous. He might make decisions quickly, but he always thinks them through before he does anything. Even if he made a bad choice, he still planned out a strategy.

"Una cosa? Una scelta sbagliata? Cazzo, c' erano solo una cosa e una scelta sbagliata." One thing? A bad choice? The fuck it was only one thing and one bad choice.

Salvatore's only getting more pissed by the word. I wonder if I opened my eyes, and he knew I could hear what they're saying, if he would calm down. Maybe he wouldn't yell at Luca in front of me if he knew I could see and hear him. Massimo sounds like he's moved closer to Salvatore when he talks.

"Salvatore, ha pagato la sua penitenza. Hai detto di averlo perdonato. Se non ti fidi più di lui, allora dillo. Lui si dimette e noi andiamo avanti." Salvatore, he paid his penance. You said you forgave him. If you don't trust him anymore, then say so. He steps down, and we move on.

Luca whispers to me as his dads speaks.

"Keep pretending to be asleep."

How'd he know?

Salvatore sounds calmer when I hear his voice next, but his tone doesn't sound like he's relented.

"L'ho perdonato. Ma ora sta per fare un'altra cazzata." I forgave him. But now he's about to fuck up again.

"Cosa stai dicendo, zio? Vuoi che rompa con lei? Che la cacci via? Lasciarla a se stessa? Sai che non farò nessuna di queste cose." What're you saying, Uncle? You want me to break up with her? Kick her out? Leave her to fend for herself? You know I'm not doing any of those things.

"Per l'amor del cielo. Pensi che si tratti di questo? Cazzo, Luca. Sono incazzato perché l'hai portata a casa tua, dove era

ovvio che si trovasse. Avresti dovuto portarla in una casa al sicuro dove nessuno avrebbe potuto guardare. L'hai messa ancora di più in pericolo. Ecco perché sono incazzato." For fuck's sake. Is that what you think this is about? Fucking hell, Luca. I'm pissed because you took her to your house, where it was too obvious she would be. You should have taken her to a safe house where no one would know to look. You put her in more danger. That's why I'm pissed.

Salvatore sounds livid. Is he as red in the face as I'm picturing him? He sounds like he's about to explode. One wrong word...

"Sapevi che l'avrei portata a casa mia. Se pensavi che fosse una cattiva idea, perché diavolo non l'hai detto?" You knew I brought her to my place. If you thought it was such a bad idea, why the hell didn't you say so?

There's a long pause before there's an answer to what sounded like a question.

"Anche tua sorella era in pericolo. Voglio scaricare la colpa su di te per quello che è successo con Anastasia. Il fatto che tu abbia infranto il voto "niente donne e bambini" ha messo in pericolo entrambe le nostre donne. Ma sappiamo entrambi che i messicani non giocano secondo le stesse regole. Loro fanno a modo loro e noi facciamo a modo nostro." Your sister was in danger, too. I want to lay this blame at your feet because of what happened with Anastasia. That you breaking the vow no women and children endangered both our women. But we both know the Mexicans don't play by the same rules. They have their way, and we have ours.

"Entrambe le nostre donne?" Both our women?

"Sì. So che non l'avrei incontrata se tu non avessi voluto che durasse. Non l'avresti portata a casa tua se non avessi pensato che sarebbe potuta diventatare la sua casa." Yes. I know I wouldn't have met her if you didn't mean for this to last. You

wouldn't have taken her to your house if you didn't see it becoming her home.

Whatever Salvatore just said made Luca relax. Both of their tones of voice have changed. I only really understood something about his house. When they were arguing, they spoke way too fast for me to catch anything.

"*La porterò nel Bronx, in una delle mie case in affitto. Matteo, tua madre mi presterebbe la sua macchina? Non credo che qualcuno del Cartello potrebbe sapere che è la sua.*" I'm going to take her to one of my rentals in the Bronx. Matteo, would your mom let me borrow her car? I don't think anyone in the Cartel would know it's hers.

Luca sounds much calmer now. I think the argument might be over, and they're coming to some resolution.

"*Non sarebbe meglio se ti accompagnasse lei?*" Would it be easier if she drops you off?

"*Non è possibile. Non con il suo piede di piombo. Era divertente quando eravamo bambini. Ora sono abbastanza consapevole da essere terrorizzato.*" No way. Not with her lead foot. It was fun when we were kids. Now I have enough sense to be terrified.

Everyone laughs, and the tension is gone. Matteo sounds like he's teasing Luca about whatever Luca said.

"*È lei che ti ha insegnato a guidare. Ora sai perché tutti pensiamo che ogni viaggio in macchina con te sarà l'ultimo.*" She's the one who taught you to drive. Now you know why we all think any car ride with you will be our last.

"*Fanculo.*" Fuck off.

"Ms. D'Amato, you can open your eyes."

Shit. How long did Salvatore know I was awake? I open them and find myself looking at Massimo before I shift my gaze to the don. Both men look like I was fooling no one. Luca's hand runs up and down my arm as his other hand continues to rest on my hip. I suddenly feel super embarrassed to still be on his lap. I shift, but Luca's grip on my hip tightens. It pulls me closer, and I feel just how hard he is. I knew he was, but if I stand up now, there's no way he can hide it.

I look at Lorenzo as he speaks, and I'm surprised at how nice he sounds after the way he busted Luca's balls about me the other day.

"Did you sleep at least a little?"

"Yeah. Thanks."

What else do I say? Why does he care? My expression must show my skepticism.

"Ms. D'Amato, I was an ass the other day, and I know it. But it was really more about giving Luca a hard time than about you. But you couldn't have known that. I'm sorry I was so rude. This has been a crappy day for you and an insane week."

"Thank you. That's certainly one way to describe things."

"My little brother has always been one for understatement."

Marco elbows Lorenzo, who shoves him away.

"*Ragazzi.*" Boys.

Whatever that one word means, Marco and Lorenzo stand up straight the moment their dad says it. Luca laughs. He speaks softly in my ear.

"My dad only has to say boys, and we know what's coming. It's not worth doing whatever we're doing when he says that."

"Are you three still afraid of your dad?"

I didn't think I spoke that loudly, but three voices answer in unison.

"Yes."

Massimo grins and nods.

"But they're way more afraid of their mama. She wields a wooden spoon like a club."

I'm shocked as I turn toward Luca.

"She's never caught us yet—on purpose—but we know the day she does, we won't sit for a week."

"You're thirty-one."

"So? She's still my mom."

"You're like a foot taller than her."

"Still don't see your point."

Now Luca is grinning too, and I know he's teasing me. He kisses my temple as I settle back against him. Another wave of exhaustion suddenly hits me.

"There are a bunch of guest bedrooms here. Do you want to take a proper nap?"

"Can I do that when we get back to your place?"

Why's everyone leaving the office suddenly? Why do we suddenly need privacy?

"Luca?"

"We're not going back to my house. It's obvious someone's watching it. They knew when I left and waited until we weren't together to make a move. I have some rental properties in the Bronx, and one of them is vacant. We're going there for a few days."

"The Bronx? Luca, I've talked to my mom once since this shit started. You know I told her I went away with a couple of girlfriends, but I can't stay gone for forever. Now you want me to stay at some place in the Bronx? She's going to worry. I have to tell her something, and I'm scared they're going to figure out who she is."

"I've had men watching her place and following her since the night we met. No one's been near her."

"How can you know that? You didn't know anyone was watching your place."

"Do you want her to stay with us?"

No. Absolutely not. But she should. Fucking-a.

"*Piccolina?*"

"If she stays with us, we can't have sex."

"We can't? Does she think you're a virgin?"

"I have no idea. We do *not* talk about that. But just like your parents weren't thrilled about me staying with you, she won't be pleased to know I'm sharing a bed with you. If she didn't know I'm not a virgin, she would now."

"The house has three bedrooms and a finished basement. I can stay down there. We don't have to do anything while we're there."

Luca sees my crestfallen expression and brushes his lips against mine.

"Abstinence doesn't excite me either, but if you'd feel better with your mom staying with us, then we can survive. Or you can sneak down to the basement, so I can fuck you. Promise not to scream?"

"How do I explain to her why we need to stay in the Bronx?"

"Tell her—"

"Another lie. This is what life is going to be like, isn't it? Lies upon lies upon lies. I'll never be able to tell her the truth about any of this, about the family I'm—"

I snap my mouth shut. I can't believe I was about to say the family I'm marrying into. Where the hell did that come from?

"Say you're house-sitting for a few days and invite her over. I don't have to be there. I won't be farther than the front yard."

"You're going to sleep in a car?"

"I won't be sleeping, *cuore*. I'll be keeping an eye on you."

"What does that mean? *Cuore.*"

"Sweetheart."

That warms me down to my toes.

"Are you really sure my mom is safe?"

"Yes. She has an around-the-clock detail. The new night desk clerk in her building is one of our guys. She has two men outside the front of the building and two at the back. Two guys follow her anytime she leaves her place."

"And she hasn't noticed?"

"None of them think so."

"Okay. I'll tell her the house-sitting part, but for now, things remain normal for her. Am I always going to have to tell her lies?"

"Selective truths. At least for now."

I take a deep inhale before I nod. What else can I say? This is part of the price I'll pay for being with Luca. I need to give this more consideration, but I can't right now.

"Are we going back to your place for the few clothes I have?"

"I texted my housekeeper to gather everything together tomorrow, and one of the guys will pick it up."

"Housekeeper?"

Luca laughs and kisses me hard. His tongue thrusts into my mouth as he grips my hair. He pinches my nipple and tweaks it before he pulls away.

"She's sixty-seven years old. She's not prancing around in a French maid's costume. I've known her since I was nine."

"That's not what I was—"

"Don't lie, little girl. I will make your ass burn for hours."

"It just surprised me. I wondered if you were going to tell me before she showed up tomorrow and likely scared the shit out of me if you were already at work."

"And you wondered just what type of woman she would be. You don't like the idea of another woman going through my clothes or judging what you have."

"Why are you reading my mind? I don't like it."

"It's exactly how I would react if you told me you had a housekeeper, and it was a guy."

"I definitely do not have a housekeeper. My place isn't big enough to need one."

"Would you rather Maria go over there?"

"If people are watching your place, it can't be safe for her to be there. And aren't they going to wonder why we don't go back?"

"I think I have a solution for that. Maria is going on vacation tomorrow. I'm pretty sure that's why she stopped by today. She wanted to hang out with you before she goes to Miami for a couple weeks. She's going with her best friend, who is a short blonde. Our family has a private jet that Maria and her friend are taking. Not just because we're rich, but because it accommodates her security detail and the things they'll take with them to protect her. Things we don't need going through TSA. I'll go with her, and it'll look like you and I are traveling with Maria. Once we take off, we'll fly to another local airfield. I get off, and they continue down to Florida. You'll be at the safe house, and I'll come back to it."

Private jet? A couple weeks in Miami? Sounds nice.

"Little one, when this is sorted out, we're going on our first vacation together. We'll fly wherever you want."

"First vacation?"

"First of many."

He waggles his eyebrows, and I go along with it. Any kind of vacation together is to be determined. I think he's only partly serious. I think he's trying to cheer me up.

"Can it be somewhere tropical? Somewhere you wear a Speedo?"

He laughs and shakes his head.

"Somewhere tropical where we can go nude."

"Oh, no. That just means sand in all the wrong places. It sucks."

I snap my mouth shut. Whoops. Luca's eyes narrow at me, and I know he expects an explanation.

"Livy?"

"Yes, Luca?"

"Who did you go to a nude beach with?"

"I didn't go to a nude beach."

Shit. Now he's really pissed. I don't want to think about him with someone else. Like it makes me want to throw something to think about him doing any of the things we've done with someone else. I hate knowing that he fucked other women at a BDSM club—more than once. I can't blame him for not liking the thought of me with someone else.

"Oliv—"

"Don't call me that, Luca. You know I don't like it. I'm not a child to be scolded, and I don't like how distant it makes you feel."

He looks surprised, and I don't think he knew he was about to call me by my full name. His jaw sets, and his stubbornness radiates from him, but he nods.

"We are going to the house in the Bronx. I'm taking you into our bedroom and stripping you bare. Then you are going to tell me just what the fuck you did naked on a beach."

"Please don't make me. I don't want to think about the past when I'm with you. If you hadn't mentioned being naked around sand, I wouldn't have thought about that memory. I wasn't really thinking when I responded."

He's silent as he puts me on my feet and stands up. I turn and put my hands on his chest. I can tell he wants to step around me, but I don't let him.

"Daddy, you don't have to fuck me to prove I don't want anyone else or to prove I've never wanted a man like I do you. You've reminded me of the same thing. I don't need to relive any memories to prove you surpass them. I already know that. I won't keep secrets from you, but I just don't want to think about what I've done with other guys when I'm with you. It makes me wish I didn't have a past."

"Why?"

"I don't know. I guess I wish—I guess it makes me sad that any of my memories aren't with you. That confuses the hell out of me, and it's really unsettling to feel that way. I don't enjoy confessing these things to you yet, Luca. But I don't want you to think I'm lying or hiding shit from you. Is this how you argue? Do you withdraw and use the silent treatment?"

"We aren't arguing, Liv."

"You weren't going to talk to me a moment ago. You probably would have given me the silent treatment all the way to the Bronx."

He wraps his arms around me and rests his hands on my ass. He appears remorseful as he looks down at me.

"Little one, I was so fucking jealous I was worried what might come out of my mouth if I said anything. I was trying to keep from fucking everything up by having a possessive temper tantrum. I was reminding myself of how fucking irrational I was being. I didn't want to say something that would hurt you. And you're right, I did want to fuck you to prove I'm the only man you need and the only one you should remember. I don't recognize this part of me. I have two brothers—basically three brothers—a sister, two cousins, and Gabriele who I grew up around. That's seven people who I've pretty much shared everything with my entire life. There were very few things that were just mine until I moved into my house. I'm used to sharing without getting upset, but there's something about the idea of sharing you with even the memory of another guy that drives me nuts."

"Do you get now why I hated knowing you fucked women at a BDSM club? You fear the comparison as much as I do. But here's the problem. I'm an only child, Luca. I've never had to share, so I don't do it well. I will never share you, not with a woman in the future or your memories in the past. You forget yours, and I'll forget mine."

I know that's not how it works, but maybe it'll soothe him before I get myself worked up thinking about him with other women. Then we'll both be pissed at nothing but in foul moods, anyway. That won't get us any-fucking-where.

"Deal, *piccolina*."

"Daddy, we've been in here alone for a long time. People must be wondering what's going on. We're being rude."

"For all they know, you fell back to sleep. Did you meet Matteo's mom, Carlotta? I think you'll like her."

"Only briefly. She and Sylvia were in kitchen making food for everyone, and I was in the living room."

He slides his hand into mine, and we head out to the living room. I didn't realize how late it was until I smell dinner cooking. My stomach rumbles. We never got to have lunch because we got shot at first. How am I able to think about that so calmly?

"Auntie Carlotta, this is Olivia. Olivia, this is my mom's best friend. I've known her since the day I was born. She was the first person other than Mama and Papa to meet me."

"It's so nice to properly meet you, Olivia. How're you doing? Do you need anything? You must be starving. Maria said you didn't have lunch."

"I'm a little hungry."

"Uh-oh."

I look up at Luca, but he's smiling at Carlotta.

"A little hungry means four courses instead of seven. You won't have room for dinner if you have one of Auntie Carlotta's snacks."

Luca leans over to kiss Carlotta on each cheek as she hugs

him. The affection between them is obvious. It's clear she's his second mom, and he's an extra son.

"Don't listen to him. He complains and yet still eats me out of house and home. Dinner won't be ready for another hour. Let's get you something to tide you over."

She ushers me toward the kitchen but shoots Luca a reproving look when he follows.

"What? I didn't have lunch either?"

"You can wait. It's too close to dinner for a snack. You'll ruin your appetite."

I laugh. It's fun seeing Luca with his family. He's so at ease around them, and they make me laugh. I feel way more welcome than I expected after how Lorenzo made it sound.

"Auntie Carlotta, I'm going to tell Mama—"

"Go right ahead and tell your mama. See whose side she takes."

Carlotta cocks an eyebrow at him, and I almost want to see him go into time out. I cover my mouth to stifle my giggle, and it sounds like I'm choking. Luca huffs as he looks at me.

"Luca, it would really help if you started laughing. Then I would be doing it with you rather than at you."

"Cheeky, *piccolina*."

Carlotta's facing the kitchen, so when Luca falls in step behind me, I shake my ass. I clear my throat to hide my yelp when he pinches it. While she goes to the fridge, I stop beside the enormous island in the humongous kitchen. It's clear she knows her way around and is as comfortable in Sylvia's kitchen as she must be in her own.

I didn't get a good view of the space last night. A Michelin star chef would be jealous. Luca slides his arms around my waist and presses his chest to my back. I feel him against me, his hard-on resting against the small of my back. For the umpteenth time in my life, I wish I were taller. I rest my arms on the counter and lean forward. It pushes my hips back just enough to taunt Luca without being too obvious.

"If you want to stay for dinner rather than me feasting on your pussy, stop teasing me, little girl."

Luca leans over me to whisper in my ear. I press my hips back and move them side to side, rubbing against him. Who the hell am I? I have never been this brazen in my life. I've always been super discreet around the families of the guys I've dated. But there's something exciting and illicit about flirting with him like this when Carlotta or anyone else in the house could see us.

The moment I can tell Carlotta finishes pulling things out of the fridge and will soon turn toward us, I straighten up. The upside of being short is the island completely hides Luca's hand cupping my pussy. He squeezes, holding me tighter.

"Eat your snack. Then we're leaving before I fuck you again in my aunt and uncle's house. Except this time, I'll make you scream until everyone knows what we're doing."

"You wouldn't dare."

"My cock wants to be inside your cunt more than I care what anyone thinks."

"Shh."

Carlotta's expression when she turns toward us tells me she knows exactly what's going on, even if I'm certain she didn't hear us.

"If you want to drive my car, Luca, you'll remember some manners. Pia or Natalia could walk in any moment. Explain that to Aunt Sylvia. See how that goes."

Luca takes a step back, and it suddenly feels cold without his body heat pressed against me. It amuses me to see how the women in his family intimidate him so easily. Nothing about any of the men seems to strike the same fear in him as his mother and aunts. I know Carlotta isn't really his aunt, but it's clear he sees her as that.

"Why do you say Auntie Carlotta but Aunt Sylvia?"

"I've known Auntie Carlotta my entire life, so that's what I called her when I was little. It stuck. Aunt Sylvia married into the family nearly ten years ago, so I was an adult."

That makes more sense. I look down when Pia comes to stand beside Luca and me.

"Luca, will you help me with my science? I don't get it."

The little girl holds up a worksheet Luca takes. He pretends to study it, his brow furrowing.

"I think I can manage."

The pair walk to the kitchen table, and I watch as he pulls out a chair for her. She thanks him, but it's obvious she's big enough she could easily do that herself. It reminds me I saw Carmine pull out Pia's chair last night at dinner, and Gabriele pulled out Natalia's. Is it just manners ingrained in all the men, or are they making sure the girls understand the men in their lives should be chivalrous? Lord, I hope they aren't setting those two little girls up for disappointment. I don't know too many guys these days who pull out chairs for women. I can't imagine there'll be any in twenty years. They put their heads together, and it's sweet to see Luca pointing out things as he explains. It's like a flash forward to him doing homework with his own daughter.

"His heart is always in the right place."

As Carlotta slides a plate of food in front of me, I turn to look at her. I pull out a stool and climb on. I feel like a kid Pia's age whenever I have to get onto any bar height chair that doesn't have a bottom rung.

"Thank you. He's really sweet to help her with her homework."

"He has a soft spot for Pia and Natalia. Pia knows she can go to Maria for help with her science too, but she loves to sit with Luca. He makes up stories and songs to help her remember things."

"Really?"

I look over my shoulder at them and see Luca pointing to something else on the paper. I turn back toward Carlotta. She was watching me as I watched Luca. It's a little disconcerting.

"Nicoletta, Maria, Sylvia, and I were born into this. You haven't met Salvatore's sister, Paola. She's Carmine's mom. But you will one of these days. We don't necessarily understand how hard it must be to have all of this thrown at you so quickly. But we know how to navigate this life and this family. If you ever need anything, just ask any of us."

"Thank you. I'm not sure that I'll be—"

"Olivia, yes, you will. You're the first person who isn't Italian and one of the kids' friends to come to dinner."

"Kids?"

I look back at Pia.

"Matteo and the others. I know they're all adults, but it's easier to just call them that when I mean all of them. You and I both know you're more than just Luca's friend. When you need help understanding this world, just ask."

"Thank you. If I ask Luca this, he'll downplay his answer. Is Mr. Mancinelli angry that Luca brought me into your world?"

"Which one? Massimo or Salvatore?"

"Well, both, but I really meant Salvatore."

"He's not angry. He would have been if Luca did nothing to help you that night. I guess none of us expected a connection between you. At least, not so fast. But the men in this family are the best judges of character. I know you know who we are, so I think you can understand why they have to be. Salvatore and Massimo both like you, and they're happy to see Luca happy. Like I said, Luca has a good heart. His father and uncle know that."

I look down at my plate before looking up again.

"You make it sound like they have to remind themselves of that. Is it because Luca's still proving himself after what happened with Anastasia Kutsenko?"

Carlotta freezes, but her eyes dart to Luca before meeting mine.

"He told you about that?"

"Enough for me to know the gist of what happened. He's not proud of what he did. I think he'll never forgive himself. I saw how it eats at him when he told me he was the reason she got hurt and that men took her. He's been as honest as he can be. I know there's plenty he'll never tell me, no matter how close we might get. I'm figuring out how to accept that. But he's been very clear that he wants me to know the man he is, for better or worse. He never wants me to feel trapped or misled. It's a lot to digest in three days."

"For these guys, sometimes three days is a lifetime."

"Do you know the details of how I met Luca?"

"Yes, and what happened on the highway in Connecticut."

"How do you live with knowing one day your sons or husband might not be the winner?"

"The fear that they might die never goes away. It's always there, but it's quiet most days. But even at its loudest, that fear isn't stronger than how much I love them. I knew I would marry within the *Cosa Nostra*, so I never looked outside it. But I didn't need to. The moment I met Domenico, I knew there was something about him. It wasn't love at first sight, but it didn't take long to fall in love with him. Growing up with this doesn't prepare you for what it's like when it's your husband or sons who walk out the door and might not come back. That said, I never want to imagine my life without having loved Dom and having Emilio and Matteo with him. That's way more important than my fear."

That's deep. Carlotta covers my hand with hers and gives it a light squeeze. I continue eating as she goes to the stove to check whatever's cooking. She gave me a lot to think about. If nothing else, it seems like everyone in this family has deep conversations with me within minutes of meeting me. Does that mean they trust me? Welcome me? I think it must.

"Are you ready to go, *piccolina*?"

"Hmm? Oh, I guess. Isn't it rude to leave without having dinner with everyone?"

"As much as I want to say the only reason to leave is so that I can fuck you in private, I really don't want it to be dark when we leave here."

"Oh."

"It's just one of my many precautions."

"After today, I don't think I'll ever argue with your precautions."

Chapter Thirteen

Luca

It doesn't take us long to say our goodbyes. Auntie Carlotta and Aunt Sylvia insist we take food with us, which Livy and I appreciate because there won't be anything at the safe house yet. We go out through the garage and take Auntie Carlotta's Volkswagen SUV. I reassure Livy that Matteo will make sure his mom gets home safely. She asks about Auntie Carlotta driving my car instead, but I explain it's too dangerous that someone would recognize it. I don't need to explain beyond that—that I don't need her going for a joyride that'll make Matteo pray for his life. She's not reckless, but she's a daredevil with a lead foot.

Livy looks out the window as we leave Queens and cross into the Bronx. The house we pull up to sits on a bit of a hill. The garage is underneath the right side of the house and appears dug into the hill. It's a modest home that matches all the others along the street. It blends in.

I pull straight into the garage. I wait until the garage door is halfway down before turning off the engine. I put my hand on her arm until the door shuts all the way. Then I let go and get out. She must realize that it's just like when she got to Uncle Salvatore and Aunt Sylvia's house. I know Marco told her not to open the car door, that one of Uncle Salvatore's men would do it since two were already waiting for them in the garage. The guy didn't step near the SUV until the garage door finished moving.

I come around the front of the car as she gets out. I push the door closed and lead her into the house. The place is furnished, but it's sparser than what I'm used to. Everything looks comfortable and clean, but it's not exactly the showroom furniture I have at my place. My guess is the house looks way more like her apartment. As we sit down to dinner, which I'm glad we brought back with us because I realize I'm starving, she asks me about Pia's science homework.

"Maria's a doctor. Why doesn't she ask her? Carlotta said you make up stories and songs. Wouldn't Maria be the best choice for science?"

"I told you I have an MBA. I do, but my undergrad was in chemistry with a minor in microbiology."

"You're a scientist?"

"Don't look so surprised. There's more to me than a cute face and hot bod."

"I know. You've got a big dick, too."

I stare at her for a moment before laughing. She said it completely deadpan, but she laughs along with me.

"I get why you have an MBA since you deal with your family's—businesses. But why chemistry? Just because you like science, and you already planned to get a grad degree in business?"

I go quiet and lean back in my chair, watching her. I'm

trying to decide whether to tell her the truth, or at least how much of it.

"Luca, you've waited long enough that you have to tell me the truth or else I'll know it's a lie you just concocted."

"There are certain parts of our international deals that make having an experienced chemist on hand useful."

She sits there for a moment before it dawns on her. Cocaine. It doesn't come from a simple plant like pot. I doubt she knows exactly how it's made, but my guess is she knows there are chemical mixtures and different steps. I wonder if she knows coke labs can blow up just like meth labs. Fuck. Does she think I know how to cook meth too?

"Livy, I don't make any of it. But I understand the recipes, so I know how much of each ingredient they need. I can calculate cost and value from that. I know how to test quality without using any."

This is the first time I've admitted to any of our illegal operations. She looks like she doesn't know how she feels about her boyfriend—I guess that's what I am—being a drug dealer. I don't think she pictures me standing on any street corners doing deals, but I'm pretty sure she guesses I oversee massive quantities coming into the country that go out on the street to get people hooked. It's as though I can hear what she's thinking.

People have probably died from the stuff his family makes or sells. Morally gray? No. Morally black. And I seem okay with it. I'm not rebelling like I thought I would.

"Livy?"

"Were you, like, assigned that and told you had to go to college for it? Do each of you have a job they expected you to fill?"

"Nobody told any of us what we had to study in college. We all picked what we wanted, but we picked majors that are useful now."

"You picked chemistry. What about the others?"

"Lorenzo majored in computer science. Marco studied electrical engineering. He's finishing his MBA right now. Maria had entirely free choice because she has nothing to do with the family businesses. She was an anatomy major and knew she wanted to go into radiology before she applied to med school."

"What about the others?"

"You mean Carmine, Gabriele, and Matteo?"

She nods.

"Carmine studied structural engineering, and Matteo studied architecture and construction management. Gabriele got his degree in criminal justice."

She blinks a few times when she hears Gabriele's. Knowing the right side of the law helps you know how to cover things up when you're on the wrong side of it.

"What's your background in?"

I'm not sure if she went to college. I suppose that's diplomatic.

"My undergrad was international marketing and consumer behavior. You're not the only one with an MBA. I continued with the marketing focus. You?"

"Operations."

She raises her eyebrows and tilts her head a little to the left as she considers that.

"I suppose that makes sense. Supply chain management and logistics. I can see how that would be useful."

"If you have an MBA, then why were you working for a liquor store?"

It's her turn to sit back. She puts her fork down and stares at me. Moments like this couldn't make it more obvious how little we know about each other. She looks like she's trying not to be insulted.

"You make it sound like I was a cashier or stocker. That

173

wasn't some little mom and pop place you held your meeting at. I worked at the firm that *major chain* hired. I was at the store that night because they were about to launch a huge campaign to celebrate the company's fiftieth anniversary. It's a franchise, so Carlos and his family owned that location, but they still follow corporate policies and take part in the big events. It was the fifth location I'd been to that day to make sure everything was ready. I'd written special ad copy and promo language for particular locations depending on their consumers. I oversaw the most profitable but most difficult franchise owners. I had a team of six people beneath me who handled other locations. I wasn't some little sample girl, Luca. I had a career."

Anger bubbles within her like a dam that's about to give way.

"I loathed Carlos, but he wasn't even the worst owner I had to deal with. He owned the place but didn't manage it, so he was rarely there. He was a jackass and a perv, but he let me do my job because he knew how much I made him. I get how consumers behave. I studied it after all. I made a few fucking changes to the layout and signage and doubled his monthly revenue. That got me a raise which has been hammering away at my student loans. Thinking about those just makes my heart pound harder. How the fuck am I going to deal with those without a job? Forbearance? Great. I'll never get out from under them. They'll fucking follow me to the grave."

She pushes back her chair and stands. She grabs her plate and marches into the kitchen. She must not be hungry anymore. She scrapes the food into the trash but appears regretful that she's wasting it. She moves to the sink, and she knows I followed her. She puts the plate down before she slams it down.

"You got an unexpected houseguest you get to bang. But really, how much has changed in your life since last week? A different enemy to murder? Same shit, different day. I can't go to my apartment. I can't see my mom. I lost my car and my job. I have bills to pay with no income. And I have no idea if all of that is what my life's come to. Am I fucking stuck not being able to go out because someone'll shoot me?"

The moment she stops speaking, she realizes what she said at the beginning. Once again, it's like I can hear her thinking.

Fuck me. A different enemy to murder. I can't believe I said that.

"Luca—"

"Don't. You said what you said. You're not wrong."

"I didn't need to say that, and I sure as shit didn't need to take all of this out on you. You didn't cause this. All you've done is try to help. I guess I felt like you'd been looking down on me all this time if you thought I wasn't that well educated."

"I never thought you weren't well educated."

"You asked about my background. That's what you say when you want to know what someone does, but don't think they went to college."

"I didn't know that. Now I do. Where'd you go to college?"

"UVA for undergrad and Wharton for grad school."

"Wharton? I went there too. I went straight from undergrad."

"So did I. We must have just missed each other since I'm three years younger than you. Luca, I see the wheels spinning. You're trying to figure out whether I was working up to my potential. In other words, was I smart enough to get a job that pays commensurate to that school's reputation?"

She crosses her arms over her chest as she rests back against the counter. That wasn't what I was thinking, but I get why she assumed I was.

"Luca, I was making six-figures. It's also fucking expensive to live in New York and have six years of school loans to pay. I live modestly, but my retirement fund is healthy. The liquor store wasn't my only client."

"I'm sorry if anything I said or did insinuated I didn't look at you as an equal. I didn't mean to."

She sighs.

"I know. There's still so much for us to learn about each other. We haven't exactly talked a ton about regular things couples do when they start dating. I guess we've got the big picture part about liking each other and wanting something special down pat. It's all the little things we need to learn."

"My life changed for the better, and yours did not. I get that. I—"

"No. Don't say that. Mine changed. Some parts are worse, but not all the changes are bad. It's better for being with you. I shouldn't have said what I did, especially throwing back in your face what you did to protect me. I'm sorry, Luca. That wasn't cool."

"Little one, it's all right. I might not have enjoyed hearing that, but you've kept your shit together ever since this started. All pressure cookers need release valves, so they don't explode. "

"You really do think about food a lot, don't you?"

I smile as we step into each other's arms.

"Daddy, are we okay?"

"Of course, *piccolina*."

"I can't believe I'm saying this, but can we just go to sleep? I'm so much more tired than I realized. It hits me in waves. I just really want to snuggle up next to you and know that you'll be beside me all night."

"Let's see if I can give you sweet dreams."

It's been nearly three weeks since we arrived at the house in the Bronx. I've gone to work each day and hated it. It all seems so boring when I could get to know Livy better. We've slowed our physical relationship down to little more than just some heated kisses. We share a bed, and we fall asleep either with me spooning her or her curled against my side and her head on my chest. We don't let go throughout the night. When one of us shifts, the other follows. We've spent the evenings talking about our childhoods, time in college, and work.

We've talked about places we'd like to visit and things we've always wanted to do. We've identified our values, goals, and ideals are the same. I wish I could say our morals and ethics are identical, but that's not possible. But they overlap wherever they can. We're discovering we're as compatible as we hoped.

She didn't believe me when I said my favorite color is steel gray until I showed her a photo of my room at my parents' house and my office in Manhattan. I learned her favorite color is periwinkle. She asked how anyone could not love it with a name as fun as that. I wasn't quite sure what shade that was, so she pulled it up on my phone. I swear it's more blue, but she thinks it's more violet.

I enjoy learning these things about her. She thinks cilantro tastes like dirt, and I can't get enough of it. We realized that when we ordered Mexican for dinner, and she nearly spat out her burrito. She pulled out a long piece of it and curled her nose. We'd gotten each other's food because I asked for extra cilantro. She ate all the pickled carrots, and I was glad to give them to her. It reminded me of the old nursery rhyme.

Jack Sprat could eat no fat; his wife could eat no lean. Between the two, they licked the platter clean.

She told me how she was a high school gymnast and cheerleader. She went on to cheer in college and was a flyer—those girls who get tossed in the air by the guys who look like they should be offensive linemen. She swears that's been the only time in her life when she's appreciated being short.

The only thing she won't talk about is her parents before they got their divorce, and she will not talk about her dad at all. I know next to nothing about them. She avoids the subject or says she doesn't know the answer to my questions. I think there's some truth to that, and she hates being reminded that she doesn't have the close family I do.

I look up as Matteo walks into my office. He was part of Maria's detail, and they just got back this morning. He came straight from the airfield here in Jersey.

"Is Maria still pissed her vacation got cut short?"

"Let's just say she swears fluently in three languages. She knows none of the other doctors asked to get the flu, but it didn't thrill her she got called back in. It was three days early, so she'll survive. I get why it annoyed her after banking three weeks of time off and not getting to use all of it."

"What about her friend?"

"Veronica? She's as fucking annoying as she's always been. She drinks way too much, gets way too loud, and then can't hold her liquor. But sober, she's a terrific friend for Maria. They have a blast together. How Maria gets past the fact that she sounds like someone murdering a crow, I'll never know."

"Tell me how you really feel."

Matteo rolls his eyes at me as he comes to sit across from me in my office at one of our Atlantic City casinos. I left at dawn to make the two-and-a-half-hour drive here. I have a breakfast meeting with some high rollers who want to invest in a casino we're opening in Reno. Matteo slides into a chair across from me and cocks an eyebrow.

"You don't look thrilled to be here either."

"You know where I'd rather be."

"In bed with a certain cute blonde?"

"Watch it."

"Come on, Luca. I didn't say anything rude. That is where you'd rather be. I didn't say what you'd rather be doing."

"Being this far away from her makes me anxious right now. It's been too quiet. The Espinozas haven't made a peep since this shit started. They just went after Livy once. Why are they waiting? What are they waiting for? They won't ignore me taking out Carlos and his guys, nor are they going to be down with a witness living. The longer they take to strike again, the more time they have to plot."

"Or it just takes them a long ass time to come up with something that might possibly but most probably won't work."

"I still don't like it. It'll take at least three hours to get back once this meeting is done. It's bad enough going into Manhattan and leaving her at the house in the Bronx. And that's only a half hour drive on a good day. Being this far away feels like it's tempting fate."

"You've had men staked out on either end of the street and the ones parallel to yours. We've got guys in cars outside the door, and men in the backyard every night. She hasn't seen daylight in two and a half weeks because you won't let her open the blinds or curtains. No one knows she's there except for us."

"I know."

I rest my head back on my chair and close my eyes. I take a deep, slow inhale, but the air leaves my lungs with a whoosh. I glance at my phone on my desk before I keep talking.

"She hasn't complained at all. She's accepted it all, but she can't stay like this. It's like house arrest. She doesn't deserve it."

"But it's keeping her safe."

"I know. I sent Lorenzo, Marco, Carmine, and Gabriele over there today. They're going to take her grocery shopping and to the pharmacy."

"All four of them? Don't you think that's excessive?"

I glare at my brother's best friend.

"No, I don't."

"Does Uncle Salvatore know you arranged that?"

"Yeah. But I didn't ask. I just mentioned it."

I glance down at my watch. My meeting's in five minutes. I know the people who're coming are already in the hotel attached to the casino. I watched all the security footage from the casino floor last night. I studied each of them, looking for any tells or little mannerisms to keep my eye out for this morning.

"I have the finished blueprints for you."

Matteo holds up a canister before pulling off the top. He gets up and walks over to the conference table before he withdraws the architectural drawings and spreads them across the oblong table with six chairs around it. I move around my desk and lean over the table. I have a basic understanding of how to read them, but I know next to nothing about drafting them or all the structural engineering that goes into a building's design. We both look up when someone knocks on the door. I fasten my suit coat's top button as I make my way to the door.

"Hello. Come in, Mr. Hamamoto. It's good to see you again."

I step aside as the Japanese card shark saunters in, casting his gaze around my office and looking down his nose at me. I don't need his money to build this casino. He's investing, not for a share of the profits, but as a down payment for us to ship cocaine from Seattle to Tokyo. There's plenty of risk for us in getting the drugs from Mexico up the Pacific coast to Washington state. The easy part is the container ship across the ocean. We have people paid off at the port authorities on both sides.

I'm about to close the door when I spot a person I could totally live without ever seeing again.

"Ms. Nishida, welcome."

"Hello, Luca. So formal."

I don't bother smiling. I'm not interested in revisiting old mistakes. Sakura Nishida and I were fuck buddies in grad school. She comes from a Yakuza family, so she and I have the worst things in common. We had an unwritten rule to never discuss our families, and since we didn't date, only fucked, they didn't really come up.

However, I ended things the morning after we graduated. My family went back to their hotel after celebrating with me after the commencement ceremony. I went to Sakura's, banged her all night, and broke things off the next morning. Was it because I was going back to New York, and she was going back to Tokyo? No. Was it because the sex got boring? Definitely not.

Oh, no. I broke it off because she forgot to hide her engagement ring. Something I'd never seen before but spotted on her bedside table. We've only dealt with each other professionally ever since. What the hell is she doing here?

"Matteo and I look forward to going over these plans with you. We break ground in three months."

Akira Hamamoto juts his chin up at my announcement. Fucker. I know what's coming.

"We haven't agreed to invest yet."

"Then you should hurry up. You know we don't need you. You need us. The investment is your down payment on the product and a guarantee that we'll deliver. This casino is going up whether or not you get involved. If you don't want an easy way to disguise our real agreement, then you can come up with something else. But the cost will go up."

"That isn't how this—"

"Oh, yes, it is."

I'm not playing games today. I want to get back to Livy.

181

Matteo gestures to the table, and we all take seats. I unbutton my suit coat, sit back, and let him take the lead as he discusses the different phases of construction. With each one he names, he tells them how much more they'll spend to buy in if they don't do it now. As I listen, I can feel Sakura watching me. I noticed she isn't wearing any rings today.

Before I met Livy, I might have considered a one-night hook up. But now, the idea of touching another woman makes me want to scrub myself in the shower. Sakura's beautiful, and she knows it. She's not confident like Livy was that night when she put me in my place about her job. Sakura's arrogant, which makes her condescending to the nth degree. She knows that too. She made an excellent project partner in grad school, but her attitude grew old fast once I had to deal with her occasionally in meetings like this.

I listen to Matteo, but my mind isn't on the meeting. My phone vibrates in my trouser pocket, where I slipped it before looking at the blueprints with Matteo. I silence it and send whoever it is to voicemail. It immediately rings again. I do that twice more. The fourth time it rings, I pull it out and glance down. It's the burner number I gave Livy.

I don't even bother to excuse myself before I stalk across the office and step into the hallway.

"Livy?"

"Luca?"

"*Piccolina*, why are you whispering? What's wrong?"

"I don't know. I spotted a natural grocer on the way back to the house from the grocery store and pharmacy. I asked if we could check it out for future reference. The guys agreed, but within five minutes of walking in, they started acting weird. They started walking way closer to me, and they were giving each other looks I didn't understand. I came into the restroom to call you, but they don't know that. Lorenzo and Gabriele are outside the door. They insisted they both come. What's going on, Daddy?"

I don't like how scared she sounds. I hate that she's hiding in a bathroom to call me. Something is very wrong, but I don't want to panic her. While she's talking, I'm already shooting off a group message.

ME

Why's Livy hiding in the bathroom? Who followed you?

CARMINE

We don't know yet. Something feels off but we haven't spotted anyone we recognize.

What feels off?

"Daddy?"

She hasn't called me that often since the first time she said it. She feels out of control, and she's looking to me to fix this.

"Yes, *piccolina*. I'm here. I'm texting the guys to find out what's going on."

"If it's nothing, they're going to think I'm crazy."

"Shh. No one will ever fault you for being cautious. Hang on. I'm getting a text.

LORENZO

It's Sergei.

The fucking bratva. Sergei's their head intelligence collector. Fuck me.

WTF? Why's he in the Bronx?

MARCO

Like we'd know.

Sabine Barclay

> Get her in the car and get her home. I'm on my way.

"Livy, I'm leaving my meeting right now, but it's going to be a few hours before I can get there."

"Why do you have to leave your meeting?"

"Because you're scared, so I'm coming home."

"Luca, you can't stop work just because I'm worried. I don't know what I can ask or say to your brothers and cousin. I wasn't sure if I was allowed to ask what's going on. I didn't mean for you to leave."

"Listen to whatever they tell you to do. You're not in danger. There's someone there none of us want to deal with, and none of them needs to explain who you are to this man."

"If there's no danger, then stay at work. You can explain things when you get home."

CARMINE

> Get off the phone with her. Sergei's getting too curious. We need to get her out before he and Anton come over here. We're in a Russian store.

> What? Fucking hell. Sergei and Anton and a fucking Russian store.

MARCO

> They never come here. And we didn't want to have to explain why we couldn't come in. Figured that should be your job.

> She would have understood and accepted no. If anything happens. If either of them says anything.

"Daddy? I hear you tapping on your phone. Tell the guys that I'm fine. We can go, but you're staying in Jersey."

184

"Liv, keep your head down when you leave. I'll be home as fast as I can."

"Luca—"

"Argue with me, and I'll take you over my knee, little girl."

"Yes, Daddy."

"Good."

"Daddy?"

"Yeah."

"Can I have a spanking, anyway?"

"Livy, I don't need to get hard right now. Shh. Yes, you can. But just get home safely."

"All right. I'll see you tonight."

Like hell.

"Bye, *piccolina*."

> We're leaving right now. Be at the house in three hours.

LORENZO

They left. False alarm.

> Don't fucking lie. I'm coming home.

CARMINE

Fine

LORENZO

Fine

GABRIEL

Fine

MARCO

Fine

They probably all sent that message at the same time. They

roll in one second after another. I shove my phone back into my pocket and return to the office. Matteo takes one look at me and stands up. He pulls the blueprints toward him and starts rolling them.

"I'm afraid Matteo and I must leave. Something's come up at one of the build sites in Queens, and they need Matteo to figure it out. I suspect I'll be signing some very large checks."

Akira and Sakura both look pissed, but I can tell it's for different reasons. Akira knows he should have shored up the deal before I came back in. I can tell he knows he missed his opportunity. Sakura looks pissed, and Matteo looks smug. She tried to bribe or threaten him, and he didn't take the bait.

"Luca, my father is intent upon investing in this project. But I don't think he'll appreciate the numbers Matteo just quoted me. He doesn't like to waste time, so it's better if you don't try another round of negotiations."

"Sakura, we aren't negotiating. The only people wasting time are you and Mr. Hamamoto. You should have agreed to our terms. Now they go up. Either you're in or you're out. That should be a brief conversation with your father."

"You know who—"

"And you know who I am."

She rakes her gaze over me, and I can tell she's shifting approaches. She smiles, and it would make most men hard. It has the opposite effect on me. The thought of spanking Livy made my dick twitch. Sakura makes it shrivel.

"I'll be in the city tonight. We could discuss this further and come to an agreement my father will approve of."

"I have standing plans. Mr. Hamamoto, I apologize for leaving so abruptly. I already know of your connection to the Nishidas but bringing your *oyabun's* daughter to the meeting to seduce me because we were once involved is not the way to make friends and influence people."

"Luca!"

I smirk at Sakura.

"Maybe you should have told your dad that's why you wanted to come rather than Mr. Hamamoto having to tell him the truth."

I knew Akira wasn't aware of my past with Sakura, but he is now. Let them both deal with her disgrace. I need to go. Matteo already has the blueprints back in the canister, and I saw him texting. He's telling our driver to bring the car around. I stand beside the door, my signal for the Japanese business-people to leave.

"I can't believe—"

"Sakura, I have a girlfriend I'm going to marry. I don't need to hide that."

I may have exaggerated it, but if Livy and I were engaged, I wouldn't hide it. And I definitely wouldn't cheat on her.

"Girlfriend? You don't date."

"I didn't until I met the right woman. Safe travels."

I close the door behind her and hurry to my desk.

"What the fuck happened?"

"The Kutsenkos know."

Chapter Fourteen

Livy

"There's a natural grocer on the corner up there. Could we go in, please?"

I'm sandwiched between Lorenzo and Gabriele. Carmine is in the front seat, and Marco is in the third row. It's a good thing I'm small, or I wouldn't fit between the giants. I'm like the valley between two mountains. But they've been super nice to me while I learned my way around the grocery store.

I called in a refill for my birth control at the local pharmacy, so we just left there. I haven't needed it since Luca and I have been abstaining. I don't think that's going to last. We needed the break to focus on more than the physical, which I'm glad we took. But we're both sexually frustrated and ready to go crazy.

I'm not much of a tree hugger, but I recognize the store name as a former client. They have my favorite granola. We should be in and out in a few minutes. Also, short of a halal or kosher butcher, this organic food chain usually has the best meat. I'm not destitute yet, so I'd like to make Luca a really nice dinner. I know he likes steak. It's not lost on me that I'm actually spending his money since he told me to keep what remained of what he gave me. He also gave me a credit card to buy the groceries. Lorenzo was going to insist that he pay until I pointed to the name on the card. Then he laughed and threw a few things on the checkout conveyer.

As we walk into the store, the guys surround me. I feel a bit like a movie star with four hulking bodyguards. It also feels excessive to the extreme. I'm so short that I bet most people don't even know I'm in the center of their tight circle.

I point us toward the cereal aisle, and they move apart enough for me to scan the shelves. I sigh.

"Could one of you get that one on the top shelf, please?"

Maybe shopping with them isn't horrible. I had to ask them to grab more than one thing in the regular grocery store. It's useful that they're all over six-feet-tall. But, hey, even my friends a few inches taller than me would have to step onto the bottom shelf to reach that high.

"Thanks."

Marco hands me the box, and I take a quick look before I drop it into the hand basket Carmine is carrying.

"Can we head over to the meat counter, then the deli, please?"

I feel like I need to ask permission for everything. I don't know whether I can just tell them what I want or if I should check first. Marco answers that for me.

"Ms. D'Amato, you don't have to ask for everything. Just let us know. If it's a no-go, we'll tell you."

"Could you all please call me Olivia?"

There I go asking for something again. From the looks on their faces, I think this is going to be the first no-go they tell me about.

"Really, the formality feels odd when I don't call all of you Mr. Mancinelli. Would Luca really object?"

I glance up as Lorenzo as he shakes his head.

"No. But we wait until the person offers for us to address them by their first name."

"A business practice or your parents' rule?"

"Parents."

All four men answer at once. It's uncanny how they do that.

At the meat displays, I search for what I want. I sense them moving closer around me. I know Carmine and Gabriele are already standing behind me, so my back is completely protected. But the air has shifted among them. I look around, but I see nothing suspicious. I can tell they're watching everything at all times, but now their eyes are darting all over the place. I grab what I want and turn toward the deli.

They're definitely walking much closer. I'm surprised Gabriele doesn't step on my heel, and Carmine isn't letting more than six inches come between us as he leads the way. Lorenzo's and Marco's arms brush against mine. We're about to pass the restrooms, and I'm getting really nervous.

"Um, would you mind if I use the restroom really quickly?"

Lorenzo and Gabriele station themselves outside the door. I duck into a stall and pull out my phone. My call with Luca takes me from anxious to terrified. I know that's the opposite of what he intended, but I'm ready to tell the guys to ditch the basket and get me in the car.

I hang up with Luca and open the door to the restroom. I can't see past the wall of men that's blocking the exit. They step apart, and we move back to where Carmine and Marco are waiting for us.

"Do we need to leave right now?"

"Grab what you need from the deli. Carmine will pay, and Alonzo will join us."

The driver. The guy seemed really cool, but I spot him near the door, and he looks completely unapproachable now. I ask for the couple pounds of cheese I'd like, and Carmine drops it into the basket. As we head toward the exit, the manager's office door opens. An enormous blond guy steps out. He could be fucking Adonis. He is one of the most gorgeous men I've ever seen, and that's saying something since there isn't a dud in the Mancinelli family. But this guy is like beyond supermodel hot. He stares in our direction, and his ice-blue eyes lock with mine.

This is one of the Russians Luca warned me about. No wonder the guys got so protective. Marco's hand goes to my lower back as he steers me to the door faster. The guy doesn't stop staring. In fact, he crosses his arms. His face is entirely expressionless, as in like a statue with no emotion. But his gaze shifts, and I know he's looking at Carmine at the checkout. Nothing changes about his face, but now malice radiates from him.

"Olivia, hurry. Stop staring and go."

Marco's hand presses me forward. My short legs do their best to keep up. No one says anything until we're in the car. Once again, I'm shuffled into the middle of the second row, this time with Carmine and Gabriele next to me. I peer out the window as we pass the building's entrance. We have no choice since it's the only way out of the parking lot.

"Was that a Kutsenko?"

Carmine glances down at me, surprised I know the name.

"May as well have been. That was an Andreyev. One of their cousins."

"He came out of the manager's office. Is that his store?"

None of the men answer. The question just hangs in the air.

"I won't ask to go there again. I'm sorry."

Gabriele offers me a sympathetic smile. Neither he nor Carmine have seemed that bad. Actually, they've been really polite and nice to me today.

"You don't have to apologize. It's not your fault. You didn't know."

"But you did."

Once again, silence looms. I look over my shoulder at Lorenzo and raise my eyebrows.

"They oversee that store."

"Oversee? Wait. Do you mean they extort? Like make them pay protection money or something?"

Fucking hell. These silences are unnerving and fucking annoying. But they also tell me plenty.

"If you knew it was a Russian store, why did you agree to taking me in there?"

Lorenzo answers since I'm still staring at him.

"Because they are never in the Bronx. They send people to deal with the stuff here. That's why we came here. We knew it was the one borough we were least likely to encounter someone."

"But you said it was a Russian store. Wasn't it risky on its own? What if the store owner recognized you?"

Marco speaks up from the front seat.

"They knew who we were the moment we walked in. We figured we'd be in and out before anything happened. We're trying to make this a nor—"

Marco snaps his mouth shut.

"A normal day for me. Seems like that's unlikely ever again. How pissed is Luca going to be when he gets home?"

"At us? We'll sort it out in private later. With you? Not at all."

I sit back and look out the window as best I can with Gabriele's bulky frame blocking half of it. We ride the rest of the way to the safe house in silence. The men don't even speak to each other in Italian. I get the distinct feeling they're gearing up for impact.

"Livy!"

The door bursts open then slams shut, and I hear Luca's loafers pounding across the foyer floor. I hurry out of the living room and stop short when I see him. His tie is pulled loose and askew. The top two buttons of his shirt are undone, and he's not wearing his suit coat. His hair looks like he's run his hand through it a thousand times. He looks like hell.

He wraps his arms around me and pins mine to my side. I can't do anything as he lifts me off my feet. He kisses along my neck and across my cheek before devouring my mouth. I struggle, but I get my arms loose. I cling to him as tightly as he's holding me. I tunnel my fingers into his hair and cup his scarred cheek. I've noticed I do that a lot. He never stops me, and it's almost comforting to me to feel it. It means I know it's really him I'm with.

I whisper when we break apart.

"Daddy."

"I'm here, *piccolina*."

"I'm all right and have been the entire time. I'm happy to see you, but you look a wreck."

"I am a wreck. That was the longest fucking four hours of my life. Fucking traffic was crazy. I was ready to get out and walk. Where are my brothers?"

I point over my shoulder at the living room. Luca looks past me, and his gaze hardens.

"Luca, don't yell at them. They tried really hard to give me a nice day. I understand now why they thought it would be fine to pop into that store. It was a fluke Sergei was there. It was scary while it was happening, but I'm fine now. I know this is something I have to accept, and I am."

"I'm glad. But you getting used to these—encounters—is a fuck ton different from my family taking you somewhere you never should have been. That's inexcusable."

"Daddy, stop. They tried to do something thoughtful for me, and they probably figured it wasn't their place to explain these things. If they'd said no, I would have had more questions none of them would have answered. That would have either pissed me off or made me freak out even more. Probably both."

"Stop defending this, Livy. You don't know what you're talking about. This isn't your place to decide."

"My place? Put me down, Luca."

"Don't get pissed with me. I'm not angry with you, so don't get testy with me."

"You said it's not my place. Is that because my daddy wants to treat me like a child? Or should I be the little woman who's ignorant of everything going on around her?"

"You said you wanted a spanking, anyway. Is this why you're pushing me? Because right now, I'm ready to rip those fucking jeans off you, spank you until you beg me to fuck you, then give you just what we both want."

"You think I'll beg you to fuck me after a punishment?"

"I know you will."

I open my mouth to ask if that's because of all the women he fucked at the sex clubs did, but I think better of it. He puts me down, but he doesn't let go.

"Luca, I don't want to cause problems between you and

your family. I want the spanking for other reasons. But I'm arguing with you because I don't want to get in the way. I don't want to be a burden to anyone."

"You are not. I told you I trust no one as much as my family to protect you. They broke that trust, and they damn well know it, too."

He slides his hand into mine and practically drags me to the living room. I try to dig my heels in, but it's useless. He shoots me a look that has me walking beside him with no more resistance.

"Non so nemmeno cosa dire a nessuno di voi, se non che mi sono fidato." I don't even know what to say to any of you other than I trusted you.

I look to my right when Matteo comes to stand beside Luca. He looks as pissed as Luca. Maybe Luca isn't overreacting after all. Maybe they both are because they haven't heard the full story. Maybe he's pissed because whatever meeting they were having got interrupted.

Matteo speaks up, but as usual, I don't understand what any of them say in Italian.

"Come se non si sentisse già abbastanza in colpa per quello che è successo prima. Ora gli fai pure credere che la donna di cui è mezzo innamorato sia in pericolo. Sappiamo tutti che la bratva non la toccherebbe, ma chi può sapere quali casini saranno in grado di creare perché tu sei entrato lì dentro? E se fosse già nel mirino? Cristo. Lui è stato un disastro per tutto il viaggio fino a qui." Like he doesn't already feel guilty enough about what happened before. Now you have him thinking the woman he's halfway in love with is in danger. We all know the bratva wouldn't touch her, but who knows what shit they're going to cause because you went in there? What if she's in the crosshairs? Christ. He was a mess the whole way here.

Whatever Matteo says, he does it with disgust. He glances

down at me before he keeps going. Luca pulls me closer as though he's afraid I'll run away while Matteo speaks.

"*La strada per l'inferno è lastricata di buone intenzioni. Nessuno di voi quattro è riuscito a trovare una scusa?*" The path to hell is paved with good intentions. Out of the four of you, none of you could have come up with an excuse?

Marco, Lorenzo, Carmine, and Gabriele listen, but none of them respond to what clearly sounded like a question. Their expressions are shuttered, and I don't know what they're thinking. But my guess is they feel like they deserve the dressing down they're clearly getting. I look up at Luca, and he's already looking at me. His expression is so pained, so filled with guilt, that I wrap my arm around him and place my hand on his heart. He looks over at his family, and I follow his gaze. I think the four guys are finally getting just how deeply this affected Luca. And I get the very distinct feeling it completely unnerves them. My guess is Luca never acts this way.

He turns away from everyone else and guides me to the stairs. I look back, and everyone watches us. As he leads me to his bedroom, he says nothing. He had plenty to say when he walked in the door, but now he's gone silent. He shuts the door behind us, but he walks straight into the bathroom and closes that door, too. I'm left standing there with no clue what to do. A few minutes pass, and I knock on the door.

"Give me another minute, Liv. I need to calm down."

I take a deep inhale and step back from the door. It's less than a minute before he steps out.

"Can you explain to me what just happened? What did you mean calm down? Are you that angry?"

"Partly. Or really, yes, but only part of it comes from being pissed at the shit decision they made. A lot of it is being pissed that they made me that scared for your safety."

"You really need to be in control that much, don't you?"

"Yes. When I don't have control, shit goes wrong. Whoever has control of the situation is the one who's coming out alive."

"You said the same thing the others did. The bratva won't hurt me."

"They won't. They will never harm women and children, but that doesn't mean you couldn't get caught in the crossfire at some point. It doesn't mean one of my family couldn't die because the bratva won't touch you. Livy, they are ruthless. They're paramilitary. The older generation was all former KGB or Soviet soldiers. Those guys trained the men our age. They move with a precision that no one else matches. The Kutsenkos and Andreyevs went through some seriously fucked-up shit growing up. They aren't right in the head now."

"Would Sergei have tried to kill them if I weren't there?"

"No. He wouldn't act alone and in public like that. What no one's told you is that Anton Kutsenko, his best friend, was there too. This isn't over."

"Do you feel calmer now?"

"Yes. If I ever tell you to stay away from me, it's because I need a few minutes by myself. I'm not prone to a bad temper or violence, but you've seen a mild version of what my life can be. If I tell you to leave me alone, it's because I don't want you to see me like that. Don't ask questions. Don't try to help. Go in another room and wait for me to come to you."

"That freaks the shit out of me, Luca."

"I know, little girl. I'm sorry. This is the shit I've dragged you into."

"I've watched you shoot men and not blink. What does a wild version mean?"

"Things I will never ever—*ever*—tell you."

I decide not to press. I decide on a different path.

"Daddy, I think you need to spank me as much as I need to be. I don't totally get this dynamic we have. But I understand you

197

won't feel better until you're back in control. I feel adrift and know I have no control. I feel like I need you to have some or else..."

"Or else what, *piccolina?*"

"I don't know. Descend into madness. I only feel safe right now when I know you have control. Even if you don't decide everything that goes on outside this bedroom or this house, you can do that in here."

"Is that why you disagreed with me downstairs? Because I warned you: I would punish you because your safety is non-negotiable."

"Not entirely. I really don't want you to lose your shit on your family. I truly believe they were trying to give me a nice day. I was scared, but I never felt unprotected. I knew I was safe with them."

"This is more about them breaking my trust than me thinking they couldn't protect you."

I nod as he pulls his tie off.

"Strip, Livy."

I watch as he goes to sit on the sofa across the room. I follow him, leaving a trail of clothes. When I'm naked and standing in front of him, I feel my excitement growing.

"Turn around and cross your wrists."

I do as he says, and he binds them with his tie.

"Come lie across Daddy's lap."

That word. The way he says it is so dark and gravelly. I clench my pussy. The entire air has shifted, and the unknown gives me goosebumps. He guides me over his lap and presses my hands up until I bend my arms.

"Move your feet apart and turn your toes inward."

I do as he says.

"*Piccolina*, when I give you instructions, you answer with yes, Daddy or yes, *caro.* Do you understand?"

"Yes, Daddy."

"Good girl."

Why does hearing him say that make me so wet? He slides his fingers along my pussy, and he knows what he does to me. He uses the wetness to tap against my backdoor. He doesn't press into me, but he runs his finger in a wide circle around the rim. Then he slides his fingers into my cunt.

"The idea of a spanking excites you a lot, Livy."

"It does, Daddy. But I got wet when you got home. The moment you kissed me, I was ready for you to fuck me."

"Do you think naughty girls who argue about their safety deserve to come?"

"You said you were going to fuck me."

"I did. But I didn't say I would let you come."

What the fuck? Oh, shit. My pussy aches so much it burns. The idea he might fuck me but not let me come makes me restless. I shift my hips, and my clit rubs against his rock-solid thigh. His hand rains down a sharp slap.

"That's just a warning to stop trying to get yourself off. Your real spanking hasn't started yet. I decide when you come, Livy. I control your orgasms just like I control your pussy. It's mine now."

"Yes, Daddy."

Do I sound breathless to him too? From that delicious chuckle, I would say I do. He rubs my clit with his fingertip. I squeeze my eyes shut.

"Why am I going to spank you, Livy?"

"Because you've told me from the start that you won't back down when it comes to my safety. You know this world, and I don't. I argued with you about stuff that has to do with your family, not me. I—"

"Wait, Livy. I am not upset about you disagreeing with me

199

about my family. You have a right to your opinion about that, and I will listen. That is not part of your punishment."

"Then I don't know why else you're doing it."

"You're right that I won't back down. But you also tried to diminish the severity of a situation you don't understand. I didn't pick my words well, but that's what I meant about it not being your place. If you decide to stay with me, then you will learn how to gauge situations. But you aren't there yet."

If I decide to stay with him. He's still giving me an out. Or rather, he's remembering that I still haven't committed. He's told me what he wants. The few clothes I have now hang in his closet or have a drawer set aside in his dresser.

"I'm sorry, Daddy."

"Ten spanks on each side. Do you remember your safe word?"

"Museum."

"If this goes from hurting to pain, then you use that word. I stop immediately."

"I know, *caro*. We both need this. I don't want to do anything that'll upset you."

"Thank you, little girl. Keep your arms bent and your hands out of the way. I will truly punish you if you move them, and I hurt you."

He runs his hand over my ass, stroking and squeezing. I feel him getting harder the longer he touches me. I know when the first spank is coming, but I'm still not prepared for the sting that radiates through my right cheek. Then it's my left cheek. He rubs the burn away. Then he spanks me again on each side.

"Those were on each side. Are you all right?"

"Yes, Daddy."

"Then you will count the rest."

"Yes, Daddy."

So begins the pattern. He spanks, I count, he rubs. We do

that from the third spank to the eighth. But there're no pauses between the ninth and tenth on each side. The tenth one lands across my pussy and makes me yelp. That's why he wanted my legs open and feet turned in. It gave him space to slap my tender cunt. I have never wanted to feel a dick in me as much as I want to feel his.

He runs his hand over me again, his touch so light. He'd covered my entire ass. Top, middle, and bottom. He nailed my horizontal crack a couple times. He helps me up and maneuvers me to sit on his lap with my ass between his thighs, so it doesn't rub or press against his pants.

"You took that so well, little one. I'm proud of you."

He wipes away tears as he cradles me against him. His touch is slow and light before he helps me to my feet.

"Stand by the foot of the bed."

I follow his directions, forced to watch him undress with no option to help since my hands are still tied behind my back. When he moves closer to me, he strokes himself. He reads my jealousy and taunts me by moving slower. Our gaze meets, and I open my mouth. I'm ready to sink to my knees, but his free hand shoots out and grasps my arm.

"You are not my sub, Livy. You do not give me sexual favors to earn forgiveness. It's already given. You don't have to do it to thank me, either. Your kisses were the thanks I wanted."

"I want to pleasure you, *caro*. Watching you stroke yourself makes me want to feel you in my mouth, against my tongue. Maybe it's because my hands are restrained, so I can't touch you on my own."

"Hmm. I think you want me to fuck your mouth to prove I'm still in control. But I think you want a little of that control back. You want to see how much I need you while you control my pleasure."

Insightful. And right. I nod my head. He holds my arm as

he helps me kneel. He strokes himself three more times before rubbing the tip of his cock against my lips.

"Open for me, little one."

He slides inside my mouth after I lick the head. I close my eyes and sigh as I wrap my lips around him. I suck hard before I move to bob my head. He grasps my skull in both hands, his fingers clutching my hair. He holds me in place as he thrusts into me over and over.

"I decide. You wanted me to fuck you, now I am."

I can barely keep up. He's careful not to be too forceful, but twice I gag. He eases back for a couple thrusts before picking up the tempo again. From his breathing and how his abs flex, I can tell he's getting close. He rips himself away from me and helps me to my feet. He steers me to the side of the bed and pulls the bedside table drawer open so hard that it nearly falls off its runners. He snatches a condom and rips it open. I can't see him, but he's quick to get it on. His hand lands between my shoulder blades and presses me forward. The moment my chest touches the mattress, he grabs my hips and pulls me onto my toes. Then he's inside me.

I moan so loudly I wonder if anyone heard me. I don't know if the guys stuck around or what. I don't even care. He pounds into me, one hand on my hips, the other gripping my bound wrists. I push back to meet each surge.

"You are my *piccolina*. Mine. I decide how to protect you. I will not back down if it endangers someone so precious to me as you. All of you is mine. I claim it all."

His teeth sink into the flesh where my shoulder and neck meet, nipping me. I whimper as I squeeze my eyes shut.

"More, Daddy. Please."

"More what?"

"All of it. Rougher, faster. I am yours. Prove it. Do what you want with me."

"You push me too far, Livy. I tell you how desperate I am to keep you safe, then you encourage me to be rougher with you. I'm so fucking scared I'm going to hurt you. But I want to give you what you crave as much as I want to take it."

"Untie my hands, *caro*. Let me turn around."

He's quick to rip away the tie before he pulls out. I scramble backward onto the bed, my legs open wide as I reach for him. He thrusts into me. I need to see him and touch him.

"I promise you I won't let you hurt me. It would devastate you, and I'm not trying to do that to you. But I crave you like an addict. And part of me always fears this is the last time we'll be together. I need it all, just in case."

Tears pool at the corner of my ears. He kisses away the ones that slide free.

"I told you, you are mine. I'm not letting go, Livy. The only way this ends is if you tell me it does. No one is taking you from me. I might claim you because being the dominant one is the role I play for us. It's who I am. But I'm not just taking. You get all of me in return. *All of me* is yours."

He stresses part of that to make sure I understand. But what's he saying? Does he mean his heart and his mind? Could he love me one day?

That pushes me over the edge.

"I'm coming, Daddy."

"I know, little girl. Fuck. Keep squeezing my dick like that... Yes... Fuck... You're so fucking tight, Liv."

He leans forward and grabs my hair, pinning me in place.

"Daddy, come in me. I'm yours."

He shudders, and I grab his ass as it flexes. The moment he's done, the roughness is gone. He's tender with me, touching me as though I'm as precious as he said.

"Luca, I'm clean. I got tested a few weeks ago."

"I have to test regularly for my club. I tested ten days before we met. I got the results the morning we met."

Our gazes lock. Since I've been staying with Luca for nearly a month, I've had my period. Part of the reason I wanted to go to the pharmacy was because it's the right day to start a new birth control pack.

"I need a solid week on my pill to be safe. After that, I want to feel your cum on my thighs as it drips out of me. I want you to mark me. I'm not going anywhere."

Chapter Fifteen

Luca

Livy is in my arms, and I'm finally breathing easy, and not just because I'm no longer panting from our—uh, energetic—sex. As the drive dragged on and on, stuck in Jersey traffic, I couldn't stop thinking about if it had been the Culiacán or the Colombians or the Irish. I want to believe Enrique would never sanction an attack on Livy or any woman, but he hasn't had his family under control recently. I know people could say the same about Uncle Salvatore with the shit Carmine got me into.

But Enrique has four nephews. Pablo is his heir, just like I'm Uncle Salvatore's. Enrique's never had kids. He's not married anymore either. I don't know what went down with that, but he was only with the woman for like a heartbeat. Pablo is his younger brother's son and his head enforcer. Pablo had a younger brother, Juan.

That fucker. He was NYPD, and a straight up fuckwad. Juan and Pablo grew up next door to Maksim Kutsenko's wife, Laura. Juan did some twisted shit when Laura married Maks.

Unrequited ego. That bag of shit was lucky that it was Maks and his brothers and cousins who got to him. If Laura had gotten to Juan—Lord, I don't even want to guess. She and Maks have twins, and Juan got way too close. Needless to say, he is no longer an issue.

However, Enrique's other three nephews, the *Tres J's*— Jorge, Javier, and Joaquin—are fucking insane. Like institutionalize them for the sake of the rest of us. They grew up in Colombia and saw shit no kid should. Pablo handles the big stuff when it goes wrong. *Tres J's* handle the local, low-level shit. They make sure people pay for their protection in Jackson Heights, the Colombian community. They hustle and oversee the dealers. But when they don't get what they want, they tear shit up. They break windows, wreck stores, trash apartments. All that shit, and they love it. Thrive on it. And that's why I wouldn't put it past those three psychos to hurt Livy.

The Irish are just as bad. They've gone through three leaders in three years. Those *feckers*—as they'd say—don't know how to get past the letter D. Donovan, Declan, and Dillan. Donovan and Declan—dumb motherfuckers with no finesse. No wonder they're dead. Dillan, though. That motherfucker could be a Russian chess master. He toys with people and moves them around like it's all a game to him. They got into it with the bratva over two Kutsenko women. They tried to pull our asses in with shit having to do with Pasha Kutsenko, Maks's cousin.

And the Culiacán take little reasoning to understand why I was ready to crawl out of my skin to get home. With three different syndicates willing to hurt Livy because we're together, plus the Culiacán already holding their own grudge, I'm kicking myself for agreeing to her going out. I'm as angry at myself as I am with my brothers and cousin. I've settled down over the past hour, but I still need to get it together, so I don't unleash my temper in a misdirected effort to punish someone else for my fuck-up.

"Daddy?"

"Yeah, *piccolina.*"

I tuck my chin and look down at her. Her head is on my chest with her arm across my waist, and her right leg over mine. I'm not really thinking about it as I run my hand over her back. It's soothing.

"Could I order some stuff?"

"Whatever you need. You know that."

She pushes up on her elbow, and her face is already pink. It's not from what we just did.

"I don't need these things. But I think we'd enjoy them."

I cock an eyebrow.

"Does my little girl want to order some sex toys?"

"Yes, Daddy."

"Let me up, and I'll get my phone."

I roll off the bed and grab my pants. I pull my phone out of my pocket and notice a couple texts. None came from anyone important enough to interrupt our shopping. I climb back onto the bed, and Livy curls up next to me, so she can see my phone.

"What interests you, little girl?"

"All of it."

I chuckle.

"What do you want to try first? Bondage? Impact? Sensation?"

"I know what bondage is, and yes, that interests me. Handcuffs, spreaders, rope. All of that. Does impact mean spanking? And is sensation like wax and those little pinwheel things?"

"Yes, to both. Impact can vary from just your partner's hand to caning."

"No. I don't want to be caned. That's a hard no."

"Livy, I would never do that to you. I enjoy seeing your ass nice and red, and I'd like to see a few raised lines. But I will never cane you or birch you. When we're done each time, I don't want any bruises left on you. I'm also not interested in inflicting that level of pain on you."

"Have you though?"

"Livy."

This is not territory I want to discuss.

"Luca, I won't get angry about what you've done in the past. I can honestly say that I won't hold any jealousy if you've caned or birched someone before. I don't feel like I'm missing out on that."

I don't want secrets where there don't have to be. I also don't want her to think I'm emotionally selective about when I let her in.

"Yes, I have. I had a sub who was into that, and it worked for us. I've done scenes at my club with partners into that."

"Were you into it with them? You say you don't want it with me, but will you miss it?"

"Absolutely not. I told you. I'm not your Dom. That is not the power exchange we have."

"Okay."

I roll toward her, my phone forgotten for a moment.

"Liv, this is the first time in my life I've wanted a true emotional connection with a sexual partner, that I've wanted something beyond sex with them. The caning and birching were solely about domination and submission. Did I enjoy that sexually? Yes. But only because the entire point of the activity was for us to get off. That's not how I see us."

"You seem to like to get off a lot."

Her lips twitch.

"It's never felt better than with you. But I enjoy it at a way deeper and different level. I enjoy it because I know you're experiencing it beyond just the physical."

"I am."

She glances down at my phone.

"Can we try floggers or paddles? Maybe a whip or something?"

I roll onto my back, and she curls up again. We scroll through a few pages of stuff, picking out things that interest us both. They'll create varying levels of pain, but none that will be excruciating. Not by their design or how I would inflict them.

"So is sensation the wax and this thing?"

She points to a Wartenburg pinwheel. It's a metal circle with tiny spikes on a pole that allows it to roll.

"Will it tickle?"

"It can. But if I blindfold you, and you don't know where I'll run it over you next, it heightens your sense of touch."

"I definitely want to try that."

"So do I. What about clamps?"

"Nipple and clit?"

"Either or both. If we get them, you must always tell me if anything tingles or goes numb. They alter your circulation, so they're not a toy, despite what they may be called. Same thing if we ever use rope. You must tell me right away if anything feels wrong. I never want to cause you permanent harm."

"I know you don't, Daddy."

"But I think you might try to take more than you can for my sake. I don't think you realize how monumentally pissed I'll be if that happens."

"Yeah, I do. With the way you reacted today, I get it."

I flinch. She's right. We keep looking through things and pick out several butt plugs, a dildo, and a couple different vibrators. I will make sure my guys at the gate don't open the packages when they arrive. I'll give them the dates and insist they set them aside. I'll be opening those before they come into the house. No one needs to know what I do to pleasure my girlfriend.

"This is an awful lot of stuff, Luca. This is way too extravagant."

"I know you made six-figures, but even at the highest end of that, you still wouldn't earn what I do. I like my house in Queens because it was just me. I hate Manhattan, but I have a penthouse there. I own properties in several other countries. No matter who I date, there's a slim chance that person would make what I do. It's not that I'm being flippant about this or trying to boast. I just want you to understand that you never have to worry that what you want is excessive. I know you're not frivolous, and I know you won't take advantage."

"How can you know that?"

"Because I saw what you picked out at Walmart when you were on the run. First, that's where you went. You also picked things on sale to make sure your money went further. I saw your regret when you threw out Auntie Carlotta's leftovers, when I made you lose your appetite. You didn't enjoy wasting the food."

"You notice a lot of stuff."

"Everything about you interests me, and I'm trying to get to know you better. But I'm excessively observant because I have to be."

"Let's just call it situationally aware. Less negative connotation to keeping you alive."

She strains to kiss my cheek, and I turn my head to snag her lips.

"Thank you, Daddy. Just because you can spend the money doesn't mean you have to or that I'll ask you to. I appreciate the splurge."

"Let's consider these an investment. How about that?"

She giggles, and it's like angels singing. But it dies when my phone rings, and Uncle Salvatore's name pops up. I didn't get to the checkout page, so I'll have to come back to the shopping cart later.

"*Ciao, zio.*" Hello, Uncle.

"*I tuoi fratelli e cugini sono ancora lì?*" Are your brothers and cousins still there?

Good question. Um...

"*Non so.*" I don't know.

"*Come fai a non... non importa. Vai a scoprirlo. Dobbiamo parlare.*" How do you not—never mind. Go find out. We need to talk.

And our little post-coital bubble pops.

"*Ti richiamo tra cinque minuti.*" Let me call you back in five minutes.

"*Non è una conversazione che può ascoltare. Non parleremo sempre in italiano.*" This isn't a conversation she can listen to. We won't always be speaking Italian.

"*Va bene.*" All right.

I hang up and sit up for a second time. This time, I'm not happy about crawling out of bed.

"I need to find out if the others are still here. We need to talk to Uncle Salvatore."

"About what happened today?"

"Probably."

If we won't be speaking Italian the entire time, it's because we'll be speaking English. That means someone outside the family is going to be part of this conversation. Since none of us speaks Russian, English is the only choice.

I hurry to dress, but I grab a pair of athletic pants and a t-shirt from my dresser. I twirl a pair of boxers around my finger before flinging them at Livy.

"Don't you dare put panties back on."

"Or?"

"Daddy will shred them."

She slips off the bed and prowls toward me. Fuck me. She's sexy as hell, and she doesn't even know it. I'm quicker than she realizes. I wrap my arm around her and swing her up to sit on top of the dresser. I nudge her legs apart and drop to one knee.

"Daddy."

It's a breathy moan as I suck on her clit. She grips the edge of the dresser as I attack. I suck and lick before my tongue presses into her cunt. My fingers slide in and rub her g-spot. It's over nearly as fast as it begins.

"Daddy, I need to come."

"Do it. Do it now, little girl."

I keep working her until she moans and whimpers. I stand and wrap my hand around her throat. I don't apply any pressure, but I hold her in place. My tongue goes past her lips as I kiss her brutally. I know she tastes herself.

"Tempt me, and I will take."

"Good."

We stare at each other, and I have never wished to live on a remote island as much as I do right this moment.

"We aren't nearly done, little girl."

"We better not be for at least another sixty years."

My grip tightens, and her head tips back.

"Livy, I will take you seriously if you say things like that. Don't tease me about that. Don't play me for a fool."

"Daddy, today should have made me run in the opposite direction. I'm not staying because I need you to protect me from the Culiacán. I'm staying because you're everything I've fantasized about. You also have your faults, but you're a better man for having them. I'm not going anywhere. Whatever comes, we work it out."

My kiss is desperate as I hold her against me.

"I have to go, little one. I need to call my uncle back once I know if the guys are still downstairs. We have plenty to talk about, but I feel the same way."

I help her off the dresser.

"I hate leaving you here, but I have to take this call without you."

"That's fine. I'll start dinner."

I kiss her cheek once she's dressed, and we're downstairs. I hear the guys in the basement. Of course. They work out to kill time. At least, they're productive time wasters.

"Uncle Sal called. Meet me in my office."

I yell down to them and turn around. I hear the thuds of their heavy footsteps. They can be as silent as church mice when they want. Otherwise, they're fucking water buffalos. Once they're all in my office—I converted the den while we're here—and the door's closed, I call our uncle. I put it on speakerphone in the center of my desk.

I get a few knowing looks as it rings.

"Would you say what you're thinking to some guy dating Maria?"

Marco's head jerks back, and he's the first to respond.

"Ew."

"Then don't say it or think it about Livy."

Lorenzo shrugs.

"Maria's our sister. Livy isn't."

I cock an eyebrow.

It's Carmine's turn to chime in.

"Don't tell us you proposed."

"No. But treat her with the same respect you would your sister or cousin. She may as well be."

She will be.

"Are you all there?"

Uncle Salvatore doesn't bother with Italian since he knows I will have followed his instructions. I answer for everyone.

"Yeah."

"I got an interesting call from Maks an hour ago."

"I'm surprised it took him that long."

"If you knew he'd call, Luca, why didn't you warn me?"

"Because I wasn't thinking about anyone or anything but getting home to Liv."

"He thinks you're holding a woman hostage."

"What?"

I look at the guys. Just what the hell happened that they didn't tell me about?

Lorenzo holds his hand up and gestures for me to take it easy.

"Calm down, Luca. We kept her in the center of the circle and kept the circle tight. Marco had his hand near her lower back. No one manhandled her or looked like they were forcing her to go somewhere she didn't want to."

I shake my head. For fuck's sake.

"Four big ass men surrounding a woman who could pass for a teenager. There was no way she was getting past any of you. No wonder he thinks she's a hostage."

"Sergei knows two of us aren't like that."

Carmine's glare is enough to make Marco raise his chin in challenge.

"Fuck you, Marco."

"I'm not lying. Am I wrong?"

Uncle Salvatore cuts in.

"Enough."

I run my hand over my face.

"What's it going to take to get them to chill out?"

"Call Maks and Sergei."

"Fine. I'm guessing they're together."

"Yes."

I grab my phone and pull up Maks's contact. What a fucked-up life we live when we have our enemies on speed dial.

"Luca."

It's Sergei.

"I'm giving you the abbreviated version because that's all you need to know. You saw my girlfriend today. She's not Italian. She didn't know who you were, and my family has learned from my mistakes."

"Mistakes?"

That's Niko. Hell. I should have known they'd be together.

"Yes, Niko. Mistakes. Piss poor choices. Fuck-ups. Whatever you want to call them. I can honestly say I get it now."

"I don't think you're even fucking close to understanding."

"Niko, she saw Carlos die. They know what she saw."

The other end of the call goes silent. Then there are several disdainful laughs before Niko taunts me.

"And she trusts you to protect her? She's fucked. Send her to us."

So, Misha or Sergei Andreyev or Anton Kutsenko can seduce her or at least try to? Hell no. They're the last bachelors out of the eight-headed hydra that is the bratva leadership.

"My point was, she doesn't know this life yet. Misguided as my brothers and cousin were, they didn't want to have to explain why they couldn't go in the store she pointed out. She's still learning, and they thought I should explain."

"Put her on the phone."

"Maks, you don't give me orders."

"Luca, put her on the motherfucking telephone before I decide she needs rescuing."

"Come near her, and you'll wish you'd gone ahead and killed me."

Niko jumps in again.

"You heard him, Salvatore. I'll put one between his eyes before bed."

"Boys."

"Salvatore, I know you aren't talking to any of us. Wrangle your puppies."

I can picture Maks as he speaks. The man is the cold-hearted Russian spy you see in Cold War movies. Believe it or not, he's mellowed since he got married and became a father. His accent is still thick even though his English is perfect. He was fourteen when his family moved to America. The rest of his family sounds the same. Straight out of a crime thriller. Well, you can fuck off, comrade.

"Stay away from her. She's here because she wants to be."

Sergei must be leaning toward the phone because his voice is suddenly louder than Maks's or Niko's were.

"If you won't let us speak to her, then we'll call Maria. Your little sister is nosey enough to know the last time you shit."

"Stay away from her."

That's not only me answering. Lorenzo, Marco, Carmine, Gabriele, and Uncle Salvatore respond.

Niko can't pass up the opportunity to take yet another jab.

"What? You don't enjoy having your women threatened? Go figure. Since you had so much fun redecorating Ivy for us, maybe we'll stop by Lorenzo's spot tonight. Maria likes happy hour there, doesn't she?"

Some of our guys trashed the place just over a year ago. It was our first introduction to Laura. She's a lawyer and kept the Kutsenkos out of jail that night. Our guys weren't all so lucky.

"Luca?"

It's Anton. He's usually the quietest in the group.

"Put her on a video call with Laura and Anastasia. Let her talk to them. If they believe her, then we do too."

"Fine."

They're the two women in that family least likely to believe anything good about us.

"She does it with none of you breathing down her neck. Have her call from Lorenzo's or Marco's phone. Laura will answer."

Marco hands his over to me, and I give him mine.

"Hold on."

"She makes the call without you."

I grit my teeth and take a breath.

"I figured as much, Anton. Hang on. She's in another room."

I look around and shrug. I hate this, but it's the easiest way to end this bullshit. I head to the kitchen.

"Livy, I need you to make a video call. The bratva thinks you're my hostage. They want you to speak to their leader's wife and Anastasia. This is Marco's phone. I have to go back to my office. They'll expect you to pan the area and prove I'm not there coercing you. I can guarantee the men will listen, but they'll do it where I can't hear you in the background. If anything goes wrong, you come and get me."

"Can't you just wait outside the kitchen?"

"They're probably going to video call me to make sure none of us are near you."

"Leave your office door open, and I'll talk loudly enough for you to hear. Turn the mic off whichever phone you're using, so there's no feedback."

I nod as I dial Niko's number. Laura and Anastasia answer on the first ring. I slip out of the kitchen and back into the office. Sure enough, Lorenzo's holding up his phone for a video call. I can see all the bratva in Maks's office, and they can see all of us. I take the phone for Lorenzo.

"She's in the kitchen."

"We know."

Maks shifts the phone for us to see Laura and Anastasia before they leave the room. I hit the mute button. Everyone on both ends of the call is silent. We must all be straining to listen. Livy's muffled, but I can still hear her from the kitchen.

"I'm Olivia. Nice to meet you."

I hear Laura speak next. She's as much a natural leader as Maks. How that marriage works is beyond me.

"Our cousin said he saw you in a Russian store today."

"Your cousin? I thought he was your husband's cousin."

"In our family, by blood and by marriage are the same thing."

"Oh. That's actually really cool."

"He said you were with Carmine, Gabriele, Marco, and Lorenzo. Why were you at that store?"

Livy pauses, and I know she's trying to decide how to answer.

"I'm not trying to come up with a lie, but I know your husbands don't like Luca, and I know at least most of why. I don't know what I can share and what I can't. I know you want to make sure I'm not a hostage, but I won't say anything that might endanger Luca or his family. I trust them. I don't know you."

It's Anastasia who responds.

"That's smart. No one thinks any of you were spying or anything like that. But why would they take you to a Russian-owned store?"

"Because I asked to go in there, and they didn't feel right explaining why not. They thought Luca should do that since he's my boyfriend. They thought it was harmless. I guess your family doesn't go to the Bronx that often."

"If they thought it was harmless, then why were they walking so close to you? They know Sergei would never hurt you."

"I know that, but I don't know who Sergei might tell outside the bratva. I guess they were thinking the same thing. I don't understand all of this rivalry and enemy stuff yet. But I know there are men who would hurt me, and I know Luca would forgive no one who let me get hurt. So, for everyone's sake, it was a good thing they stuck close to me. I'm not a hostage. I'm with Luca because I want to be."

There's a pause before Livy continues.

"I can tell you don't believe me. Your faces say it all. This isn't some weird thing where the victim falls in love with her captor. Luca and I met in a messed-up situation, but I'm with him because I want to be. I can leave whenever I want. I'm here because I choose to be. I don't know how either of you met your husbands, so maybe you're worried about me because of your own experiences. Or maybe you're just worried because of what happened to you, Anastasia. I can get either of those possibilities. But, however you wound up with the men you married, I believe you chose them. That means you figured out how to live with who they are. You can't fault me for doing the same."

I hear Laura next.

"Have you met Sylvia?"

"Yes."

"I'm going to tell you the same thing she told Heather, who became my sister when she married Aleks, one of Maks's brothers. If anything ever happens, and you can't get to Luca or his family, you come to one of us. When I say that, I mean any of the wives, our husbands, and our family. That includes our parents. Coming to us will not protect the men in Luca's family from the men in ours. That's their business. But if you think you're in danger, our doors are open. You will get the same protection as any of the women in our family have until Luca can come to you."

"Why are you telling me this?"

"Because you're entering a world where you will never know more than a sliver of what's really happening. The business is supposed to stay between the men, but it doesn't. I may not like Luca or anyone in his family, but I respect your choice to be with him. That choice doesn't mean anyone gets to hurt you for it."

"Thank you."

Anastasia speaks up.

"Maks will give Salvatore all of our numbers. *You* put them in *your* phone. Only use the first letter of our first name. Nothing else to identify us. Call if you need us. Any of Luca's drivers know how to get to all of our houses. We all have homes in Sylvia and Salvatore's neighborhood. If anything changes and you need to get away from Luca, we'll protect you."

There's a long pause, then I struggle to hear what Livy says.

"I pray it never comes to that, but I believe you. I have nothing to offer you other than the same thing in exchange. If you ever need anything, whether or not I'm with Luca, I will do what I can. Thank you."

I hear nothing more, so I turn the mic back on and look at Maks, who's holding the phone now.

"I assume you heard all of that, Maks."

"Just like you did."

"Satisfied?"

"Luca?"

Livy calls out to me.

"Yes."

"Do I give this phone back to someone? Or do I stay in the kitchen?"

I glance at Maks before turning toward the office door.

"Come here, *piccolina*."

She's hesitant when she gets to the door. I hold out my free hand. I turn the phone toward her.

"Livy, this is Maksim Kutsenko."

"You didn't lie, Luca. They look exactly the same except for the hair." She squints. "Who's that behind you, Maksim? They don't look like Sergei, but they look exactly like you, too."

Maks doesn't need to check.

"Those are my other cousins, Pasha and Anton. They're from the other side of the family."

She looks around the room at the guys in my family and me.

"There's a lot in this world I've entered that I don't understand. But the genetics in your two families is the most mind-boggling."

Carmine looks enough like my brothers and me to pass for one. Matteo looks a lot like us too, but not as much as Carmine, since we're not related by blood. Gabriele is the only one who doesn't look a lot like us, but he shares the same coloring as us.

Maks and the others in his family laugh, and the guys around me do too.

Her smile drops, though. She takes the phone from my hand and brings it closer. Her tone is totally different now.

"I know why you can't stand Luca, and I know he deserves it. I choose to believe you were all being good Samaritans today. Do not try to get between Luca and me again. I won't give you the benefit of the doubt twice. Fool me once, shame on you. Fool me twice, and I won't forgive you."

She stares at Maks and doesn't blink. She's in a battle of wills with a man who makes the devil look like a pussycat. Who is this woman?

Chapter Sixteen

Livy

The call ends, and I look at everyone in the room. I hear a noise on a phone on the center of the desk and realize there's another call still going. I almost jump when I hear Salvatore's voice.

"I wish I could have seen Maks's face."

"I appreciate the women's offer of help if I ever need it. Maybe they insisted upon talking to me, but how would they know I exist if not for their husbands? I don't appreciate being manipulated, and that's what Maks and his family did. They used me to get to your family. Apparently, I can be grateful and unreasonably pissed at the same time."

Salvatore's voice comes through the speaker again.

"Sylvia had a sister who was attacked, assaulted, and killed because of the family she was from and the one she married into. She was pregnant. She got separated from her guards, and she ran. She passed families where she could have begged for help, but she knew they wouldn't open their doors to her. She and her baby died because of that. It's Sylvia's rule that all women and children have shelter in our home. I agree with her, though she'd do it even if I didn't. She explained that to Heather, Aleks's wife, a few months ago. It seems the Kutsenko women are of the same mind. You can trust them, Olivia. They're the only ones you can trust."

I'm watching Luca as Salvatore speaks. I feel the sadness in the room as much as I hear it in Salvatore's voice. Luca's nodding as his uncle speaks. Part of me wants to know the full story of what happened to Sylvia's sister, but I would never ask, and I know it's probably better not to hear it. Then again, maybe I need to understand the full extent of the danger I'm facing. I don't know.

Luca's observing me just as intently as I am him. I can tell the longer I say nothing and don't move, the more apprehensive he's becoming. It makes me really stop and think about how this must be for him. I've had boyfriends since college, but he has dated no one in years. He's let no one into his life like he has with me. He has a damn good reason not to. He's out of his depths on how to be a regular boyfriend, and then he's trying to navigate bringing a woman into the Mafia. Stressful doesn't even touch how this must be for him. The situation has mired me in my own fears and doubts. I haven't considered his position nearly enough.

I open my arms to him. I offer the comfort this time. He steps forward, and I pull him close. I make sure my body is entirely relaxed against his, but I hug him tightly. I feel the tension ease from him as I run my hand up and down his back. I lean away so I can see his face. I don't make a sound as I mouth the one word that finally washes the fear from his eyes.

"Daddy."

"Olivia."

And the moment shatters. I almost forgot Salvatore was on the phone.

"I admire your pluck. Most men wouldn't stare down Maks. You fit in well with our family."

I turn my head toward the phone. Does that mean I just got the don's blessing?

"Thank you. I am not timid by nature."

"Good. This world will eat you alive if you are."

In the spirit of not being as mousy as I think they believe I am, I push on.

"I may have met Luca because I was in the wrong place at the wrong time, and that's made me depend on him. But I am skeptical and untrusting by nature. The fact that I haven't run says a lot about the faith I'm putting in your family. I've watched people die and have people who want me to die. That's scary. But I am not easily intimidated. By anyone."

I'm looking at the phone while everyone else is looking at me. I raise my eyes and meet each man's gaze, Luca's last. I don't think it was Laura's and Anastasia's offer to help me that pulled me out of my haze. It was Maks and his men, using me to get to Luca and his family. They might genuinely want to protect me, but they also didn't pass up an opportunity to have a go at the Mancinellis. They can do that at someone else's expense.

Salvatore has been gracious to me, but I know he's also suspicious. It makes sense, but so am I.

"We will keep that in mind, Ms. D'Amato."

Now we're back to formality when he called me Olivia a few minutes ago. Fine. He doesn't sound disapproving. Just the opposite. That's the warmest he's sounded to me yet. I'm still watching Luca, and he nods. He doesn't shift his attention when he speaks.

"Uncle Salvatore, is there anything else?"

"Not right now. I will see you in the morning. *Ciao*."

"*Ciao*."

Six voices respond before Carmine hands the phone to Luca. He slips it back into his pocket as I look around again.

"I didn't get past peeling a few cucumbers for a salad. I'll finish making dinner. Are all of you staying? Would you like to join us?"

Five sets of eyes turn to Luca, and five broad grins spread across their handsome faces. It's Lorenzo who answers.

"Sure."

Luca's left eye narrows.

"We don't have enough food in the house for all of you."

Marco laughs.

"We took Olivia grocery shopping today. You have plenty of food."

"Leave."

His brothers, cousin, and associate—whatever Gabriele is if he's not a friend—laugh, but they file out the door. I whisper up to him.

"Luca, they can stay. I'd like to make dinner to say thanks for today."

"And I'd like you naked and sitting on my dick while I feed you dinner."

My mouth falls open before I whip my head around to make sure no one heard him. If they did, they're pretending not to. Luca leans forward to whisper in my ear.

"The moment I'm not worried you'll scald yourself cooking, your clothes are coming off. Your pussy is my appetizer."

"Is sex all you think about?"

"That's your fault."

"What did I do to make you think of sex right now?"

"Besides breathing, you stood up to Maks and my uncle. That's fucking hot as hell. I'll meet you in the kitchen as soon as I get rid of the idiots laughing at me."

I turn back toward the door and see all five guys still chuckling. They know Luca's in a better mood than he was, so they're having a little fun at his expense. I don't doubt he's going to have something to say to them tomorrow, but for now, he's at ease.

"Bye, guys."

I wave as I walk past and head back to the kitchen.

"Be downstairs at six tomorrow. We'll talk then."

That was not a friendly invitation. I suspect none of them will enjoy their workout.

We're soon working together to make dinner, and it feels completely natural as we move past each other to get what we need. He offers to grill the steaks I got, which I appreciate because it's turned frigid after a few weeks of pleasant weather. While I finish making the salad and cooking the vegetables, he cleans up as we go along. It means the island is completely clear once we set the table.

Before I can complain the food will get cold, he's pulling my clothes off. He has no trouble lifting me onto the island, which means I have no chance to refuse. But we both know I won't. His index finger and thumb on his left hand pinch my clit, while he does the same to my left nipple. He squeezes until I squirm.

"Lie back, Livy."

"Yes, Daddy."

"Fuck, *piccolina*. I like how that sounds better each time you say it."

"Does it make you hard?"

"You know it does."

"Does it make you want to fuck me, Daddy?"

My smile drops as I moan. He answers me with his tongue thrusting into my pussy. He flicks it several times before he pulls back a couple of inches.

"Pinch your nipples. Now."

I'm quick to obey. I roll them between my fingers, then pinch and twist. With his fingers still tight around my clit, I'm discovering how the clamps we plan to order will probably feel. His now free hand pushes my legs wider. Then his fingers are stroking my g spot. His pinky is pressing against my backdoor.

"Daddy, may I come?"

I haven't really asked in the past. But I like how it deepens this dynamic we have.

"Not yet, little one. I'll tell you when *I* decide we're done. I'm starving, and I haven't nearly finished my first course."

He drops his head back to my pussy. His tongue should be a fucking national treasure. The way he uses it makes feeling him go down on me totally different from any of the guys in my past. It was like they were fumbling around in the dark compared to him. Every touch, every slow pause, every minute of unpredictability heightens my need. I squirm, trying to slow my need to come.

"Please."

I'm begging.

"Please, what?"

"Please let me come, Daddy."

I think he can tell I'm sliding past arousal to desperation and frustration.

"Come, little one."

He lets me rock my hips before he rubs my clit. The sensation rushes back into it as he hits just the spot I need.

"I'm coming. Fuck. I'm coming."

My body goes lax as the euphoria wanes. It's not super sexy, but Luca's quick to wash his hands before he strips. Holy hell. I think he might be harder than I've ever seen him. How is that even possible? He lifts me off the island and thrusts into me.

"Let's have dinner."

Dinner? Food is the last thing I'm thinking about right now. Each step he takes to the table rubs my sensitive clit against his pubic bone. He sits, then guides my hips to rock on him as he reaches past me to snare a bite of salad. He brings it to my mouth before snagging one for himself. We go back and forth as he feeds me one bite, then feeds himself the next. We laugh as it gets a bit awkward for him to cut the steak. I grab a fork while he chews. Now we feed each other.

"Daddy, I need to come again."

The ache's been a slow burn throughout the meal, but I'm on edge now. I grind against him, and he groans.

"Come whenever you want, *cuore.*"

Sweetheart. He hasn't called me that since the first time he said it.

"Are you close, *caro?*"

"I've been close since before the guys left."

"I want to make you come."

"You will."

We're nearly finished eating, so we soon forget the last few bites as we move together. I brace myself with my hands on his shoulders while his roam all over me. As I feel my orgasm rip through me, I suck his tongue. I do a Kegel, and I feel his breath hitch. He lifts me off, and I'm quick to stroke him until his cum coats my lower belly. We look down between us for a moment before I fall forward for another kiss.

"A week, and then I'm filling you with my cum, just like you said. When it drips down your thigh, you'll remember your pussy and everything else belongs to me."

"Yes, Daddy."

If anyone else said something so insanely possessive, I'd be saying peace out. A lot of it is just hot, dirty talk, but there's just enough sliver of truth for me to feel safe once more after a shit-tastic day of being terrified again. He knows that, and he gets what I need. He holds me pressed against him, and I close my eyes. They remain that way as he carries me upstairs and into the bathroom. He doesn't put me down until we're in the shower. He's about to turn off the water when I stroke him until he's spinning me around and trapping me against the wall.

"I told you if you tease me, you better be ready for me to take what you offer. Tonight's just your pussy. Soon it'll be all of you."

He drops to one knee and spreads my ass cheeks. His tongue glides over my pussy and up to my asshole. He gives it a quick flick before licking my clit. His thumb presses against the puckered skin until the tip slips in.

"Luca?"

"Have you been fucked back here before?"

"Yes."

"Did you enjoy it?"

"It was okay. Not a favorite."

"We put several butt plugs in the shopping cart. We still need to check out on the site. Are you all right with trying them?"

"Of course. I wouldn't have agreed to them if I wasn't."

He stands and presses his body against mine again. I angle my hips, and he slides into me.

"I look forward to seeing any of those plugs in you, knowing it's getting this fine ass ready for me to fuck."

"Do we have to wait until they come, Daddy?"

"Livy, I'm not a small man. I don't want to hurt you. I'd rather wait until you've had a plug in for a while and are ready for me."

I look over my shoulder.

"Luca, I get how important my well-being is to you, but your need to protect me can't always negate what I know I'm capable of doing. I've never worn a plug before, but I've had anal before. I want this with you tonight."

"That's fair."

He sounds very hesitant. I let it go for now as I press my hips back.

"Daddy, please."

He moves inside me, and we're both panting soon. As I get closer, I beg to come. He rubs my clit and pushes me into my orgasm. I clench around him.

"Livy, I'm close. I have to pull out."

"Use your cum to lube me."

That surprises him. I know it does because he hesitates. Then he withdraws, spreads my ass cheeks, presses the tip into my backdoor. I feel his cum shoot into me, then he eases into me. He's so careful, and I'm so impatient. I thrust my hips back, taking him. His hand slams down on my ass.

"You are not in control, *piccolina*."

"I'm sorry, Daddy."

"You will be."

His hands alternate sides as he spanks me. We're both still turned on despite just coming. It keeps him hard as he rocks his cock inside me.

"Now you are truly mine, Livy. All of you is mine to pleasure. Your orgasms are mine to give and take. There's no part of you I haven't had."

"And there's nowhere I haven't taken you. You're all mine, Daddy."

"Yes, I am, Livy. I'll never let go."

"Don't you dare."

I'm so close to confessing how I feel. There's a heavy pause, and I wonder if he's thinking the same thing. He kisses my neck as he wraps an arm around my middle. The heel of his other palm rubs my clit until I scream and tremble. I feel him come again.

"*Cuore*, I'm going to try harder to be the man you deserve."

"Daddy, you are exactly the man I deserve. I don't want you to change."

"I hope you always think that."

I hope I do too.

Luca slips out of bed as I wake from my sex-induced coma. I could barely keep my eyes open after our shower sex. I know Luca slipped downstairs to clean up the kitchen a little and turn off the lights. He wasn't gone long. I was the one who started our next round. I straddled him and guided his cock into me, but the moment I slid all the way down, he took control. The complete abandonment I can enjoy when we're together is its own type of euphoria. I don't have to think about anything but the pleasure I receive and what I want to give in return.

I sleep peacefully when I'm next to Luca, which I obviously didn't do the second night in the room at the other end of the hallway. I'm in some altered state of being while we're fucking, and dare I say it? Making love sometimes. Sleep and sex. Those are the only times of the day when my situation isn't wreaking havoc on my emotions. I know we're not in a Dom/sub relationship, but I submit, and I know that. I like it. I need it, even.

That give and take between us satisfies needs in us I don't think either of us realized. I believe Luca when he says that what we're building differs from his previous experiences. It sure as shit differs from anything I've ever had. None of my past relationships lasted because it always felt like something was missing. Not that I stopped getting along with the guy or that we were incompatible. It just felt like a void that's been growing with each year. Luca fills that gaping hole.

"Are you going downstairs to work out?"

"Yeah. The guys'll be here in a few minutes."

I look at the clock on his side of the bed. 5:50. Such an ungodly hour, but it's actually twenty minutes later than when I usually get up.

"Are they always on time?"

"They know they better fucking be today."

I sit up and inch across the bed to kneel in front of him. I rest my hands on his bare hips.

"I don't think you slept as well as I did. You're fired up already."

"I slept."

I wait for him to say more, but he doesn't. Instead, he slides his hand between my legs. He wakes up hard every morning, but for the month when we weren't doing more than kissing, we both ignored it. Now I wish we'd woken up earlier. But he's trying to distract me.

"Daddy, are you angry all over again?"

"You know how you told me about those nightmares you had the second night you were here? I had some similar to those."

He cups my nape and brushes a soft kiss against my lips as his fingers dip inside me. My hips press forward of their own volition.

"I need you, Livy."

There's a hint of desperation in his voice that I'm not used to. He's usually so unwaveringly certain about everything that the few times I hear this doubt, it shakes me. He sits beside me, and I straddle him like I did last night. But this time, he holds me against him. Kneeling, I'm tall enough for him to rest his head against my chest.

"Daddy, did those nightmares really upset you that much?"

"Yes."

I guide one of his hands to grip my ass while I guide the other to hold my breast to his mouth. He latches on as I ride him. My sole purpose is to get him off. I don't even care if I don't come. I want to take care of him right now. It's disconcerting to see him this vulnerable. Last night, he was clearly upset. He was angry and stressed out. He was fearful for me. But he never seemed vulnerable like this.

I lower my head to whisper to him.

"I would take a week's worth of birth control pills today if it meant you could come inside me. You need to feel me like this, feel us connect like this as much as I do. Daddy, let me take care of you sometimes. I want to."

"Oh, Livy."

It's a reverent whisper before he goes back to sucking my nipple.

"Daddy, do you need us to keep going slowly? Or do you need to be rough?"

"I don't know, *piccolina*. I just need you so badly."

"I'm not going anywhere. Remember, we said we'd figure out whatever comes together. No one is going to take me from you either. You won't let them. I'm not scared anymore, Luca."

And I'm not. I just realized it as I say it aloud. I'm really not. I'm not suddenly foolishly thinking I'm untouchable or immortal. I still have a healthy fear of death, and I'll always worry about Luca when he leaves the house. But I'm not the scared woman I have been since I met him. I hate seeing him like this, but I know he's like this because he fears failure. He'll do anything to make sure nothing happens to me. That gives me confidence I didn't have before. Confidence that I can survive the Culiacán. Confidence that I can have a future with him.

A future. Part of me still thinks I'm completely fucking bananas to consider that with a guy in the Mafia, a guy I barely know. But the concept of soulmates wouldn't exist if there weren't truth to it. The idea of love at first sight wouldn't exist if there weren't truth to it. I'm done having these conversations with myself. I'm drawing a line in the sand in my mind. Unless something happens otherwise, my future is with Luca. There. I said it. It's done.

"Little girl, I'm close. Hop off."

I lift myself off and like last night, Luca comes across my belly.

"Luca—Daddy—I'm not letting go."

My thumb runs over his scar on his left cheek.

"You know, you're the only person I ever let touch it."

"Why do you?"

"Because there's no part of me I want to keep from you. Unfortunately, that's impossible. There are so many parts of my life I'll hide. I don't want to hide the scar. It seems so insignificant between us, considering everything else. And you always sigh when you touch it. It's not pity. It's like it comforts you."

"It does. Your mom didn't tell me how you got it except for something to do with Matteo's older brother. I'd like to know, but I'm not asking you. And I won't ask anyone else. But when I feel it, I know it's you I'm with. It's already familiar to me, and I can never doubt it's you. I've never been into the bad boy type before, but holy fuck. You make it so hot. Even without a scar, you radiate masculinity. With it—I don't know. I guess anyone who could withstand the injury that gave you this scar must be tough as hell. That's sexy as fuck to me."

"Little girl, we may never leave this bed. Kiss me."

Chapter Seventeen

Luca

It took extreme willpower to leave Livy with just that last kiss. I heard the guys arrive fifteen minutes ago. Let them wait for me. I'm in basketball shorts and a t-shirt. As I make my way to the basement gym, I have socks and sneakers on. I own this home, but it's a place we've used as a safe house several times. Various people have stayed here, so I invested in equipment.

I have weight machines, free weights, a treadmill, a high-end spin cycle, and a rower. We all have spaces like this in our places, but usually only my brothers and Matteo come over to work out with me. Carmine and Gabriele usually aren't welcome. I'm only making an exception today because I have to deal with yesterday.

"I need to be able to trust all of you with Livy. I can't be with her around the clock. It's not practical, and it wouldn't be good for us. But I can't leave her with guys I can't depend on to not put her in situations like yesterday. I get you didn't mean any harm, but what if it were some other bratva member not in

235

Maks's family? Can we truly say they wouldn't do something and then hope for Maks's forgiveness? I can't take those kinds of risks with her. I'm pissed and hurt that you did."

I dive straight in. After grabbing the wrist wraps and winding them over my hands, I walk over to the boxing speed bag in the corner. I was in a lot of underground bare-knuckle fights when I was a teenager and in college. It's money from my wins that paid for most of grad school.

It surprises me when Gabriele walks over to me. He's not hiding behind Carmine for once. Not that the lumbering ape could hide despite Carmine being as big as me.

"We know we fucked up. But none of us has had a girl-friend since at least college. I know I haven't really been serious about anyone since I was a senior in high school. This is unfa-miliar territory for us, too. We thought we had control of the situation, and we thought we were keeping it from being a big deal. We don't know what you've told her, so we figured it was better that you do the explaining the way you want. Luca, if we'd said no, she would have asked questions. She might have been satisfied with us saying nothing, but I doubt it. Did you want us to be the ones who laid it all out for her?"

"That might have been your reasoning, but you still made a shit decision. How about next time you just say, 'no, Luca will explain later,' and leave it at that? She knows enough to accept that. She knew that much yesterday. Considering how we met and why she started staying here, I'm pretty fucking sure she would have been fine with that."

I look at Lorenzo and Marco, who are at the flat bench. Lorenzo was spotting Marco while he bench pressed. I expect the most from them. They're my brothers. Matteo's a *capo* and has been as long as Lorenzo and Marco. Carmine finally got promoted to that, even though I disagreed with Uncle Salvatore's decision.

Even though all four of them hold the same rank, I hold Lorenzo and Marco to a higher standard because we share the exact same blood. I know they feel that way about me, even Marco, who's as close to Matteo as he could be as best friends. I already trust them with my life, and one day, I'll trust them to lead beside me. Until yesterday, that was enough. It's not anymore.

Marco wipes his forearm across his forehead as he speaks.

"Look. None of us disagree with you that we majorly fucked up. But Gabriele's right. All of this is new for us. We protect Maria, our moms, and our aunts. But they know this life, and they aren't women one of us loves. Don't bother denying that. I know you're about to. Mama and Papa fell for each other almost right away, so did Uncle Sal and Aunt Sylvia, and Auntie Carlotta and Uncle Domenico were the same. It runs in the family."

No one mentions Carmine's parents. My aunt Paola had an "indiscretion" as they would say. She got pregnant with Carmine when she was nineteen and unmarried. Uncle Salvatore wasn't the don yet, but he was the underboss. He did everything he could to keep the old leadership from forcing Auntie Paola to marry Carmine's dad. Cesare Ciccone isn't a bad guy, but he and Auntie Paola are oil and water. They weren't that serious when Auntie Paola got pregnant, and they never would have gotten married if they hadn't been pushed into it.

Bitter doesn't even begin to describe them. They didn't actually get married until after Carmine was born. Auntie Paola agreed to name Uncle Cesare as Carmine's father on the birth certificate, so there was no need for an Acknowledgement of Paternity. But it meant she could ensure his last name was Mancinelli, not Ciccone. They didn't give Cesare any choice. It was concede to that and marry Auntie Paola or die. My grand-father was unbending.

Having the Mancinelli last name might be a blessing for Carmine when he's dealing with people outside the *Cosa Nostra*, but the old school members have never forgiven him for being illegitimate. As though he had a choice. It made him the black sheep of the family from the day he entered the world. He lived up to it for years.

People's expectations were so low that he figured there was little point to being anything other than what they assumed. At least, that's what most people thought. He accepted being Uncle Salvatore's lackey and everyone's whipping boy. He played it off as though he were too dumb or too spoiled to care or know better. All the while...The smug bastard manipulated everyone. Me included. I just knew it while others didn't.

"I don't know how I feel yet, but I expect you to keep her alive long enough for me to figure it out. We are nothing if we can't trust each other."

I look at Carmine and Gabriele.

"This was the one thing I thought I could rely on you for."

"You know what? Fuck you. Let them deal with your girlfriend."

Carmine juts his chin toward Lorenzo, Marco, and Matteo.

"She's not my problem. You don't think I'm good enough to guard her, Cousin, find someone else who will. I don't give a fuck what happens to her. Gabe and I are good at what we do. Let someone else take our place, but don't cry to us when someone rapes her and leaves her ass on a corner."

A sound at the top of the stairs makes us all turn.

"Livy!"

I whirl toward Carmine and draw back my fist.

"Luca, no!"

I hear her feet clatter down the wood steps. She jumps

down the last three and runs toward me. She yanks on my forearm and steps between Carmine and me.

"Move, Livy."

"No. Put your hand down, Luca. Now. I mean it."

She pushes against my chest, and I take a step back as I lower my fist. She spins around and steps up to Carmine, who's a foot taller than her.

"You're fucking lucky I stopped him, and you're even luckier I have the restraint not to knee you in the junk. Fuck you. You want to be pissy at your cousin because you're butt hurt that he's pissed you put me in danger, fine. Don't use me to take it out on him. I kept questioning why people think you're so bad when you've been so nice to me. Now I get it. You are an asshole. If you couldn't care less if I get raped and murdered, then I don't want you anywhere near me. Next time, I won't stop him."

She glares at him, and her anger pulses from her. It's the same defiance she showed Maks yesterday. I knew she was tough the night we met. Then I underestimated her when she agreed to my protection. I guess I equated her acceptance of my help to weakness and an inability to stand up for herself. She needs me to protect her from guns and knives. She doesn't need to be sheltered. I get the difference now.

She spins in the other direction and looks at the other guys before she looks back at Carmine.

"I'm here now. If guarding me is going to cause a rift among you, then I'll stay here at the house. I can accept that. We all know Luca won't let me go anywhere without at least one of you because he trusts you more than anyone else. You wouldn't have been with me yesterday if he didn't. If you can't live up to that trust or I'm too much of an inconvenience, then just say so now. None of us need you knocking each other's teeth out or breaking noses. *I'll* relieve you of guarding me."

"Ms. D'Amato—"

Carmine starts, but his head jerks back when Olivia rolls her eyes at him.

"Olivia, I said that shit because *I was* being pissy. I would never want either of those things to happen to you. You know I never would have said it if I knew you could hear. That doesn't make it okay, but I wouldn't have. I didn't mean it. I'm sorry."

I snort.

"Now you know how to apologize. Who knew it would take my girlfriend to make your balls drop?"

Carmine's eyes narrow, and his lips thin. I smirk.

"Luca, you're not helping."

Livy puts her hand on my folded forearms and presses against them.

"Whether it's me personally or you just don't want to be stuck protecting someone who isn't family doesn't matter to me. Tell Luca now whether you'll accept being on my detail or not. Luca, you respect their decision. You don't give them shit or hold it against them. I want them to choose."

"There are no choices, Livy. That's not how this works."

"It is now that I'm in the middle of it. You will not force your family to do something just to accommodate me. And you will not hold it against any of them if they don't want to help. I'm serious, Luca. I will not be in the middle of this, so later everyone can blame me for wrecking your family. I've been blamed for that since before my birth. I'm not dealing with that bullshit again. So, decide."

What the hell does that mean? That's the most she's ever alluded to about her family. Is it a situation like Carmine's? Do her parents blame her for her birth? No. She's close to her mom. But she said she hasn't dealt with her dad since she turned eighteen. Does he blame her for being born?

Matteo, ever the shit disturber, grins.

"Are you always this feisty?"

"Feisty? I'm not a fucking horse that needs breaking."

Matteo smiles even wider, as if she proved his point.

"I'll guard you if you'll marry Luca right now. I'll gladly watch you put him in his place every day for the next sixty years."

Livy notches up her chin, but I see the amusement in her eyes.

"Go figure you're still single."

"You wound me, *ragazza*."

She looks over at me, but it's Matteo who explains.

"It's like *chica* in Spanish. It literally translates to girl."

"Do any of you speak Spanish?"

I slide my hand onto her waist as I step closer.

"We all do."

"*Que te la pique un pollo.*" I hope a chicken pecks your dick.

She tells my friend to fuck off with the politest smile. The tension eases when Matteo laughs so hard he chokes. Then everyone gives him a hard time. She got her point across, and she lightened the mood. I lean down to whisper in her ear.

"Little girls don't give their daddies orders. Your ass is mine when we get upstairs."

She turns toward me, and I wrap both arms around her as I continue to whisper.

"But thank you for stopping me from beating the shit out of my cousin."

"They won't be mad that I got in the middle?"

"No. Just promise me if you ever leave me, you don't wind up with one of them. They've all fallen in love with you."

I'm only half joking.

She goes up on her toes and puts her lips against my ear.

"None of them are good enough to replace my daddy."

I don't care who's watching. As I kiss her, I lift her off her feet and guide her legs around my waist. I'm walking toward the stairs as I thrust my tongue into her mouth. She sucks on it lightly, and I can't help but groan. When I reach the bottom of the stairs, I stop.

"Be ready in ten minutes. I'm taking my girlfriend out to breakfast."

I look back at Carmine and Gabriele and cock an eyebrow. They both raise their chins, and I nod. Just like that, we're back to homeostasis. I don't like them, and they don't like me. But we trust each other about keeping Livy safe.

Our food's just arrived at the little hole in the wall diner in Little Italy near my Bronx rental house. Livy looks around the table as we all lean back and groan. We pull out our phones and read the group text.

> **PAPA**
>
> Maks's men intercepted a shipment last night. Sal says it was while you were all on a call with him. He distracted you. Lorenzo and Carmine were supposed to be at the docks, not listening to Maks and Sergei hand you your asses.

I look up to see how the others are taking my dad's message. None of us are going to point out that Uncle Salvatore was distracted, too. Fucking bratva bastards. How'd they even fucking know about that shipment? We didn't know it was coming in until I was driving back from Atlantic City. A storm at sea helped get the boat filled with counterfeit jewelry here early. There's a million dollars' worth of product—that is at black market retail price, not its actual value. The shit's only worth a few grand in raw materials.

ME

The garage?

Yes. Now.

I look at the guys at the table. Fucking hell. I'd hoped to avoid this conversation for a few more weeks. But I honestly knew better. This is unavoidable.

"Livy, we have to take this to go."

"What happened? Is everything okay?"

"It will be in a little while. I'll explain what I can when we're in the car."

I look at Matteo, and he nods. My dad and uncle will expect the others to go with me. With only one family member with her, Livy won't leave the house. I signal the waiter, and we get carry out boxes. Livy only has one, but the rest of us each have three. Our fucking pancakes are going to be soggy shit by the time we get to them. But, since we don't know when we'll get to eat again, we'll survive.

Gabriele drove this morning, so we pile into the SUV. Livy sits between Lorenzo and me. Once we're on the road, I glance around the vehicle before I settle my attention on Livy. While the others pretend not to pay attention, I know they're listening to every word. I have to be delicate in what I say. I have to tell my girlfriend just enough for her to understand without her knowing much.

"We have an issue at work. A problem came up we need to take care of. I might be home for dinner, or it might be a couple days. I won't have my phone on, so I won't be getting calls or texts. Matteo is going to stay at the house with you. If anything happens, someone will get in touch with him. If I'm going to be away more than two days, I want you to stay with my parents."

"Where are you going? Why would you be away for a few days without your phone on?"

"I don't think I can tell you more than that. I need to think about what's safe for you to know."

"This is Mafia business, not your legal stuff."

"*Cosa Nostra.*"

This is the first time I've corrected her.

"What's that?"

"We're the *Cosa Nostra*. Only people outside us call us the Mafia. It means 'our thing.' It's specific to Sicilians."

Livy nods as she considers what I'm saying. She sighs but remains quiet. I suppose she's waiting for me to say more, but what can I say? I want to ignore the questions she asked, but she stares at me intently.

"Our issues are with some rivals. They got involved where they shouldn't have. We need to figure out the extent of the issue and deal with it."

She darts her gaze to the front seats, where Carmine sits next to Gabriele. Her lips twist from side to side before she nods.

"With only Matteo guarding you, I need you to stay at the house. I'd feel much better if you'd stay inside."

Her eyes widen, but she says nothing. I take her hand and entwine our fingers before I rest our hands on my thigh. We ride like that until we get to the house. I'm tempted to say goodbye with a quick kiss while standing in the driveway, so I don't keep the others waiting. But a couple of them nod as I help Livy out of the car. Matteo climbs out of the third row and follows us into the house. I steer her into my office.

"*Piccolina*, I'm sorry this is happening."

"It's something I'm going to have to get used to, isn't it?"

"Yes. Like I said, if I'm going to be gone for more than two days, I want you to go to my parents. It means something's gone wrong, and it's a bigger situation than we planned for. If anything happens and somehow you get separated from Matteo, you go to my parents or Uncle Salvatore and Aunt Sylvia."

"If I get separated from Matteo? You said I have to stay here. How—"

"If you have to run, Livy. If something happens to Matteo, and you have to run, you go to them."

"Luca..."

She's shaking her head and trying to back away from me.

"I can't stay and explain more. I'm sorry, but I have to go. This has to come before us. It's my duty."

"What if I can't get to your family? Do I go to the bratva?"

My expression hardens, and that only makes her eyes widen further.

"Whatever this is, is because of them."

I don't answer. I just continue to stare at her. She nods and wraps her arms around me.

"Please, just be careful, Luca. I don't want anything to happen to you. I'm not ready to let go of a future with you."

"Do you really mean that, little girl?"

"Yes, Daddy. I didn't say it last night, but I decided. I'm committed to us. Not just right now, but for good."

"Livy, I wish I could stay. Nothing should go wrong. I'm going to a controlled place where my family and I are in charge."

"Luca—"

I see it in her eyes. It's not the right time for either of us to say it.

"I know, *cuore*. Me too."

Tears well in her eyes before I kiss her. What she doesn't

know is that word can mean more than just sweetheart. It can mean heart.

I pull away from her, and we walk back into the foyer.

"I'll see you later."

I lean down and kiss her cheek.

"Bye, Daddy."

Why does that sound so final?

"We have a problem."

I state what no one wants to hear. I'm in the garage's office with Uncle Salvatore and my dad. It's a location that isn't on any city maps, and the neighborhood conveniently forgets it exists. It's convenient for them because they get paid well each month to ignore us. This is where we come when we need to dispose of complications. It sits on land that backs up to the East River. We can see Manhattan from the office window.

I say what's been on my mind since my dad's text came in.

"How did Maks know about the shipment? I'm certain someone told him to look out for it. How else would he have known which ship to board?"

My dad looks toward the bays where we have four bratva members strung up attached to the garage door opener. The clatter of the doors when they open and close muffles the screams while the men feel like their arms are being ripped from their shoulders as they dangle from the machines. He's still watching them as he speaks.

"You think we have a leak?"

"Yes. I think some of their concern about Livy was legit. But why did they wait several hours to contact us?"

Uncle Salvatore grunts before he points to some of our men.

"Any idea who?"

I shake my head.

"Barely anyone outside our family knew this shipment was coming. Even if, somehow, Maks and the others heard a ship was on the way, how did they know it would dock early? How did they know it was coming into Philly and not here?"

We know no one in our immediate family would ever betray us. So, who overheard something, spied somewhere, or bribed someone to get this information? We have people on our payroll at the New York and Philadelphia ports. Was it one of them? I'd rather believe that than someone closer to us.

The *Cosa Nostra* is like any other Italian Mafia organization. We have a hierarchy. It's actually pretty similar to the bratva. The cartels also have chains of command. It's only the Irish who are a loose fucking mess. That's why they're a constant shit stain. We have a don; the bratvas have a *pakhan*; and the cartels have a *jefe*. What do the Irish have? A fucking skipper. That's not even a term that's really used.

My family are all Made Men. The only way to become a Made Man is to be a Sicilian or Italian. Once you are one, you're essentially untouchable unless the don or underboss gives permission for your death. My brothers, my cousin, and Matteo are all capos—*Caporegime* or *Capodecina*—captains. They're Uncle Salvatore's right-hand men as much as I am. I deal with things that the don isn't available to. In my family, our *capos* report to me as often as they do Uncle Salvatore.

They lead our *soldati*, or soldiers, and assign them to various operations. My guess is it's a *soldati* who squealed. They're among the lowest ranked Made Men. Whoever this is, better believe Uncle Salvatore and I will give that permission.

I seriously doubt it was an associate—a non-Sicilian or non-Italian allowed to join our ranks. It's the third lowest rank in the Mafia, and they aren't Made Men, so for a betrayal like this, they guaranteed their death with no permission needed.

Uncle Salvatore continues to look out of the office's double-sided window into the garage bays where Gabriele is taking a tire iron to a guy's ribs. We've strung these men up for twenty hours, but they're Russian. They'll last longer than that.

"Give Gabriele another hour with them. If they don't talk after having almost every bone crushed, then we waterboard them."

Gabriele has always followed Carmine's lead, which usually means he went as astray as my cousin. But he's an excellent interrogator. He's technically a Made Man too, but being outside of the don's family and his shit choices have always kept him from rising to being a *capo*. Being an enforcer technically puts him at the bottom of the barrel with guys who aren't Made Men.

However, he's more patient than most for extracting information. He's also stronger than any other guy I know, and there's not a weak one in our bunch. One punch from him can break the strongest bones in a man's body. As a result, he's remained an enforcer. Normally, that position is even lower than an associate, a non-Sicilian or non-Italian. Uncle Salvatore has made an exception and elevated his role to just below a *capo*—a no-man's-land of his own. Everyone knows seeing Gabriele means an excruciating death for their crimes.

I took him with me the night I met up with Carlos because Gabriele is not trigger-happy during those types of meetings. He's unlikely to escalate a business situation, and his size intimidates without him doing anything. If Carlos hadn't gone after Livy, but he'd caused any other trouble, Gabriele would have ensured the Culiacán representative understood he didn't lead the negotiations. If only he had that patience with street fights and low-level hustles. He throws punches, then asks questions. Hence why he isn't a *capo*.

Uncle Salvatore and Papa look as much alike as I do my brothers. My mom's genes didn't get a whole lot of say in our appearances, but I think they got the stronger say in Lorenzo's personality. Marco and I are somewhere between our parents, but Lorenzo is more of an observer and is the slowest to anger. But when he gets there—holy fuck, watch the fuck out. Fucking forget a cat five tornado. You'd rather stand outside naked during one of those than face my baby brother. He'll handle the waterboarding. My dad looks at his older brother before he shares his reservations.

"They're more likely to survive Gabriele and Lorenzo than anyone else could. The bratva don't break. Be done with them. We need to focus our attention inward to make progress searching within our own ranks. We—"

We all freeze when the garage's front door swings open. Uncle Domenico and Uncle Cesare are running toward the office. Something is very wrong. The look on Uncle Domenico's face tells me everything. I burst out of the office and run to meet the two older men.

"What happened to Matteo and Livy?"

"They're safe, but you need to come to your parents' house. Olivia's all right, but Matteo's hurt."

"What the hell happened? If Matteo's hurt, how is Liv safe?"

I look between them, impatient to understand what happened. My dad hands me my suit coat as Uncle Cesare explains.

"Paola feels badly that she hasn't met Olivia yet, but she's getting over the flu. She called me and asked me to run a plate of desserts over to your house."

Technically, Uncle Cesare and Auntie Paola are still

married since we're Catholic. But they haven't lived together in ten years, not since Carmine left for college. Everyone turns a blind eye to what they do with their private lives. Despite their bitterness, they're actually nice to one another now that they live apart and could almost be called friends.

"I got to your house, and Matteo was just making the introductions when a Molotov cocktail came through the kitchen window at the same time there were gunshots. We both got Olivia down and between us. Matteo took shrapnel from the island that exploded. It didn't take long to realize the gunshots were aimed at the men in the car outside your house and the ones in the backyard. We got Olivia to the garage and into the car. She got down on the floor by the backseat. I drove. As we came out of the garage, someone shot Matteo in the arm. Some of the glass cut Olivia's hands, which were protecting her head. They're at your parents' house with your mom and Carlotta. Sylvia should be there by now."

I look at Uncle Domenico, who looks wrecked as Uncle Cesare describes what happened to his son. My sister isn't the only doctor in the family. Auntie Carlotta is a general surgeon and handles all our injuries. We have to be a minute from death before we agree to going to the hospital. Doctors and hospital administrators ask too many questions. Gunshot wounds and stabbings result in the police. We don't need anyone poking around too much.

"You should be with Matteo."

"Carlotta sent me away. She said my pacing was annoying."

I can believe that. Uncle Domenico hovers worse than a mother hen when his kids are sick or hurt. You'd think he was the one with the MD with the way he watches over her shoulder and points things out. She's threatened to suture his mouth shut before. She probably would.

My dad rests his hand on my shoulder, then squeezes.

"Go."

Normally, I wouldn't leave the garage without a shower and changing into completely fresh clothes. We never leave in what we're wearing when we get here. It's a good thing we're rich for how many custom suits we go through. But we can't afford to bring any DNA evidence out with us. We're all making an exception this time. I already got cleaned up and changed a few hours ago after my turn with our guests ended. I haven't been outside the office since then, so basically in a sterile environment.

When we get outside, I slip off the surgical booties I wear over my shoes and toss them in a burn bin by the door that's there to collect anything we might still have on to prevent any evidence leaving with us.

We have to cross Queens to get to my parents' house, and the drive feels even longer than the one back from Atlantic City. Uncle Domenico's driving, and I'm in the front passenger seat. Uncle Cesare is behind me. Neither Uncle Domenico nor Auntie Carlotta are really my aunt or uncle, but it was just easier for all of us as kids to use uncle and auntie as signs of affection and as honorifics. Second Cousin Once Removed Domenico is a ridiculous title.

"Why are they at my parents'? Why not your place? Was Auntie Carlotta already there?"

"We knew you'd feel better if Olivia was with your mom rather than anyone else. Carlotta and I were still at our house, so I drove her there."

He's right. I do feel better knowing Livy is with my mom. My parents have the same level of security as Uncle Salvatore and Aunt Sylvia. There are guards all over the property, and not only is the community gated, so is their driveway.

We're not as bad as the Kutsenkos and O'Rourkes, who all live practically in family communes. My parents live one neighborhood over from Uncle Domenico and Auntie Carlotta and five minutes from Uncle Salvatore and Aunt Sylvia. It's handy when there's an emergency in the middle of the night. It was super handy when we were all younger because there was always a playmate within walking distance.

I'm out of the car before it's even in park. This is the second time I'm running into a house frantic to find Olivia.

"Livy!"

Chapter Eighteen

Livy

Thank God Luca is here, but he sounds as frantic as he did yesterday when he got back from Atlantic City. Scratch that. He sounds worse. I thought he'd panicked last time. Compared to right now, I'd say he was barely anxious then. He bursts into what I found out is his mother's study and skids to a stop. Carlotta and I are sitting by the window for the natural light as she plucks tiny shards of glass from the back of my left hand. My right hand already has some gauze wrapped around it.

He comes to squat in front of me, not interrupting Carlotta. I lean into his embrace as best I can and loop my free arm around his neck. We hold each other until Carlotta whispers that she's done. He lifts me from my seat and takes my place, holding me against him. We exchange a polite kiss, aware of his parents and Matteo's.

"Where's Matteo?"

He's looking at me and running his hand over my hair. It's Nicoletta who answers.

"He's up in his room."

I learned Matteo has had his own room since he and Marco were old enough for toddler beds. They'd shared a crib when Matteo was here, and it was nap time. No wonder they're inseparable. It also means Nicoletta and Massimo's house is as huge as Salvatore and Sylvia's. There's the master, five bedrooms for their kids and Matteo, plus three more guestrooms. The master is tucked away on the ground floor in one wing, and two of the guest rooms are at the opposite end of the house. The other six rooms are upstairs. As I look at everyone gathered and how close their family is, the huge houses make sense. They're a sign that home is where you hang your hat.

"Can I see him?"

Carlotta nods.

"Yes, but I knocked him out with some pretty strong painkillers. He's asleep."

"Then I won't disturb him. Livy, are you okay?"

"A couple little cuts on each hand, but otherwise, I'm fine. A bit shaken, but not hurt."

Luca's slow to agree, but eventually, he nods. I look over my shoulder as the others leave, and Nicoletta closes the door behind them.

"Oh, little girl. I'm never letting you out of my sight again. Only bad shit happens when I do."

"That's not true. You had several days at work where nothing happened while I stayed at the house."

He shoots me a look that says I'm not helping. He's so gentle when he lifts my hand to his face and eases my bandaged palm against his scared cheek.

"Daddy, you're here now, and everything is better.

I lean forward and start the kiss, but he soon masters me as he crushes me against his chest. Once again, that need for

254

control drives him. It's as though merely kissing me and dominating our intimacy can demand that everything will be all right, that I'll be all right. I gasp as he lifts me and presses me backward onto his mother's desk.

"Luca, we can't do this here."

"If we don't do it here, then everyone will know we're doing it upstairs because that's the only place I'll go with you."

"Your mom offered your room to me if I want a nap."

That shocked the hell out of me. After all the fuss that I expected after hearing Lorenzo talking about their parents disapproving of me staying with Luca, I never imagined Nicoletta would offer me her son's room instead of a guest one.

"I'll fuck you in there, too. But right now, Daddy is going to make you come right here."

"Luca, no. This isn't—"

He lifts me off the desk, turns me around, and presses me forward as he yanks down the pants I'm wearing. Some more clothes arrived while he was in Atlantic City yesterday. I'm not wearing panties since he shredded two pairs that I wore after he told me not to. He hadn't been kidding. He's not kidding now, as he lands his hand across my ass.

"*Piccolina*, this is for pleasure, not punishment. If doing anything else in here truly bothers you, then we won't. But this is a reminder that I lead. You do not."

"I know, Daddy. I want this too."

His hand rains down two more spanks, his large palm covering most of my ass.

"Why do you want it?"

"Because I don't have to think about anything but what you're doing right now. Because it reminds me you're always trying to please me, and you're not too into anyone—me included—stopping that. Because I enjoy submitting to you and knowing you're taking care of me. That is one of your ways of showing me you care. You know spankings make me wet, and I know you're going to make me come. You'll help me forget for a little while."

"That's all correct, little girl. You did nothing wrong earlier or right now. I want to pleasure you and distract you. Just concentrate on how your body feels right now."

He lands five more slaps across my ass, and I wonder if anyone can hear them since they ring through the air and fill the room. Then he's rubbing the scorched skin. I look back over my shoulder.

"Daddy, you can take me like this if you want."

"As much as I love watching my cock sliding in and out of your cunt, I need to see you, Livy. I need to hold you."

I stand up and turn around. I kick off my shoes then pants. As I talk, I unfasten his belt and pants.

"You're really very sentimental, Daddy. You're a big softie at heart."

"Only with you, *piccolina*. No one else would ever say that."

"Oh, no. I think you're a big softie with all the women in your family."

"Not like I am with you, though there is one part of me that's never soft when you're nearby."

I wrap my hand around his cock and stroke.

"Definitely not soft. Daddy, do you want to fuck me?"

I shoot him what I think—hope—is a coy smile. I squeak as he lifts me onto the desk, presses me to lie down, then drags my hips to the edge. He thrusts into me, and he slides in with ease. I know he could see how wet I was while he was spanking me.

"Do you want *me* to fuck *you*, little girl?"

"Every minute of every day."

I can tell he's restraining himself, holding back from letting loose like he has. I'm certain it's the little bit of discretion he has. No need to push his mother's desk across the room. With each thrust, he circles his hips before withdrawing.

"Livy, I'm going to do better protecting you. I swear. I don't want—"

His jaw clenches as he stops himself.

"You don't want me to leave you."

I guessed right. That was what he barely kept himself from saying. I can see it in his eyes even before he nods.

"I'm not going to. I can't. And I don't mean because of all the shit that's happening outside our doors. I mean, I can't let go of you now that I know you. I can describe all the things I like about you and what I admire, but I can't find the words to explain why that makes you the only man I've ever seen a future with. I don't want to give that up, Luca. I won't give it up."

"Livy, I feel the same way. I just know."

He kisses my neck and up to the sensitive skin behind my ear. He lifts my hips off the desk and slams into me. That self-control slips just enough to send me over the edge.

"Daddy, I'm coming. I didn't ask. Will you spank me for it?"

"Tonight, little girl. Tonight, I'm going to do way more than just spank you. I told you all of you belongs to me. I'm going to remind you."

Along with the clothes that arrived, so did the toys that Luca overnighted. We discovered that just before we left for breakfast. The guys all showered, and so did Luca and I, so it took more than an hour for us to get out the door. One guy brought the boxes from the guard shack at the driveway gate to Luca just as we were about to leave.

We knew what they were since the guards left the boxes sealed. Marco started to ask what was in them since packages never get delivered to a house without security opening them first. Luca gave him a look, and my face flushed bright red. Marco snapped his mouth shut and went to get in the car. The other guys followed. We took a quick peek. I'd already put everything away before the attack.

That makes me pause. The house. It's mid-morning, and Luca was gone overnight. Matteo slept in one of the guest bedrooms.

"Are we going back to the Bronx tonight?"

"No."

He grunts the single syllable before he pulls out and coats my shaved mound with his cum. We look down, then our gazes meet. The same thought crosses our mind.

Soon. In a few days, there'll be no pulling out.

My thoughts go further than that.

One day, maybe we'll make a baby.

Luca's hand rests on my belly. Maybe I wasn't the only one thinking that.

"Could you imagine that, Livy?"

"I am right now. I told you, I've dreamed of us having a family. Only once was it a nightmare."

"I'll never have children out of wedlock, Liv. I've seen what that's done to someone in my family. I won't do that to my kids. And I want what my parents have. I'm not asking now because there's still way too much for you to learn and think about. Divorce doesn't happen in my family. For all the things we overlook in our faith, we don't break sacraments. I don't want either of us to be miserable for the rest of our lives. And I will never agree to living a separate life from my wife where we both fuck whomever we want. I will never be unfaithful. *Never.* I also don't want a loveless or sexless marriage."

"Luca, I feel the same way. My parents thought they loved each other, but they got married because my mom got pregnant. She wanted to make sure I had my father's last name because she's old-fashioned. But my parents were a horrible match once real life set in. I already told you my dad was horrible to my mom, and I saw all that. I don't think you would ever be that way. Your sense of honor is way too strong, plus your family would never forgive you. I don't want either of us to rush this and wind up like my parents. I don't want to make my kids go through a divorce and two separate homes, but neither do I want them to grow up in a home where their parents can't stand each other."

He ran tissues over me as we talked, and now he shoves them into his pocket as I sit up. He helps me off the desk, and I pull up my pants as I slip my shoes back on. He watches me as he speaks.

"I decide things quickly, but I'm not impulsive. I wouldn't have said any of that if I hadn't already given this hours of thought. More than hours. It's on my mind even when I should focus on other things. When this shit with the Culiacán is over, and I will make it end, I want you to live with me permanently. I'm not asking for that now because I never want either of us to wonder if I asked or if you agreed out of necessity. But that's where I want this to go."

"I thought no one cohabitates without marriage in your family."

"They don't, but I want to continue to ease you into this. I want you to know there's a way out before there isn't."

I swallow and nod. I want to tell him I'll give up my Brooklyn apartment right this minute. I want to call my mom and tell her I'm moving. With no work to do, just time watching TV and looking out the window, I've thought about this nonstop too. Maybe I should say that.

"Luca, I want that too. I can consider this rationally, setting aside the current danger, and think about what our life would be like without the Culiacán after me. Whatever happened that kept you away through the night didn't have to do with me. It was business as usual for you. It shocked me how easily I accepted that. I'm still shaken from having a bomb explode a few feet away from me, but I remained calm through it all. I'm calm now. I haven't thought once about leaving or pushing you away."

"Little one, we're going to spend the night here. Maybe two. Then we're going back to our real home here in Queens. Obviously, someone knows you were at both of my houses, so hiding out in the Bronx is pointless. I'd rather have you in a house that has maximum security around the clock."

"Do you think Cesare and Matteo know who it was?"

"I didn't ask. If I found out on the way here, I would have been beyond reason. I needed to focus on you, not what I'm going to do to them."

"Retaliation is inevitable, isn't it?"

"Any strike on us gets a response. That's how all syndicates operate. That someone attacked you—Livy, don't ask me what I'm going to do. I won't tell you, and I won't lie either."

"I trust you to do whatever you need to. I won't try to change you. I'm entering your world, not the other way around. I know you can never leave. You'd be a target and dead within the day. I also don't think your family would ever leave you unprotected. None of you have the luxury of leaving this behind, so I'm accepting you as you and as a mafioso. I know I can't have one without the other."

He tucks hair behind my ear and cups my jaw.

"Livy, I'm falling in love with you."

"I'm falling in love with you, too."

It's not a solid declaration, but it's the truth for both of us.

"It's been a rough morning, and you're getting shadows beneath your eyes. We both need sleep. But I need to talk to my family before I can come up to bed. Do you know which room is mine?"

"Yeah, your mom told me. But can I sleep in there now that you're here?"

"I don't know."

"I'll respect your parents' wishes, but I'm worried I'm going to have nightmares again. Maybe it was just that one night because it was all just starting, and I didn't understand what was happening."

"If you have a single bad dream, and we're in separate rooms, you call me or come get me. I don't care what anyone else says. I will not leave you alone if you're scared."

"Thank you, Daddy."

"I'll always take care of you, *piccolina*. Never doubt that, and I will never take your trust for granted."

When he says things like that, I think I already love him. Dear God, don't let me be wrong to put my faith in him.

We walk out to the living room, and it surprises me to see Matteo lying on his stomach on a couch. I know he has some stitches and several adhesive bandages on his back even though I can't see them through his shirt. Luca smirks, and I know the taunting is about to begin.

"Aren't you supposed to be tucked into bed? I thought your mama already read your bedtime story."

Luca helps Matteo as the injured man sits up.

"Mama's bedtime story was a shot of Dilaudid. I only woke up because I was starving."

"Your stomach. Jeez. My mom never has enough food in the house to feed you."

I'm certain Luca would say something a lot stronger than "jeez" if there weren't so many—adults—in the room. Grown-ups? Parents? I'm not really sure how to refer to them since none of them are my relatives.

I elbow Luca as I smile at Matteo.

"Thank you. I wish it never happened, but I appreciate you protecting me."

"Of course. Even if you do have rotten taste picking him over anybody else."

"*Fanculo.*"

Luca whispers to his friend. I look at him as Matteo snorts. Luca keeps his voice down.

"It means fuck off."

"Be nice to Matteo. He helped save my life, and he puts up with your bad temper. I can only imagine what he endured in the car the other day, stuck with you for four hours."

"Endured? Stuck? Ouch, little one. You wound me."

"Don't start kissing them better until you're in private."

Matteo pretends to retch. Luca shoves his shoulder, and I reach out to pull his hand back.

"Ow. I'm telling. Mama!"

"Oh my God, are you both five?"

I turn as Nicoletta walks over, answering for the friends.

"Pretty much."

Carlotta ignores her son. Luca crosses his arms and jerks his chin toward Matteo.

"He's not that hurt if he's worried about eating. He'll survive. He was making fun of me, Mama."

Now I can't help but grin. I know they're joking, but I can picture what they must have been like as kids. I pinch Luca's ribs.

"Ow! Livy, what the heck?"

"You're older. You should know how to behave better."

He scowls at me, and I wink. He wraps his arm around me and easily picks me up until I'm eye level.

"Uncle Sal is right. You'll fit in just fine."

He puts me down, but he pinches my ass once he does. I

dart a glance at his mom, who's no longer paying attention to any of us and has gone back to talking to Carlotta. He looks back at Matteo.

"Are you really all right?"

"Yeah. A few stitches across my right shoulder blade that will itch more than hurt. Nothing that deep. The bullet grazed my arm. My mom was just being cautious. A few other cuts she needed to wash out and cover. She only gave me the painkillers to knock me out. Plus, no matter how many times she's done it or how gentle she is, stitches still hurt like a motherfucker going in."

"She gave you the shot before she started?"

"Yeah."

"Pussy."

"*Fanculo.*"

It's Matteo's turn to curse. I infuse all the authority into my voice that I can.

"*Ragazzi.*" Boys.

I'm a little louder than I intended, but we hear the others laughing. Luca still has his arm around me and squeezes me closer.

"Mama, what have you been teaching my girlfriend?"

Nicoletta laughs.

"That's all her."

It's all me. I babysat a lot as a teenager. There was a family with three sisters, so I had plenty of practice sounding stern. I'm about to explain that, but Salvatore and Massimo arrive. I look past them to see if Luca's brothers, along with Carmine and Gabriele are with them, but the older men are alone.

"Stay here, Livy."

"No, Luca. She needs to hear this."

I look up at him, then I really examine Salvatore's and Massimo's expressions and body language. Luca takes my hand, but I don't budge. I shake my head as I see exhaustion and sympathy enter Luca's dad's and uncle's eyes.

"My mom?"

Salvatore nods.

"Where is she?"

I lunge forward toward the archway to the living room. I need to see my mom.

"Olivia, we'll take you, but you need to hear this first."

I lean back against Luca as he pulls me to his chest and wraps his arms around me. I don't know if it's to comfort me or to restrain me. Maybe both.

"Is she dead?"

"No. Our men got her out of her place in time. But they tossed a Molotov in there since she's on the ground floor. Her apartment caught fire, and it was already too far gone for our men to do anything. Their only priority was getting her out. As far as she knows, they're neighbors who ran in to help. She's at the hospital."

"Does she know what caused the fire? Does she know it was an improvised bomb?"

"Yes. But she doesn't know who did it."

"Culiacán? Did they attack Luca's house, too?"

"We believe so."

"How'd they find my mom?"

She hasn't had contact with anyone from Mexico since she ran away as a teenager. She barely has anything to do with the Mexican community in Brooklyn. She steers clear. I don't know enough about her family to understand why she won't talk about them. I just know she grew up in an orphanage and was badly mistreated. A Catholic organization got her across the border when she was eighteen. They helped her become an American citizen as soon as she was eligible. She even thought about becoming a nun, but the Mother Superior knew it wasn't my mom's calling. She was faithful as a kid growing up in the church-run orphanage, but she became devout after they brought her here. Getting divorced is a sin she's never gotten over.

"We don't know."

I bring my attention back to Salvatore as he answers. I want to scream at him. How the fuck do they not know? Men were supposed to be watching her. How did they not see someone until after her place was going up in smoke?

"I want to see her."

"Luca can take you. We made sure the ambulance transported her to a hospital where we have people."

Have people. In other words, people on their payroll. People who won't involve the police. Right now, I'm not feeling so confident about Salvatore's people.

"Come on, Liv. Let's go. We'll talk in the car."

I turn my head to look up at Luca, and for a heartbeat, I consider pushing him away. Even running from him. Leaving him and all this shit behind. But the idea is gone in a flash. I sink against him and draw strength from his steadfastness. Luca's family didn't do this. The Cartel did. My mom was in danger because of what I saw, not Luca or any of the *Cosa Nostra*. She's alive because of the Mancinellis.

"We can't go in the car alone, can we?"

"No, *piccolina*. But we'll go in one of the town cars. You and I will be alone in the back."

We left the house in the Bronx in such a hurry that I barely grabbed my purse from beside the garage door. I didn't grab a coat. Nicoletta lends me one before we head out to the driveway. The driver holds the door open for me, and I slide in. Luca follows. The moment the door closes, he lifts me onto his lap. It reminds me of our drive back from Connecticut. I slept most of the way. I curl up against him, my arms tucked between us.

"Little one, I knew nothing about your mom until just now."

"I know, Luca. You would never keep that from me or simply forget. But could you tell from Salvatore or your dad just how bad it is? Am I going to get there and find out she's closer to dead than alive?"

"I don't know. It's serious, but I don't think it's life threatening. If it had been, they would have at least warned me in Italian if not told you."

"Daddy, this could have happened, even if I'd disappeared. It probably would have happened sooner to flush me out. I don't know what I would do without you. I don't know that I could do this on my own. I mean, I would see my mom in the hospital. But I just don't know that I could hold my shit together. I know I can because you're going to be with me."

"We're going to make sure they properly take care of your mom. When you're confident she's well enough, I'm taking you away. We're going out of the country somewhere. Not only do I want you farther away from the Culiacán, but I want you to have a chance to breathe. Is there somewhere you've always wanted to go? Anywhere in the world."

"You can't just up and leave work."

"I'm going to."

"But—"

"Is my little girl really going to tell Daddy what he can and can't do?"

He asks with a smile, so I know he's teasing. He isn't making this a Daddy Dom/little girl thing. We're not truly like that. But there's just enough of an edge to remind me I like how we are.

"I would never presume to do such a thing, Daddy."

"Liv, my family is extensive enough that they can spare me for two weeks."

"Two weeks? That's too much, Luca. That's too long and too extravagant."

"How about I tell you all the places my family and I own, and you pick one of them?"

"You make it sound like a long list."

"It is."

"Um... Is there anything in the south of France? I've always wanted to go there, and I want somewhere warm."

"I have a house in the hills above Nice and a boat docked in Saint-Tropez."

"That works."

"All you'll need is a toothbrush and sunblock."

"I know they have topless beaches there, but I need at least a bathing suit."

"Don't worry about that. The house and boat both have spots where I can fuck you under the Mediterranean sun."

"Luca!"

I look toward the privacy glass that was already up when we got in the car.

"They can't hear us. That's the point of it. I could be fucking you right now, and they would be none the wiser."

Tempting until I remember why we're in the car. He must think of the same thing because he presses my head against his chest and kisses my forehead.

"Luca, it's going to take a little while before we can go. If my mom can't go back to her place, then she needs a place to stay. She's going to expect that to be my place in Brooklyn. The insurance company might put her up in a hotel, but how the hell is she going to explain this to an adjustor?"

"You're going to have to do more than just introduce me as your boyfriend. You can tell her how wealthy I am. My legal wealth, which is what I live off of, comes from the businesses I own and very good investments thanks to Lorenzo. I will take care of fixing her place or getting her a new one. She doesn't need to involve the insurance company."

"How will she explain to the police why she isn't involving them? If she tells the cops who her daughter's boyfriend is, she's going to get sucked into this further. They'll explain who you are. She doesn't even know we're dating. How am I supposed to go from being single to having a boyfriend who's willing to shell out thousands of dollars to a woman he doesn't know?"

"We'll figure it out as we go."

That's the best he can say because we just got to the hospital.

Chapter Nineteen

Luca

My head's pounding. This is the worst headache I may have ever had. It started the moment Uncle Domenico and Uncle Cesare arrived at the garage. It went away once I was with Livy. Now it's back with a vengeance. Motherfucker. I grit my teeth as I stand beside Livy as she asks about her mom. We're told which floor to head to, and when we get there, I spot three of my guys discreetly hanging out in the waiting room. They can't stand outside Livy's mom's door, so this is the best they can do. I squeeze her hand and tilt my head. She follows my gaze, recognizing her driver from her grocery trip. She shoots Alonzo a tight smile before we keep walking down the hall.

"Mom?"

Livy calls out softly after she opens the door.

"Ivy?"

I'm not used to anyone calling her that, so it feels off. But I'm certain her mom will think the same thing the first time I slip up and call her Liv or Livy.

She pushes aside the curtain, but I hang back. I don't want to invade the woman's privacy. Livy walks over to the bedside, then notices I'm not next to her.

"Mom, I brought my boyfriend, Luca. Can he meet you?"

"Of course."

Livy steps where I can see and gestures for me to come forward.

"Hello, Mrs. D'Amato."

"Mom, this is Luca Mancinelli."

Something flickers in her gaze as it sharpens. She knows my last name. She shifts her attention to Livy before looking back at me.

"Does she know?"

"Mom?"

"Yes."

Livy and I speak at the same time. I rest my hand on her lower back.

"Olivia, she recognizes my last name. She knows about my family."

"Olivia?"

She whispers it as she meets my gaze. Why does she look hurt? Doesn't she realize I'm trying to be as respectful to her mom as she was with my parents? She focuses on her mom, but I feel the tension in her body that wasn't this extreme a moment ago. I press my hand against her back, letting it rest there.

"Mom, are you okay? What happened?"

Livy's mom isn't looking at her. She's glaring at me.

"My guess is your boyfriend happened."

"Mom!"

"How long have you been together?"

"A little while."

"Olivia, answer me."

"A few weeks, Mom."

Mafia Heir

"Interesting how the Good Samaritans who got me out of my apartment had Italian accents. I thought nothing of it, but now I get it. So, who targeted me? The Russians? The Colombians? The Irish? The Albanians? The Mexicans? Which of your friends tried to kill me?"

"Mom."

Anguish fills Livy's voice, and I hate all of this for her. But maybe her mom being knowledgeable enough to name at least half of the syndicates means it won't be so hard to explain. Wishful thinking, I know.

"We believe it was the Culiacán."

Something flashes in her eyes again, but I don't know her, so I don't know how to read it. She turns her head toward Livy, but she's still watching me. Livy takes her mom's hand, and finally Mrs. D'Amato focuses on her daughter. It's as though she's dismissed me.

"I'm fine. But this ends right now. He will get you killed. You are now a target to all of those killers. The moment I'm out of here, we leave."

"Leave? I'm not going anywhere. Where do you think you're going?"

"California. As far away from New York as we can get. Canada might be better. Olivia, none of them will just forget about you. If they know about me, they know about you." She glowers at me. "Or are you going to forbid that? She obviously knows plenty now that this has happened. What're you going to do to her when she leaves you?"

"Mom, stop. I've known who—what—Luca is since the moment we met. I witnessed something, and Luca protected me. I never went to Long Island, and I wasn't house-sitting. We've been dating since we met. But he has made it clear since the very beginning that I can walk away at any time."

Livy's mom snorts.

"Seriously, Mom. I've met his family. I won't be swimming with the fish wearing concrete shoes. His family won't kill me for what I know. I know very little, but Salvatore Mancinelli won't order a hit on his nephew's ex-girlfriend."

I hate her using that term even remotely about her. Girlfriend, fiancée, wife. Those are the acceptable ways to describe her.

"Nephew? You're the don's family?"

"Yes."

I'm not getting into any specifics if I don't have to. This is bad enough. She doesn't need to know I'm next in line for my uncle's position.

"I'll give you a few minutes. Olivia, come and get me when you're ready."

"No."

"Stay."

Both women respond at the same time.

"Stop calling me Olivia. You know I don't like it."

Her mom interjects immediately.

"What's wrong with your name?"

"Nothing. But Luca calls me Liv or Livy."

I just realized that I've never once told her that my full name is Luciano. No one calls me that except for my priest. I don't think anyone in my family has said that name except at my baptism and confirmation.

"Mom, tell me what happened."

"I was asleep, but I woke to the sound of something exploding. I think the window breaking actually woke me. Whatever they tossed came in through the dining room window. I got out of bed and threw on some clothes. By the time I crossed the room, I could hear the fire. I burned my hand on the doorknob because it was already scalding."

She holds up her bandaged hand, and that's when she notices Livy's bandages.

"What happened to you?"

"Something similar."

"What? Tell me now, Olivia."

"Finish your story, Mom. Obviously, I'm in better shape than you."

Her mom's deep inhale tells me how hard she's fighting not to lose her temper.

"I realized how serious it was, so I ran into the bathroom to grab a bath towel. I soaked it in the tub and threw it over my head. I grabbed a hand towel and soaked it, too. I used that to open the doorknob, but I still burned my other hand. I'd only taken one step into the hallway when a man wrapped something around me and guided me toward the door. There were two more guys with smoke extinguishers making a path for us. An ambulance and firetruck showed up within a minute or two of us running out to the street. Half the complex was evacuating. I can't wait to explain this to the property manager."

Livy runs her hands over her face, leaving them over her nose and mouth. She turns tear-filled eyes to me. I draw her closer, and she turns into my chest. Her mom is beyond pissed as she watches us, but I'm not rejecting Livy when she needs me. She takes three shuddering breaths before she twists to see her mom. She doesn't let go of me, so I don't let go of her.

"You are going to tell me what happened to you now."

"Luca's brother's best friend and his uncle were at the house while Luca was finishing up work. Someone tossed an explosive into the kitchen window. They got me to the car in the garage, and we left. Some glass cut my hands while I was crouched on the floor."

She's selective in her truth.

"Why were those men at the house if Luca wasn't?"

"Matteo was my bodyguard today. Cesare brought over some desserts his wife made. She's getting over the flu and was too tired to come over after baking all morning. Luckily, they were there."

"If you weren't involved with Luca, they wouldn't have needed to be there."

"If I weren't involved with Luca, I'd be dead."

Livy snaps her mouth shut and closes her eyes.

"Mom, I came out of work and found Carlos Espinoza talking to Luca. Carlos tried to kill me. Luca protected me and gave me what I needed to get away from the city and the Culiacán. I didn't get far enough away fast enough. They came after me and, thank God, Luca worried something else would happen to me. He rescued me when the Espinozas found me. They were about five seconds away from shooting me. Luca has been protecting me since the moment he first saw me."

Mrs. D'Amato recognizes the Espinoza name, and she reacted the same way when she heard about the Culiacán. Anyone could have heard about the Mexican Cartels since they're in the news. But knowing the Espinozas are Cartel is too specific.

"You're wondering why I know the name. I grew up in Mexico and didn't come here until I was a young adult. No one from Chihuahua doesn't know the cartels and the families involved. I know enough to stay away."

"Mom, this is no one's fault but Carlos's family. It's not yours. It's not Luca's or his family's. It's not mine. But Luca can help, and he's already offered."

"I don't want your blood money."

I force myself not to react. I keep my expression relaxed, and I keep my breathing steady. I don't need my heart to race and Livy to hear it.

"Mrs. D'Amato, I own six car rental franchises. I own a

quarter of an Atlantic City casino. I own the land that will soon be a Reno casino. And I have investments that make enough that I never need to work another day in my life. All of my family has legitimate businesses. What you're talking about is money that gets reinvested into our community, paying our construction workers, our salvage yard workers, our—"

"Soldiers who extort people and kill them when they don't pay your uncle. I told you, I grew up in Mexico. I know how mafias work."

"We are not the Mexican Cartels in Mexico. We keep our business between men, and we keep it off the street. The danger Livy's in now is because of them. The other syndicates know better than to target our women and children."

"You really believe she's going to be part of your Mafia world, don't you?"

"Mrs. D'Amato—"

"It's Ruiz. I never took my ex-husband's name."

Now she corrects me.

"Ms. Ruiz, we've played as nicely with them as we're going to. We didn't escalate it. They did. We will end it. Once the Culiacán are no longer a threat, Livy won't be in danger anymore."

"Ridiculous. She'll always be in danger. The Russians—"

"The Ivankov bratva never targets women and children. Never. The family that leads them doesn't tolerate any violence toward women and children from inside or outside their organization. They're the only people I would ever tell Livy to go to if she couldn't get to me or my family. The Colombians have an interesting connection to the Russians these days because of a woman who married the Russian leader. They won't touch any women and children because they're desperate to stay on this woman's good side. There's history between the families. The Albanians won't do anything because they're not strong enough to defend themselves against the Russians. The Irish have too many internal problems right now to target anyone connected to my family."

That's a longer lesson in syndicate politics than I would normally give. But I know we're about ten seconds away from Ms. Ruiz demanding Livy pick between her and me. She watches me, and I have a sudden sense that we've met before. Or maybe it's because I feel like she can actually hear my inner thoughts. It's fucking bizarre.

"Ivy said you've only been dating a few weeks. You're already in love with my daughter, aren't you?"

"Mom."

Livy hisses the word, but I talk over her.

"Yes."

Livy and I look at each other. It was only an hour ago that we said we were falling in love. Neither of us said we were in love. But the truth is out now, and neither of us denies it. I can see my feelings reflected in her eyes.

"I love you, Livy. I didn't want to rush you earlier, but I know how I feel."

"Same for me. I love you, Luca."

I kiss her forehead when all I want is to swoop her into my arms and make love to her. I know we've already done that. I mean, I can tell the difference between us fucking and making love. I know we both can. Obviously, our bodies figured it out before our minds. Or at least, our bodies acknowledged it before our minds.

"Mom, Luca will help you with your place. Or we can find somewhere else for you."

Ms. Ruiz is silent for a long time. When her shoulders sag, she suddenly looks ten years older than she did a moment ago. What did she just decide? Is she going to stop trying to break us up?

"This will not end. If it's not the Culiacán, then it will be someone else. Are you really prepared for this to be your life every day?"

"Ms. Ruiz, this isn't typical. Most days, the women in my family go to work, run errands, see friends, spend time with family. All the things the average person does. They are removed from this world because there's a mutual understanding that women and children are untouchable. The Culiacán are causing trouble now, but they don't have the strength in New York to fight any of us for long."

I watch Livy's mom as she considers what I say. If she grew up around the cartels in Mexico, I can't blame her for not believing me. They aren't as discriminate about who they target. They leave their messiest work in the street to intimidate locals. Keeping what we do private is far more intimidating in New York. People fear what they don't know. Their imaginations run wild, and that keeps people in line.

"Mom, I've met most of the women in Luca's family. He's telling the truth. There are two doctors, and both women work in this hospital."

She must have learned that while Auntie Carlotta was taking care of her hands. That makes me pause. I wonder if Maria is here or what time she'll get here.

"Ms. Ruiz, would it help to speak to my sister? She's a radiologist here. If she's not on a shift now, she will be soon. My mother's best friend is a general surgeon here. She's the one who fixed up Livy's hands. She could speak to you."

Once again, something I don't understand flickers in her gaze. She's hiding something. I don't like surprises, and I'm certain whatever her secret is, it'll be something I don't appreciate. I'm extending a fucking olive tree by suggesting she talks about our life with people in my family.

But I want her to accept me, and I don't want her to make

Livy choose. I wouldn't accept her picking me over her mom. I don't know how I would survive it. But I'm as adamant about not coming between her and her mom as she is about not coming between me and the rest of my family.

"No. I don't need that. You offering says enough. I don't want to put you in an awkward position with your family."

Did I just sigh with relief? I hope neither of them noticed.

"Mom, what do you want to do? You know I would normally offer to have you stay with me at my place, but I haven't been there since all of this started. It's about as safe as going back to your apartment. Would you like to stay with Luca and me at his house in Queens? Do you want to stay at a hotel? Luca's house has security around the clock patrolling the entire property. He can arrange for a security detail outside your hotel room and outside the building."

Livy's mom shifts her gaze to me, and there's something patronizing about her expression. As though she thinks I won't really do what Livy offers. Or maybe she believes I'd only do it, so I can keep fucking her daughter. I glance down at Livy, but she doesn't seem to notice what I do. Maybe I'm reading way more into it because she knows her mom way better than I do. If she sees nothing, then it must be my imagination.

"And just how would that work? Wouldn't people ask questions if I have some guy standing outside my door at all hours? I think that screams target."

Livy looks up at me again.

"Ms. Ruiz, there are plenty of hotels in New York where you wouldn't be the only guest with personal security outside their door."

"Fancy."

"Mom."

Livy hears that condescension as loudly as I do.

"You are welcome in my home, Ms. Ruiz. There are two other guest rooms besides the one Livy chose."

Which is true. We just have to get Livy's things into that room before her mom arrives. Livy's sly when she presses her heel down on my toes. Hard. She's not in agreement with my suggestion, but we both know her mom would flip if we shared a room. The woman can barely tolerate me being in the same room as Livy. But I get it. She's Liv's mom. She's not being any more protective of her daughter than I am of my girlfriend. If the situation were reversed, and I was in the hospital and Ms. Ruiz dropped all these bombs, I would be livid. I try to remind myself of that.

"Thank you for the offer, but I have someone I can stay with who I know no one will suspect. I have a friend who is a nun, and I know she'll let me stay with her on Staten Island."

Livy looks doubtful at the suggestion.

"How are you going to get there?"

I cut in.

"We can get you wherever you need to go. We can get you out of the hospital without anyone seeing you."

Ms. Ruiz shifts her gaze between Livy and me before she locks eyes with her daughter.

"Thank you. I appreciate that, Luca. Olivia, I won't be there long. We'll figure out something more permanent. Canada would be best. I'll have to see what it takes to move there."

I cock an eyebrow. We can make that happen and appear entirely legal. Ms. Ruiz's lips flatten.

"Letting you take care of that would probably be best. I suspect you can make me disappear and reappear in a foreign country with no questions."

"Something like that. Let Livy know when you're ready to

leave Staten Island, and I'll see that everything is taken care of. When will the doctors discharge you? I can set up a driver."

"They said this evening. They just wanted to observe me."

I debate whether to tell her I plan to take Livy on vacation soon. That might be salt *and* lemon juice in an open wound.

"Mom, we're going on vacation soon. Luca and I will be abroad for a week or two. Once I know you're settled and safe, then we can go."

"Vacation?"

I guess we're talking about it now.

"Yes. I'd like to get Livy away from New York until things calm down."

"Will you let me know when and where you go?"

Livy looks over her shoulder at me.

"Of course, Ms. Ruiz."

"Thank you."

"Mom, do you want me to spend the day with you?"

"No. You look exhausted. You need sleep too."

Livy hesitates before she nods. Mother and daughter hug before Livy steps back and slides her hand into mine.

"It's going to be okay, Mom. Luca won't accept anything else."

I hope I live up to that.

"Livy, I'm going to take you back to my parents' house in the morning. I'm going to be gone for a couple days, and I don't want you alone at home."

I definitely think of the house in Queens as our home. It's not my house or my place. It's ours. I alluded to Livy having her own room, but that will never happen again. The only place she's sleeping is our room.

"Where are you going?"

I don't answer. She twists in her seat to look at me, relying on the streetlights we pass to illuminate the town car's backseat enough to see me. We wound up spending the day with Ms. Ruiz after all. I stepped out much of the time to give mother and daughter privacy. I also had work calls to make and emails to deal with. I worried Ms. Ruiz would push the issue about Livy and me breaking up, but she didn't. I think Livy explained more about us because she warmed to me and was friendly by the time we left.

"Are you going back to that place?"

I return her stare. It's always best if I say nothing aloud. Plausible deniability and all that. I'm not confessing to any premeditated crimes, and she's not knowingly abetting a perpetrator.

"And I won't be able to reach you while you're gone."

"If there's an emergency, Uncle Salvatore or one of the guys will let me know. If I can, I'll come to you right away. If I don't, it's because I truly can't get away."

"Is there anything else I should know before I stay with your mom and dad? Is there anything I shouldn't say?"

"I wouldn't describe how much you like it when I eat you out."

"Luca!"

She playfully swats at me. I already have my arm around her shoulders, so I tug her closer and press my lips to hers. It's a searing kiss that makes us both forget everything that happened that day. I unfasten my belt and reach between us to unfasten hers. Then we're easing down onto the seat. I know this is a foolish risk I take every time we ride without our seatbelts, but somehow I feel an unreasonable sense of invincibility in our vehicles.

I push her pants down her thighs and off before trailing my

fingertips along the silky skin. I find her cunt, and it's already getting wet. I don't press into her, instead rubbing along her pussy lips. The heel of my hand rests against her clit, and she tries to wiggle closer.

"What do you want Daddy to do, *piccolina*?"

"Anything. Everything."

It's a frustrated, breathless whisper. I grin, and I know she sees me because she lurches upward to kiss me. I move my hand away from her pussy and catch her wrists, raising her arms over her head.

"Hold on to the end of the seat. Do not move your hands, little girl."

"And if I do?"

"I will spank you and edge you all the way home. Then I will make you watch me jerk off until I come. Then I'll say goodnight."

"Daddy."

Now it's a whimper.

"Then follow my instructions if you don't like that outcome."

"I will. I promise."

"Do you though? I know you'd hate the last part, but I think you want a spanking, and I think being edged excites you as much as it frustrates you."

I ease my fingers into her, but I move excruciatingly slow. I barely swipe my fingers against her g spot before I withdraw. I do it over and over, careful not to touch her clit.

"Daddy, what do I need to do? I want you so badly. I ache. Everything burns, and I feel like I'm on fire."

"What do you need me to do?"

"Anything. Just more of whatever it is."

"Do you want me to finger fuck you?"

"Sure."

"Do you want me to lick your cunt?"

"Sure."

"Do you want me to stick my cock in you and fuck you until you can't see straight?"

"Desperately."

I unfasten my pants and push them past my hips. I grab her waist and lift her so I can thrust into her easily. I pound her as she continues to cling to the end of the seat. We're getting rough fast, and now I worry I will slam her head into the door. I lift her as I shift to sit again.

"Hold on to the headrest. Fuck me, little girl. Ride, Daddy, but don't come until I tell you to."

"Daddy, I already need to come."

"I know. But we still have twenty minutes until we're home. You're going to last that long."

"I'll try."

"I know you will."

But I know she'll never succeed. I'll let her come before then if for no other reason than I won't last that long. She rises and falls on me with an urgency that excites me even more than anything we've shared before. She lasts ten minutes before she moans.

"Daddy, please may I come? I need to. I'm trying not to, but I'm so close."

"Yes, little girl. Come."

"Are you going to spank me for not making it home?"

"Do you deserve one?"

"Yes."

The single word lingers in the air until my hand lands against her ass. I'm unrelenting, even if I'm not spanking her that hard. I grab her flesh with both hands after every three or four slaps. I love the feel, having to spread my fingers wide to cover it all. I love the way her hips flare, giving me something to hold on to when I fuck her doggy style.

"Harder. I want you to spank me harder."

"Your wish is my command."

"No."

She stops moving and looks down at me.

"I don't want to command you, Luca. I don't like that even as a joke. I have no idea how anyone could control a man like you. The idea of even trying is stressful. I'm not helpless and incompetent. I can figure things out on my own and take care of myself. But when we're together, I get a break from that. You know you don't have to fight to gain or keep control with me, and I know I don't have to worry if I'm not in control. I know I can tell you what I need. I don't always have to ask. But I won't command you to do anything. It implies there's a consequence or a punishment if not obeyed. That's not the outcome I want with us."

I draw back my hand and strike her ass with enough force to press her hips against me. Her breath catches as her clit rubs against my pubic bone. I do it again and again.

"I will always give you what you need, and I will do my fucking best to give you what you want. That's what being your daddy is about, providing and protecting. I know you can do shit on your own, and I'm fucking proud of how resilient and determined you are. You can always tell me anything, *piccolina*. If you don't like that joke, then I won't make it again. I never want to make you uncomfortable or question our dynamic. What do you want right now, *cuore*?"

"I love you so much, Daddy. May I touch you?"

"Yes. I need that, too. I love you, *cuore mio*."

"That means my heart, doesn't it?"

"Yes. That's what you are."

She leans in and kisses me as I alternate sides as I paddle

my hand against her ass. I feel the moment she comes, and I'm so fucking tempted not to pull out. But I never want to trap her. We'll decide together when we're ready for a *bambino* or *bambina*. She's still kissing me as I lift her off my dick. Our groans are ones of frustration, not pleasure. We continue to kiss as she strokes me until my cock stops pulsing.

She whispers in my ear as she settles on my lap.

"*Mi corazón para siempre.*" My heart for forever.

Once we're cleaned up, she nestles against me. We arrive at our house, and I carry her up to our room, strip her, and make love to her all over again. Our skin's glistening with perspiration as I hold my phone, and we reorder all the toys and implements we picked out but had to leave behind. I don't know when I can get back over to the house in the Bronx, and I'm not sending anyone to pick up the things I plan to use while I fuck my girlfriend. I refuse to let any man think about that, and it would humiliate Livy if a man or woman saw what we chose. This time, we pick the overnight shipping. Our bodies have cooled, and we pull up the covers to snuggle together as we fall asleep.

Tomorrow. My revenge will come soon enough.

Chapter Twenty

Livy

How the hell did it get to this? I kept asking myself that over and over as Luca and I rode back to his house in Queens. At least I was until we made love. Even with how hard he spanked me, there's a marked difference between our lovemaking and fucking. I don't know why that one word—command—set me off. I hated hearing it. I knew he was joking. But it felt so wrong that it shattered the moment. I guess I really don't enjoy thinking of Luca as anything but in charge. Even when I've seen him at his most emotionally raw, he's never struck me as weak.

I know Salvatore issues commands that Luca must follow. I'm not completely trapped in my fairy tale. But I seem to compartmentalize that. His dominant personality is a constant reassurance to me. And frankly, the fucking sexiest thing I've ever seen. Knowing that one day he'll be the don is impressive and intimidating at the same time.

I've never been drawn to men in power. I don't look for

men with high-powered positions or wealth. It's never meant much to me. And it's not Luca's role or his affluence that makes me a moth to his flame. It's his aura. I imagine it scares the shit out of most people, and others see it as arrogance. But, to me, it's his certainty that he'll love me and provide for me in all ways, always. I want him to know I don't take that lightly.

"Luca, you've said you see us together in the future. One day, you'll be the don. If we are together, what does that mean for me? How will I know what to do? How to be a wife you're proud of?"

"I'm proud of you now. Just be who you are already."

He kisses me as we step out of the shower. We're getting ready to go to his parents. I still need to pack an overnight bag.

"You know that's not what I mean. I don't really know what Sylvia does. I mean, I know you always say the business is between the men. But does she have a role in your community? Does she have responsibilities for the wives and children?"

"She's a lawyer. It's ironic because Maks's wife is too. The heads of the two strongest syndicates married attorneys. She handles all our legal business dealings. My dad handles the ones that aren't and those that might waver between the right and wrong side of the law. Her hands are spotless."

"Oh."

Why am I continually shocked by the women's careers? Do I expect them to just sit around all day doing nothing? Do I expect them to be in hiding? No. That's not it. It's that they're so damn normal. There's nothing average about a lawyer and two doctors in the family, but that seems so average in the grand scheme of the world.

"Do Salvatore and your dad know how serious you are?"

"How serious *we* are. Yes. My dad told me I'd found *the one* when we had dinner at Uncle Salvatore and Aunt Sylvia's."

"He did? But I'm not Sicilian. I'm not even Italian despite

my last name. Won't your children need to be fully Sicilian? Would that mean they pass your children over for Marco's?"

"You see yourself having kids with me, Livy? Not just in your dreams, but in real life? Not just a passing idea, but truly?"

"Almost every time we have sex."

"So do I. Some people might not like it, but no one outside of my family would care. Besides, your name sounds so Italian you could have been born there."

Luca finishes getting dressed, and I'm almost done with my makeup. He grabs a bag from the bottom of his closet. He holds up clothes to me, and I nod or shake my head.

"But I'm half Mexican and half American. Is fifty percent really enough to satisfy your community? Will being part Mexican be a problem? The whole rivalry thing. That we met because your enemy is causing trouble."

"I dare someone to speak against you in front of me or Uncle Salvatore. And fucking may God have mercy on their souls if they're stupid enough to do it in front of my mother or any of my aunts or my sister. They'll wish it was in front of a man. The women in my family will eviscerate them."

I can't help it as my lips twitch and a smile breaks through. The women in Luca's family don't lack confidence or self-assurance, but none of them come anywhere near matching the men's size and strength. Yet, listening to Luca, I believe him. No one crosses a mama lion with her cubs. Maria has no children, but I can tell she'll be like that, too.

"Don't be surprised if you receive a wooden spoon at your first baby shower."

"What?"

First? I just dropped my cosmetic pouch in the overnight bag. Good thing I just packed it, or I would have dropped it on the floor.

"It's a running joke. None of our moms have ever struck us, but we didn't know that when we were really little. By the time we did, they'd come up with more creative punishments that often made us wish they'd just spanked us."

"First baby shower? Isn't it rather gauche to have more than one shower? Aren't you supposed to keep what you get with the first and pass it down to the younger ones? And these days, don't parents just get what they need? Who has a shower for more than one kid?"

"Shower. Excuse to get together and eat too much. Six of one, half a dozen of another."

"But you get together at least once a week."

"That's just the immediate family."

"Oh."

I haven't met Carmine's mom or Matteo's brother, but that makes almost twenty in Luca's immediate family. I can't imagine adding to that with extended relatives.

"Just how big is your family?"

"You've heard of a family tree. We have a family vineyard. We're all cousins of some degree or times removed. Or such close friends that we may as well be relatives."

"You said you were trying to arrange a marriage with that woman in Chicago. Did Salvatore and your dad plan to arrange one for you? Did I get in the way?"

"No. That practice is over. Mostly."

"Mostly?"

"Yeah. There's a woman Carmine's supposed to marry, but he's been evading it for years."

"Does he know her?"

"You know how his nose has a slight bump? She broke it when he was twelve. He went back to Sicily with Gabriele for the summer, and he knocked her into a wave. She clocked him.

She hasn't been a fan since. She's been avoiding him as much as he has been her. A match made in heaven."

"Wow. And he's the only one? You said his parents didn't want to get married, so why would they arrange a marriage for him if theirs was a disaster?"

"They didn't. It was my grandfather who insisted. He swore that was the only way Carmine could truly belong in our family. If he married to strengthen us. But once he died, Uncle Salvatore forgot about it."

He uses air quotes around forgot. Carmine gives me the most distinct playboy vibes of all of them. If Luca hasn't had a girlfriend since like college, I don't think Carmine has ever had one. I don't think he could commit to one. I think he likes to flutter and pollinate as he goes.

We leave the bedroom and head down to the kitchen. We don't linger long over breakfast. We're back into a town car, and I realize the driver isn't alone up front.

"Is that Gabriele up there?"

"Yes. He's your bodyguard for today."

"I need one at your parents'?"

"I'd just feel better, at least for today. My parents have plenty of men patrolling their property, but you know I'm only comfortable when a guy in my family is with you. Gabriele is like adopted family. I need more information to assess going forward. If anything happens, stay with my mom. My dad will take care of it."

That sounds just about as ominous as anything Luca's ever said. His dad might be well into his fifties, but I wouldn't mess with him. What he lacks in Luca's size these days, I'm certain he makes up for in experience. I can tell that he's leaner than he was in his younger days. I think he was once as big as Luca, but he's not a small man by any stretch. Neither is Salvatore. It's just obvious they aren't working out twice a day. Maybe only once a day.

It's still early when we arrive, barely eight o'clock. But the house is bustling. I didn't expect everyone to be there. Luca and I have a second breakfast, and I'm ready for a nap. We just had cereal at his house—our home as he keeps correcting me—but Nicoletta has eggs, bacon, pastries, and crepes. She moves around her kitchen with ease, and everyone acts as though this is the norm. Maybe it is.

"Livy, I love you. I'll see you in a couple days. If it'll be longer, I'll get a message to you. I'm going to miss you, *piccolina*."

"I'm going to miss you too, Daddy. I love you. Please be careful."

"I will. I'm coming back as soon as I can. Then we're packing for our trip. I'm going to try to make the arrangements while I'm gone. If I don't have time, then I'll do it as soon as I get back. Love you."

He gives me a kiss that should only be shared in private. Luckily, we're in his mom's study. I glance at the desk and try not to think about what we've already done. We had sex this morning when we woke up and a second round in the shower. That should tide me over. Maybe.

"Love you, too."

We head back to the foyer, and he gives me a discreet peck before I watch him leave with Lorenzo, Marco, Matteo, and Carmine. Massimo and Cesare must already be outside since they said they would all ride together. Salvatore is already wherever they're going.

Maria is sipping her tea in the kitchen, so I wander back in there. Carlotta and Sylvia are headed to work. I'm not sure where Nicoletta is. We realized once we got here that Luca's parents aren't staying here today. All the guys said their goodbyes to their moms and aunts before Luca and I stepped into the study. It made me realize that the older generation was here in case it was the last time they saw one or all of them. It was a sendoff of sorts. I feel comfortable being frank with Maria.

"Your aunt Paola wasn't here. Won't she worry if she didn't get to say goodbye to Carmine this morning?"

"He and Gabriele stopped by on the way here. Gabriele's parents moved back to Palermo about five years ago, so Auntie Paola and Uncle Cesare are the only parents he has here now. He's as close to them as Matteo is to my parents."

"What's your aunt like?"

"Uncle Salvatore but a woman. Believe it or not, my dad is the laid back one in their family."

I smother my laugh, but Maria's expression tells me it's okay because she finds it just as funny.

"My dad's as laid back as a lawyer gets, I suppose. He's the quietest of the three."

"He's the quiet one? Salvatore seems to only use the fewest words he needs."

"That's only because he's still trying to make a good impression on you. Give it a few more days. You're family now, so be prepared. You won't understand half of it because he switches back and forth between Italian and English all the time."

"I'm family now? Luca and I aren't that—"

"Bullshit. Pardon my French. You're as good as married at this point. He wouldn't have brought you into our world if he wasn't certain, and you sure as fucking shit wouldn't stay if you weren't certain. Besides, you're living together, and no one thinks you're in a guest bedroom. My brother has never had the same woman back twice to his bedroom."

"Are you the blunt one in the family?"

"Hardly. That's Auntie Paola. Like I said, she and Uncle Salvatore are a lot alike."

Shit. If this isn't as blunt as their family gets, then what is? And if Luca hasn't brought the same woman back twice, does that mean he always went to Diana's place? Or did they only go to their club? Why'd I have to think about that? She hasn't crossed my mind in days. That just soured everything.

"I know Luca wants you to stay at the house, and my mom is at work, so I took the day off."

"What does your mom do?"

"She's a financial data analyst. Lorenzo is the most like her. He got his interest in math and his personality from her."

"Really?"

Because he seemed like an asshole when I met him, and Nicoletta is like the nicest woman ever once I got past her ice shield. Maybe they aren't that different after all.

"Yeah. Neither of them gets upset over much, but when they do—batten down the hatches. Mama says Lorenzo was such a mellow baby and kid that he never really had to learn how to calm himself down, so when he explodes, he takes a while to get over it. But it takes a lot to wind him up. Like he's the only one who can tolerate Carmine and Gabriele and hasn't punched either of them."

"You tolerate them."

"I like them. Gabriele moved here when he was ten. He spoke no English, and he was easily six inches taller than the kids his age. They teased him mercilessly at school because, back then, he was a gentle giant. Carmine stuck up for him, and they became best friends."

Maria pauses and watches me as we sit together at the kitchen table.

"What has Luca told you about Carmine's parents?"

"Not a whole lot."

"Auntie Paola got pregnant at nineteen, and my grandfather forced her to marry Uncle Cesare. They were just having a good time. They didn't intend to shackle themselves to each other. Auntie Paola insisted Carmine have the Mancinelli name, not the Ciccone one. She refused to say I do until after Carmine was born. She thought she was protecting Carmine by making sure he had that last name. Uncle Cesare is on the birth certificate, but since they weren't married, she got to choose which name Carmine got. In some ways, it has protected him. But mostly, being illegitimate has made people look down on him. The older generations I should say. People our age couldn't give two shits. But they treated him like crap as a kid, and Gabriele stuck out, so the boys did things on their own. Since no one expected much of them, they didn't try hard to do anything but get in trouble. Once people figured they were spoiled and stupid, they got to do whatever they wanted until they were old enough for Uncle Salvatore to put them to use. Then they got the shit jobs."

"I can understand that. Why do you see them differently?"

"I had a horrible horseback riding accident at the beginning of high school. I wound up in the hospital for a few weeks. I broke several bones and punctured a lung. It's what made me interested in radiology. Carmine used to come to the hospital every day after school to tutor me and keep me company until I fell asleep. He understood I was lonely and bored. My brothers already had after-school jobs or were doing things for Uncle Sal. They couldn't stay as long as they wanted, but Carmine did. He refused to do several things Uncle Sal ordered him to until I stepped in and told him how much I needed Carmine's visits. I was in a lot of pain while I healed. He used to hug me when I cried during physical therapy. He was so gentle. Always careful not to squeeze or wrap his arms lower than my shoulders. For a while, I felt closer to him than I did my own brothers. Then he went back to being a dickhead, doing stupid shit I couldn't overlook."

Wow. That's a lot to take in. In a selfish way, it makes me glad my parents got married before I was born, even if it was a similar situation with my mom getting pregnant unexpectedly. I wonder if Salvatore and Massimo would have accepted me if I were illegitimate. Would Nicoletta and Sylvia and Carlotta? It makes me realize how little I know about this family that I'm entering. It's a reminder of how insane and short my relationship with Luca has been.

"Were Carmine and Gabriele ever close with your brothers and Matteo?"

"When we were really little, yeah. I can remember all of us playing together, but that was well before Gabriele moved here. Those are my really early memories."

"And now? After everything with Anastasia and the Kutsenkos?"

"I don't know if that's reparable. Luca's guilt is still eating at him, and he's resentful. I don't know what happened between them about fifteen years ago, but that's when everything really turned bad. My other brothers don't know either, but they know Carmine knows something that neither he nor Luca will tell. They resent that because whatever it is, they believe Carmine's the reason he and Luca won't share it. Matteo's been on the receiving end of Carmine and Gabriele's jealousy because he fit in with the family so well and has always been a nephew to Uncle Sal, not Uncle Sal's second cousin's kid. Carmine and Gabriele have been assholes to Matteo because they're jealous. For how close we are, there's a lot of resentment festering beneath the surface."

I'd say so. Paola and Cesare. Carmine and Gabriele toward Luca and his brothers, and that's reciprocated. Same between Carmine and Gabriele versus Matteo. I'm certain Salvatore resents Carmine being a fuck-up and being stuck accepting

Gabriele. Yet, they also seem like a genuinely happy and loving family when they get together.

"Do they put that shit aside when they have to do whatever it is they're doing today?"

"Yes. For all Carmine and Gabriele's faults—and I can recognize them all—they are good in situations like this. I don't know what they do or what makes them good at it, but no one excludes them. It's a given that they'll go too. It's the more—refined—parts of the family businesses that they seem to suck ass at."

That's reassuring. I don't want Luca out there doing God knows what with shit bags who are likely to get him killed.

"Where is Gabriele? I haven't seen him since the guys left."

"He's probably in my mom's study, reading. When he's not working or working out, he likes to read. He doesn't even own a TV and doesn't have a subscription to a single streaming service. It's uncivilized, I tell you."

Definitely more than meets the eye.

"You have an MD, and your brothers have grad degrees. What about Carmine and Gabriele?"

Maria gazes out of the window, and I wonder if she heard me.

"I don't know if anyone outside the immediate family knows this, but Carmine went to Stanford. He got in there and several other places, including every Ivy League school. Uncle Sal sent him away for four years. He got in trouble at the end of high school and nearly wound up in prison. Some people thought he died. Other people thought he was in jail. Auntie Paola and Uncle Cesare went out to visit him for all his breaks and holidays. Since he studied engineering, Uncle Sal insisted he work in our construction business. Matteo's an architect, and Carmine is a structural engineer. He designs the buildings, and Carmine manages all the construction sites. The trouble he got into was bad enough that it cost Uncle Sal a couple million to keep him out of prison because they wanted to try him as an adult. He's been too busy working to pay Uncle Sal back to go to grad school. His little stint in Sicily a few months ago hasn't helped."

What the fuck did he do to get exiled for four years? I have so many questions. But Maria is already volunteering a ton. I don't want to push it by asking and making her clam up.

"Gabriele's a lawyer or will be. He just needs to pass the bar. He took time off between undergrad and law school. Before everything with Anastasia happened, he'd almost earned Uncle Sal and my dad's trust. They talked about him working with Aunt Sylvia. Now who knows? I keep telling my dad that Gabriele's ability to get in trouble and always get out of it makes him the perfect person to work for my dad. You know he's a lawyer too, right?"

"Yes. Your uncle's chief advisor. A *consiglie*-something or other."

"*Consigliere*. Papa handles the stuff Aunt Sylvia can't go anywhere near."

I've heard it said that mafia comes from *mia famiglia,* or my family. If that's the case, then it's true. The Mancinellis definitely keep it all in the family. It's a fucking tarantula's web. Do they even spin webs? Whatever. It could be one of those massive spiders from Australia that's the size of a person's head. It's whatever web one of those could spin. It's fucking sticky and complicated and unlike anything else. Except for maybe the other syndicate families. Sounds like the Russians are super similar.

"If business didn't get in the way, do you think your family and the Kutsenkos could be friends?"

Maria's head jerks back as she looks at me as though I've lost my mind. Then her brow furrows.

"We probably would. Our families are a lot alike, which is why we're such rivals. But never take that for granted, Olivia. Never trust them. I know the women offered you help, but don't go to them unless you truly believe you'll die if you don't. They are heartless. The men and the women. Any woman who could marry into that family—she has ice in her veins. The men are—they may be insanely fucking hot, but they're literally killing machines. They have no emotions whatsoever, and they move like soldiers. Lock step about everything. They're brutal too. Never let the bit of charm they can show when they want to fool you. They won't hurt you, but they will use you in a heartbeat to get to Luca. When you run into them at social events, which will be inevitable, never be out of Luca's reach or always be near one of the other men in this family."

That isn't scary or anything. Fuck.

"What about the Colombians and Irish?"

"Enrique is on his way to being a fine-looking silver fox. He smiles more than any of the other leaders, but it's an act. It's meant to be disarming. To anyone who doesn't know him, it is. But he grew up in Colombia. He didn't come here until he was in his twenties. His younger brother came at the same time and still goes back there often to handle business. Enrique doesn't have any kids, but he has nephews. Pablo's okay, but he's totally different from when we were all kids. He's dark now. Like—I don't even know. He's intense in a way the guys in my family aren't. I think he has to do all the worst stuff all by himself."

"What do you mean worst stuff?"

Maria stares at me. It's the same expression Luca gives me. Don't ask questions you already know the answer to. But I don't know.

"Maria, I don't know what that means. Luca hasn't and will never tell me. Is it like in the movies? Torture and shit like that?"

She keeps looking at me, but her head tilts to the right. It's like she's waiting for me to figure it out, and she's getting impatient. Like I shouldn't be so dumb. Excuse me for not knowing the sick and twisted shit she clearly doesn't think twice about.

"Why do you think Luca and the others don't have their phones on?"

"So, they aren't interrupted."

"When you were on the run, did you turn off your phone?"

"Yeah."

"Why?"

"Because—so they can't be tracked."

"Why wouldn't they want to be tracked?"

"No one can find out where they go or what they're doing."

"Exactly. Olivia, did Luca tell you anything at all?"

"He said there's somewhere they go that's under their control. If he's ever gone more than a couple days and it wasn't planned, it probably means something went wrong, and it's not under their control. I'm to come here if that happens."

"It isn't some café where they're sipping espresso. I don't know what goes on there, and I don't want to imagine it either. Save yourself the nightmares and don't ask or picture it. But people who wrong my family never make the same mistake twice."

That only makes me morbidly curious about what Luca's doing right now. Curiosity killed the cat. I don't think I have enough lives left to be nosey.

Chapter Twenty-One

Luca

I grip the steering wheel as the SUV eases down the street, surprisingly quiet for its size. With all the special protective after-market features we have customized, you would think it sounds like a bear lumbering down the road. But it's practically as quiet as a hybrid. Ironically, all the syndicates use the same body shop to customize their vehicles. The near silence doesn't calm my nerves. I'm driving the first vehicle, and Marco is behind the wheel of the one in my rearview mirror. Lorenzo drives the third.

None of the vehicles have their headlights on, and there are very few streetlights. We're counting on that, but it makes the night vision goggles I'm wearing essential. I'm counting on my brothers wearing theirs, so no one rear ends anyone. I'm usually much calmer when we set off on these missions, but I feel more pressure to succeed than ever before. This needs to end tonight.

We spent all the daylight hours at the garage as our soldiers brought in one Culiacán member after another, but the senior most members never visited us. I didn't expect that they would. They've burrowed their way underground. Carlos and his brother, Arturo, were barely midlevel men. Manuel, who led the attack on the highway, was the equivalent to a *capo*—a *lugartenientes* or lieutenant. I've even heard them called plaza bosses. They run their designated areas and make sure business stays on track. That's basically the same thing Marco, Lorenzo, Carmine, and Matteo do.

The Culiacán here in New York are reinventing themselves to adapt to the way things work in America. Their hierarchy has shifted. The days of Pablo Escobar and El Chapo are gone. They're taking a page from some of the southern Colombian organizations and creating smaller groups led by a *celeno*, or manager. That's Edgar Espinoza. That motherfucker is the one who ordered Arturo and Manuel to go after Livy. I already guessed that, but some of their men don't do well when they're tortured. They squeal like *cerdos rellenos*—stuffed pigs.

We're after him now. And wherever Edgar is, his father, Santiago, is sure to be there petting his lapdog son's head. Edgar is so desperate for his father to take him seriously that he begs for attention like a puppy chained outside during a storm. Santiago is the New York *jefe* I'm interested in. Cut the head off the snake.

"Up there on the right."

Carmine has always been a nosey little shit, but it makes him good at surveillance. Lorenzo hacked into the city cameras to help track Edgar and Santiago down, but it was Carmine's drone that got us the heat signatures we need and the audio to confirm their location. He's always loved expensive toys. If we paid taxes on our shit, he could write this off as a work expense.

We all have earpieces in, so we can communicate despite being in separate vehicles. I tell my brothers my plan.

"I'm pulling off at the next left. It'll give a clear line of sight when we get out."

Carmine is in the front passenger seat across from me. Gabriele would normally be right behind him, but it's one of our associates since he's guarding Livy. I'm trying not to think about the fact that Matteo's brother, Emilio, is behind me. If I didn't need everyone on this mission, I wouldn't have picked him to come. His ass could have stayed in Jersey. We have four soldiers with us, making the backseats cramped with three muscular men on each.

Marco and Matteo—who insisted upon coming despite his injuries and only with his mom's approval—are in the second SUV with their six men, and Lorenzo is with Uncle Salvatore, our dad, Uncle Domenico, and Uncle Cesare. They have three more men with them. It's rare that Uncle Salvatore, Uncle Cesare, Uncle Domenico, and Papa come out on missions with us, but this is their way of proving they've accepted Livy. They only come out when it's personal. When it's about family.

We'll wait in the cars while Papa and Uncle Salvatore make their way to the rooftops of the buildings on either side of us. They have eyes like nighthawks. They claim it's because they ate their carrots as kids. Whatever the reason is for their perfect vision in their fifties is irrelevant. Their keen eyesight and years' of experience developing their patience make them the best snipers we have.

Uncle Salvatore's voice fills my ear.

"Wait for us."

Once any of us leave the SUVs, we'll switch to Italian if we have to talk. Preferably, we only use hand and arm signals. The two senior-most members of our family and organization move like wraiths through the night as they pick the buildings' locks they each enter. Then they're out of sight.

"*Alfa in posizione.*" Alpha in position.

Uncle Salvatore has his spot chosen.

"*Bravo in posizione.*" Bravo in position.

Papa's set up in his. They'll provide support to take out anyone who flees the building and to take out anyone who might hear us coming. They'll make sure there aren't any guns pointing at us when we enter the room where Edgar and Santiago are watching TV. Having your bodyguards gunned down through windows makes a statement and announces our arrival, but it safeguards us too.

I look to my right, where Lorenzo stands across from me. Marco is behind him, and Matteo is behind me. Carmine forms the vertex of our V with our other men filling in around us. It's a formation we've practiced plenty of times. It'll move us across the street, allowing Matteo and me to watch anything approaching from the left, and Marco and Lorenzo watch anything coming from the right. Carmine watches what's head-on.

Normally, Gabriele would be beside him, but I'm glad he's with Livy. I don't have to worry about her, and I can stay focused. I ignore the fact that Emilio is in Gabriele's spot. The only time I think about my scar is when Livy touches it, or I'm close enough to Emilio to take a knife to his throat. Uncle Cesare and Uncle Domenico will guard the vehicles and watch for anything coming from behind. That might be the most important job of all because we'd be royally fucked if we had no means to get away.

I give the order.

"*Andiamo.*" Let's go.

We're dressed in black with our tactical gear on. Each of us has our NVGs pulled down so we can see in the dark. We carry our rifles, but we each have a handgun holstered to our thigh. We have bullet-proof vests on that carry a flashlight, zip ties, and a small first aid kit. Most of us also have a knife fastened to our belt. If it's not there, then it's in a pocket. There's not a man in this group who's left their house without a knife since they were twelve.

We're approaching a half-constructed apartment building the Colombian Cartel owns—or more accurately Pablo Diaz. What the fuck the Mexican Cartel thinks they're doing here is beyond me. My only guess is they know we're coming, and they think that holing up here will cause the Colombians to come after us when we shoot the building up. Short sighted, since that might happen, but they'll be dead first.

Carmine's advancing forward to breach the door, but we hear a thud to the right. A man's body falls from an alleyway onto the sidewalk. Given the angle, I'd say that was my dad's handiwork. Thanks, Papa. That's one lookout down.

My cousin tests the door, but it's locked. We expected that, but it never hurts to check. Carmine slides the telescopic camera beneath the tiny crack where the two doors meet. He looks at the screen on his left wrist. He shakes his head. The lobby is clear. He picks the lock, and Lorenzo and I each pull open a door. Our men push forward, guns raised and ready. Lorenzo and I resume our positions at the head of the squad. I use my index and middle fingers to point to my eyes, then to the property manager's office. Two of Lorenzo's guys break off to check it. I signal for two of my guys to check the mail room. All four return, shaking their heads. All clear.

Marco's guys know to cover the elevators and the front door while two of Carmine's men head to the back door. No one is coming in or out. The rest of us creep up the stairs, our heads on a swivel to watch what's above and below us. One would think the Culiacáns would hide out in the basement where it's harder to get heat signatures and leaves fewer entry points for us. But no. The dumbasses picked the third floor. They aren't fleeing anywhere any time soon.

We get to the apartment where we know they're hiding, and we can hear voices inside. They sound normal, as though none of them have a care in the world. Dumb fucks. They think they're safe from us. That they could attack my woman and her mother, and that they could hide out here as though they were in the right. Fuck that shit.

Lorenzo is still across from me and on the right side of the narrow hallway. He slides his hand into his vest to pull out the percussion grenade. He sets it, and I reach out to push the door open just enough for him to toss it in. Everyone plugs their ears, and I shut the door. The sound vibrates through us, surely deafening everyone in the room. It'll stun and disorient them long enough for us to make our way in.

We hear three screams, and we know Uncle Sal or my dad took people out. They must have tried to rush the door. I kick it open, and Lorenzo's side pours in, all moving diagonally to the left. Once the last man is in, my side floods through the door, bearing right. Carmine and his remaining guys surge forward.

We move with ease that comes with hours of practice and drills. Bodies fall left and right. But as we sweep the semi-finished apartment, no one spots Edgar or Santiago. The drone confirmed they were here. It saw them through the window. Neither Uncle Salvatore nor Papa has radioed that anyone left. I get to the door to the master bedroom, which is shut.

"*Sei.*" Six.

Matteo pats my shoulder, telling me he has my six, my ass. I kick the door open and jump back. Bullets spray the wall across from me. If I hadn't expected the gunfire, one of them would have hit me. Matteo's crouched next to me, firing out several rounds before I make my move to enter the bedroom. At this point, we're working in pairs to sweep the apartment. Matteo checks the bathroom while I yank open the closet doors. Nothing. Those men who just shot at us were guarding someone. I look around, stopping to study the bed.

I point to it, then make a fist. I'm telling Matteo to wait. I go to the door and catch three guys' attention and signal them to come inside.

"È un letto a scomparsa. Solleva il telaio." It's a Murphy bed. Lift the frame on three.

The men get into position, two on each side. It's the type that lowers from the wall. With the way it's made, I can tell there's a space between the mattress and the floor. Maybe a closet or just nothing, but I sense someone is there.

I hold up my index then middle finger. I point to the bed with my index finger at my count of three. They yank upward, and I aim my rifle. What do you know? Two little rabbits hiding in their warren.

"Get up."

I point the rifle barrel at Edgar's head, knowing the threat will spur Santiago into action. He can't afford to lose his son and only heir. It won't matter after today since they'll both be dead.

"Face the wall, hands on it, feet apart."

The guys release the bed once the two Mexicans stand. Matteo and I keep our guns trained on our captives while the other three guys frisk Edgar and Santiago, collecting the array of weapons the two fuckers never got to use.

"Kneel, hands behind your head."

They follow my next set of orders, and their wrists are zip tied. We rejoin everyone in the living room, dragging out two prisoners. I sweep my gaze around the destroyed unit, checking to see if any of the wounded or dead are ours. Nope. Italians, in general, might not come to mind when thinking about efficiency. But the Romans did coin the words vendetta and vindictive. You know: Caesar, Ides of March, the knife in the back. All of that. My people have refined retribution to both an art and a science.

Lorenzo drags out an older man I don't recognize, but his features are similar enough to Santiago's, meaning he's a relative. This guy hasn't aged well, so for all I know, he could be Santiago's father or brother. The head of the entire Culiacán Cartel still lives in Mexico, so I doubt it's him. *El Cazador*, the hunter, isn't leaving his palatial home near Chihuahua to hide in some half-built apartment building in Brooklyn.

I pull my pistol and put it to Edgar's head.

"Who's that?"

Silence.

"You can decide whether you bleed to death after I shoot both your legs and your arms or you can have a quick death with a bullet through your temple. Who's that?"

Not smart to test me. I put a bullet in his right thigh, making sure not to hit his femoral artery. I don't want him passed out or dead too fast. He howls with pain.

"Do you believe me now? Who's that?"

I'm making a statement to the two older men as much as I am to Edgar. He can try to hold out, but it's pointless. They can try to hold out and make him suffer. Either way, he's dead.

"He's my nephew."

The stranger speaks up. I smirk at Santiago. His brother would defend Santiago's son before Santiago would. I say as much.

"Were you fucking Santiago's wife twenty-seven years ago? Is that why you're protecting this shit stain and Santiago isn't?"

Holy shit!

"I'm right. Now this makes it interesting."

I saw something in Santiago's eyes when I asked, and this nameless man's eyes confirmed it.

"Did you know you're a *bastardo*? No? Ah, the things deathbed confessions tell you."

I shoot no-name in the thigh in the same place as I wounded Edgar. I won't do more than that here. We need them to live long enough to get them to the garage. I don't need them making a colossal mess in the SUVs.

"Brother of Santiago and fucker of other men's wives, do you have a name?"

"Ricardo."

"Dick. What a fitting nickname. We're going to move our chat to somewhere more spacious."

I nod my head, and men drag the three captives to the door. Our cleaning crew has already arrived and will make it appear like nothing ever happened here. They'll repair the damage and scrub the DNA.

When we get to the SUVs, Uncle Salvatore, Uncle Cesare, Uncle Domenico, and my dad are already there. Uncle Salvatore and Papa have disassembled their sniper rifles and are sitting on the backseat, each eating a sandwich. Fucking hell. My brothers, cousin, and friends were the ones who ran up and down three flights of stairs. Papa grins as my brothers and I stare.

"*Non preoccupatevi. Vi abbiamo conservato quelli che non ci piacciono.*" Don't worry. We saved you the ones we don't like.

"*La merda delle piante.*" Plant shit.

They left us the veggie ones. It's not that we don't all eat our healthy servings of fruits and vegetables every day, but these suck. Tomato, alfalfa, mushrooms, and cucumber. My mom craved them each time she was pregnant, and she still thinks they're wonderful. It's always a fight over who *doesn't* get to eat them. Every other food my mother makes is a battle to see who can have the most. My dad and uncle undoubtedly took the sardine sandwiches, which Carmine and Marco love. They probably also each had a roast beef one, which Lorenzo, Matteo, and I like. I scowl at my dad.

"*Te lo ricorderò quando sarai vecchio e rimbambito. Farò in modo che tu possa mangiare solo questi per pranzo ogni giorno.*" I'll remind you of this when you're old and senile. I'll make sure you only get these for lunch every day.

"*Continua. Non saprò comunque cosa starà succedendo.*" Go ahead. I won't know what's going on, anyway.

"*Tu e Marco siete stomaci ambulanti. Probabilmente è l'unica cosa che saprete che sta succedendo. Non lo dimenticherò, papà.*" You and Marco are walking stomachs. That's likely the only thing you'll know is going on. I won't forget this, Papa.

"*Allora è un bene che vi abbiamo conservato questi.*" Then it's a good thing we saved you these.

Uncle Salvatore grins as my dad finishes teasing me. He holds up a bag of Auntie Carlotta's Italian wedding cookies. They're the ones dipped in the creamy glaze and have sprinkles. It's a near feeding frenzy as we all step forward. Papa, Uncle Cesare, Uncle Domenico, and Uncle Salvatore toss a bag to each guy on the mission.

While we've been bickering, a couple guys bandaged Ricardo's and Edgar's wounds enough to get them into the SUV without bleeding out. Santiago's in the middle. They're crammed into the back with the third row up. There's barely room to shut the liftgate. Cozy family time for them and for us. Like in the Seinfeld episode, but instead of soup, "no cookies for you."

We pile into our vehicles and make our way to the garage in Queens. The three SUVs pull into the bays, and we unload our three visitors. Carmine's men strip them and get them strung up to the garage door openers. It's always important to stretch and limber up before physical activity. With their arms stretched as far as they'll go, Carmine opens and closes the doors a few times. The sound of the gears and clatter of the metal doors drown out the men's screams.

Uncle Salvatore gestures to us leaders.

"All of you, into the office."

We file in, and it's a tight squeeze with so many men over six-feet-tall and with shoulders broad enough to make us look like an NFL first-string lineup. Except we look like this without the pads.

"We have to call Enrique and let him know what happened. Luca, they went after your girlfriend. You're leading the mission. You make the call."

We have a satellite phone for the few times when we need to reach the outside world. I dial Enrique's number.

"Hello."

"Enrique, we did some housekeeping for you. Shall I send the bill to you or Pablo?"

"Luca? What the fuck? It's the middle of the night."

"Did I interrupt something?"

"My fucking beauty sleep. What the fuck do you want?"

"Guess who I just found having a sleepover at Pablo's new building?"

"Fucking tell me. I'm not in the mood, Luca. Either spit it out or clean up the mess I make at your mini mall project."

"Cranky. Santiago, Ricardo, and Edgar Espinoza had friends over in a third-floor unit in that building Pablo's got half-built in Brooklyn."

"*Malditos hijos de puta.*" Fucking motherfuckers.

It sounds like he's getting out of bed or something. Then I hear him tapping his phone and a ring tone.

"*Tío?*" Uncle?

"Luca's on the line. They just raided your site in Brooklyn. The Espinozas were hiding out there."

"How much damage did you bastards do?"

I roll my eyes and exhale.

"You're going to cry foul to us? You know we cleaned that shit up and left it nicer than your men can build. You should be more concerned about why the Culiacán thought they should use your place."

"Obviously to stir shit between us. Why do they matter to you?"

"They're targeting my girlfriend."

There's a long pause then both assholes laugh. Pablo's choking on his laughter as he speaks.

"What poor, innocent girl have you duped into dating your sorry ass?"

"At least my woman isn't running off to marry a Kutsenko."

Touchy subject, I know. Sumiko had already broken up with Pablo when she met Pasha. But it's still a sore spot for Pablo. It was the first woman he'd dated in like a decade. My guess is, she dumped him for the same reason all women complain about when they meet any of us from this world. We're too emotionally closed off and uncommunicative. We are. When we find the woman we want to let in, we know we've found the one.

"What time does your crew start at the mini mall? I'll be there thirty minutes before them. That's all I need with the shit job your crews do, laying drywall."

"Pissy, pissy, Pablo. You're missing the point."

"No, I'm not. Unlike some people, I can do more than one thing at once. While you're still practicing how to walk and chew gum at the same time, I'm already dealing with the Culiacán."

"We have Ricardo, Santiago, and Edgar. Whatever you're

planning to do won't matter with them gone. We're giving you a generous heads up. Clearly, they think they can sit at the grown-ups' table. They might be the fastest growing Mexican Cartel, but they're still new compared to your family and mine. If you want your turn to strike, then do it. But if you wait around, I will leave nothing for you."

Enrique speaks next, and I take a deep breath. I want this conversation over. I want to get back to the men hanging out there, get whatever info I can, and get home to Livy.

"How gracious. Who's this woman, Luca? Is she why you retaliated? If they're after her, you know you can't rely on what's worked in the past."

"You don't need to know anything about her other than we're serious. I will do whatever it takes to defend her, and I don't give a rat's fucking ass if that disturbs whatever turf war you're in with the Mexicans. She saw Carlos die after he tried to kill her. They won't give up easily, and I know what they'll do to her. We're going to do it to them first."

"Wonderful. Salvatore, I know you're there. Calm his foolish ass down. No one needs heads literally rolling down 5th Avenue. This isn't TJ or Bogota. Keep it civilized."

"I'm here, Enrique. This is Luca's mission. I don't disagree with anything he's said, and if he wants to treat the Culiacán the same way they treat their enemies, then I see no reason to stop him."

I jump back in.

"Pablo, do you want to have a go with them or not? If it's a no, then we're going to sweep up the rest of them and deal with this."

"Leave us Ricardo."

"Can't. We're at our place."

No one who comes as our guest leaves alive. There's no handing off prisoners once someone's been inside here. The three men had hoods on from the moment we loaded them into the SUV until we strung them up here. They don't know where they are, and we're keeping it that way.

Pablo huffs.

"Fine. Leave Josue. I'll deal with him."

"Who's that?"

"Ricardo's son."

"Did you know that Edgar's really Ricardo's son, too?"

"That's old news, *cabrón*." Asshole.

The civility didn't last long.

"Well, aren't you special to know already? Do whatever it is by noon. That's as long as I'm willing to wait."

"Fine."

The call ends, and my eyebrows shoot up and down. It is what it is. Just like always. We dance around each other when we need something and kill when we want something. That's how it is among all the syndicates. Add a new dance partner or target, and it gets messy. No one wants to be the one left cleaning it up, so we extend each other professional courtesy when it suits us.

"Carmine, can you get a drone to follow Pablo? We need to know what happens with Josue."

"Yeah. If he picks that overpass by the river, it'll be hard to keep it out of sight while getting close enough to pick up conversations."

"Do what you can."

Carmine nods and cants his head toward the bays. Uncle Salvatore nods. My cousin starts working over the three cartel members. We all took our tactical gear off during the conversation. So, Carmine has no trouble swinging his arms to land punches. This is just a warmup.

The office window only allows us to see out while no one— our guests—can see in. Lorenzo watches what's going on through the window just like the rest of us, but he asks the sixty-four-thousand-dollar question.

"Do we keep this in New York, or do we take it to Mexico?"

"Depends on what we learn from them."

We watch Carmine gesture for us to join him on the floor. I step next to my cousin, who's standing in front of Santiago.

"Repeat what you just said."

Carmine has a pair of pliers around the man's nose, which he squeezes and twists.

"A'wite. A'wite."

Carmine eases the pressure, but he doesn't remove the tool.

"Your little bitch isn't who she claims to be."

What the fuck does that mean?

"And who is she really?"

"Ask her about her family."

"Why?"

He goes silent. Carmine practically rips the guy's nose from his face. It's halfway across it, broken beyond repair. Not that it matters. But he says nothing. I grabbed a bunch of bamboo shoots as I left the office. I move to Ricardo, and Lorenzo releases the prisoner's right hand. My brother holds Ricardo's hand still as I slide two reeds under his nails.

"I've met a few people who have made it to a second hand, but few do. Only two Russians have lasted to having their toes done. You are nowhere near what those men were. You can end your agony now."

I slide a third one under Ricardo's fingernail. He howls and flails, but it does him no good. He's not going anywhere. I wait, but nothing is forthcoming. I repeat the process with his fourth finger.

"Find out from her."

He's trying to sow the seeds of doubt, but I'm certain Livy has kept nothing from me willingly. She knows unnecessary lies would break us. There are enough half-truths and lies of omission from me. She wants us as much as I do. I'm certain of it. But it wouldn't surprise me if there's something about her family that she doesn't know. I got that feeling when I met her mom.

"None of that shit matters now that we have her."

I lunge at Edgar when what he says registers. I wrap my hands around his throat.

"Your empty threats only antagonize me. That's not a good idea since I control how you die."

I step back and draw my gun. I fire a shot into his left thigh. He pisses himself. We all laugh. I shoot his right arm, and he bursts into tears. I know he's on the edge of passing out.

"Santiago, you didn't raise much of a man if he's pissing himself and sobbing. Will he shit himself when I shoot his other arm?"

I don't wait for an answer. I put a bullet in Edgar's left arm. I wait for him to pass out before I draw my knife. I inflict a dozen shallow cuts on his chest and abdomen. Ones that revive him long enough for him to howl before he passes out. I give him another dozen on his back, waking him until he drops back into unconsciousness.

"I can keep going, Ricardo. Do you want to watch your son's agony? Santiago, you raised him as your own. You've kept him at your side ever since you came to America. Your leash isn't more than two feet long. Are you going to put him out of his misery?"

"You think too highly of yourself, Mancinelli. Mexican Cartels kidnap people off the street in broad daylight all the time. No one ever finds them."

"Because you own your Federales. No one trusts them, and they make more money on your payroll. That's not the case here."

315

"But we don't need to snatch anyone, though. We're more resourceful than that."

That leads me back to thinking we have a leak. But who?

"You're paying one of our men. You'll be ash in a few minutes, so there'll be room to deal with them soon enough."

I gesture to Matteo, and he lights a massive industrial furnace that we don't keep to heat the building. Carmine and Marco get Edgar down and carry his passed-out ass to the fire. They swing him enough for him to wake yet again.

"Papi!"

Edgar cries out just before my brother and cousin swing one last time and let go. We all watch in silence. My family in disinterested silence, and the Espinozas in horrified silence. The smell of burning skin and hair permeates the air, making everyone's nose curl. It's my least favorite way to dispose of people because of that. But he's still screaming in there.

"Who's next?"

I cross my arms and rock onto my toes, my lips turned down in a mocking frown. Ricardo spits in my direction, the rope he dangles from making him sway.

"You better hurry and get home. If you don't, you won't save her like last time."

I force myself to appear unfazed when my heart speeds up.

"Nice of you to volunteer."

Carmine and Marco deal with Ricardo, leaving Santiago trembling so hard, he looks like he's having convulsions.

"Well?"

"Once she's in Mexico, there's nothing you can do. You'll never find her. She's always been ours."

What the fuck does that mean?

I walk over to the table near Santiago and pick up a machete. There's a variety of implements and tools here for me to choose. I speak to any of our men when I give the order.

"Take him down."

Lorenzo and one of his men oblige, holding Santiago up when he nearly collapses. I take the knife to his dick, letting it drop to the floor. His scream fills the entire garage.

"Pick it up and put it in your mouth."

"No. What? No."

"Do it."

I stab him in the balls. He obeys. The moment it's in there, I lop off his head. It rolls to the floor after three slices as his body crumples.

"Send his head to *El Cazador* with a note that he can eat a dick."

I drop the machete back onto the table and hurry into the office. I'm stripping off my clothes as I go. I get into the shower and scrub myself as though I'm going into surgery. It's the only way to get all the splatter off me. I'm in and out in five minutes. My brothers are under their own showerheads at the same time as me.

"I need to see Livy."

No one argues with me, and my brothers hurry out to the SUVs. Lorenzo sticks out his hand, and I give him the keys. Once we're three neighborhoods over from the garage, we turn our phones on. Immediately, they're pinging.

GABRIELE

Had to leave the house.

Twenty minutes later.

With O. No one else was there with us. Will update.

Ten minutes later.

> If I don't hear from you in five minutes, I'm
> sending someone.

That was three minutes ago.

What the fuck happened between scooping up the Espinozas and offing them? We were only in the garage for like an hour. Not even. I hit Gabriele's number on speed dial, my leg jiggling as I peer out the front passenger window. The moment I hear him answer, I speak.

"Gabe, where are you?"

Chapter Twenty-Two

Livy

Maria just got called in to work. Apparently, 'tis the season for the flu. Another one of her colleagues had to call out sick, but this time because their kid got it. We had a good chat this morning, then we watched a movie. I'm worried about my mom, and I really want to talk to her. She texted my burner that they had released her from the hospital, and she made it to Staten Island. Other than good and be careful, what can I say? Definitely not much over a burner.

"I'm sorry I can't stay. I can't believe how many times I've been called on my days off. I know the bug is going around, but this is crazy. I have a date tonight, so I'm not coming back here after work."

"You date?"

Shit. That was rude.

"Sorta. I go out and have fun, but it never lasts long. My family has plenty of regular jobs, but most guys figure out pretty quickly that despite the lawyers, doctors, and investment advisors, we're still *Cosa Nostra*. When your uncle's the don, that makes it extra hard. I either can't bring them home to meet my family, or they're too terrified to meet them."

"Do you see yourself with someone within the *Cosa Nostra*? Like maybe from somewhere else?"

"I don't know."

She tries to play it casual, but there's something I can't quite read. Is there someone she's into, but she can't date him? Or does she want him, and he doesn't want her? I don't think we're at the point where I can dig that deep. I don't want to be rude—ruder.

"You have plenty of time."

"Yeah. I'm not worried. For now, I go out with someone until it's not fun anymore. I don't even date that often. It's been like six months since I've been out with someone before this guy. This is our third date, so it'll run its course pretty soon."

When she puts it that way, I feel rather sad for her. I don't know which is the worst part. She knows it's not going anywhere; she knows she's going to call it off soon; or she's so used to it that it doesn't appear to faze her. I watch her gather her purse and coat before I walk to the door with her. We give each other a quick hug, and I realize I love Luca and want a future with him because of the man he is, but I also wouldn't mind a future with him, so I can have Maria as my sister. I never minded being an only child, but hanging out with her and seeing Luca with his family makes me realize what I missed.

Once she's gone, I feel lost. It's not my home, so I can't go poking around. I know there's a gym downstairs, and I brought some clothes to work out in. I've watched two movies since she left, so I'm not really in the mood to watch another one. I don't want to interrupt Gabriele, who worked out and then retreated into Nicoletta's study, so I can get a book. I don't even know what's on the shelves. I just saw there were a lot of books the last time I was in there. I've read everything on my mobile app, and I don't want to log into my phone, anyway. That also means no streaming music while I work out. I can live with that.

I jog upstairs to Luca's room where I'm staying and hurry to get changed. It's the middle of the night now, but I'm not sleepy at all. Not even a little. Despite no one to talk to, my mind isn't idle. Lying in bed alone will only make me miss Luca and give my mind an opportunity to run wild worrying about him.

It's only five minutes later that I'm in the basement and lifting weights. Focusing on my form and counting my reps keeps my mind off everything else. Every time my mind drifts, I make myself restart my set. That gets me on task right snappy. I'm sweating by the time I hear the basement door open.

"Olivia!"

Gabriele's voice is urgent, and I hear him clattering down the steps. I look over my shoulder, and his expression freezes me. The only thing that seems to move are my eyes. They dart around. But surely my heart has stopped. The determination and menace on Gabriele's face threatens to send me into a panic. The only reason I'm not freaking out is that I can tell it's not directed toward me. Something's happened?

"Is it Luca? Is he all right?"

"What? Yes. This isn't about him. We have to go."

"Where? Why?"

I've put the dumbbell back on the rack and grab the towel I took from the bedroom's bathroom. I swipe it across my forehead, but Gabriele plucks it from my hand and tosses it aside. He practically drags me across the basement until we get into the unfinished section. I didn't even know this was back there.

"Gabriele, what's going on?"

"There's been a plausible threat."

"What does that mean? Gabriele, tell me what's happening. You're freaking me out."

"I will, but for right now, we need to be silent and move."

I watch him grab a flashlight from a shelf near an old-fashioned metal door. It's the sort you would see on an old school furnace. The kind that's only half the wall high and rounded at the top. Gabriele reaches beneath the shelves next to the door and pulls out a key. He unlocks the door and drops the key back beneath the shelves.

"Are we hiding?"

"We're escaping."

What the ever-loving fuck? Escaping from what? The who is easy. The Culiacán. But what did they do? And how are we getting there?

"Keep your head down. I'll go first and lead the way. Don't let go of my hand. Are you afraid of cramped spaces?"

"Would it matter if I were?"

"No."

"Good thing I'm not."

Gabriele flicks on the flashlight and opens the door all the way. He has to bend nearly in half to get through the doorway. It's like he's entering a gnome's house, and he's a giant. I only have to stoop. It shocks me that once we're into what I realize is a tunnel, we can stand upright.

"Pull the door shut, Olivia. Make sure it clicks. That way it locks."

Locks? What if we can't get out on the other end? I'm certain there's no cell signal down here. Is this to be our grave? I roll my eyes at myself as I yank the door shut, and it slams louder than I expected.

"Come on."

Gabriele reaches back his hand as he speaks. I slide mine into his, surprised at how gentle he is. It's like a child putting her hand in a bear's paw, but he's careful not to crush it when he tightens his hold. I don't ask questions because I have no idea if our voices can carry. We walk for at least three or four minutes before we come to another door. This one is more like a garage door. It's on rollers, and there's a chain Gabriele pulls to raise it. It's pitch-black outside. There are no house lights or streetlights nearby. I can't see my fingers in front of my face since Gabriele turned off his flashlight the moment the door was open.

He pulls the door shut once we're both out, but he's careful not to make a sound. They keep the rollers and chain well-greased for something that must be a hundred years old. Perhaps Massimo and Nicoletta have replaced them. I know the house was built in the early 1920s. I suspect I just went through a bootlegger's tunnel. I think whoever owned the house during Prohibition either smuggled booze in or out of the house. The door in the basement would have looked like it led to a working furnace back in those days. When I glance over my shoulder, the coiling door hides behind climbing ivy Gabriele held aside for me. It's completely disguised.

I can barely make it out in the dark, but Gabriele puts his finger to his lips and gestures for me to follow him. I reach out and grab the back of his suit coat. I can't see and don't know where I am or where I'm going. He slows his pace a notch, realizing I'm struggling not to trip since I can't watch the ground and am not familiar with the path. He seems to know his way without thinking about it since I can tell he's texting. His phone is completely dark, but I can feel how his arms move as his fingers tap out a message. I hope it's to Luca.

We're entering a park that separates the neighborhood Luca's parents live in from Salvatore and Sylvia's neighborhood. It's at least a mile wide, so I can't see the houses well. There's enough light from the moon and stars for me to tell now that there aren't any buildings obscuring them. I glance back once more and realize we came out of what now appears to be a shed, except it's not within the wall around the house. It's about five yards past it. Massimo and Nicoletta must own the land between their house and the park. This strip of land means no one can build close to their house. It's like their version of a moat.

Gabriele reaches back and grasps my forearm, pulling my hand from his suit jacket. He stops and waits for me to step abreast of him. He points toward a dense group of trees, and we hurry toward them. He winds us through the tree trunks, and it's clear he's been here so many times he could probably navigate in his sleep. I nearly stumble when he comes to an abrupt stop. I'm unprepared for him to jump and pull a rope ladder from the branch above us. I look up and realize there's a structure in the tree.

"I'll hold it still while you climb. Keep your head down at the top."

I look around, more confused than ever. But I follow his directions, and I appreciate he holds it still, or I would have swung around and made no progress. When I reach the top, I crawl forward on my hands and knees until I reach the opposite end. Gabriele's right behind me, making quick work of the rope ladder. He crawls forward, and even though I can't see very well, I can picture how ridiculous he must look in his custom-tailored suit.

There is not a single man in this family who buys his suits

off the rack. Their shoulders are too broad, and their torsos are too trim to get things that fit as well as their clothes do. Besides, the fabric alone must cost a fortune. Never mind the labor that must go into all of it. I've seen inside Luca's closet. It's insane how many suits he has. I got the distinct impression he's not unique in his family with his wardrobe. Since none of them strikes me as fashionistas, it makes me wonder why Luca has so many clothes.

"Olivia, are you all right?"

"Yes. What's going on?"

"I'll explain everything, but I'm waiting for Luca to call. He has two more minutes before I send someone to get him."

His phone vibrates in his hand, and he answers on the first ring. Luca talks over him, his voice the most demanding I've ever heard.

"Gabe, where are you?"

"*La casa sull'albero.*"

My guess is he said the treehouse. It's sorta close enough to Spanish for me to understand. I squint as though that might help me see better in the dark. I can make out some shapes, and I realize that it's more like an enormous tree fort. Luca, Gabriele, and the others must have played here as kids. I can't believe it's still here and in such good shape. No one must have played in it for like twenty years.

Gabriele whispered his response to Luca's question, so my boyfriend gets the hint. I can barely hear him since Gabriele has his phone to his ear. Is Gabriele afraid someone can hear us? Is that why he's using Italian? Does the language really matter if someone finds us here?

"*Sto arrivando.*" I'm coming.

"*Venite in uno dei vostri affitti. Qualcosa che nessuno saprà riconoscere.*" Come in one of your rentals. Something no one will recognize.

325

I think that was something about not being recognized. I can't remember who it was, but whoever told me Spanish and Italian were similar enough to understand one if you know the other was a fucking liar. I have no clue what Gabriele means.

"*Mi ci vorranno almeno trenta minuti.*" That will take me at least thirty minutes.

Whatever Luca is doing will take thirty minutes. I don't want to be up here for half an hour. I didn't grab my coat, and now I'm freezing. Gabriele must realize that a t-shirt and leggings aren't much to keep me warm in the dark in late winter. He slips out of his suit coat and hands it to me. I feel badly taking it until I slide it on. The amount of heat the man must generate is astounding. I feel like I've just been wrapped in an electric blanket. But does that mean he'll get cold even faster?

I whisper so quietly I almost don't hear myself.

"Thank you."

"*Lasciatemi parlare con Livy.*" Let me talk to Livy.

Gabriele passes me the phone.

"Don't say anything. Let me do the talking, *piccolina*. I'm coming as soon as I can. I don't know what's going on, but I will get to you as fast as I can. Trust Gabriele. He'll keep you safe. No matter what happens, do not get separated from him. Are you wearing the bracelet I gave you this morning?"

While we said our goodbyes in his mom's study, Luca gave me a bracelet. He apologized that the first piece of jewelry he gave me was something with a tracker in it. He showed me how once it fastened around my wrist, we can only take it off with a special key, which he put in his parents' safe. He explained all the women had bracelets or necklaces with trackers. He went on to tell me that all the men have trackers in their belts. Knowing this didn't ease a single fear. Instead, knowing ratcheted them all up into overdrive. I think half the reason he kissed me was because it calmed me down.

"Yes, D—"

I catch myself. Hearing Luca's voice is reassuring and soothing. I feel safer knowing he's on the way. I can do this.

"I'm going to hang up now. Stay with Gabriele. He knows what to do. No matter what, do not get separated from him."

He's said that twice. Why? What does he think is happening? What does he know could happen?

"I love you, Luca."

"I love you, little one. I'll be there soon."

I hand the phone back to Gabriele, who says goodbye before he slips the phone into his pants' pocket.

"Are you warm enough, Olivia?"

"Yes."

I'm not, but I won't complain.

"Aren't you freezing?"

"I'll survive."

"Gabriele—"

"I said, I'll survive."

There's no bite to his tone, but it certainly leaves no room for me to argue. I burrow further into his suit jacket, drawing my legs up to my chest. I'm leaning against wood planks that make one of the fort's walls. I close my eyes, and suddenly all the exhaustion that wasn't there earlier slams into me. I should have gone to bed at a reasonable time and gotten some rest. Lord only knows when I might get to sleep now.

I listen to the night air as a light, but frigid breeze rustles the surrounding leaves. A couple of nocturnal birds call to each other, and I wonder what species they are. Definitely not a recognizable owl hoot. The air is crisp, so I try to convince myself that it's refreshing. I'm not doing well at that. My teeth chatter, and my skin prickles with goosebumps. It's an expansive black abyss beyond the tree house. The only visible light is so far in the distance that it looks miles away, even though I know it's coming from Sylvia and Salvatore's neighborhood.

If we're this close to them, why can't we go there? The girls. Gabriele won't take me there because of Pia and Natalia. He won't endanger them, even if I know he's committed to protecting me. I wonder why he doesn't take me to Carlotta and Domenico's since that's even closer but in a different direction. What is going on? The wait, with no end in sight, is making me jumpy.

I close my eyes and try to calm myself, but it's shattered when there's a bird call beneath the tree. Why's it coming from down there? Gabriele's crawling across the treehouse and tossing down the ladder. Insanely, I'm more focused on how his pants are going to be filthy, and he's likely to rip the fine material, than who's coming up the ladder. I refuse to get my hopes up that it's Luca. It hasn't been long enough, has it?

"*Piccolina?*"

Thank fucking God.

I lurch onto my hands and knees and crawl toward his voice. He lifts me as he stands. I wrap my arms and legs around him and hold on for dear life. He shuffles his feet forward to keep from tripping, then he turns and eases down to the floor. He opens his suit coat to me to huddle into, but I lean back and slip off Gabriele's.

"No."

"Take it, Gabriele. I have Luca now."

I drop the jacket onto his lap. He's sitting shoulder to shoulder with Luca. I press my body against Luca, and he envelopes me in his muscular arms. It's as though nothing can get through them to get to me. They're an impenetrable shield. He strokes my hair as I rest my head against his chest, his steady heartbeat that reliable balm to my anxiety.

He turns his head toward Gabriele, so he doesn't have to speak loudly.

"What happened?"

"A package addressed to you arrived. The guys at the gate diffused it, but it means someone is around."

"Who delivered it?"

I listen to this shocking news. A fucking bomb? Molotov cocktails weren't enough. Now we're into actual real explosives.

"That's the worst part. It was some kid. He couldn't have been older than thirteen or fourteen. He had no clue what he was carrying."

"Do you think he was a recruit or just some teenager trying to make a little extra cash?"

"The latter. The guys at the gate said he was too unaware of his surroundings to have been trained for anything like this. That's what tipped our guys off that something was wrong. I mean, besides the ridiculous hour, but plenty of courier services deliver 24/7."

Only somewhere like New York. Most normal couriers probably keep typical business hours. I can't imagine a courier service in some Podunk town in Alabama or Idaho is making deliveries at four in the morning. Normal people are asleep right now.

"I brought a Corolla and switched out the plates. We should be good. I'm going to take Livy to a safe house near Philly. We'll fly out as soon as we can tomorrow."

I lift my head.

"Fly out to where?"

"It's time to take that Mediterranean vacation, *piccolina*. We need to get away for a while."

Luca turns his head to look at Gabriele. I want to know what he says, but he switches to Italian because I can't know.

"*Eravamo in garage da appena un'ora. Come facevano a sapere di dover prendere di mira Livy ora? Come facevano a sapere che dovevano vendicarsi?*" We'd barely been at the garage for an hour. How'd anyone know to target Livy right now? How'd they know to retaliate in the first place?

"*Qualcuno sta sicuramente parlando.*" Someone is definitely talking.

"*Ma chi?*" But who?

Luca's question hangs in the air. I don't know what he asked, but I know it was something from his inflection.

"I'm going to go down first, then I'll help you. Gabriele will follow us."

I shift off of Luca's lap and follow him to the opening with the rope ladder. He disappears as quickly as he appeared. Gabriele helps me as I scoot backward and reach my foot out. Once I'm certain where to place my hands and feet, I make my way toward the ground. I'm about halfway down the ladder when large hands grip my waist and lift me into the air. Luca sets me on my feet, and our lips meet. His kiss is possessive and desperate. He's scared.

His voice never wavered. His heartbeat was steady. His hands weren't clammy. Nothing indicated the fear I taste in this kiss. Our tongues tangle before I suck on his. The world slips away for a few seconds. Neither of us—no. I don't notice Gabriele stepping next to me. Luca notices everything, but it feels like his attention is solely on me. We pull apart, and I look behind me as Gabriele tosses the ladder back over the lowest branch. I turn to gaze up at Luca and go up on my toes. He leans forward.

"Daddy, everything's going to be all right now that you're here."

"Little one, Daddy will always come for you. Always."

"I know. What now?"

"We get out of here. Gabriele, Marco and Lorenzo are two streets over. They followed me here. I'm at the end of the block."

"I'll walk with you to the car, then I'll find them."

Luca leads the way, and I walk between them. From the back or from the front, I doubt anyone can tell I'm here. Thank heavens for small blessings. In this case, it's literal. I'm rarely glad to be so short, but now's a good time to appreciate it. They both have their guns drawn, and they're walking with them raised and ready to fire. I know Luca's is pointing to the left, and Gabriele's is pointing to the right.

I can see the car Luca brought. It's about the most average looking car that's on the market. It's got to be at least a decade old and is that kind of burnt rust hue that's a sort of nondescript color but not as simple to describe as white or black. I hear the car unlock as Luca presses the button on the fob. He's reaching for the backdoor when a gunshot rings out. We both spin around in time to see Gabriele lurch forward. He stumbles but spins around, firing into the distance. His gun makes no sound.

Another shot blasts, and it pings against the car right next to the door for the gas cap. Four more shots hit the metal as Luca knocks me down and covers me with his body. When he arches up to take a shot, I raise my head.

"Down."

He snaps at me. I put my face on the ground and cover my head with my arms. I know he and Gabriele are shooting back, but no sound is coming from their weapons. It's disconcerting because all I can hear are the bullets landing near us.

"*Figlio di mignotta.*"

I'm pretty certain Gabriele just growled, "son of a whore." From a couple other conversations I've heard the guys have, I think it really means motherfucker. I try to peek around my arm, but I can't see him.

"*Mi hanno colpito ancora.*" They hit me again.

"*Dove?*" Where?

Luca sounds concerned, but is he asking about a bird?

"*Parte anteriore e posteriore della spalla sinistra.*" Front and back of my left shoulder.

The front and back of something. I lower my left arm and turn my head. Fucking hell. I can see the blood pouring out of Gabriele's wounds. It drenches the left half of his shirt.

"Luca, he's gushing blood. We have to get him to Carlotta or a hospital."

"I know, but they're closing in on us. Gabe, can you get in the car?"

"Go without me."

"That's not fucking happening."

I don't know why they switched to English. Is it so I can follow along? Actually, I don't think either of them realizes which language they're speaking. They switch between the two so easily and fluently that it's whatever language comes to mind.

"Livy, I'm going to roll off you. Get in the car and get down. I'm going to put Gabe in the front passenger seat."

Luca's moving as he speaks. I stay crouched low to the ground and open the door. The moment I do, the window shatters above my head. I squeeze my eyes shut and my press lips together as hard as I can to keep from screaming.

Where are Luca's brothers? Why don't we hear sirens? Surely, plenty of other people can hear what's going on.

"Give us the *puta.*"

I freeze. Whomever this guy is, he just called me a bitch. Definitely not here to help. As though the Spanish accent didn't give it away already. I dive into the car and slam the door shut behind me. I crawl forward and push the door open across from me and scramble out. When Luca and I hit the ground as the bullets first started flying, the key fob landed beside me. I scooped it up, and now I'm trying to get to the driver's seat and get the engine on.

The moment I get the door in front of me open, someone drags me out. My knees hit the ground, and this time I can't hold in my scream.

"Livy!"

"I'm all—"

The fist that lands against my left cheekbone makes my head ring.

"Livy!"

"You should teach your *zorra* to keep her mouth shut unless she's sucking cock."

I went from a bitch to a whore. The man who has his hand in my hair also grabs his crotch and thrusts his hips toward my face. It's my turn. My fist slams into his dick, and he howls with pain. I scramble to my feet as he tries to hold on to me. I bring both of my hands down as a single fist and land it on the inside of his elbow. He lets go of my hair, and I shove him as hard as I can. I yank open the driver's door and look across the car.

The scene in front of me makes any nightmare I've ever had look like the sweetest dream. There are ten men, all with their guns pointing at Luca and Gabriele. One of them steps forward and swings his foot back before kicking out at Gabriele's head. Even with bullets in his shoulder, Gabriele is a force to be reckoned with. He grabs the guy's foot and calf, then snaps them. I'm fairly certain I'd see bone poking through the skin if the guy pulled up his pant leg.

Luca doesn't have his gun in his hand anymore, but I see him reaching into his pants' pocket. He pulls out his switch-blade and snaps it open. When a man rushes forward to take it from Luca, he slices the guy's inner thigh. Blood geysers from the wound, and the man collapses. From the way it gushes, Luca must have sliced a major artery.

It shocks me how gracefully he gets to his feet, moving in front of Gabriele with only his knife in his right hand to defend them both. He's methodical about the way he slashes and thrusts to keep our enemy from encroaching any further. I reach across the center console and pull on the door handle. I stretch as far as I can to get the door open.

"Gabriele."

I hiss his name, but he's edging toward unconsciousness. He's bleeding far worse than I realized, and I thought he was gushing the last time I looked. He struggles to get to his knees, but he wavers. Luca spreads his arms, trying to shield Gabriele while he staggers to his feet. He more tumbles than sits in the car.

"Luca, get in."

I have the car on and am tugging Gabriele all the way onto the seat. He's barely able to lift his legs. I look past him when I see movement across from Luca. A man walks forward, ignoring Luca as my boyfriend slices this guy's chest. The cartel member puts a gun to Luca's forehead. I tense, waiting for the moment Luca's brains explode in front of my eyes.

But that doesn't happen. Before I can comprehend what is happening, Luca's kneed the guy, grabbed his arm, and twisted the gun back toward its owner, forcing the guy to shoot himself in the temple. Luca fires off several rounds, making the cartel members even more unpredictable as they spray bullets in our direction.

"Livy, go!"

"No. Not without you."

"Little girl."

I can't do it. I can't leave him behind.

Even if I wanted to, the opportunity is gone. An SUV pulls

up in front of me. For a moment, I thought it was Marco and Lorenzo, but that's not who gets out of the vehicle. This man's closer to Salvatore's age, and he carries himself with the same arrogant swagger you'd expect from a mafia boss.

"*Bajad las armas, gilipollas. Son inútiles si están muertos. Incluso el mono.*" Put the guns down, assholes. They're useless if they're dead. Even the ape.

Gabriele grunts and mutters, so I'm the only one who hears him.

"*Mamahuevo.*" Cocksucker.

"*Sácalos del coche. Has perdido demasiado tiempo. Ya tenemos a los otros dos.*" Get them out of the car. You've wasted too much time. We've got the other two already.

The other two? Does that mean Marco and Lorenzo?

The guy I got away from pulls me out of the car a second time. When his arm recoils, this time I'm prepared. I stomp on his foot and punch him in the throat. I'm lucky that he's five-foot-eight on his best day. I wouldn't be able to reach him otherwise.

"*Que te folle un pez.*" I hope you get fucked by a fish. It loses something in the translation. Or maybe not.

There's an aura about this older man that makes me need to regain my dignity and assert myself. I don't want to stand before him, cowering or controlled by someone holding onto me. I face him, and our gazes meet. There is something insanely familiar about him, but I have no idea what. I can't pinpoint it. Where we're standing, there are streetlights every few yards, and his car's headlights reflect off the trees. I can't make out all his features' details, but enough for them to send a chill down my spine.

"*Vámonos. Necesito que vayas al garaje ahora.. Es casi el amanecer.*" Let's go. I need you to hit the garage next. It's almost dawn.

I don't know which garage this man is talking about, but the air around me shifts. I look back at Gabriele and see through the windshield that he's suddenly extremely alert. Luca's got a gun in his right hand and his knife in the left. He keeps his back close to the car as he eases around to me. He blocks me from the group of men and their leader. I whisper to him, hoping no one can hear.

"What's he talking about?"

"Something he should know nothing about."

"The garage? Is that the place you control?"

"Livy."

There's my answer. But that begs another question: How the fuck does this man know about it?

Chapter Twenty-Three

Luca

What the fuck is going on? How does Jesus Espinoza know about our garage? And why the fuck is he in New York instead of his palace near Chihuahua?

"*Estás muy lejos de casa, cabrón.*" You're a long way from home, fucker.

"*Sabe tu papi que estás fuera más allá de tu hora de dormir con la sancha?*" Does your daddy know you are out past your bedtime with your sidepiece?

He's talking to me, but he's looking at Livy. He's watching her as he insinuates I'm cheating with her. I can't see her because she's behind me. I keep my arms raised, a gun in my right hand, and a knife in my left. I shift to keep her behind me, but she steps around.

"*No sabía que los hombres de tu edad pudieran permanecer despiertos hasta tan tarde. ¿No deberías estar roncando en tu mecedora?*" I didn't know men your age could stay up so late. Shouldn't you be snoring in your rocking chair?

"*Si fueras mi—*" If you were my—

"*No soy tu nada.*" I'm not your anything.

"Livy, stop."

I know she's trying to give me time to think, but I don't want her antagonizing this man. He literally makes heads roll. He decapitates people who get in his way and leaves the heads in village and town centers to make a point. It's hard to see his expression clearly, but he reacted to her last comment. That's what's making me anxious. It was something more than thinking Livy's rude or annoying. Something deeper that I can't figure out.

"*Te estás follando a un cerdo italiano, pero me hablas como si fueras mucho mejor.*" You're fucking an Italian pig, but you speak to me as though you're so much better.

Jesus takes several steps forward, forcing me to shift my gun from pointing at Jesus's men to him.

"No closer."

"Shoot me, and I'm dead. But then so are you. Who's going to take care of your *chica*, then?"

Jesus tugs on his shirt cuffs before adjusting his tie. He's a caricature of a mafioso with his mannerisms. He's ridiculous, but neither should he be underestimated just because he looks like a joke.

"Mancinelli, you and your woman can get in the SUV on your own, or we can stick you in the trunk of that piece of shit car you arrived in and strip her naked to sit among my men. Your choice, but in the meantime, your friend's going to bleed out while you're fucking around."

I know the situation is serious with Gabriele. I'm trying to drag this out just long enough that they leave him behind. Our family will find him thanks to his tracker. They have to be on their way. Why aren't they here yet? Where are my brothers? Is that who Jesus meant when he said they have the two others? I guess it takes a shitstorm like this for me to acknowledge Gabriele is as good as family. I don't want the fucker to die.

Livy steps a little closer to me and whispers.

"Why haven't the police come? They didn't have silencers on their guns."

"Because they're paying the cops to stay away from this neighborhood, and so are we. Gunshots are the one thing they're paid the most to ignore."

"But your family...Wouldn't they come?"

"I don't know. My mom texted my brothers and me to say she was going to stay with Auntie Carlotta and Uncle Domenico. I think she wanted to give us the house to ourselves. She said Papa would join her whenever he finished."

I'm watching everything going on around us. Jesus's men surround us, but he only has the one SUV. At first, I don't know why we're waiting around. Then I realize he doesn't want to leave without an escort.

"I wondered why she hadn't come home. But what about Sylvia?"

I'll keep talking if it keeps Livy from freaking out.

"She and the girls are probably with Auntie Paola. They were going to eat there. Sometimes Natalia falls asleep just after dinner. When that happens, they stay over. All of our homes are big enough to accommodate overnight guests, and no one thinks twice about it."

It's true. We don't always just walk into one another's homes unannounced, but it's not unusual for people to crash in a guest bedroom if they're tired or just up too late to drive home. *La mia casa è la tua casa.* My house is your house. It's not just a Spanish phrase.

Jesus waves a dismissive hand in Gabriele's direction as he speaks.

"Sácalo del coche y haz algo para no manchar de sangre los

asientos. Que asco." Get him out of the car and do something to keep from getting blood all over the seats. Disgusting.

Looks like my stalling tactics won't work. Livy and I watch as two guys haul Gabriele out of the car. His head lolls from side to side, but I know him. He's not nearly as feeble as he's pretending to be. He's lost a lot of blood, but I've seen him with way worse injuries, winding up the last man standing in a fight. I was concerned earlier, but the bleeding has slowed.

"Livy, just do whatever he says. We can't risk him separating us."

"Yes, Daddy."

I know she's putting the most faith in me when she calls me that. It means she's depending on me to protect her and give her a sense that I have control over the situation. We both know I don't, but she needs that reassurance.

"*Piccolina*, do what Jesus says without argument. Once we're in that SUV, we're at his mercy."

"All right."

I watch as the two men practically drag Gabriele, as he hangs like dead weight between them. He's fucking with them, and they don't even know it.

"Put your gun down, Mancinelli. The knife too."

I follow Jesus's instructions. I turn toward Livy, and I remember she has no coat on. I shrug out of my suit jacket. One guy who'd been pointing his gun at me steps forward. He's aiming his pistol at me again, but I ignore him just like I did before.

"What the fuck do you think you're doing, *ese?*"

"I'm giving my girlfriend my jacket. She's freezing."

I ease the coat around her, holding it as she slides her arms into the sleeves. It drowns her, but that's what we need right now. I keep my voice low, so no one but Livy can hear me.

"Let me see the bracelet."

She sticks out her wrist, and I slide my hand up the sleeve. There's a gold plate on the band, and it's engraved with a wolf standing beside two boys. Romulus and Remus. The plate is thicker than it appears, and there's a tiny catch on the right side. I press it, and it activates the emergency alert. Not only will it allow my family to track us, but it'll notify them that something's happened. While still turned away from the cartel members, I press the little catch on the back of my belt buckle to do the same thing. With both our trackers activated, my family will know it's not a mistake.

I wrap my arm around Livy's shoulders as I guide her toward the SUV. Gabriele is already inside, sitting in the second-row. Two men climb into the third-row before flipping the other half of the second-row seat up. Livy goes in the middle, and I follow her. She's smushed between Gabriele and me, but I'm glad about that. I don't want any of those men touching her, and she's still safest with Gabriele on her other side.

"*Avresti dovuto promuovermi.*" You should have promoted me.

My head whips up from helping Livy secure her seatbelt. Gabriele lurches forward, his hands wrapping around the man's throat, yanking him backward in the driver's seat. Everything happens quickly, and Livy's trapped in the middle. I reach across her and into Gabriele's pants' pocket. Fortunately, I'm sitting to his right, and he's right-handed. I know his knife is in there. I pull it free and flick it open. While he's strangling the guy, the men behind us are trying to restrain us. But Gabriele and I are way stronger.

I stab and slash, cutting through his carotid artery and his jugular vein. I'm making sure he's dead. This motherfucking son of a fucking bitch piece of fucking shit is not taking our enemies to the garage to ambush my family or my men. I lean so far forward my lips are practically touching his ear. I want my voice to be the last thing he hears before he arrives in Hell.

"*Spero che il diavolo ti scopi il culo con le sue corna.*" I hope the devil fucks you in the ass with his horns.

Gabriele sits back while I pull the knife free. I wipe it on Gio Ambrosi's shirt. I've known this twat my entire life. He was one of Carmine's friends. They used to hang out together before Gabriele, Carmine, and I wound up at the vineyard. Gio expected to get a promotion when Carmine stepped into his role as a *capo*. He started wheedling Carmine to tell—not ask—but tell Uncle Salvatore that he deserved a better cut from the jobs he did, and he demanded more respect.

Carmine laughed at him. I was there. My cousin warned him not to repeat what he said because if it wasn't me who killed him for it, Uncle Salvatore would do it personally. Gio was a Made Man, but that didn't mean it entitled him to shit. He thought being so close to Carmine for years warranted him being treated better than most of our men. Dumb fuck. It got him worse treatment because he associated with Carmine.

And when push comes to shove, Carmine always sticks to family before friends. Gabriele and Matteo are the only two friends who have been promoted because of their relationship with my brothers or cousin. Even then, Matteo is family, and Auntie Paola and Uncle Cesare practically adopted Gabriele.

Blood splattered everywhere, and I look at Livy, who's got it sprayed across her. Some of it got in her hair, but she must have used my coat to cover her face because it's clean.

"Who was that?"

Gabriele answers before I can. His voice is raspy and strained. He's suffering from the exertion now.

"Someone who deserved a far worse death. *Un Giuda. Un voltagabbana. Un traditore.*"

Loyalty—even when it's misguided—is everything to

Gabriele. He calls Gio a Judas, a turncoat, a traitor. The moment we recognized him, there was no other outcome than his death. But he was lucky that we're trapped in this SUV, and Gabriele's injured. We were merciful.

Livy looks at me, her unique brown and gold eyes huge.

"He was a friend of Carmine's, and Gabriele spent a lot of time with him since we were kids. He thought he was more important than he really was. He sold us out."

At least now we know who the leak was. He shared our secrets with Jesus and the Kutsenkos. Hopefully, we only had one hole to patch and not a sieve.

Gabriele and I are sitting back now as though I didn't just kill someone. The men in the third-row are still threatening us in Spanish, but I'm ignoring them. Jesus comes over to the front passenger side and opens the door.

"*¿Qué cojones acaba de pasar?*" What the fuck just happened?

No one answers. It's obvious. But Jesus's men don't want to admit that they couldn't stop Gabriele and me, and he and I feel no need to confess.

"*Que alguien lo quite de en medio y conduzca ya el puto coche.*" Someone get him out of the way and drive the mother-fucking car already.

Everyone watches as men carry Gio to a car that just pulled up. They dump him in the trunk and slam the lid shut. One of Jesus's men curls his nose as he gets into the SUV's driver's seat. He doesn't enjoy sitting in another man's blood. Oh well.

I glance down at my watch, thinking we must have been out here for at least an hour. Nope. Not even twenty minutes. I've lived a lifetime since turning on my phone and seeing Gabriele's texts. I wonder where we're headed as the driver puts the vehicle in reverse. Now that Jesus doesn't have someone to give him directions, what's he going to do with us?

He knows better than to think we'd ever give him the address or directions. He could threaten Livy, but he knows we'd just take him straight to one of our stash spots where we have men standing guard.

I also want to know what brought Jesus *"El Cazador"* Espinoza all the way to New York City. I could ask who he's hunting, but it's not like he's going to give me a straight answer. So, I bide my time. We leave the park area between the two neighborhoods where my family lives, and we head toward the highway. I feel Livy jump when police lights and sirens turn on. The driver is doing nothing wrong, so I know these cops have been waiting to make their move. They're on our payroll.

"Muévete de una puta vez." Get the fuck moving.

This beast isn't like our SUVs. It roars as the driver hits the gas. There's no slipping quietly into the night. Police cars are pouring onto the road, following us as the driver speeds up. We enter an industrial complex I recognize. This is not our territory and not where we need to wind up.

Now he's swerving and weaving, trying to keep any of the patrol cars from boxing him in. I wrap my arms around Livy to keep her from slamming into Gabriele, who tries not to flinch with each jostling movement.

Jesus snaps at the driver after his head bounces off the window.

"Más rápido no significa que nos maten." Faster doesn't mean get us killed.

Livy cries out, but it's too late.

"Watch out!"

The driver has no chance to avoid the spike strip a cop throws out in front of us. He swerves, making the tail end swing out. The front two tires go over the Stringer, or tire deflation device. They blow, but the guy doesn't slow down. Instead, he slams on the gas. The SUV spins, colliding with a police car and nearly pinning an officer between the patrol car and this SUV.

Losing the front two tires sends the SUV careening across the street as we end up in a tailspin as the clearly inexperienced guy behind the wheel steers in the wrong direction. Anyone who's driven in snow or rain knows to steer into the skid, but he's doing the opposite. Guess the weather's always nice where he grew up.

"Gabriele, get down. Brace yourself."

Once more, I'm covering the top of Livy. The impact comes as we hit a police van, then we're rolling. A pea in a tin can doesn't even begin to describe how it feels. I've been in several car accidents but never a rollover. I'm doing everything I can to protect Livy while trying to keep an eye on Gabriele. I move to hold on to Livy tighter when she struggles, then I realize she's reaching for Gabriele. She leans over him, while I lean over her. She keeps his head from taking the brunt when the car finally stops with the driver's side on the ground.

"Nobody move."

No shit. None of us can. Fucking police.

The driver's either unconscious or dead because he's pressed against the steering wheel, causing the horn to blare. Jesus grabs the man's shirt and yanks him back. The way he moves like a ragdoll, there's no way he's alive. The fuck nut didn't have his seatbelt on. He's lucky he didn't fly through the windshield, which is completely shattered. I hear groans from the men behind us.

"Put your hands where we can see them."

Livy grimaces as she turns her head toward me.

"How the fuck can they see anything?"

"I know. Are you all right, *cuore*? What hurts?"

"Everything, but nothing serious."

"Livy..."

There's an edge to my voice that tells her she better not be downplaying anything for my sake. She whispers to me, but I know at least Gabriele hears.

"Daddy, I'm all right. Honestly. I'm going to be sore everywhere tomorrow, but I don't have any injuries. You protected me."

"Because I love you."

"I love you too. What's going to happen once we get out of this?"

"For you, hopefully straight to one of Aunt Sylvia's guest bedrooms where Auntie Carlotta can give you a full examination. For the rest of us..."

"Are they going to arrest you?"

"Maybe. Gabriele?"

"I'm alive. You're still stuck with me."

"I guess that's not so horrible."

Gabriele grunts as he tries to look in my direction. His words are a bit mumbled as he speaks.

"You need a neurologist. Clearly, your brain got rattled."

"You took care of Livy and took two bullets protecting her. I won't overlook that. Thank you."

"She has horrible taste, but that can be forgiven. She makes up for you."

"*Fottiti.*"

"What does that mean?"

I grin at Livy.

"Screw you."

She whispers in my ear, definitely making sure no one else hears.

"If you're offering..."

"Is that all my *piccolina* thinks about?"

"Better than thinking about the mess we're in right now."

"When I get you alone—watch out, little girl. That wolf on your bracelet won't be the only one in your bed."

"Our bed."

I love how she corrects me. She's right. The only his and hers are our sinks.

We hear other cars arrive, so Livy and I stop talking. I strain to hear, and it shocks me when I hear more Spanish, not Italian. Why the hell are they here?

Chapter Twenty-Four

Livy

I don't recognize that voice. It's not Mexican Spanish, but it's definitely Latin American. I look at Luca in confusion.

"It's Enrique Diaz."

"Why?"

"I don't know."

The vehicle rocks, and suddenly, we're tossed back to the other side of the vehicle as people right it. I look past Luca, and there's a police officer with his rifle pointed at Luca's head. I look to my left, and the same is the case, except it's pointing at Gabriele. The liftgate goes up, and cold air blasts into the confined space. It revives me a little now that the adrenaline is wearing off. I feel shaky and nauseous. I don't dare tell Luca that. He'll explode, and he'll probably wind up on Rikers Island.

The officers open the side doors and order us out of the vehicle. Gabriele and Luca each hold up a hand while they slowly ease off their belts. The officer standing beside Luca tries to restrain him once he's out of the car, but Luca's elbow flies back and lands in the man's nose. Other officers rush forward, but Luca's lifting me out of the car. He scoops me into his arms and ignores everyone around him.

"Mancinelli?"

"Yes, Diaz. What the hell are you doing here?"

"Me? Why were you in Espinoza's car?"

I watch Enrique as he looks around. This is the most bizarre scene. There are five cruisers with at least eight cops on the scene. Three more cars surround the SUV we were in and the others Jesus had with him, but it's not the cops who're going through those cars. They're men I don't recognize at all. They're taking stuff out of the trunks and ripping out the back seats to lift stuff out.

"Luca, is that coke?"

"Yes."

"Why are they doing that? Who are they? Feds?"

Luca snorts.

"Enrique, your men are dressing a little too shabby these days. Livy just asked if they're feds. You need to pay better, so they don't look like they got their suits at some discount store."

"Piss off, pretty boy."

Ruggedly masculine, dripping with testosterone-filled sex appeal—yes. Pretty boy—no. I look up at Luca and wonder if it's actually a dig at him because of his scar.

"Don't hate me because I'm beautiful."

Luca's goading Enrique, and I don't get why. I don't get why the police still have weapons pointed at us while Enrique's men are taking kilos of cocaine out of Jesus's cars. Where is Jesus anyway?

I look around before tapping on Luca's chest.

"You can put me down."

"No."

"Luca, I can stand on my own."

"Whenever you're not in my arms, shit goes sideways, and I'm praying you're not dead."

He tightens his hold on me. Poor man. He appears cool as a cucumber, but he's fighting to hold his shit together. I wish we could go somewhere private where he could breathe and realize that I'm safe just like him. At least, I think we are. No one has shot us or cuffed us.

"Put Ms. D'Amato down, Luca. We need to talk. I'm not pleased to be woken in the middle of the night again. I'd just fallen back to sleep."

I'm not sure if Luca bristles because Enrique issued him orders or because Enrique said my last name aloud. Could it really be a secret at this point? Does it even matter?

"Luca, Gabriele needs medical attention. Whatever's going on has to wait. He has bullets in him."

"Ms. D'Amato, one of my nephews will drive you and Mr. Scotto to Dr. Mancinelli's house."

Mr. Scotto? Is that Gabriele's last name? I guess I figured he was a Mancinelli too. And which doctor? Carlotta or Maria?

"My girlfriend isn't going near your batshit nephews."

"Fuck you, *hombre*."

Some guy flicks Luca off before barking orders to a teenager about being careful not to puncture any of the bags.

"That's Javier. He's one of the *Tres J's*. Javier, Jorge, and Joaquin. Stay away from them, Livy. They're fucking sadists. They should be locked up in isolation somewhere. They're menaces to society."

Wouldn't people say that about Luca and the men in his family? This entire scene is fucking insanity. Members of three syndicates, surrounded by police, are shuffling a few million dollars' worth of coke among cars. How does this even happen?

I nearly jump out of my skin when I witness a man

standing apart from the others aim his gun at Jesus's men and put a bullet between each of their eyes. He just moves down the row, not dropping a beat between targets.

"Luca?"

"Don't look, *piccolina*."

"But who is that?"

"Pablo. He's my equivalent among the Colombians."

"He's one of Enrique's nephews, right? Is he the *Tres J's* brother?"

"Older cousin."

I need someone to map this shit out for me. There's so damn many of them in all the families. Maybe they're all good Catholics after all because birth control doesn't seem to be a thing. Then again, Carmine is an only child, and so is Gabriele. At least, I believe they are. Matteo only has one brother. But Luca is one of four.

There are four Kutsenko brothers and four cousins. Maybe Eastern Orthodox are like Roman Catholics. I think I remember something about Pablo having a brother. So, two there and then Pablo's three cousins. I wonder if there are others.

My mind's wandering. Is it because I'm too fucking exhausted to see straight? Or is it my mind's coping mechanism to block out watching a series of assassinations?

Tires squeal and everyone spins around to see yet another black SUV approaching. I'm already confused about which ones belong to Enrique and which belong to Jesus. Who's coming now?

"Thank God."

Luca's relief doesn't match his sprint to the side of the road with me still in his arms. He has us duck behind a strange car, and I notice Gabriele crawling toward us. He has his suit coat wadded up against his chest. When he gets to us, he groans as he lies down. He's doing his best to keep pressure on his wounds.

"About fucking time they showed up."

What's Gabriele talking about?

"Who?"

"Carmine and the others."

I listen to glass shatter and screams of pain. There must be bullets flying, but unlike before, there are no sounds of gunshots. The weapons must all have silencers.

"Luca! Gabe!"

Matteo's running toward us, firing his gun at I don't even know who. I hear several tires popping, but I don't know on which vehicles.

"What the hell happened to you?"

"I got shot, you dumb fuck. But they're flesh wounds."

I don't know about all that. Flesh wounds shouldn't bleed that much, but I'm not contradicting Gabriele. Instead, I look up at Luca and keep my voice low.

"You have to put me down. Gabriele's getting weaker. He needs Matteo *and* you to help him."

"I know. I can't let you stay behind. Stay where the three of us can shield you."

"Just get Gabriele to a car and let me watch my own back."

Luca glares at me as he nods. He and Matteo hoist Gabriele onto his feet. Everything has caught up to him, and he's deathly pale. I see the alarm on both Luca's and Matteo's faces. Luca wraps his arms around Gabriele's chest, and Matteo turns away before he grabs an ankle in each hand. It's clumsy and slow, but Luca and Matteo realized what I did. There's no way Gabriele can raise his left arm high enough to get it around either of their shoulders, and he's too close to passing out to make his feet work. I stay close as we run toward a Porsche 911. I didn't see this earlier, and it's not pointing the direction the vehicle Matteo got out of came from.

"Whose car is this?"

I ask as I hold open the passenger door as the guys help Gabriele into the seat. Matteo's running around the front to get to the driver's seat as he answers.

"Joaquin's. I've been waiting to do this for ages. I cloned his fob like two years ago."

I watch as Matteo reaches beneath the vehicle, then stands with a little magnet box in his hand. He slides off the lid, and a fob drops into his hand.

"The moment wasn't truly right until now."

This is only a two-seater. I look around. What the hell do Luca and I do? It's fucking chaos everywhere. I spy Carmine, Marco, and Lorenzo, along with men I don't know, in a fight with Pablo and the *Tres J's*. Both sides are dressed in tactical gear rather than suits. There are dead bodies—Colombians, Mexicans, and cops—strewn across the industrial complex's parking lot. Enrique is plowing his fist into Jesus's face over and over. All the while, Luca and I are stepping away from the Porsche Matteo is stealing. He revs the engine several times before putting it in gear. The tires squeal, and that breaks up the fight.

I quickly figure out which one is Joaquin since he's screaming profanity I don't even know. He orders his men not to shoot. He'd rather someone steal his car than damage it. What the hell? I don't get any of this.

I thought Jesus's men got Lorenzo and Marco, but they got out of the same car as Carmine. I guess he and the other soldiers with him found the vehicle Lorenzo and Marco were in and freed them.

"Come on, Livy. We need to get to one of our SUVs."

As we run across the industrial yard, passing storage

containers where Enrique's men put the stolen coke, I realize Luca's relatives started the fight with Enrique's nephews as a distraction. The *Cosa Nostra* are stealing the coke from the original thieves, the Colombians. We get into the SUV that doesn't have drugs in it. The moment the liftgates slam closed on the other vehicles, I hear a whistle. Lorenzo, Carmine, and Marco fall back, signaling their men to do the same. As the *Cosa Nostra* men climb into their various cars and SUVs, the Colombians realize what's happened.

"*¡Hijo de puta!*" Son of a bitch!

Enrique ducks out of the way as Marco leans out the window of the SUV we're in and shoots out the tires of the car Jesus is being shoved into.

"What the hell just happened, Luca?"

I want answers. Now.

"My best guess is Jesus arranged a meeting with Enrique to sell that coke to him. When the bomb they sent to my parents' house didn't go off and Gabe got you out, Jesus scrambled to change the plans to deal with us and still make the meeting. Enrique never intended to buy shit off Jesus. Those police are on several payrolls besides the City of New York's. They were there to arrest the Culiacán, but the Colombians always intended Jesus to be Enrique's. He can have him. The police knew to force Jesus and his men into that industrial park because Enrique owns it. If the coke had stayed in the shipping containers, it would have been on one of their ships to Europe this morning."

He doesn't need to tell me it'll be on one of the Mancinellis' ships instead.

"But what about all those police officers?"

Luca looks at me for a long moment, and I'm uncertain whether he'll answer.

"They chose money over common sense. Either they were

in debt and needed cash or had to pay off some other debt to Enrique. I recognized all of them, Livy. They were on our payroll, too. Three of them worked for the Irish, and two more on top of those three worked for the Russians. These were dirty cops who played a game that was bound to get them killed. This wasn't the first time out for any of them, either. They knew."

It makes sense. But what's wrong with me that I can reason out why their deaths are—acceptable? Reasonable? Expected? I'm not stunned at all when I think about watching Pablo shoot those Mexican Cartel members. They're the bad guys, right? But it sounds like the cops were too? They weren't doing anything to help us. They held no loyalty to Luca and his family.

But Carmine, Lorenzo, and Marco killed men, and so did the soldiers who work for them. Doesn't that make the Mancinellis bad guys, too? Bad guys. Am I seven? But what else do I call them? They're all criminals. It's just a question of whether they're the current enemy.

My fucking head hurts. No one else is talking in the vehicle, so I lean against Luca and close my eyes. He strokes my hair, and I feel myself relaxing. I'm more mumbling than whispering, but I manage to ask Luca what time it is.

"Coming up on six."

"Where are we going?"

"Uncle Salvatore's. I'm going to be in a meeting with him and the others for a long time. I want you to sleep as much as you can. We're still going away, little one. While Jesus is alive, there's a threat. We have to figure out what's going on between the Colombians and Mexicans. Enrique is keeping shit from us, and that's why he just lost almost three million in product."

"Three million?"

That's fucking insane. Maybe it's because I'm so tired, but I can't conceptualize three million dollars' worth of coke. Maybe if I'd seen all those kilos in one place rather than pulled out of cars and shipping containers.

I don't stop myself from dozing off during the drive. Luca helps me out of the car and guides me to the front door. Marco's leading the way, so he walks in without knocking or ringing the bell. Lights are on throughout the house, so no one's sleeping. I step aside when Nicoletta hurries toward us. I try to give her space to hug her son, but she pulls me into her embrace, and I sag against her. She wraps her arms around Luca and me, and I draw a different sense of relief and safety from her. She smells and feels like a mom. I would never say that out loud, but she does. It's soothing.

But whatever benefit Luca drew from it is over the moment he straightens. I follow his gaze to a man who looks just like Matteo, but with hair a few shades lighter. This must be Emilio. I glance up at Luca, and his jaw clenches so hard that I can see the muscle or tendon—whatever it is—bulge.

"Livy, this is Matteo's brother, Emilio. Emilio, this is my girlfriend, Olivia."

"It's nice to meet you, Livy."

I don't like that.

"Olivia."

I'm quick to correct him. I can't tell if he's subtly antagonizing Luca or whether he's just too forward. Maybe it's both.

"I'm sorry. I thought you went by that, and Luca was just being formal. I go by Lio."

I can tell something is on the tip of Luca's tongue, but he's keeping it to himself.

"It's nice to meet you, Lio. It's still Olivia to everyone but Luca."

"How sweet. Since we already shortened Luciano to Luca, do you have a pet name for him?"

I never considered whether Luca was short for something. "Yes."

Emilio waits for me to elaborate, but I don't. I lean against Luca, and he wraps his arm around me tighter. I'm too tired to play games or interpret hidden messages. I just want to fall into bed and be done with today. Carlotta walking over makes me so relieved I almost cry.

"Do I need to take a look at you? You were outside in not nearly enough clothes for way too long."

I look down at what I'm wearing. I have Luca's suit coat on over a t-shirt and leggings, which have grass stains and mud on them, not to mention a man's blood. I was freezing in the tree-house. After that, things were too confusing and unstable to think about whether I was cold.

"Nothing some thick blankets and a bed can't fix. How's Gabriele?"

"Both bullets passed through. That boy has always been practically indestructible. But that doesn't make it any easier for me to stitch him up. One of these days..."

Carlotta swallows and shakes her head. She blinks several times, and I step away from Luca to hug her.

"I'm certain he knew he just had to make it home to you, and you would fix it all."

She nods and offers me a watery smile. Sylvia joins us.

"Luca, you know which room you and Olivia can use. Olivia, are you hungry?"

I think about that for a moment. I am, but I'm way sleepier.

"I'd really just like to go to bed. I should shower first, though."

I don't have any clean clothes to change into.

"I'll put some clothes on the bed while you're in the bathroom."

"Thank you."

Luca slides his hand into mine and leads me toward the stairs.

"Uncle Sal, I'm going to get Livy settled. Then I'll come back down."

"Take your time. Olivia, are you all right? Does Carlotta need to examine you?"

"I didn't get hurt. I'm just tired and dirty."

Salvatore walks across the foyer to where Luca and I stand at the base of the stairs. His voice is gentler than I've heard before, except for when he talked to his daughters.

"We're going to settle this, Olivia. No more looking over your shoulder or being scared. I don't know what's going on between the two cartels, but your involvement is done. After today, neither will catch you in the middle."

But will being with Luca put me in the middle of other fights? I scan the family standing in the foyer and the living room. It still surprises me how normal these gatherings feel. Not quite Norman Rockwell, but just nice. I see Carmine talking to a woman I haven't met, so my guess is she's his mom. All the women are here except Maria. None of them look like they're trapped between warring mafias or stuck in lives that make them unhappy. Just the opposite.

"Thank you, Salvatore. I trust you and Luca to sort it all out."

He looks like he's about to walk away when he thinks better of it. His brow furrows for a moment before he meets my gaze.

"I hope you know that each of our houses is as much a home to you as it is to Luca and all the kids. Sylvia and I consider you our niece. Hopefully, you'll think of us one day as your aunt and uncle."

I don't know what possesses me.

"Salvatore, may I hug you?"

He stares at me for a moment before he smiles. I've only

seen him do it a couple times, but it's like looking at Luca now. It gives me a glimpse of what Salvatore must have looked like twenty years ago. How'd he make it into his forties without being married? He opens his arms to me.

"Thank you—Uncle Salvatore."

I try it out, not sure whether I just crossed a line. He said he hopes I think of him as one. He didn't say I could call him one.

"Uncle Sal."

He gives me a quick squeeze that I return, then we step apart. I take the hand Luca offers, and we make our way to a guest bedroom.

"Do you want to take a bath, Livy?"

"I'm afraid I'll fall asleep in it. I'll take a shower to rinse off. I don't want to dry my hair, but I'll have to. I'd rather wash that tomorrow, but I have—stuff—in it."

"*Piccolina*, I wish I could share that shower with you, but I have to go back downstairs."

"I know, Daddy. Will you wake me when you come to bed?"

"Do you need something now?"

"Later. When we don't have to rush."

"All right. The bathroom is on the other side of the walk-through closet. You should find everything you need already in the shower and towels hanging on the racks. Aunt Sylvia believes beds should be cozy year-round. Do you want me to turn on the electric blanket to warm the bed?"

"Oh, that would be fabulous. Yes, please."

I strip out of the filthy clothes and look around for where to put them. I don't spot anywhere, so I fold them and put them on top of the dresser. I know Luca is watching me, so it tempts me to tease him. I bend straight over and pick up my shoes. They don't need moving, but I know he enjoys the view.

A steel band wraps around my waist the moment before his

hand lands on my ass. He rains down five hard slaps that press me onto my toes. Then he lifts me off my feet and carries me into the bathroom. His hand between my shoulder blades tells me to lean forward as he comes to stand at the end of the counter. He unfastens his belt and pulls it free. I mentioned one night that the idea of being spanked with his belt—marked by him—intrigued me. Now he holds it up.

"Do you want to try this?"

"Yes, *caro*."

"What's your safe word?"

"Museum."

"Have you ever been spanked with anything before?"

"Only your hand."

"Livy, this will hurt. No matter how light I go, it will leave welts, and it will burn. There's nothing wrong with telling me to stop if you need me to."

"Daddy, I won't do more than I can. I promise."

"All right."

He coils most of the belt around his hand, tucking the buckle within his palm. There's only about eight inches of leather hanging loose.

"You will count each one and ask for another."

"Yes, Daddy."

He positions me, and I inhale, trying to relax. But nothing could prepare me for the searing pain that ricochets through my lower half.

"One. Another, please, Daddy."

"Are you okay, *piccolina*?"

"Yes. Another, please."

He spanks me five more times. I count and ask for each one. When he's done, he drops the belt to the floor and twists my hips so I can see my ass in the mirror. Welts cover every inch. They're deep pink, almost red, and puffy. But I know they will settle and only be tender. He swore from the beginning that he would never bruise me, and he never wanted lasting marks. He's examining his handiwork, and I know part of it is arousing to him. But another part worries that he's inadvertently hurt me.

"Daddy, thank you for my spanking."

I try to ease his worry.

"Your pussy is dripping, little girl. I thought you were sleepy."

"I am, Daddy. At least my mind is. You haven't used my pussy in a while, so I guess that part of me is well rested."

"Is that so?"

I press my lips between my teeth, trying not to laugh. I squeal when he squeezes my ass hard. He steps behind me and yanks my hips back. Then I feel him thrusting into me. His hand wraps around my throat. We haven't talked about breath play, which I want to try. I just don't think tonight is the right time. His hand rests heavily without constricting.

"You teased Daddy when he was already hard for you. You know I need to be in a meeting right now. Instead, I'm balls deep in my little girl. I think you need a good fucking to make sure you have the patience to wait until Daddy can really take care of you."

"I need you, *caro*."

"I know, *cuore*. I need you, too."

He kisses along my neck as he pulls me up to rest his chest over my back when he leans forward. We watch ourselves in the mirror above the sinks.

"How many more days?"

"Shit. I don't have my pill to take in the morning."

"I'll make sure you have everything you need when we wake up. So how many days?"

"Four."

"Fuck. That might kill me."

"We could go back to condoms for those four days."

"Yes. I don't want to keep pulling out. I love how good it feels to be bare inside your pussy, but I hate ending the moment."

"Same."

I swallow my moan as his thrusts press his cock against my g spot. I whimper when he pulls out, but he spins me around and lifts me. I wrap my legs around his, locking my ankles just beneath his chiseled ass. He tips me back onto the counter, and I grip the edges to balance. He kisses behind my ear and back down my neck. He feels so good that I'm tempted to tell him to come inside me and take the chance.

But we aren't even engaged. I'm not repeating what happened to my parents or Carmine's. When Luca and I have kids, it'll be because we've already committed to each other officially and for life, and we've talked about having a family. In depth, not just in passing.

"Harder, Daddy."

"The counter—"

"And I are fine. Harder."

"Who's in control?"

"You, *caro*. But I know I can always tell you what I want and need."

"And I'll always put your wellbeing before anything else."

"My wellbeing says I need fucking harder."

My earnest tone makes him laugh, and my heart skips a beat. I cup his face and dive in for a kiss that soon consumes us. He lifts me again, but this time he lowers us to the floor. We're on a fuzzy mat, and it's actually pretty comfortable. He kneads my tits as he pounds into me.

"Is this what you need? You want me to fuck you until

you're sore, and all you can think about every time you move is how much you want me back inside you?"

"Yes, Daddy."

"One of these days, after we're married, I'm going to fill you with my cum, and we're going to make a baby."

"I want that. I want the kids, the yard, and the picket fence. All of it. But before that, I want to convert one bedroom into a—"

I snap myself back into reality before my fantasy tumbles out of my mouth.

"Into a what?"

I moan and writhe, hoping he thinks I'm too close to coming to remember what I was about to say. But he pulls out, and I whimper. I flail and reach for him.

"What do you want to turn the bedroom into, Livy?"

I'm suddenly too nervous to say it. He lowers himself onto his forearms and presses gentle kisses across my cheek.

"What's wrong, Liv? What do you want? It's our home, so we can do whatever makes you happy."

"Maria told me earlier that you never brought the same woman back to your bedroom more than once. I don't want to know whether she was right, but it made me wonder if you always went to Diana's or only to your club. I'm curious about what somewhere like that is like, but I don't want to go anywhere where I'm going to run into women you've fucked. It would ruin it, and frankly, it would make me insecure as fuck. I want to change one bedroom into a playroom or sex room or whatever they're called. I want to do tons of kinky shit somewhere that has no memories of other women for you."

"First, we can make a sex room wherever you want in the house. I'll clear out the entire basement gym and theater to make a huge one. I—"

"No! You are not explaining to the guys why they can't work out with you anymore."

He laughs and thrusts into me. He holds himself still, even as I attempt to flex my hips.

"Second, none of my subs came to my house. I did not mix those parts of my life. I will tell you the truth, so you never hear it from someone else and wonder why I kept it from you. I have a studio in Manhattan. That's where I would meet them. I put it on the market while I was in the car on the way to Atlantic City. It's already under contract. I haven't thought about my past, Livy. I don't want to. I only want to think about now and our future. Will things bring memories to mind from time to time? Of course. But I'm not interested in living in my memories."

"Same, Daddy. I want to live in the moment and plan for our life together."

Our kiss is passionate, but it's also tender. The tone shifts, and we're no longer fucking. We're making love. We move together until I can't ignore my need.

"*Caro*, may I come?"

"Yes. I'm on the edge, Livy. Don't hold out."

I move with him until I feel the tightening in my core. My eyes drift closed, the sensations so intense that I can only handle a couple of my senses at a time.

"Yes. I'm coming. I'm coming. Oh, Luca."

I strain and tense as pleasure bursts through me. Luca keeps thrusting, and that temptation to tell him not to pull out sweeps over me again. But it only takes one time.

"Let go, Livy. I have to come."

He jerks back and fists himself, but he's already coming. Did he start while he was still inside me? Ropes of cum leave cream across my tits and belly. We both look at it before Luca helps me to my feet. It's only now that I realize he's fully clothed and I'm fully naked.

"You're late for your meeting."

"I don't care. I should shower quickly."

He strips off his clothes while I turn on the water. I step into the shower, then he follows me in. We do nothing but scrub ourselves. He gives me a quick kiss as he leaves the bathroom. I didn't realize he had clothes here, but he grabs some from the dresser.

I'm more than halfway asleep by the time I'm drying my hair while sitting on the bed. Sylvia left some pajamas for me. I'll wear them in the morning. If I put the PJ pants on to sleep in, they'll wind up around my ankles. I'll need to roll them over several times since I'm five inches shorter than her. Either way, I appreciate her kindness.

I hear a phone buzz, so I drag myself off the bed and look around. I head back into the bathroom and realize Luca dropped his while we were having sex. I wake up the screen and see a text message just came in. I can only see the preview. I know how to unlock it because Luca's lent it to me before. But I won't invade his privacy. I only want to know if it's urgent and needs his attention now.

I walk back into the bedroom just as the door opens. I jump and crouch beside the dresser, relieved when I see that it's Luca since I'm naked.

"Your phone just buzzed. I was checking whether I needed to bring it downstairs."

I hand it to him.

"I just came back for it. Who's the message from?"

"I don't know. I didn't read the preview."

He unlocks the screen and turns the phone so we can both see it.

PABLO

Talk to your future wife. She's not who she seems.

My brow furrows.

"Luca, what does that mean? I'm not hiding anything from you."

"I know, *piccolina*. Pablo's just stirring shit. It's part of their retaliation for tonight. They're fucking with me because they know better than to come near you. But they're counting on anything to do with you will set me off."

"Are you going to respond?"

"Not to the text. I have to go back downstairs. We're about to call Enrique and Pablo. I don't know how soon I'll be up here."

I cannot stifle my yawn.

"Okay. Hopefully, you can get some sleep before the night is over."

It's after six. We're a little late for that, but I hope he comes to bed soon. He needs the rest as much as I do. We share a quick kiss, and I climb into bed as he closes the bedroom door. As I get comfortable, I can't help but wonder about that text.

What does Pablo think he knows about me?

Chapter Twenty-Five

Luca

Gabriele's passed out in a guest bedroom, doped up with narcotic painkillers. He has an unreasonable pain threshold that scares Auntie Carlotta. She's convinced one of these days, he'll push himself into the grave. She insists that just because he claims injuries aren't that painful doesn't mean they aren't serious. She knocked him out as much to ease any pain he might feel as to keep him immobile, so his body can rest.

The remaining men gather in Uncle Salvatore's office. I just want to be upstairs with Livy. I know she's safe here, but I can't stop worrying. I feel like I might be ill. Would she be better off somewhere far away and not connected to this life? Or would ending things and sending her away just make her an unprotected target? At this point, I'm certain it's being a target. But my conscience screams at me.

It surprises me when Carmine comes to stand beside me near Uncle Salvatore's desk. There are plenty of seats, but I'll fidget. I'm forcing myself not to pace.

"How's Olivia?"

"She's all right. Exhausted."

"Can we talk later?"

I watch my cousin, and I'm even more suspicious than usual. Carmine shakes his head and looks away for a moment before our eyes lock.

"We are not the same people we were as teenagers. We're not even the same people we were six months ago. I'm done with playing the puppeteer out of spite to everyone in this family. Watching you get beaten every day in Sicily was too much even for me. I admit I didn't feel any remorse when Uncle Sal had a go because I was still so fucking bitter. But Lucenzo was a mad man. He was the same manipulative fuck I became. Watching him was a painful look in the mirror. And seeing you with Olivia makes me envy what you have. I don't want Olivia, but I'd like to have a relationship like you do. What woman wants the family shitbag? What family would welcome me into it?"

I want to believe Carmine, but there's so much history between us. Shit no one knows but us and Emilio. I shift my attention to Emilio as he sits with Matteo. I noticed he wasn't with the others when they came to get Livy, Gabe, and me. I figured he'd slinked back to Jersey. But nope. Here he is. If anyone is truly the black sheep of the family, it's Emilio. But he's not as closely related to Uncle Salvatore as Carmine and I are.

"Yeah. We can talk."

"Should we include him?"

"Fuck no. Let me get through talking to you and not killing you. Then I'll possibly consider talking to him."

Besides the fight he and I got into that left me with the scar along my cheek, he drank and partied way too much in high school. He wrapped his BMW around a telephone pole and nearly killed the three girls in the car with him. He was so drunk, his blood alcohol level was almost too high to register. The ER docs have no idea how he didn't poison himself. That experience sobered him up, but it wasn't enough to make him stop being a douche.

"Luca?"

I didn't realize Uncle Salvatore was talking until he said my name.

"Sorry. Just thinking."

We hadn't started the meeting yet when I came downstairs the first time. We were scattered between the kitchen and dining room, all of us starving. We were about to head into the study when I realized I forgot my phone. I pull it out now.

"Pablo texted me while my phone was upstairs. It's a veiled threat. He said I need to talk to my soon-to-be wife because she isn't who she seems. He's fucking with me by using her as bait. He won't actually touch her, but he knows he can wind me up by talking shit about her. There's nothing she's hiding."

Papa nods as he speaks.

"We know that. He's bullshitting you because he can. We've all spent our adult lives discovering people's lies and extracting them. Nothing about Olivia gives any hints that she's hiding something. She may not have had time to tell you everything about her life, but she isn't keeping something from you.

"Let's call Enrique and Pablo and figure out what the fuck he means."

I dial Pablo's number. It's the first speed dial contact in my phone that isn't my family. Pablo grew up in Jersey, but we've known each other since we were kids. We played on the same soccer team. We used to get along when we were playing pee-wee sports. That was before we understood we could never be friends. That may as well have been a million years ago, but his number was the first one outside my family that I saved in my very first phone.

"*Hola, Luca.*"

"Hello, Pablo. I got your text."

Silence hangs in the air. Pablo and I wait each other out. He knows I want him to explain, and I know he wants me to ask. Neither of us is giving an inch. I speak first, but it's to address another issue.

"Enrique, we gave you a heads up about the building in Brooklyn as a courtesy. We left Josue to you. You might have mentioned you were sixty-nining the Culiacán."

"Who we do business with is not your business."

"I'd think you'd think twice about getting into bed with them when they had no problem shooting up your place after luring us there."

"Jesus and Josue are learning that was a poor choice."

I scoff.

"You won't kill the head of the Espinoza family. That's what's bad for business. Are you sitting with him sipping shit tequila right now? Hello, Jesus."

There's a noise in the background, but no one says anything. That's all the confirmation I need that Jesus is there. What condition he's in is a guess. There was nothing pretend about the way Enrique wailed on his face, but the *jefe* is still breathing.

It's Pablo who speaks next, and I want to reach through the phone and choke him.

"The only business you need to worry about is giving back our product."

My family laughs. No one on either side of the call believes that's going to happen.

"It's the price of peace. You hid the fact that you're in bed with the cartel that's tried to kill my girlfriend. Do you know what they've done?"

There's silence. This time I decide to fill it.

"They chased her down on the interstate, caused an accident that could have killed her, then tried to take her. They shot at her while she was out to lunch with *my sister*. They tossed Molotov cocktails into our home and her mom's. They caused a fire there that would have killed Livy's mom if our guys hadn't been there. They sent a bomb to my parents' home, and then you saw the shitshow that was tonight. How about I call Laura next, Enrique?"

"Don't play games with me, *cabrón*." Asshole.

"What games? I think she told you something along the lines that if you fuck up again, the next time she sees you, she will carve her initial and her sister's out of your arm with a butter knife. I think she'll count doing a multi-million-dollar deal with a family intent on hunting down and murdering a woman as a pretty big fuck-up."

"The deal started months ago."

"And you could have ended it once you knew, which I'm certain was practically the minute I met Livy."

Uncle Salvatore steps in, and I hold the phone out to him. The call is on speaker, but it's easier if he takes it.

"You would never pay for that coke. You could've told us you planned to screw them over. Then you wouldn't really be as guilty as this makes you look now, and we could have let this go. But you sided with them, and they are our enemy. Enrique, this isn't some petty little tiff. You and I are not on good terms."

If anyone else heard Uncle Salvatore say that to them, they would know he had ordered a hit on them.

"I do not run my business by being concerned about you."

"Good. Then you won't be concerned that your product is already on its way to Europe."

"A ti no te parieron, te cagaron."

Enrique's phrase literally means, you weren't born; you were shat. Basically, it's a wordy way to call Uncle Salvatore a motherfucker. I laugh, but there's no humor in it. It's purely condescending.

"What did you think was going to happen when we found out? Even if we never found out about that shipment, we still would have retaliated. We know you know that."

Pablo interjects, and I want to roll my eyes, but I make myself listen.

"Luca, listen to me. We haven't been friends since we were six, but that doesn't mean I can't throw you a bone once in a while. When I texted you, I wasn't threatening Olivia. You need to talk to her mom. I only found out tonight how complicated all of this is, but Olivia's mom needs to tell you. I'm certain there's plenty my *tío* and I don't know. It's better coming from Ms. Ruiz."

I definitely don't love that they know Olivia's mom's last name isn't the same as hers. It means they've looked into her or heard more than a passing comment about the woman. I look at my dad, then my uncle.

They both frown but nod.

"Fine."

"Sooner rather than later, Luca. For both their sakes."

I signal we need to wrap this up by twirling my finger in the air. I want to get back upstairs to Livy. We both need sleep before I can think about dealing with any of this. I would walk out now, but we're using my phone.

"Fine, Pablo. Enrique, you fucked up. Now you have to accept the consequences of siding with the wrong people. You're not getting shit back from us, and you should be glad we aren't doing more."

I hang up the call. Fuck. Gabriele isn't here, so he can't tell the rest of them about Gio. I turn to Carmine, and I have a moment of regret having to inform him. But they'd grown apart since Carmine's promotion.

"Carmine, we found who's been selling info to the bratva and the Culiacán. It was Gio."

Shock, then shame, flash across his face. He stares at the floor as he nods.

"He's dead?"

"Yes. He was Jesus's driver. He was going to take Jesus to the garage."

The room is silent as we watch Carmine. He shoves his fists into his pants' pockets.

"Did he shoot Gabe?"

"No. We didn't know he was involved until they had us in the SUV that rolled. One of Jesus's men was behind the wheel for that. He was already dead. I don't know who shot Gabe, but Gio definitely wasn't around for that."

Carmine looks past me at our uncle.

"Do you want me to deal with his family?"

Uncle Salvatore watches me for a moment before he responds.

"Yes. Make sure we provide for his widow and boys. Find out what his brother knew."

"I'm going to check on Gabriele. I'll go to Gio's house in a couple hours. I don't want to wake Theresa and the boys this early with the news. I'll wait until the boys are at school and tell her alone."

His head is down as he crosses the room. When we were younger, I used to believe Carmine was incapable of remorse. Then I realized he was the master performer and could hide his emotions, only displaying what he wanted the world to see. But the man striding to the door is neither hiding nor pretending. His guilt is very real. When I shift my attention to Uncle Salvatore, I know he sees the same thing I did. He's going to let Carmine's shame be his punishment. He kept Gio too close to our family and then the bastard crossed us.

"Get some sleep, Luca. You can sort this out with Olivia's mother in a few hours."

I don't need telling twice. I stuff my phone in my pocket and head toward the stairs. I'm crossing the foyer when a guard who patrols the grounds opens the front door. I recognize the bags he's carrying.

"Vinny, did you have any trouble?"

His face flushes, and I frown. That's when I notice the box tucked under his arm. Oh, fuck me. The stuff we reordered arrived, and the guys at the gate opened the box. How could they not when they knew about the bomb threat that happened at my parents' place?

"No. Mikayla grabbed Ms. D'Amato's clothes, and I grabbed yours. Mikayla got whatever was in the bathroom, too."

He hands everything, including the box, over to me. He practically sprints back out the door. I can only imagine the conversation he and his wife had on the drive over here. I peek in the box and flinch. Nothing is in its original packaging. I wonder if it would be better to dump everything into my bag and claim I put it all there. If I don't, she'll assume Vinny and Mikayla saw it all because they packed the rest of our stuff. Either way, she'll know security opened the box to search it. Fucking hell.

I carry the box up to the room and ease the door open. I take in my beautiful girlfriend sound asleep, her just below shoulder length blonde hair is mostly back to its normal color and strewn across the pillow. The silky skin of her bare arm and shoulder is exposed as she holds the covers tucked around her. I drop the bags and the box, not caring about them now. I strip out of my clothes and slide into bed beside her.

"Daddy?"

"Yes, little one."

I wrap myself around her, and she nods in her semi-asleep state. She sighs as I spoon her.

"Don't let go, Daddy."

"I won't, *piccolina*. Go back to sleep."

She drifts back into a deep slumber, and it's only seconds later before I join her.

Chapter Twenty-Six

Livy

I come awake to the feel of Luca wrapped around me. I bask in the moment's serenity. Tucked away in this bedroom within a house that feels more impenetrable than a medieval castle, the world exists far, far away. I'm cozy as my back absorbs the heat Luca radiates. His bare skin's against mine. I wish I could wake up just like this every morning for the rest of my life. That would be bliss.

"Did you sleep well, little one?"

"Mhmm. I felt you get into bed, but I was too sleepy to really understand what was happening."

"I know. But I'm glad you got the rest. You needed it."

I roll over in his arms and caress my hand over his shoulder, chest, and upper back. There are deep shadows beneath his eyes, and he's clearly far more exhausted than I am.

"Did you sleep, *mi vida?*" My life.

That's a new one. I've never called him that, but it feels so right.

"Oh, Livy."

He groans as he rolls forward, pressing me onto my back.

"Is that really how you think of me, *cuore mio?*"

"Of course. If I'm your heart, then why wouldn't you be my life? The love of our lives."

"I love you so much, Livy. You don't still feel like this is too rushed?"

I rest my hands on his shoulders, our gazes locked.

"Luca, where's this coming from? What happened while I was asleep?"

"Nothing. I just worry you'll wake up one morning and think this was a horrible mistake brought on by the circumstances."

"Do you worry about this all the time? That I'm going to leave you?"

"There're certainly plenty of reasons you should."

I press his shoulders until he shifts away, and I can sit up. I tuck the sheet and comforter under my arms.

"Luca, I don't know why things happened the way they did. We're both Catholic and believe in God. Maybe it was Him. I don't know. But there have been hours with little for me to do but think and pray. I know it hasn't been that long, but I feel so calm after I pray. There are no doubts I'm ignoring or trying to rationalize. There's no fear I'm trying to forget. My heart and mind are peaceful every time I think about my decision to be with you. I'm not going anywhere."

"I'd describe it the same way. I've prayed a lot, too. I'm always embarrassed to say that because I feel like such a hypocrite to claim I have a deep faith when I ignore so many of the fundamental tenants of our faith. But I still believe, and I still find reassurance in prayer. Whenever I ask about us and pray for guidance, the same peace always comes. I'm where I'm supposed to be. I know being in love isn't enough, Livy. Especially not in this world."

"Luca, are you asking me if you're enough? The answer is yes. You're everything to me."

"Thank you, *piccolina*. I needed to hear that. I don't want to lose you."

I would say the only way he could lose me is if someone took me, but that feels like it would flagrantly tempt fate. We do *not* need that.

"I sent a guard and his wife back to our place to pick up some stuff. I spotted your birth control pills when I checked earlier."

He points toward two bags on the bench at the foot of the bed. There's a plain box with one small label on it. It takes a couple seconds, then my eyebrows shoot to my hairline. I push back the covers and crawl to the end of the bed.

"Luca, they opened this!"

"I know. I'm sorry, Livy. I didn't think to text the guys and tell them to set it aside. After the bomb threat, I doubt they would have."

"Fuck. How many of them do you think saw what's inside?"

"Two. Whoever was at the gate when the delivery arrived would have opened it. Then V—"

"Don't say his name. I want to look all of them in the eye and not know who saw our sex toys."

I sit back on my heels as I pull things out of the box, realizing they have unpacked most of the items to ensure no one smuggled anything dangerous within the packaging. I glance at the door before laying everything out on the bed around me. Luca walks to the door and listens. He must hear no one because he opens the door a crack despite being naked. He shakes his head when he looks at me. He shuts and locks the door before prowling back to the bed. His entire demeanor has shifted.

"What do you want to play with first, little girl?"

"We can't do that here! Someone will hear us."

"The girls are at school, and Sylvia has court today. Uncle Salvatore has meetings scheduled all morning. Anyone else who spent the night probably left at least an hour or two ago. It's midmorning already. We have the house to ourselves, Livy."

"Isn't there stuff you need to do? Do you have to go to that place?"

"No to both. My brothers will have filled in for me or cleared my schedule. If I'm needed there, then someone will call to tell me. No one has, so I'm not."

He checks his phone to be certain before he climbs back onto the bed.

"You haven't told me what you want to try first."

"All of it."

Luca laughs, and it's that deep, dark, sensual sound that shoots straight to my pussy. I look at the bed's headboard. There are wrist cuffs he could wrap around the headboard's post. I hold them up. He takes them and puts them on my pillow. I pick up a bar and pull the ends until it slides and doubles in length. I definitely want to try this spreader. I hand it to him.

Then I examine the various impact implements. I select a flogger, a paddle with holes punched through the wood, and a cat-o'-nine-tails. I push aside a few things to find the eye mask and ear plugs. While doing that, I find the Wartenburg pinwheel. I run it over my palm, then my nipple.

"Are you stealing my fun?"

"Never."

I hand it to Luca and press my shoulders back, arching to push my tits toward him. He doesn't start where I expect. He places it a couple inches behind my ear, gradually rolling it along my neck, along my collarbone, through the dip between my collarbones, then down the valley between my tits. He moves unhurriedly as he runs it around the circumference of my right breast, making each circle smaller as he draws closer to my nipple. By the time he reaches it, it's tightened into a dark nub. It prickles as he crisscrosses and swirls the pinwheel over my nipple.

He repeats what he's done on the other side. While he pays attention to my left breast, I roll and pinch my already puckered right nipple. Once they're both tight and sticking out, I hand him clamps.

"I won't make these too tight. If it tingles in a bad way, you tell me immediately."

"I know, Daddy. You will be beyond monumentally pissed if I get hurt."

"That's putting it mildly, little girl."

He fastens them on, and I lie back, my thighs dropping open with my knees bent. He grips my thighs and lifts me to reposition me how he wants. He settles on his belly, blowing cool air on my clit. He licks, sucks, and flicks it until I'm gripping the covers in my fists.

"Please, Luca."

"Who?"

"*Caro*. Please, *caro*."

He grazes his teeth over the bundle of nerves, and my hips come off the bed, trying to gain more pressure where I need it. He pulls back and snaps the clamp onto my clit. I whimper.

"It's just a new sensation. It doesn't hurt. It just surprised me."

From here, he positions me as he wants. He rolls me onto

my belly, drawing my arms over my head. He fastens the cuffs around my wrists, chaining me to the bed. He connects the spreader to my ankles, forcing my legs as far apart as the pole allows.

"Your ass could make me come just looking at it."

He trails his hand over my flesh before landing a hard slap that cracks in the otherwise quiet room. Since we're alone, I don't hold back. I moan, letting him know how much I like it.

"You like that, don't you?"

"Yes, Daddy."

"What shall I use instead of my hand?"

I feel him climb off the bed. He opens a plastic package, but I can't see what he's doing. Even when I try to twist and look over my shoulder, I can't make out what he has. He moves to stand beside me, and I hear a bottle cap flip open. I know it's lube, but it still makes me shiver when the cool liquid drips between my ass cheeks. He uses the moisture to help his finger glide around my backdoor. The tip presses into the puckered hole. Then his fingers are pressing my ass cheeks apart, and he pours lube directly into my asshole.

"You've taken my cock before, but I won't start you with the largest plug."

Now that he's standing beside me, I can watch what he's doing. He drips lube onto the rubber plug that has a fake crystal on the flange. He's so careful as he eases it into me, pausing to watch me for any sign that I'm hiding my discomfort. I'm not. I'm relaxed but moving rapidly toward impatient.

"Please."

"Please what? Take it out?"

"No!"

He chuckles before pushing it all the way in. I know it's not the largest one we ordered, but I feel full. He twirls it, and I try to grind my clit against the mattress. His hand lands across my ass.

"*Piccolina*, you will not get yourself off. You don't come without my permission. If you do, I will deny you any orgasms until tomorrow. Plus, you have the clamp on. I don't want you to move the clip and accidentally pinch the wrong part of your clit."

"Yes, *caro*."

My toes flex and wiggle as I wait for what comes next. He eases the eye mask on before slipping in the left earplug.

"Daddy, can we try the ball gag too?"

"If that's what you want. Show me you can snap your fingers with the cuffs on."

I don't know why being cuffed would keep me from snapping, but I do it.

"I'll snap if I need to safe word."

"Good."

"Luca, lift the mask for a moment."

He does what I ask, and I twist as best I can to see him.

"I don't want this to stress you out. The whole point of why we're like this together is so you have control because you crave it, and I can let go of trying to cling to control that doesn't exist for me. If you can't stop worrying you'll hurt me, then you're never going to feel in control. Just the opposite. This will make you miserable. You couldn't have been this worried about your subs. I mean, I'm certain you were careful, but you're a bundle of nerves."

"They were there to take whatever level of pain I wished to dole out because it got them off, which got me off. I didn't love any of them. I didn't care about every single thing about them, every breath they took, every heartbeat. I want to give you the perfect first time with real BDSM, Livy."

"Daddy, it's perfect because it's with you. We're finally

alone and able to explore. I trust you completely. When we're like this, all I have to focus on is how you make my body feel. I can forget about everything else and enjoy the attention you lavish on me. It should be the same for you. You can forget about everything else and enjoy knowing that you control every sensation, every moment of ecstasy and agony I experience. My body is yours to do with what you want. I am yours."

"Liv, I never want to disappoint you."

"Keep loving me the way you do, and you won't. Release this hand."

I shake my right one. He does as I say, and I immediately wrap my palm around his cock.

"Livy."

I ignore the clear warning in his tone. Maybe getting him off will get him to release his doubt. Maybe pushing him to take control will recenter both of us.

"Did I say you can touch me? Did I tell you to jerk me off?"

"No, so I'm hoping this warrants a very hard spanking."

I lean forward and lick the tip of his cock. He fists my hair and thrusts into my mouth, brushing my throat. His hand lands across my ass.

"You want me to fuck you? Now I am."

I can barely keep up as he presses my head forward as his cock fills my mouth, resting heavy against my tongue. I love the feel. I love that I'm pushing him to these limits of his self-restraint because he desires me this much. I keep stroking him as I suck.

I moan around his cock and kick my legs, lifting them together because of the spreader. He just used the cat-o'-nine-tails on me. It slices through the air again before the thongs swish across my upper thighs, ass, and lower back. He's unrelenting in his speed, but I know he's not being as forceful as he could be.

"I'm going to come down your throat, and you are going to swallow all of it. Then I'm sticking that ball gag in. You are a naughty little girl, thinking that you can play with Daddy's cock whenever you want."

He leans forward and kisses my cheek before he whispers in my ear.

"The way you give head might kill me and send me straight to heaven. I know why you did that, but if you ever think to be the one in the lead again, I'll paint your ass red for real, then fuck you in it. Do you understand, *piccolina*?"

"Mhmgble."

It's a garbled sound as I try to signal my agreement. The best I can do is suck harder. I try not to choke as his cum shoots down my throat, and I can't catch my breath as he holds my head in place. He pulls out and quickly positions the ball gag. Then he pulls the mask back over my eyes and puts in the other earplug.

The sensory deprivation heightens what I experience. I don't know what's coming next, and I can no longer ask or see. The pinwheel glides up my left instep before it weaves over my calf and thigh before he skims it the length of the division between my ass cheeks. He draws figure-eights on my lower back. He presses it so lightly against my skin as he moves up my back that I shiver.

I'm so intent upon the sensations the pinwheel creates that I'm unaware of what his other hand is doing until the paddle strikes my right butt cheek. Holy fuck. Ho-lee fuuuuck. That fucking hurts. My fingers and toes curl and flex over and over. He nails my left side, then alternates for three more on each side. The pinwheel stops, and I sense he shifts position. Then the paddle lands across my horizontal crack, pushing my ass upward. I kick both feet again.

Just when I fear I'm going to need to snap, he tosses the

paddle aside. He bends my legs and climbs onto the bed. He pushes my heels toward my back and slides his tongue along my pussy. I scream behind the ball gag. Everything is so sensitive and aroused. I'm clutching at the pillow beneath my hands. I want to touch him, but I can't. I want to enjoy every inch of him like he's enjoying me, but that's not my decision to make. I revel in the frustration that creates while the aching need to be closer to him sends my emotions into a tornado. They blow left and right, unpredictable, and wreaking havoc in their path. I writhe and tremble until he twirls the plug.

I try to draw my knees under me, so I can push my hips upward. Luca pulls back, taking his magical tongue with him. Instead, he takes the flogger to my pussy. He swats it six times before he dives back in. I'm screaming and moaning, sweat dripping between my shoulder blades. I shriek when he lifts my hips and flips me onto my back. I bounce on the mattress as he moves around. I can't guess what's coming next.

Two cold metal balls slide into my pussy. Ben Wa balls. Three of Luca's fingers follow and roll the oversized beads against my g spot. With the earplugs in, I don't anticipate the vibrating wand that buzzes against my clit. He releases the clamp, and all the feeling rushes back in. The wand and Ben Wa balls send me careening toward an orgasm that I battle to control.

I suddenly have this overwhelming need to pee. I'm struggling against it, and I wonder if I'm going to squirt for the first time ever. Do I snap and admit that I might not be able to stop this orgasm and warn him? Or do I ride it out and discover what happens? If I snap, he'll stop immediately, then I'll never know. I focus on breathing through the intense sensations until my body arches off the bed.

He turns off the wand and removes the balls, but his fingers pinch my clit mercilessly. He's doing something with his other hand, but I can't tell what. Then he's pulling the ear plugs out, ripping off the eye mask, and unfastening the gag, which he flings toward the wall. He pulls me toward him before flipping me back onto my belly. His hand comes around my throat, and this time he squeezes.

"Snap if you need to."

"Yes, Daddy."

He continues to tighten, but I can still breathe. His other hand positions me with my hips up before his cock surges into me.

"You came, didn't you?"

He loosens his hold enough for me to speak.

"Yes, Daddy. But it's never been like that before. I thought I might squirt. I thought I could breathe through it. I had no control over that."

"You've never come like that before?"

"No. Only for you."

His hand tightens again, and I can hear my pulse in my ears.

"You are mine, Olivia. You know I will kill for you. I will torture for you. I will do anything I fucking want to keep you safe. No one will ever stop me from taking care of you. I will love you until my last breath. You are everything I have ever wanted and needed. There is no one but you. You destroy any self-control I have."

"Dddee."

He lets go.

"Daddy, show me."

"Fucking hell, Livy. You know I won't. I'll hurt you."

"And could you fucking trust me one goddamn time? I will safe word if I need to. But stop putting distance between us when it doesn't need to be there. Fuck me the way you want because it's exactly what I want too."

"You don't know what you're asking."

"Then fucking show me. Fuck, Luca. When are you going to understand that I want it as rough as you do? Stop thinking you want anything between us more than I do. Who the fuck are you to think your feelings are stronger?"

"That is not how my little girl speaks to her daddy."

"Then fuck me hard enough to shut me up."

"Livy, it'll take a long time to forgive you if you push me to where I hurt you."

"And it hurts that you won't listen to me and trust me. This is the one thing I need most right now. Please, Luca. Please."

His grip tightens around my throat again, and his other hand clutches my hair. His body presses me into the mattress, practically smothering me. My hands and feet are still restrained, so I am fully at his mercy.

"May I come?"

"Yes, *piccolina*. I'm going to get you off until you simply beg me to stop because you can't do anything more than lie there and breathe."

He's fucking me so hard that the entire bed shakes. It slams against the wall over and over. I pray we aren't wrong and that someone is still at the house. His weight keeps pressing me further into the mattress, and pain blurs the pleasure. But I don't want him to stop. Just the opposite. I want more. I want this complete domination of my body. This animal wildness that he can't get enough of me. That no other woman has driven him to this point. That he finally loses all the vaunted control he carries with a death grip. By having complete control over me, he can let go of the control he has over himself and be free. I don't know if that makes sense to anyone but me, but I get that's what we both need.

His hand tightens another notch, and I start to see stars.

Just as panic nips at me and blackness dances at the corner of my eyes, my body explodes.

"*Caro!*"

I scream, but I barely make a sound because he's crushing my throat. My body goes rigid, and he immediately lets go.

"My sweet little girl. You're so fucking beautiful every minute of every day, but watching you come is magnificent. Your trust is everything to me. *Tu sei il mio desiderio più profondo.* You are my deepest desire. I love you."

He hasn't slowed. If anything, he's more frenzied than ever. He keeps whispering in my ear.

"I can't stop, Livy. Every moment of desire, longing, lust that I've held back since we met is coming out. I'm still scared I'm hurting you. Please don't let me do that."

"Luca, I would never betray you or cause you guilt and shame on purpose. I want this. Don't stop. I'm close again."

And I am. He grunts as he grips my chin and turns my head, so he can nip and tug my earlobe with his teeth.

"Your tight little cunt is going to take my cock over and over. Once I shoot my cum into you, I won't stop. Day after day. Week after week. Month after month. Year after year. You will sleep filled with it. You'll go to the fucking grocery store with it in you. And you will sit and make nice with our families while it drips down your legs. Do you know why?"

"Because my pussy belongs to you, Daddy."

"That's right. And who does my dick belong to?"

"Me."

"You and only you."

He grazes his teeth over my shoulder before kissing the trail he left.

"Come again, Livy. Squeeze the cum from me. I'm wearing a condom."

"Thank God. I don't want you to pull out ever again, Luca. I want us to come together."

"We will, little one."

He pounds into me. The last threads of restraint snapped for us both.

We cry out together. I realize he laced our fingers together as his cock pulses within my pussy. We lie, panting for a couple minutes before either of us can speak again.

"Daddy?"

"Yes, *piccolina*."

"Nothing has ever—I hope—Was this—"

I stutter each time I speak, and now I suddenly feel self-conscious and embarrassed. What if I just made way more out of this than what it was?

"Livy, nothing has ever been like that. I hope it was as good for you as it was for me. Was this the best you've ever had?"

He says all the things I wanted to.

"Nothing compares. I've never felt so desirable and sexy. Feeling you finally lose the last bits of restraint because you wanted—"

"Want. Not past tense. Want. Right now. Always, Livy."

"Last bit of restraint because you want me that much feels so incredibly empowering when I've felt so lost and out of control."

"And at the same time, I felt like I had complete control over you because you couldn't move, even breathe, without me allowing it. I've never felt more in control than just now."

"That's what I wanted for us."

He pulls out of me, and I whimper. He's quick to remove the cuffs and spreader. He grabs everything and puts it all into one of our bags. Only the butt plug, which he just took out, the Ben Wa balls, and the foam wand go back into the original box. There's a small plastic bag that he puts the condom in. I watch him drop a bottle of toy cleaner in there. Then he slides under the covers with me.

"I called you Olivia earlier. Did that bother you? I didn't realize it until after it came out."

I have to think about that for a moment. I don't know when that was.

"I didn't notice. Does anyone call you Luciano?"

He grins.

"My priest. The only other two times that I know that someone else called me that were on my baptism and confirmation. Emilio was being a dick."

This isn't the right time to ask, but I want to know what happened between them.

"Daddy, can we take a nap before we face the world? I know we need to see my mom."

"A nap, then a hot bath together. How does that sound?"

"Blissful. Will you hold me while I sleep?"

"Livy, the aftercare has never been so significant to me as it is with you. After what we just did, I'm not ready to let go of you yet. Not just because I want to be sure you're all right, but because I don't want to sever the emotional bond we have. But tell me if I'm being too clingy."

I'm getting groggy, and I yawn. I slap my hand over my mouth and cringe.

"I wore out my little girl, didn't I?"

"Yes. I'll put suction cups on your hands and feet, and you still won't be too clingy, *caro*. The only place I ever want to be is where we can touch. I'm the stage five clinger."

I yawn again, and he draws me closer. He strokes my hair, and I twitch as I slide into sleep. I'm not entirely sure what I'm saying.

"I hope you plan to marry me soon."

"Is that what you want?"

"If you don't ask soon, I'm going to ask you. Is it husband-daddy or daddy-husband? "

My eyes are closed as I babble. I hear Luca laugh before he kisses my forehead.

"Don't worry, Livy. I'm asking you sooner than you think."

Chapter Twenty-Seven

Luca

I stand behind Livy on the stoop of the small Staten Island walk up. I suppose I assumed all nuns lived in rooms at churches or cloistered away somewhere like a monastery or abbey. I never imagined one would open the door to a four-story urban row house. Livy extends her hand.

"Sister, I'm Olivia D'Amato. I'm here to see my mom."

"Welcome. I'm Sister Hannah. Your mom is staying with me."

"Thank you for helping her."

The nun offers Livy a kind smile, but she's not so quick to warm to me. I'm about to cross the threshold when Sister Hannah raises her hand.

"Give your weapons to your driver. You are not bringing them in here."

"I already did, Sister. I'm unarmed." *And unnerved.*

I haven't left my house without a weapon since I was twelve. It kinda freaks me out. But I say nothing as we follow the middle-aged woman farther into the building. We walk down a hallway until we come to a rear unit. Sister Hannah unlocks the door and ushers us in.

"Mom?"

Livy calls out, and Ms. Ruiz steps out of the living room. The apartment is modest, but very comfortable. No cots or threadbare blankets and hairshirts here. I took a couple Medieval Literature courses in college to get a break from the science and math. Apparently, I was impressionable back then.

"Ivy!"

Livy dashes forward and embraces her mom. I hang back, not wanting to intrude. Sister Hannah offers me a drink, but I decline. Livy reaches back to me while holding onto her mom with her other arm. I come to stand next to her, but I don't take her hand. I try to respect her mother and the doubts the woman clearly possesses. They radiate from her expression and the clearly stiff posture when she sees me.

"Mom, I'm so glad you're okay."

"I am, but what about you?"

"It's been a couple more challenging days, but I'm safe with Luca and his family. Those challenges are a part of why we came. Mostly, I couldn't wait to see you, but I have some questions."

"I expected as much."

Hesitation, then resignation, settles into her eyes. She nods and leads the way to the sofa and armchair.

"Pablo Diaz is the Colombian *jefe's* nephew. He sent Luca a text saying I'm not what I seem, and that Luca needs to know who I really am. I don't get what that means. I've hidden nothing from Luca.

"You'd both better sit down. This is so much more complicated than you can imagine."

We walk to the pullout loveseat, and I wait for Livy and her mom to sit before I do. It's as uncomfortable as it looks. I feel badly if Ms. Ruiz is stuck sleeping on this.

"Luca, you may as well call me Maritza."

My brow furrows. Oh, fuck. Oh, shit. Oh, hell. Holy fucking shit in hell.

"You figured it out, didn't you?"

"Figured what out, Mom?"

"Luca knows your father."

"No, he doesn't. He would have said so."

This got complicated fast. So much for small talk. This conversation can only go badly or horribly. There's no other option. I rest my hand on her back.

"Livy, remember when I asked you about Danny D'Amato?"

"Yeah, and I said I didn't know anyone by that name."

"Livy, he's your dad. You don't have to hide that anymore."

I hate thinking she kept something from me after all. If I know who her mom is, she must realize I know her dad, too.

"I'm not hiding anything. My father's name is not Daniel D'Amato. I don't know who that is. My dad's name is Dante."

"Yeah, Danny for short. Your eye color made me ask. When you said you didn't know anyone by that name, I figured you were some distant relative whose family got out."

"Got out?"

I can't blame her for being completely baffled. My moment of hesitation was for nothing. She's genuinely clueless.

"Through marriage or something else and left the *Cosa Nostra*."

"My dad doesn't go by Danny, and he's not *Cosa Nostra*."

"Yes, he is Olivia."

Livy's head whips around as she looks at her mom. The pain of betrayal fills her eyes. I wish I could hold her, make this better. But this is so much more complicated. Maritza was right. I continue explaining.

"Livy, your dad is fully Sicilian. He's worked for my family since he was a kid. He's a couple years younger than Uncle Salvatore and my dad. But he got hurt about twenty years ago. A bullet punctured his lung, and he's had breathing trouble since then."

"Twenty years ago? That's around when you got divorced."

She looks at her mom, and the pieces are falling into place in her mind. Her mom picks up where I leave off.

"Your dad and I never should have gotten married, but when they forced him out because he got shot protecting Luca's dad, he grew more unpredictable and bitter than he already was. Salvatore was the one who insisted he sign the divorce papers, but he wouldn't listen to me when I said I didn't want Dante anywhere near you. He made sure the courts granted your dad partial custody. Since Dante never hurt you beyond scaring you, Salvatore was unbending about it being important that you had a father. He wasn't wrong."

"Yes, he was. I never speak to Dad anymore. I made sure he couldn't contact me the moment I turned eighteen."

"He accepted that because it was what you wanted, but being in your life protected you. Your dad has a lot of problems that he's refused to get help for. Luca, he's been lying to your uncle for years. He gave me the money Salvatore paid for him to see a psychiatrist. He insisted I use it for Olivia, since he would never see one. Once Olivia cut ties with him, Salvatore stopped paying that money. Ivy, Salvatore gave him the money, hoping medical treatment would protect you from his outbursts. He thought he was helping Dante salvage any type of relationship your dad could have with you. The only reason I kept quiet was that I knew your father would never lay a hand on you. But that doesn't make up for the way he talked to you."

"I'm twenty-eight, not eight. You never thought you should explain this to me?"

"Your dad got an envelope under the door each month. Other than that, he's had nothing to do with Luca's family. When he was no longer useful, Luca's family pretended like he didn't exist."

I cut in.

"Is that what he told you?"

"Yes."

"Maritza, Danny has always worked for us. He stopped being an associate who—takes care of things—but the ties that bind were never severed. That store he owns is a front."

Livy looks at me in confusion. I close my eyes for an extended blink and sigh.

"Liv, your dad launders money for us. He doesn't do the things you've seen me do, and he hasn't since he stopped being strong enough to fight back. But we still employ him."

Livy sits back and stares at her mom. Maritza and I are silent as Livy digests everything she's learned. When she sits forward, she rests her elbows on her knees, her hands cupping her cheeks as she stares at the floor.

"Is there anything else about Dad I should know?"

"No."

"Goo—"

"Olivia, that's just one side of your family. I'm not done."

Livy rears back.

"What does that mean?"

"The reason your dad and I got married was to make sure you got his name. Olivia D'Amato sounds as Italian as Olivia Ruiz does Spanish. The difference is your dad wasn't running from a mafia. I was. My parents were from rival Culiacán families, but back when they married, the families were allies. The alliance was brief, and it fell apart when I was a kid. My mom's family killed my dad, and his family retaliated by killing my mom. I wound up in an orphanage my dad's family controlled. I was five when my parents died, so I didn't understand why I got better treatment than the other kids—and better is relative. I didn't know who my parents were."

Maritza's lips press together while she fights to keep her composure.

"When I was fifteen, men started following me to and from school. They would say obscene things to me, make offers and threats I didn't understand. I told my priest and the nuns. They told me to never go anywhere alone, and that there was nothing they could do to stop them. When I was sixteen, my grandfather on my dad's side acknowledged me. I suddenly had a family and a home. The moment I left the orphanage, I became the rope in a tug of war. Both of my grandfathers tried to arrange marriages to men old enough to be my father. Of course, no one consulted me. They just sent men to kill each other."

Maritza's voice catches, and she gazes out the window. She's reliving some memory because fear flashes across her face. Her voice trembles as she continues to speak.

"One nun from the orphanage had a friend who was a sister at an orphanage in Baja. She had a farmer smuggle me from my grandfather's house in the back of a fruit truck. I traveled four-teen hours to Mexicali. It's a border town a few hours east of San Diego. The nun picked me up and took me to Tijuana. I couldn't stay there though. It was my mom's side of the family that ran TJ. I stayed hidden at the church in TJ for three weeks. I basically lived in a closet."

Her gaze darts to the narrow hall closet we passed.

"Then a priest from Tucson arrived with legal documents to get me across the border. I never knew it, but I had a distant cousin on Border Patrol in Arizona. She sponsored me and helped me immigrate. Once I had my citizenship, she and her now-wife helped me move to New York. I disappeared here. Ruiz is my mother's name. Espinoza was my last name before I left Mexico."

"You mean this somehow related me to Carlos?"

"Third cousins. You shared a great-great-grandfather."

"What the hell, Mom? You knew I went to his stores. You knew I had to work with him."

"And you were blonde before whatever color I still see hints of. You got your blonde hair from your father's mother and your eyes from your paternal grandfather's side of the family."

Livy's washed out most of the temporary color from her hair. Apparently, it's lasted longer than the ten washes she expected. But she's blonde again.

"Did the Culiacán come after you because they know I'm with Luca? Or did they come after you because they discovered you're my mom and that you ran away from them?"

"Either. Both. I don't know."

Livy covers her face with her hands. I rub her back because I don't know what else to do. Maritza watches Livy, and I watch Maritza. This is some fucking twisted shit. How the hell do I excuse myself to call Uncle Salvatore and explain this fuck storm?

Livy turns her head toward me as though she can read my mind.

"You need to tell Salvatore all of this. Should you call my dad and tell him what's going on? Should he know what happened to my mom?"

I look at Maritza.

"I have to tell my uncle, but it's your decision whether anyone tells Danny."

"You need to tell him. He's still Olivia's dad. If for no other reason than he could wind up a target, too."

"Livy, are you all right with that?"

"What choice do I have? Seems like I've never really had one. How ironic that I never knew I descended from two—no, three—mafia families, and I wind up in love with the *Cosa Nostra* underboss."

One of these times, I'm going to have to correct her about the word mafia and what context she should use it in. Sicilians are *the Mafia* with a capital M. Other people use the term with a lowercase m to denote organized crime groups. None of them are mafia with an uppercase or lowercase m. They're syndicates. Potato, potado except to anyone in the Mafia. That's why we prefer our real name, *Cosa Nostra*. Now is not the time for a lesson in semantics.

I pull out my phone and dial Uncle Salvatore. I debate whether I should speak English or Italian.

"*Ciao, Luca.*"

"*Ciao, zio.* Livy and I are with her mom."

I decide on English. It seems rude to use Italian, and it seems like all the secrets are out of the bag now.

"I just found out Livy is Danny D'Amato's daughter. She didn't know that Dante went by Danny for short."

"I know. I just found out, too. I had a hunch and went knocking on Danny's door. I knew those eyes couldn't be a coincidence, and I couldn't ignore it anymore. How is Maritza? Put me on speaker."

"My uncle would like to talk to you."

I hit the button.

"Maritza?"

"Hello, Salvatore."

"Were you badly hurt the other night?"

"No. My hands got burned, and I had smoke inhalation. I'll be fine within a couple days. I already feel back to normal."

"I went to Danny's. He shared something he's been keeping from me for a while. You did too."

"Salvatore?"

"Yes, Olivia."

"Are you going to punish my dad?"

"No. For your sake and because he didn't piss away that money I gave him, I won't. But there are no more chances."

"Thank you."

Livy collapses against me and buries her face against my chest. I feel her sobbing. I can't reach Maritza to give her the phone, so I awkwardly hold it up while trying to comfort Livy. I give up and lift Livy onto my lap, so I can hug her while putting the phone high enough for everyone to hear and for the mic to catch anything Maritza says.

"Salvatore, this could be as much about me as it could be about your family."

"I know. Maritza, we need to find you somewhere safe to live. You know it may not be in New York anymore."

"What?"

Livy jerks around so fast that I almost drop the phone.

"Ivy, Salvatore is right. To keep us both safe, I may need to move. That's why I mentioned California before."

"You're just going to leave me?"

"Of course not. But if my family knows about both of us, I'm not safe and neither are you. Luca and his family can protect you, though."

Livy looks up at me, then strains to whisper in my ear. I lean forward.

"If she becomes your mother-in-law, then will your family protect her?"

"We're going to protect her no matter what. But that might

mean she moves. I don't know yet. If things work out the way my family and I plan, no one in any Mexican Cartel is going to come anywhere near either of you. It'll be hazardous for their lives and their businesses."

How do you say you're going to kill someone without saying you're going to kill someone? There you go.

Uncle Salvatore's voice comes through the speaker.

"Maritza, are you okay with just my men?"

She sighs, and her lips tighten into a pucker as she considers my uncle's question.

"Danny, please come to Staten Island."

"Dad?"

"Hi, *chica.*"

"Mom, how'd you know he was on the call?"

"Ivy, I've known Luca's family for nearly thirty years. This isn't the first call I've been on with Salvatore."

"Maritza, I'll come if you need me there, but I won't come into the apartment if you don't want."

Danny sounds anxious, and I know he's expecting Maritza and Livy to reject him.

"I'd feel better if you were in here with me."

"Mom?"

"*Mija,* for all your father's faults and how dysfunctional we were, the one thing I've always known is the same thing you know to your core about Luca. Your dad will always protect you and me to his last breath. That's why Salvatore made sure the judge granted your dad partial custody. From the outside world, I'm safest when I'm with your dad."

"This is all so fucked-up."

Chapter Twenty-Eight

Livy

Neither of my parents comment on my language, and I didn't even notice until Luca flinched. I normally wouldn't swear in front of them or Salvatore.

"Dad?"

He says nothing, so I look at my mom instead.

"No. You are not going near him, Mom. You haven't seen him in years. Keep it that way."

"Olivia, that's why no one will suspect me going to him."

"Absolutely not. It's a hotel or Luca's family. You are not going near him."

"He has a place here on Staten Island that he never uses. It's a studio from before we got married that he rents out these days as a vacation rental."

"How do you know that?"

"Just because I haven't seen him doesn't mean we haven't talked. He's still your dad, so I give him updates every once in a while."

I stare at my mom. There are way too many revelations today. I offer a jerky nod. I look up at Luca. I want to know what he thinks of this. This can't possibly be a good idea. My parents are oil and water, plus Luca said my dad doesn't do this stuff anymore. He murmurs against my ear.

"Your parents are right, *piccolina*. The reason no one's come near you is because your dad protected you. It's why even Uncle Salvatore and I didn't know the connection. You might be done with him, but he's never been done with you. With how good he is at laundering money, it doesn't surprise me he successfully kept you away from anything connected to the *Cosa Nostra* and kept the Mexican Cartels from finding your mom. I knew of your mother and had heard her name, but he's never once said your name. I knew he had a kid, but I knew nothing else."

I'm trying to digest everything Luca and my mom told me. My dad wasn't the deadbeat I often thought of him as. He's a criminal instead. He's a humongous liar, but if I can accept all of Luca's half-truths and lies of omission, then I can understand why my dad never told me the truth.

"Dad?"

"Yes, *chica*."

Now that I know he's fully Sicilian and likely speaks Italian fluently, it's odd to hear him use that Spanish word. I assumed it was because of my mom and how she only spoke Spanish to me as a kid.

"That's why you used to scare me. You couldn't tell me the truth about why I had to do everything just so. That was your way of protecting me."

"I'm sorry. I didn't know how else to do it. You were so young that it was the only way I thought I could impress upon you the things I knew needed doing without explaining it to a kid. I feared you'd slip up one day by accident and admit something if you knew it. When you were a teenager, I felt like I couldn't lighten up in case you stopped thinking my rules were so important. I could live with you rebelling once you were eighteen because you left for school. You naturally lost yourself in the crowd."

This changes every-fucking-thing in my life. Neither of my parents are who I thought. My entire childhood has a totally different context now. I look at my mom, then stare at the phone as though I could see my dad through it. If my dad's coming over here, I'm not sure how I feel about seeing him. As I shift my gaze back to my mom, I'm not sure how I feel about being in the same room with her.

"I can accept all the lies you told me when I was a kid because I know this world enough now to understand why you did it. Dad, I can even accept and forgive how difficult this must have been, and that you did the best you knew how. But I'm—I don't even know—angry, hurt, confused—about why you didn't tell me once I was an adult. Dad, you thought I was safe in college, but I never would have known if I wasn't. Mom, you knew I worked with distant family. What if I'd said something that connected you to Carlos's family? How could you leave me so utterly unprepared?"

Anger, stemming from the hurt and betrayal, bubbles up from my gut, burning a path behind my ribs, threatening to spew forth in a tirade. I need to go. I need to leave. I look up at Luca, and I don't care if anyone hears me.

"Daddy, take me home. Right now."

"Livy—"

"Right now, before I say things I can't take back, especially in a nun's home. Take me, or I'm going by myself."

Luca leans in and puts his lips to my ear.

"Do not give me ultimatums about your safety, *piccolina*. You will discover a side of me you won't enjoy. This changes everything. We will leave, but everything about how I plan your future security is different. Never threaten to go somewhere by yourself, and never, ever be foolish enough to do it. Do you understand me, Livy?

I turn my head to whisper to him.

"Yes, Daddy. But please get me out of here. Pp—pp —plea—"

I stutter as the swelling lump threatens to block my throat. I bury my head against his shoulder as I lose the battle not to cry. Through all of this, I've only cried a couple times. The dam is about to explode, not crumble. I shift to stand, and Luca helps me.

"Uncle Salvatore, I'm taking Livy to our house, then we're flying out. Lorenzo, Marco, Matteo, and Carmine agreed to come with us. Alonzo and Vinny agreed to the assignment."

My mom shakes her head.

"You're going on that vacation now? There are plans we need to make. You're safer here, Ivy, where you have all of Luca's resources to protect you."

I turn to my mom, glaring at her.

"You can make your own plans and tell me about them after. If Luca thinks we should get away, then I'm going where he takes me."

I take a shuddering breath and slide my hand into Luca's and turn toward the door. Then I freeze and whip back around.

"Who is Jesus Espinoza to us?"

"Your uncle. My brother."

I sway, and Luca wraps his arms around me. I hear Salvatore through the phone, but he may as well be a million miles away.

"That's a detail you should have told me, Dante."

"I didn't know. Maritza, how have you kept that from me?"

"I never told you anyone's name from my family. Ivy, why are you asking about him? Salvatore, who is he?"

It's Luca who answers.

"Your brother is now the *jefe* for the entire Culiacán Cartel. He has been for a decade."

The color vanishes from my mom's face, and it's so startling that I rush to her.

"Mom?"

I clutch her hands in mine, and they're freezing. She looks deeply shaken for the first time during this conversation.

"Does he have a scar over his left cheekbone, just beneath his eye?"

I think about it.

"Yes. I think so. It was faded, but I think I remember seeing that."

"He's supposed to be dead. He supposedly died in a street fight when he was fifteen, and I was ten. He ran away from the orphanage a couple months after we arrived."

Salvatore speaks up, and I dread whatever comes next.

"Maritza, I never knew he lived in an orphanage. I know your grandfather raised him. I didn't know he was your brother."

Mom closes her eyes, but tears leak from beneath her lashes.

"They took him and left me. They didn't want me until I was useful. A virgin bride for some old man. Salvatore, if he knows about me, then he knows who Ivy is. Was he responsible for the attack on my apartment and on Luca's house?"

I don't correct her since it is his, but I know she meant to remind me it's not really my home. She doesn't think this is going to last.

"No. That was Santiago and Edgar."

"Santiago? He has a brother named Ricardo. That one?"

"Yes."

There's a heavy silence that makes me anxious.

"Who are they, Mom?"

"They're distant cousins so many times removed I couldn't count. I went to school with them, even dated Ricardo for a few months. But it was Santiago who was the final straw that convinced the nun to help me escape. Santiago tried to take me after school one day. He wanted to ransom me to either side of my family or either of the two men negotiating to marry me. He wanted to sell me. Ricardo found me and brought me back to the orphanage. He swore he would punish Santiago one day so he would never forget."

Luca clears his throat.

"He did. He was Edgar's biological father. He slept with Santiago's wife."

"Mom, would your brother hurt you?"

"I don't know. I ran and never looked back. But he did the same thing. He never tried to contact me once he was an adult, and I was still stuck at the orphanage."

I look back at Luca. Dare I ask and let my mom hear my question?

"Luca, did Jesus send that bomb?"

"What?!"

My mom and dad both exclaim.

"I met Jesus last night because someone sent a bomb to Luca's parents' house while I was there. Luca's friend was my bodyguard, and he got us out. But then Jesus and his men stopped us just as Luca, Gabriele, and I were getting in the car. Gabriele got shot twice."

My dad cuts in.

"Carmine's best friend?"

"Yeah, Dad."

"Did he survive?"

"Yes."

That makes me pause, and I look up at Luca. Fucking-a. Was he at the house earlier? Was he there recovering? If he was, there's no way he didn't hear us. Luca shakes his head and mouths, "his house."

I have more questions.

"If Santiago and Edgar handled the improvised explosives, is it possible Jesus doesn't know I'm related to you, Mom? Could he not know you're here?"

"I don't know. Maybe."

"All of this because I didn't walk out of work five minutes earlier or ten minutes later. I can't believe how this has escalated. If they know I'm with Luca, they must know I won't tell anyone what I saw. Why haven't they given up? Just let it go?"

Luca answers those questions.

"Because they're worried you could still go to the cops and deny I was involved at all."

I suppose. I'm back to wanting to leave, but this time, it's because I'm suddenly so tired. This latest news that my own uncle's trying to kill me sapped every bit of energy.

"Dad, how soon are you going to be here?"

"I'm in the car with Salvatore. We're about five minutes away."

Do I want to see him? I didn't a few minutes ago, but now I do. I actually want a hug from him.

"Luca, I'm super tired. After I see my dad, can we still go, please?"

"Of course, *cuore*."

Salvatore's voice is kind as he explains what comes next.

"Olivia, I have men following us. They'll stay outside while your mom gathers her things, and they'll escort your parents to your dad's studio. They'll stay and position themselves in a few places in the neighborhood. No one is getting close to your mom."

I want to point out that someone got close enough to deliver a bomb. Then I remind myself that if Massimo didn't have his gate and patrols, no one would have found the bomb before it exploded and killed Gabriele and me.

"Mom, are you okay with that?"

"Yes, *mija*. I told you, no one will protect me better than your dad. And I trust Salvatore and his men."

I walk back to the loveseat and sink down onto it. Luca wraps his arms around my shoulders, and I slump against him. I close my eyes, focusing on how he's stroking my arm and kissing the top of my head. We remain that way until we hear someone knock on the door. It's obvious the nun isn't happy to have more mafiosos in her house, but my mom slipped out when Luca and I sat down. She told Sister Hannah that she's leaving. She went to pack.

Now I'm alone in the living room with Salvatore, Luca, and my dad. I stand up, unsure of what to do. Then something propels me, and I wrap my arms around my dad. He holds me tight, and I have a memory of the fleeting moments when he'd comforted me as a kid. He still wears the same aftershave. I knew he had respiratory trouble, but now it makes me wonder if some of his highhanded, over-the-top rules were because he knew he couldn't defend himself or me if it ever came to a physical confrontation. He did what he could to prevent that.

There's no two ways about how fucked-up it was that he used to point a knife at me and threaten me. I'll never not have those memories. I can't condone or excuse that decision. But I guess I have an explanation now, and I can accept it.

"*Chica?*"

"Yeah."

"I'm sorry for so many things, everything. Every moment of

every day, I've loved you, but I've also feared for you. It scared me a *Cosa Nostra* rival would get you or someone from your mom's past would find you. I will regret nothing more than parenting you that way. Once you became an adult, I knew I couldn't exert that control over you. The protection I was so desperate to give you ended because I went about it all wrong. But I've kept an eye on you always. Through your mom and sometimes trusted friends. I couldn't just stop keeping the only person I've ever loved safe."

That makes me sad to know he never loved my mom, but it doesn't surprise me. I'm certain she never loved him. But it's still hard to hear.

"Dad, we'll figure out something going forward. At least I know. That goes a long way."

"I'm so, so sorry, *chica*."

"I know. I'm sorry I refused to speak to you. I did it out of spite. I never meant to go years without talking to you, but I never told you that either."

"I took it for what you intended it to be. You wanted me away from you and out of your life, so I respected that, at least directly. Indirectly—" He shrugs. "I couldn't."

"Were there ever times when you were right to have done that?"

He's quiet for so long that I lean back so I can look up at him.

"Yes."

Salvatore's been inconspicuous. But now he demands an answer.

"When? Who?"

"I took care of it, Sal."

"That doesn't answer either of my questions, Danny. When and who?"

"Donovan about five years ago."

My brow furrows.

"Donovan O'Rourke? What does he have to do with this?"

Luca steps forward, sandwiching me between him and my dad. I get a sense of what men who've wronged Luca face. There's such palpable menace radiating from him as he glowers at my dad.

"What the hell does Donovan O'Rourke have to do with Livy?"

"Luca, you know him? I went out with him for like a month years and years ago."

He looks like his head is about to explode.

"Luca?"

He ignores me.

"Danny, why the hell did Donovan get anywhere near Livy?"

"He targeted her because he got pissed that he lost ten grand to me at a poker game. I laundered that money and gave it to you, Sal. He claimed I cheated, which I didn't. He thought he'd go after Olivia to get back at me. She dumped him, and I called the feds. It led to that raid on one of his warehouses in Rochester. He backed off."

Luca is fuming. He paces the length of the room, which isn't very long. His hands are fisting and unfisting, and he's worrying me.

"Luca?"

"I bet I know how all this shit started. Did you meet Dillan O'Rourke?"

Chapter Twenty-Nine

Luca

I hate thinking of any O'Rourke names on the best of days. Thinking about any of them connected to Livy spikes a rage inside me that threatens to consume me. I think I get how the Kutsenko men have felt when their women faced threats from unseen enemies.

"I met Dillan a few times. He's Donovan's cousin."

"Was. Donovan's dead."

I watch her for any reaction. Surprise, but no regret or sadness. Good. I don't think I could handle it if she had even one soft feeling left for him.

"What happened?"

She's naturally curious but not concerned. Okay. Breathe.

"He tangled with someone he shouldn't have. Maksim Kutsenko."

"He's Irish. Do they work for the Russians or something?"

Her naïveté on this would boggle my mind if I didn't

remind myself that she knew none of this existed before the night we met.

"Livy, he used to run the Irish."

"The Irish?"

"Yeah. Like we're *the* Italians. He was a mob boss."

"No. Not when I knew him."

Livy shakes her head.

"Was his father, Liam, still alive?"

"Yeah."

Then it was quite a while ago. She must have been right out of college, but she said she went straight to grad school.

"Liv, when did you go out with him?"

"Summer after I graduated college, before I left for grad school."

Un-fucking-believable. I force my jaw to relax as I glance down at the floor. Then I look at my uncle.

"This is payback for the bit of help we gave Maks and Bogdan."

Uncle Salvatore's lips flatten, and I know he's cursing up a storm in his head in English and Italian. He's keeping it to himself out of respect to the nun who lives here. His gaze darts to the crucifix on the wall several times before he responds.

"For Olivia and Maritza's sakes, I almost wish we hadn't helped them."

"Luca, I don't understand what you mean. I haven't seen Donovan in years. I didn't even know he was dead."

"This is indirectly about Donovan. Dillan is the one who did this. That piece of—work. Donovan would have had him do a complete background check on you. He probably never found out anything about your mom's side of the family, but it means Dillan has known all along your connection to the *Cosa Nostra*. When he found out you and I are together, and he found out what happened to Carlos and the others, he decided to play chess with us. The manipulative—"

I'm finding it exceedingly hard not to swear. I need to think of this apartment as church. That's the only place I can guarantee I never use profanity.

"Livy, he's been moving us all around the way he wants. He's probably doing business with the Culiacán, just like the Diazes. He would have heard that you and I were involved. He must have told Edgar and Santiago that you're Dante's daughter. When their attacks didn't work, and you were still alive, it escalated within the Cartel. Jesus got involved, and I'm certain Dillan was on the phone or meeting with Jesus in person to give him the play-by-play. What I don't know is if Jesus or Dillan know you're related to Jesus."

She listens to me intently, and I can tell she's having a hard time believing me. But she doesn't know Dillan like I do. He's another one I've known since I was really young. He played on the same soccer team as Pablo and I did. He used to find ways to fuck around, then always managed to get Pablo and me blamed for it while looking like an angel. A tattle-taling angel. *Leccaculo.* Kiss ass.

"Is it sorta like if only he would use his genius for good rather than evil?"

I exhale a disdainful puff.

"Something like that."

I turn to Uncle Salvatore and wait to see what he has to say, but he's watching me. He's going to let me make the calls on this since Dillan went after my girlfriend.

"We need to know whether Jesus knows who Livy is and whether Dillan told him."

"Luca, I want to see my uncle. I want to look him in the eye and ask if he tried to kill his own niece, if he allowed men to try to kill his own sister."

"You are not getting anywhere near him, Livy. There's no discussion about that."

"Yes, there is."

I inhale and grit my teeth. I don't want to argue with her in front of other people, and I don't object to her disagreeing with me. But she doesn't know what she's asking.

"Salvatore, is it only in the movies where the mafia bosses have sit-downs? Or does that happen in real life? Is there such a thing as neutral territory?"

"There is. But I don't think it's wise to trust Jesus or Dillan. I agree with Luca. Olivia, it would be extremely ill advised to go anywhere near Jesus to find this out."

"Livy, can you live with a phone call to start?"

She hesitates, then nods. Her mom walks into the room and looks around.

"What did I miss?"

"Mom, Luca believes a man named Dillan O'Rourke is involved."

"Is he related to Liam and Donovan?"

Livy's brow furrows before she closes her eyes and sighs.

"I suppose you were involved with *Cosa Nostra* stuff while you and Dad were married. That would have been nearly ten years. I hadn't thought about that."

"I was as involved as any wife might be. I knew names and a few things, but never anything significant. I preferred it that way, and your dad wouldn't have had it any other way. It would have been too dangerous."

Dante speaks up for the first time since he hugged Livy.

"Itza, we should go. We can pick up anything you need on the way. I want us settled at the studio before sundown. I know that isn't for a few more hours, but I want the men to have plenty of time to survey the area. I need to go over protocols with them. I don't want to do any of that in the dark."

I watch Livy's parents, and they must have come to some kind of peace over the years because there's no hostility between them despite how Danny treated her. I don't see reconciliation, but I also don't see any hint of volatility. He picks up Maritza's overnight bag. There couldn't be much in it since I know she hasn't been back to her apartment. We already have a crew working in there, and an exorbitantly paid property manager who makes sure no one asks questions.

"Dad, can you give me a minute with Mom, please?"

"Of course, *chica*. Itza, I'll be by the building's front door."

Uncle Salvatore shakes Maritza's hand and follows Danny out.

"Do you want to be alone?"

I keep my voice low. Livy shakes her head.

"Mom, are you safe with Dad? Honestly? Tell me the truth."

"Ivy, your dad drank way too much back then. He was bitter about life. There was someone else he wanted to marry, and he blamed me getting pregnant for ruining that. He ignored the fact that she married someone else while he and I were still dating. Then getting hurt protecting Massimo and feeling like they'd demoted him stole his identity. He felt useless. Too much machismo. We're both older and see life very differently. Your father is a different man. One I almost don't even recognize, but it's for the better."

"Why didn't you tell me any of this?"

"Would you have believed me? Would you have seen him to learn for yourself?"

Livy looks at the floor.

"Probably not."

"You wouldn't have."

"But, Mom, you could have tried. Maybe it would have

worked, and I could have had some type of relationship with him before now and not out of necessity."

"Hindsight is always twenty-twenty."

"I suppose. Mom, have you forgiven him?"

"Forgiven, but not forgotten. He never went to therapy, but he worked on himself a lot. We've talked through a lot of stuff over the years since you left home."

"I can't believe how much you've kept from me."

"It's always been to protect you."

Mother and daughter look at one another before Livy hugs Maritza. It's definitely not as warm as the hug when we arrived. My heart breaks for Livy, and I'm committed to be here for her as she works through how betrayed she feels.

Livy breaks the silence.

"All right. If anything changes, tell Salvatore. He'll help. I'm certain, and if he doesn't, Sylvia will. Go to her. They'll let us know, and I'll help you sort it out when we get back."

"You're still going on vacation?"

Maritza looks aghast at me.

"Liv, we may need to postpone. If this involves Dillan, then—"

I have some serious shit to fuck up for him. And I can't do that while I'm on vacation with my girlfriend. If she weren't with me, there's plenty that I could fuck up for the O'Rourkes in Europe.

Livy stares at me, but she says nothing. She knows what I mean. She says another goodbye to her mom, and I give Maritza a one-armed hug and an air kiss. We haven't worked up to anything more. We go our separate ways outside. Maritza and Danny get into one vehicle while Uncle Salvatore, Livy, and I get in another. Maritza and Danny leave in an SUV while the rest of us are in a limo. The privacy glass is up as always.

"Olivia, I wondered all along if you and Danny were related. I was fairly certain you were, and I even suspected you might be his daughter. He never referred to you by name, insisting he keep his family separate from everything *Cosa Nostra* once you were born. He was adamant. I ran a background check on you, but I didn't look into your family, so I didn't know for sure. Luca knew I would do that, but he didn't ask."

She just nods, but I wonder if she feels I betrayed her too by allowing my uncle to dig into her past. She'd said she wasn't Italian despite her last name, and she said she'd had little contact with her dad in years. Knowing her mother was Mexican seemed like a reason not to dig too far into her family. Since she hadn't known more than her mother was an orphan who was eventually sponsored to come to the U.S., that didn't seem exceptional either. The church my family attends has sponsored an orphanage near Mexico City for years.

"I figured you had. Since Luca didn't address it, and you didn't insist I leave, I knew you had found nothing. I sorta wish you had dug into my family. Some of this could have been prevented if you and Luca had known my family connection sooner. Can we call Jesus?"

I pull my phone out and call Enrique. Livy looks up at me in confusion, but the Colombian *jefe* answers before I can explain.

"*Hola, Luca.*"

"I'm with Uncle Salvatore and Livy. We just saw her mom and dad. Put Jesus on."

"*Apasiguate.*" Calm down. "You don't issue me commands."

"I know you haven't killed him, so put him on the phone."

I ignore his comments. I can tell when the phone is put on

speaker. There's some shuffling and noise in the background, then Jesus is there.

"*Si.*"

The arrogance.

"Do you know who I am?"

Livy jumps straight into it.

"I do now. I did not last night."

"Do you regret it? Or are you going to try harder to kill me?"

"Your mama was blunt like this when she was *muy pequeño.* I couldn't see your face clearly when we stood on the street. It wasn't until you were leaving that I got a clear view. Then I knew. The blonde hair distracts from how much you look like your mama."

I look at Livy. Now that Jesus mentions it, I see the similarities. Her hair and eyes keep it from being obvious. But the shape of her eyes, nose, and mouth are like her mom's. She got her face shape and cheekbones, along with her eye color, from her dad.

"You haven't answered my question. Nostalgic or not, do you regret it? And are you going to try harder to kill me?"

"*La única persona a la que voy a matar es a ese cabrón que mintió y dijo que una antigua mula se follaba al subjefe de la mafia.*" The only person I'm killing is that fucker who lied and said a former mule was fucking the Mafia underboss.

I don't know if his English isn't good enough to say all of that, or if he thinks Uncle Salvatore and I won't understand, or he just prefers it. I want to be sure he knows I understand everything.

"*¿Era Dillan O'Rourke?*" Was it Dillan O'Rourke?

"*Si.*"

Livy leans closer to the phone.

419

"*¿Cómo conoces a este hombre?*" How do you know this man?

"*Negocios.*" Business.

I jump in again.

"*¿Negocios como los que tenías con Enrique?*" Business like you had with Enrique?

"*Pensó que dándome esa información sobre una supuesta mula conseguiría hacer un trato con él en su lugar. Casi lo hizo.*" He thought giving me that information about a supposed mule would get me to make a deal with him instead. It almost did.

There's the sound of skin hitting skin, then a grunt before Pablo speaks.

"*Diles lo que realmente planeaste, mentiroso de mierda.*" Tell them what you really planned, you lying sack of shit.

There's a long pause before it sounds like a metal pipe hitting something and a sharp exhale.

"*Si las cosas no se hubieran jodido con el accidente y el trato con los Díaz y los Mancinelli, se suponía que los O'Rourke robarían la cocaína de los contenedores de transporte a cambio de esa información y de pagarme por la cocaína. Se suponía que pensarían que esos kilos eran nuestros y que habíamos hecho un trato con los colombianos para alquilar el almacén. Nunca habrían sabido que la coca era robada.*" If things hadn't gotten fucked up with the accident and dealing with the Diazes and Mancinellis, the O'Rourkes were supposed to steal the cocaine from the shipping containers in exchange for that information and paying me for the cocaine. They were supposed to think those kilos were ours, and we'd made a deal with the Colombians to rent the storage. They never would have known the coke was stolen.

"*Bastardo codicioso y ambicioso.*" Greedy and ambitious bastard.

Uncle Salvatore mutters under his breath, so only Livy and

I hear him. Jesus planned to get paid twice. Enrique was supposed to pay Jesus, then put all the cocaine in his shipping containers. When Dillan robbed Enrique, Jesus would have claimed to Enrique that once the products were out of his hands, they weren't his responsibility. He was never going to tell Dillan he originally sold the drugs to Enrique. But Dillan would have truly stolen them, and Jesus wouldn't have gotten his second pay day. I wonder how long it took Pablo to get that info out of the man.

The first problem for Jesus was believing the Colombians were going to pay. Enrique always planned to steal from Jesus.

"*No creas que ni a ti ni a Enrique os vamos a devolver una mierda. ¿Qué cree Dillan que pasó con el cargamento?*" Don't think either you or Enrique are getting shit back from us. What does Dillan think happened to the shipment?

Enrique grumbles and huffs.

"*Ese hijo de puta tuvo las pelotas de decirme que le entregara a Espinoza, para que le tocara a él.*" That motherfucker had the balls to tell me to hand Espinoza over, so he could have a turn.

Enrique huffs again, then his voice calms.

"*Luca, Dillan confirmó que Olivia es sobrina de Jesús. Él sabe quién es ella y su madre. Va a seguir usando eso, incluso cuando Jesús esté muerto.*" Luca, Dillan confirmed Olivia is Jesus's niece. He knows who she is and her mom. He's going to keep using that, even when Jesus is dead.

Livy turns panicked eyes to me before looking back at the phone.

"*¿Vas a matar a mi tío?*" You're going to kill my uncle?

"*¿De verdad piensas en él como tu tío?*" Do you really think of him as your uncle?

"*No, pero ahora que sé que lo es, no puedo desconocerlo.*" No, but now that I know he is, I can't unknow that.

Silence fills the car, and I know everyone but Livy is waiting for me to explain. I switch to English.

"Livy, he wronged two bosses. Enrique doesn't care about Dillan, but Jesus has proven untrustworthy and a shit stirrer. No one can ignore that. If it weren't Enrique, it would be Dillan."

She sits back and looks out the window as we cross the Verrazzano-Narrows Bridge from Staten Island to Queens.

"Luca, what do I tell my mom?"

"Livy, she'll understand. Where she grew up...Marrying into the *Cosa Nostra*..."

"But she thought he was dead, and now he's not. What if she wants to talk to him or see him?"

"She could have said that before we left."

"She didn't have time to process it. What if she wants to after she thinks about it?"

We both look down at the phone when Enrique speaks. He sticks to English too.

"Olivia, your uncle's fate is sealed. But if your mama wishes to talk to him, then I'll wait."

"Thank you."

She leans over and whispers to me.

"Does this mean I can use my regular phone again?"

I nod. She reaches into her purse and pulls it out, then turns it on. It pings over and over, so she's quick to silence it. I can only imagine how many messages she has after disappearing for nearly a month and a half. I watch as she shoots off a text to her mom.

LIVY

> I know where Jesus is. Do you want to talk to him? He doesn't have long.

While she waits for a response, Uncle Salvatore addresses Enrique.

"What are your plans for O'Rourke, Diaz?"

"The kind that is none of your business."

"He didn't wrong you this time. He's going to claim he's a victim, too."

"That motherfucker is always crying victim."

"Diaz, he's mine. He went after my family, my niece."

Tension I didn't realize I held fades away. He not only already considers Olivia family, but there's no qualifier on it. No niece-in-law. Livy's head shoots up, her eyes wide as she looks at my uncle.

She mouths, "Thanks, Uncle Sal."

Her smile is radiant. The brightest I've seen in days.

"Diaz, you have Espinoza, even though his men went after my niece. I'm letting you have him without a fight. Dillan and his shitbag family are mine."

"Fine."

MARITZA

Yes. How can I?

The text comes in, and Livy once again looks to me.

"Enrique, I'm adding Maritza to the call. She wants to speak to her brother."

I dial the number I see on Livy's phone.

"Hello?"

I nudge Livy.

"Mom, you're on a call with Salvatore, Luca, and me. Enrique and Pablo Diaz are on the other line with Jesus."

"Chucho?"

I recognize the nickname for Jesus, but I'm used to Chuy instead.

"*Sí, hermanita.*" Yes, little sister.

Sabine Barclay

"Dejaste que me mintieran. Lloré durante semanas. He encendido una vela cada año en ese día. Recé por ti cada semana en misa. Lo he hecho durante casi cuarenta años." You let them lie to me. I cried for weeks. I light a candle on that day every year. I pray for you every week at Mass. I've done that for almost forty years.

"El abuelo me mandó tres años a un agujero de mierda donde aprendí cosas que ningún adolescente debería aprender. Cuando volví, nadie me reconoció. Ya no era un niño, rogando por ver a su hermanita. Estaba demasiado metido en este mundo. Luego hicieron la misma mierda pero contigo. Dijeron que estabas muerta. Imagina mi sorpresa cuando veo a una mujer que podría haber sido tú hace veinte años. Pensé que eras tú hasta que me di cuenta de que era demasiado joven. Entonces supe que tenía que ser tu hija." Grandpa sent me away for three years to a shithole where I learned things no teenager should. When I came back, no one recognized me. I wasn't a boy anymore, begging to see his little sister. I was too far into this world. Then they pulled the same shit but about you. They said you were dead. Imagine my shock when I see a woman who could have been you twenty years ago. I thought she was you until I realized she was way too young. Then I knew she had to be your daughter.

"Y te la llevaste de todos modos." And you took her anyway.

"No la vi claramente hasta después del accidente. Al principio no lo sabía. No lo habría hecho. Anoche habría sido muy diferente si lo hubiera sabido. Podríamos haber cenado juntos esta noche." I didn't see her clearly until after the accident. I didn't know at first. I wouldn't have. Last night would have played out far differently if I'd known. We might have been having dinner together tonight.

"¿Por qué debería creer algo de esto? Tú mismo dijiste que no eres quien eras. Nunca solías mentir, pero has hecho una

424

carrera de ello." Why should I believe any of this? You said yourself you aren't who you were. You never used to lie, but you've made a career out of it.

"Diaz, dile lo que encontraste en mi cartera." Diaz, tell her what you found in my wallet.

"Una vieja foto de dos niños. La niña tiene un balón de fútbol y el niño un cerdo de peluche. Están intercambiando. El niño es mayor." An old photo of two kids. The girl has a soccer ball, and the boy has a stuffed pig. They're trading. The boy is older.

Maritza sobs into the phone. I hear Danny consoling her, then she's muffled for a moment.

"Fue tomada la mañana que dispararon a papá." That was taken the morning they shot Papa.

"Lo he guardado todo este tiempo, hermanita. No importa lo que me haya pasado, siempre me he asegurado de recuperarlo. No voy a ninguna parte sin él. Diría que me entierren con él, pero..." I've kept it all this time, little sister. No matter what's happened to me, I've always made sure I've gotten that back. I go nowhere without it. I'd say bury me with it, but...

That only makes Maritza sob harder.

We pull up to our home, and I want to get Livy inside. So much for our vacation and leaving this afternoon. We have to deal with Dillan.

"Enrique, we're home. My family will deal with Dillan. You deal with the Culiacán. But whatever you do, make sure it doesn't make Livy a target again."

Maritza clears her throat and sniffles.

"Jesús, te amo, hermano mayor." Jesus, I love you, big brother.

"Itzy, te amo, hermanita." Itzy, I love you, little sister.

"Ve con Dios a mamá y papá." Go with God to Mama and Papa.

"*Os cuidaremos a los dos.*" We'll watch over you both.

I won't ruin the moment by pointing out that they're overly optimistic that he's headed to Heaven. He's headed south of a different border. Far, far south.

"*Adiós, tío.*" Goodbye, Uncle.

"*Adiós, Olivia.*" Goodbye, Olivia.

There's nothing left to say, so I hang up. We head inside, and the next two hours are a blur. Everyone comes to our house. My aunts, uncles, siblings, parents, and cousins, plus Matteo and Gabriele. He should be in bed, but he refuses. He's determined to be a part of whatever we do to the O'Rourkes. He won't admit it, but he wants revenge for them putting Livy in danger, not him. I figured out that the bomb likely came from the O'Rourkes after the guard who opened and diffused it met with the men in my family and me. It was the O'Rourke's hallmark. Either they sent it and used a Spanish-speaking kid to deliver it, or they gave it to someone in the Culiacán.

It's dark when we leave. I've said my goodbyes to my parents, my aunts, my uncles, and Livy. None of my uncles nor Papa are coming on this one. Gabriele's finally agreed to stay with the cars. The Kutsenkos have taken out several Irish warehouses on the docks. The O'Rourkes most profitable pub mysteriously had a gas leak that blew it sky high. It's easy to think there isn't much left to fuck up. Oh, but there is.

We start in Jersey. They have a microbrewery, and we hit that first. We slip in and flip the valves, letting every liquid out. Beer that's on tap. The stuff that's still fermenting. Anything in a barrel. It's several inches deep on the floor. It'll do a small fortune in structural damage along with costing them thousands in product. On the way out, we smash everything we pass in the dining area, then all the windows. Matteo cracked their safe and took everything out of there.

Next we hit a bakery in Brooklyn that's a front for their

counterfeiting. We do another smash and grab, taking all their equipment. They have machines to print cash, fake passports, fake IDs, and fake credit cards. We use one of the industrial ovens and make it look like a gas leak. This business isn't under the O'Rourke name, so the similarity between this place and the Dubliner won't be obvious to most people. Let the fucking Kutsenkos think we copied them. Fuck if I care.

While we're in Brooklyn, we head to Bay Ridge, or "Little Ireland," where the O'Rourkes own several Celtic import stores on Third Avenue. We don't give a shit about any of these shitty little tchotchkes. We destroy everything we can find. We know one store is owned by an Irish-American cop's wife. Oh, well. Let that remind the po-po who live in the O'Rourkes' pockets that we haven't forgotten about them.

Finally, we leave the city and head out to Rockland County. Pearl River is probably considered the most Irish city in America. More than half the residents claim some sort of Irish ancestry. And not the "everyone's Irish on St. Patty's Day." It's the "there's an Irish dance school on every corner." Tempting to hit up those since the O'Rourkes own several, but we don't target things to do with kids.

They're into real estate here. While it's also tempting to go after several properties, we're not giving them any reason to file an insurance claim on properties they're flipping. We hit their construction companies instead. They won't report the stolen equipment. They legally registered none of that shit, nor do these have all the licenses they need. They have no recourse.

I'm driving as we enter Queens, and Carmine is sitting next to me. We still haven't talked, but we should. When we get to my house, I'm eager to go upstairs to check on Livy, but I hang back.

"Carmine."

"Yeah?"

It's fucking freezing out again tonight, but I point around the house. We head to the backyard as everyone else is filtering out and heading to their places. We get to the pool, and I sit on the lounger where I found Livy the second morning she was here. That seems like so long ago, even though it's barely been a month and a half. It's insane.

"You wanted to talk."

"Luca, I've treated you worse than anyone else. I'm sorry."

"Why this change of tune? You've held a gun to my temple since I was fourteen. That was more than half a lifetime for me, and nearly half for you."

He's twenty-eight to my thirty-one, so he was eleven when he started fucking up my life. Manipulative prig from the start.

"I told you. I don't want Olivia, but I want what you have. It's been obvious since the moment I saw you together. I want what half the Kutsenkos have. I didn't enjoy looking at Lucenzo and seeing myself forty years down the road. The people who made me a resentful child who grew into a revenge-seeking adult are dead. *Nonno* can't look down on me anymore. Lord knows that man's in the bowels of Hell. He's not looking down on anyone. But the rest of them can't give me shit for being the *rifiuti illegittimi.*"

Illegitimate waste.

That's what the grandfather we shared as well as his paternal grandfather called him. Neither were happy that their children had to marry one another, and they hated Carmine before he was born. His father's father swore Auntie Paola trapped him and lied. He was convinced Carmine wasn't Uncle Cesare's. He's looked just like Uncle Cesare since he was born, but Mario-Andrea Ciccone would not be convinced otherwise. Our grandfather claimed Auntie Paola slummed it by ever going near Uncle Cesare, and he was convinced Uncle Cesare got her pregnant to get her inheritance. Because our grandfather was the don, everyone followed his lead.

"Luca, I was so scared that day. I was barely eleven. I wasn't supposed to be at that park. I didn't want *Nonno* to find out I'd disobeyed him and followed you. When it happened, I knew you wouldn't tell on me because then you'd have to admit what happened. But once *Nonno* died five years later, I wasn't as terrified if someone found out I'd been there. It became a way to feel powerful when everyone still looked down on me. I didn't feel so worthless when I thought I could control you."

"So, you used my fear of anyone finding out to fuck me over as many times as you could. When I wanted to refuse to involve Anastasia, you threatened to not only tell Uncle Sal but to fucking tell the Kutsenkos. Things weren't supposed to go that far with Anastasia. If I'd known what was going to happen, I would have confessed my sin rather than deal with the fallout from Chicago and the Podolskaya."

"You and me both."

We stare at each other.

"Why were you there that day, Carmine? Why'd you follow me to the park?"

"Because her little sister was supposed to be there, and I had a crush on her."

"You had a crush on Iskra?"

"Yeah. But she liked Bogdan. I wanted to convince her I was better."

We went to school with the Kutsenkos. I'm the same age as Maks, and Carmine is the same age as the youngest brother, Bogdan, who is the same age as his cousin, Misha Andreyev.

"You thought you'd convince a bratva Elite Group member's daughter to like you more than the boy being trained to one day be part of the Elite Group. And how did you think the *Cosa Nostra* don's nephew was going to do that?"

429

"How the fuck did I know? I was eleven. I thought she was really nice and smart."

"But you got in an argument with Iskra."

"No, I didn't."

"But Klara was yelling at you and pulling you away."

"Because Iskra told me she'd be my girlfriend if I kissed better than Bogdan. I didn't know until days later that they'd never kissed. She'd timed it so Klara would find me. She wasn't that nice after all."

"It would have been fine if you'd gone home when I told you to, but you refused."

"I thought Iskra still wanted me there. I thought she was going to explain to Klara that she liked me after all."

I snort. That wasn't what happened at all.

"Instead, she put a gun to your head, Carmine. She was seconds from pulling the trigger. What was I supposed to do? Watch her kill you? You knew I would never let that happen. I wouldn't let that happen now."

"I'm sorry, Luca. I didn't know you'd have to kill her to stop her."

We're silent, both of us lost in our memory of that night. Emilio and I went to the park to get drunk with some friends we had in common with Klara. I liked her friend, Min-jun, and I hoped to talk to her.

"And I didn't know Emilio was fucking her and believed they were in love."

I run my finger along my left cheek, down to my jaw.

"I still have nightmares about that, Luca. Seeing Klara pull that gun and point it at me. Then you rushing forward, pushing her away. How you two fought, and the gun going off. Then Emilio—"

Carmine looks out at the pool. I see his Adam's apple bob in the dim light from the lanterns around the pool, and the light from the patio.

"I never imagined Emilio would defend her instead of you. I never imagined he would turn on the family like that."

"He was certain he loved her. Now that I have Livy, I get why he did it. But he was too drunk to think rationally. If he'd been sober, proclaiming his love and avenging her, then I might accept his claim. But it was intoxicated lust every time they were together. If he'd been sober, he wouldn't have done it. And I'm guilty of having never tried hard enough to stop him from drinking."

"I knew you didn't kill Klara on purpose, but I knew your shame from killing any woman would give me power. So, I exploited it."

I sigh. No one besides Emilio, Carmine, and I know what happened that night. Iskra ran off when Klara pulled the gun. None of our friends had shown up yet. Despite my gushing blood, and Emilio being drunk off his ass, we dealt with Klara's body. I wiped the gun clean, and we took her to her car. We left the gun with her. Iskra never knew about the fights, so we let her family think it was suicide. I discovered the next morning that Emilio couldn't remember most of it. The only part he remembered was slicing my face.

He and Carmine took me to Auntie Carlotta. He dumped me in the living room to bleed all over the carpet and sofa. It was Carmine who yelled for Auntie Carlotta and Uncle Domenico. Emilio went up to his room and passed out. Uncle Domenico found Emilio's bloody knife on the bedside table. That's how they figured out Emilio cut me.

"And we all kept each other's twisted secrets. You never told that I killed a girl. I never told that Emilio cut me, even though everyone knows. And he never told anything. I still don't believe he remembers nothing. He did that purely to save his own ass."

"And we've kept those secrets for a decade and a half. I will keep yours, Luca. That won't change, but not to lord it over you. I'll do it because I caused it all."

"No, not really. Klara and Iskra did. Iskra was a foolish little girl, just like you were a foolish little boy. Klara was high and a hothead."

"Thank you for saving my life that night."

I nod.

"You saved mine too."

We both stand and look at each other. At the same time, we stick out our hands and grasp the other's. A moment later, we're embracing for the first time in sixteen years. He is a different man from four months ago, and so am I.

"I forgive all of it, Carmine. Just don't play me for a fool. I won't forgive a second time."

"I won't and thank you. What about Emilio? Could you ever reconcile with him?"

I shake my head as I inhale. That fight wasn't his only fuck-up. Uncle Salvatore relegated Emilio to our small-time businesses in Jersey. He comes on missions sometimes, like the one the other night, because he's still a good soldier. But he's proven himself untrustworthy too many times.

"How are he and Matteo so fucking different?"

"If they didn't both look just like Uncle Domenico, I'd say someone switched Emilio at birth. But it's jealousy, Luca. He knows he can never be the heir, the underboss. But that's what he wanted. Because you were best friends, he saw all the ways people treated you better. Being practically part of the don's family wasn't enough for him. He's always been self-destructive, but after everything with Klara, you stopped covering for him."

What Carmine says makes sense. I look toward the house.

"Go inside and see your girlfriend. Are we leaving in the morning?"

"That's the plan, assuming the O'Rourkes don't figure shit out before we can get to the airfield."

"I can't believe Uncle Sal agreed we could all still go with you."

"He wants Livy to have a nice time, and he feels the same way I do. She'll never be safer than when family guards her."

"Thank you for trusting me."

"Goodnight, Car."

"Night, Luke."

We haven't called each other those nicknames in sixteen years. I make my way upstairs while Carmine goes to the driveway and his car that's still parked there. I strip and slip into bed.

"Daddy?"

"Yes, *piccolina*. I'm home."

"Are you all right?"

"Very. I'm sorry I woke you."

Livy reaches and turns on the bedside table lamp before rolling into my arms.

"Luca, I remember what I said the last time you slipped into bed. I was half asleep, but I was serious."

"I know. But little girls need to have some patience."

I silence her with a kiss until she's breathless. I grab a condom from the bedside table and slip it on before slipping into her. We both sigh. I've truly come home. Not to my house, but my home. That's Livy's arms.

"This is where I belong, *piccolina*. I love you."

"This is where *we* belong, Daddy. I love you."

Epilogue

Livy

I've never flown in a private jet. We just arrived at a private airfield near Nice after traveling on the Mancinellis' luxury corporate plane. I never imagined just how comfortable airplane seats could be, but real leather goes a long way. There was a private cabin in the aft, and Luca and I took advantage of it after takeoff. I'm officially a member of the mile-high club. To my great and ecstatic surprise, it was Luca's first-time making love and fucking in the air. He reminded me he hadn't had a girlfriend in a decade, so he'd traveled with no women outside his family.

"Luca, this is breathtaking."

"It is."

I shift my gaze from the spectacular view of the Mediterranean to my handsome boyfriend, who's watching me. He slips his arms around me, and I step closer.

"I can't believe we're here and have two weeks of sun and

relaxation ahead of us. A blissful escape from everything. Thank you, Daddy."

"I'm excited to have two weeks of your attention."

It's been three weeks since everything finally came to a head, and Luca discovered who was really behind the Culiacán pursuing me. Ignorance has been my bliss. He's told me nothing about what's happened, and I haven't asked. The only thing I know for certain is the Diazes released Jesus, who returned to Mexico with a clear understanding that he'll forfeit his life the second he returns to New York. I'm certain Uncle Salvatore—I've gotten used to calling him that far faster than I accepted the idea that I have a *Tío* Jesus—and Luca would prefer they keep their business out of the city. However, that's unlikely.

I know Uncle Salvatore did this for my sake and my mom's. I appreciate that he convinced Enrique. I don't know how I would manage the guilt of knowing that Uncle Salvatore let someone kill Jesus to avenge me. We're not the only ones the Culiacán will steer clear of. They're giving the Colombians a wide berth too. Things were contentious with the Diazes the first week, but I suspect things are back to their normal simmering hostility between the syndicates—not mafias. Luca explained the difference.

"What do you want to do first, *piccolina*? The beaches in Nice are pebbly, but we can go further along the coast."

Luca took me back to my apartment a few days after Jesus's capture. I packed up everything and moved into Luca's house. It truly became our home when we interspersed my belongings with his. A tiny—okay, major—part of me worried that the shine would wear off once my need for constant protection went away. That we wouldn't feel the same way. We don't. It's so much better. Without the constant fear and strain, we've grown closer with more time to talk and spend time together as a normal couple.

"Do you believe in soulmates, *caro?*"

He grins. I know that was a random question, not at all an answer to his.

"I have you in my arms. Of course, I do. I know people could make the argument that after going so long without dating, I'm confusing love and infatuation. But I'm not. I've likely thought about our relationship and our life together more than most people do after months, even years, of being together. Intuition has saved my life countless times. It's what kept me from dying and only winding up with this."

He touches his left cheek. He finally told me what happened with Emilio and Carmine. He shared the story the morning after he and his family dealt with the Irish. He and Carmine won't broadcast it to the family, but they're on noticeably better terms. The unacknowledged bitterness and friction I sensed when I met everyone has virtually disappeared. Uncle Salvatore and everyone else take their cues from Luca. His reconciliation with Carmine means everyone else has welcomed him more than ever before.

"I feel the same. I admit it was lust at first sight, but love came shockingly fast. I know we are meant to last, Luca. I'm pretty sure most couples believe that when they say they're soulmates, but we connect in ways most couples never imagine."

I lean in for a kiss, and it's explosive. Luca turns me, and I lean against the balustrade that separates us from a steep drop practically off a cliff. He grasps my bare thigh and hooks it over his hip. It's chilly in the south of France as we approach spring, so I have a wool coat on, but I'm wearing a dress. And no panties. He scooped those up and threw them away when I was packing my apartment. When we got home, I marched straight into our room, gathered his boxer briefs, and took them to the outside trash can. My crossed arms and smug look got me a spanking with the cat-o'-nine-tails, and I loved every second.

"I think the first thing I want to do is make love outside."

"I can make that happen, little girl."

I reach between the two of us and unfasten his belt and pants. His cock springs free, hard for me and only me. He slips his fingers between my legs.

"You're so wet, *cuore*. I just spent eight hours fucking and making love to you, but you still need more. Greedy little girl."

"Greedy Daddy. You're still hard after fucking me in the car from the airport."

He lifts me with ease, and I wrap my legs around his waist as he thrusts into me. We sigh together.

"That moment when you enter me is almost as good as coming. To finally feel you deep inside me."

"To know we're one. I could hold you like this, just enjoying being inside you. It's like infinity. No end and no beginning to us. Just one."

"You're quite a romantic at heart, Daddy."

"Only for my *piccolina*."

I hold on to the railing as he surges into me over and over. But this position satisfies neither of us. He carries me, bouncing on his dick, to a table beneath a canopy. I lie back, watching him. He's not in his typical suit and tie. He looks like that first morning after I arrived at his house. He's in a sweater that clings to every muscle, and jeans that show off a way too fine ass. My hands roam over him, enjoying every ridge and valley of muscle, until he snares them and lifts them over my head. He pins me to the table, his cock thrusting deeper until there's nowhere left to go.

"I want your cum. I want to feel you even when we're done. Harder."

"Whatever my little girl wants, Daddy's going to give her."

Fortunately, it's a stone table, or he would push it across the patio. I moan, uncaring if anyone hears us. His family and the two other guards we brought did a thorough sweep of the property before Luca let me out of the car. Now they're somewhere inside the sprawling villa.

"You're mine, *cuore*. Every part of you. Mind. Heart. Body. Soul. I will give you pleasure until my last breath."

"I claim all of you, too. I want all of it, Luca. I will never share. I will never take for granted what it means for you to let me in."

"I know you won't."

"I'm really close. May I come?"

"Yes."

He growls, and I know he's barely holding on. He kisses me as his grip on my wrists tightens, and his fingers dig into my hip. He's in control, and I love it. I crave it. Even with everything back to my new normal, I'm happy ceding control to him. Knowing he needs it as much as I do, choosing to trust him. Basking in his love and attention is empowering in its own way. Even when he's being so dominant, I never feel like anything less than an equal partner because I know everything he does is to give me happiness and show his deep-seated feelings for me.

"Daddy...Yes...Oh...So close. So—More...I'm coming."

"So am I, *piccolina*. Fuck, you're so fucking tight."

Our kiss carries on even after our orgasms wane. We're breathless from the kiss and the exertion when we finally break apart. He lifts me, still buried inside me, and sits on a nearby chair.

"You still haven't told me what you want to do?"

"There's a perfumery in Grasse I'd love to visit. Would that be too boring for you?"

"Of course not."

"I promise not to spray too many samples on you."

"That's what we have my brothers for. Spritz away on them."

"You're such a mean big brother."

He waggles his eyebrows and appears so boyish. His grin is lopsided, and he's so relaxed. I run my fingers through his hair, and he turns his head to kiss the bit of my wrist that's not covered by my coat sleeve.

"And I will teach our oldest child how to be just as horrible."

One day. We've talked about it, and we're not in a rush.

"Come on. I know a wonderful restaurant where we can have lunch along the way."

It takes nearly forty-five minutes to get there, but it's this amazing hole in the wall type place. It surprises me to hear Luca and his family speak fluent French. We're seated outside with another amazing view but of the countryside rather than the sea.

"I think I'll have the *fougasse*. I saw—"

I gasp as I shut my menu and look over at Luca. I cover my mouth with my hands, but he draws my left hand away, running his finger over my ring finger. I stare at my boyfriend, down on one knee, and I struggle against the tears that threaten.

"I'll do my best to never lie about anything when I can avoid it. I didn't lie when I said I would ask you soon. I've been planning this since practically the day we met. I knew I would bring you here. My family and I have been coming to this restaurant since I was a child, so it holds many sentimental memories. I hope this is the first of many we share. I love you, *piccolina*. I want you and the rest of the world to know that I don't say that mildly. I want you and everyone else to know that I want nothing more than to spend the rest of our lives together. I'm yours. All that I have and all that I am. Livy, will you marry me?"

I nod and throw myself at him, nearly knocking him over.

"Yes, Luca. Right now. Right this very minute. I love you for the person you help me be. I love you for the person you let yourself be with me. I love you. Yes, yes, yes. All the yeses, Daddy. Yes!"

He cups my face with one hand while the other still holds my left hand. He's still running his finger over mine as we kiss. When we draw apart, he reaches into his jeans pocket and pulls out a small box. He flips it open, and I gasp for a second time. It's the most stunningly gorgeous piece of jewelry I've ever seen. The stones must be flawless, and the filigree is unlike anything I've seen before.

He takes it out of the box and slips it on my finger, and all I can do is stare at it, then at Luca, and back and forth.

"Do you like it?"

There's hesitation in his voice, and I launch myself at him again. This time he's prepared and catches me, then brings me to my feet.

"It's spectacular, Luca. I can't imagine a ring I could love more. It's perfect."

"It had to be for my Livy."

I cup his face, brushing my thumb over his scar. He was right. It is soothing. I'll always know it's him, and in his arms is where I belong.

Discover how Carmine Mancinelli made a horrible impression on Serafina Carosi when they were ten. He reinforced it when they were eighteen. Now they're twenty-eight, and Carmine is done with being the family dirtbag. He's ready to turn over a new leaf and prove to Fina that he's not the man she assumes in *Mafia Sinner*.

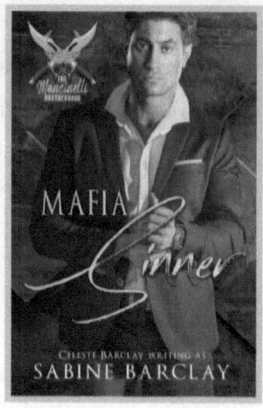

She disliked me when we were twelve. She loathed me at eighteen.

Now I'm not the man she thinks I am.

Now I'll make her mine.

Let them try to keep us apart.

Let them test us.

No one threatens what's mine.

I'm the man she will turn to.

I'm the man she will want.

I'm the man who will save her.

I'm the man who will push her to her limits, then give her everything she desires.

Meet Carmine and Fina.

Thank you for reading Mafia Heir

Sabine Barclay, a nom de plume also writing Historical Romance as Celeste Barclay, lives near the Southern California coast with her husband and sons. She loves her days at the beach soaking up way too much sun, a good Netflix binge, and a strong hot chai. Her heroines are independent women who can defend themselves but love their Alpha heroes who want nothing more than to protect their soulmates in her Mafia Romances. She's Gen Y/Oregon Trail and loves creating engrossing contemporary romances that will make your toes curl and your granny blush.

Subscribe to Sabine's bimonthly newsletter to receive exclusive insider perks.
https://bit.ly/sabinebarclayfreebie

www.sabinebarclay.com

Join the fun and get exclusive insider giveaways, sneak peeks, and new release announcements in
Sabine Barclay's Facebook Dubious Dames Group

Do you also enjoy steamy Historical Romance? Discover Sabine's books written as Celeste Barclay.

The Mancinelli Brotherhood

Mafia Sinner **BOOK TWO SNEAK PEEK**

Carmine

"This place is supposed to be amazing. Like award-winning amazing. I can't wait to try the lemon cupcakes. And I hear they have the most incredible Italian wedding cookies."

The type that is dipped in a creamy glaze with sprinkles. I shake my head.

"Don't let Auntie Carlotta hear you say that. She'll never forgive you. Then again, say it loudly. I'll take your share."

My cousin Maria rolls her eyes and elbows me in the ribs as I hold the door open for her and her best friend, Veronica. We've just arrived at a specialty bakery near Maria's place in Manhattan. Froofy is how I would describe it. It looks like a Hallmark movie vomited in here. But who am I to turn down a cupcake? I've already spent my requisite two hours at the gym this morning, so the calories don't count, right? I almost roll my eyes to match Maria. I think that's one of the most asinine jokes I've ever heard.

As my gaze sweeps the place for any threats to Maria, and I suppose Veronica too, I spy the most delectable ass bent over to unpack a box. The things I would do while tapping that ass. Fuck. I haven't had this visceral a reaction since I was like sixteen. But I can't help it. I almost need to adjust myself. I turn my attention to a window display.

"Good morning. Welcome to *Morso Migliore*." Best Bite.

She's Italian. Like from Italy. I can tell from her accent. I shift my focus to her and stop dead. My hand self-consciously moves to the slight bump on the bridge of my nose. I glance down at Maria and catch her wicked grin. Fucking hell. She knew. She did this on purpose.

I look back at Serafina Carosi and have an even stronger reaction to the front of her than the back. Curvaceous. Voluptuous. Rubenesque. Fucking hot as holy fucking hell on the fucking hottest day in August. And her expression tells me she still thinks she's looking at shit on her shoe when she focuses on me. My heart's racing now that the initial shock's worn off.

"*Ciao, Maria. È passato molto tempo.*" Hello, Maria. It's been a long time.

Her greeting is sincere when she smiles at my cousin. Then she looks at me, then my best friend, and back to me. Her lip practically curls when she recognizes Gabriele. From how he moves to stand farther down the counter, as though he's looking at the pastries, I can tell he feels the Arctic wind too.

"Carmine, Gabriele."

"*Salve, Serafina.*" Hello, Serafina.

My greeting hangs in the air as I approach the counter. A magnet draws me to her when it should repel me. It's because we're such opposites. My north pole—my tongue—would love to meet her south pole—her pussy. I nearly shake my head to clear my mind of my ridiculously inappropriate daydream.

I'm close enough to see her translucent gray eyes with the green flecks take on a wary hardness. Her hair is much shorter than it was ten years ago. But it's still the same rich honey brown that it was then and when we were twelve. She was adorable as a kid. She was hot when she was in her late teens. And she's fucking gorgeous now that we're twenty-eight. I find my tongue again since it's not where I want to put it.

"*È passato molto tempo.*" It's been a long time.

"*Sì. Solo un decennio.*" Yes. Only a decade.

She says that as though it hasn't been nearly long enough.

The Ivankov Brotherhood

Bratva Darling

BOOK ONE SNEAK PEEK

LAURA

As I sit across from the four Kutsenko brothers, I press my lips together to keep from drooling. No four men should be so strikingly handsome. Not all from the same family, anyway. I fight a valiant battle against letting my gaze drift toward the eldest, Maksim, whose ice-blue eyes bore into me. After years of negotiating billion-dollar investment contracts while facing countless ruthless businessmen, I've learned to keep my expression studiously blank. But it's a true struggle today. Instead, I focus my attention on the squirrelly lawyer sitting across the conference table. While he's disingenuous with each comment, he's a good negotiator. But I'm better. How cliché am I?

While I feel Maksim watching me, I focus on Dmitry Yakovitch as he continues to argue the merits of the venture capitalist company I represent, RK Capital Group, merging with Kutsenko Partners. What he means is the merits of Kutsenko Partners acquiring RK Capital Group, then stripping it and making it another money-laundering shell corporation. While most people in New York have little awareness of the Russian mafia, I do. The Kutsenko brothers' names appear on no titles or deeds anywhere in New York City, but it wasn't difficult to determine which shell companies likely belong to them. Their assumption that I'm unfamiliar with them is proving beneficial to me as they continue to whisper amongst themselves in Russian. I think they may even believe they're convincing me that they don't speak much English.

The senior partners of RK Capital Group know who I'm negotiating with, though they may not know I'm aware of these Russians' more nefarious operations. They've given me the go-ahead to agree to a merger with an eventual acquisition, but only for the right price. A price to the tune of twenty billion dollars. Considering an investment firm like Goldman Sachs is worth nearly one-hundred-and-twenty billion dollars, my clients' asking price appears reasonable.

"Mr. Yakovitch, I shall stop you now." I raise my left hand, pen caught between my index and middle fingers. When I have his attention, I lean back in my chair and casually twirl the pen over my index finger and thumb. "Fifty billion is my clients' asking price. You know that. Your clients know that. RK doesn't oppose the merger. What they oppose is the insulting offer you've made. It's nearly noon, and I'm hungry, Mr. Yakovitch. I have a delicious ham sandwich waiting for me. I even have three chocolate chip cookies waiting for me. If we aren't going to make any progress, I shall let you go, so I can move onto my eagerly anticipated lunch."

I cant my head just enough for me to appear as though my gaze rests solely on the opposing attorney's face, but I can see each Kutsenko brothers' reaction. My face battles yet again against showing my emotions as I fight not to smirk. Their muted but surprised expressions confirm what I already know.

"Please tell your clients to make a reasonable counteroffer, or I will conclude this meeting and enjoy my ham sandwich and cookies."

Dmitry glares at me before turning to Maksim and his three brothers. In rapid Russian, he doesn't interpret my suggestion. Oh no. There's no need for that. I can't catch every word because his voice is too low. But I catch something along the lines of "The bitch refuses to budge. What now? A fucking ham sandwich. More like a stick up her ass."

Maksim swivels his chair to look at his brothers. In Russian, he says, "Fifty billion is ridiculous. She's not so stupid or naïve not to know that. My guess is they'll settle for twenty billion. We offer fifteen."

"That's barely better than what we already offered," Aleksei, the second-oldest brother, argues. "She'll be eating the fucking sandwich and dipping her cookies in milk before we walk out the door. We need the buildings."

"We offer twenty, Maks," Bogdan, the youngest, insists.

As I watch the brothers discuss, their voices barely lowered, I pull my lunch sack from the black leather satchel by my feet and set it beside my laptop. It's a ridiculously pink floral bag with an embroidered monogram, the L and D overlapping. It's an empty prop, but they don't know that. I watch as five sets of eyes narrow. I offer a smile that would appear innocent in any setting other than this meeting. It's patronizing, and I know it.

Bratva Sweetheart

Bratva Treasure

Bratva Beauty

Bratva Angel

Bratva Jewel

www.ingramcontent.com/pod-product-compliance
Lightning Source LLC
Chambersburg PA
CBHW020004120726
47903CB00004B/1125